# THE CHRISTMAS ONE NIGHT STAND

## L. STEELE

# 1

---

## Zara

"No."

"What do you mean, no?" The man sitting next to me in the driver's seat of his car, the man who represents so much of what I hate on every level, glares at me.

"Exactly that." I glance out my window. And why did I agree to him taking me out to dinner? Why didn't I turn him down? Why did I rise to his challenge when he asked earlier if I was scared? I may find him attractive, but I'll never find him appealing—not even if he were the last man on this planet. And especially not when he stands for everything I hate.

Hunter Whittington is the very embodiment of entitlement. He comes from old world money and has been groomed to take his place as the Prime Minister of the United Kingdom. He belongs to that class of Oxbridge educated, elitist, stuck-up, pain-in-the arse, wankers who thinks it's their right to rule and dominate. A grumphole who's highly popular with the old-boy's network, perceived as cunning, ruthless and lethal, while also appearing to not give a damn about anything. Well, except for being very insistent I attend this dinner with him.

"I thought we were agreeing to a truce for this evening?" Mr. Posh-tosh drawls.

I toss my hair over my shoulder. "I agreed to have dinner with you; doesn't mean I'm going to be all docile and pleasant."

"Pity, because when you smile, you're actually quite charming."

I scoff, "That the best you can do? Your compliments leave me cold."

"When I compliment you, you'll know it," he drawls. "That was simply me, stating a fact."

"And this is me, stating that I'm already regretting being here with you."

He flips on the indicator, then turns off the motorway and onto a secondary road. He's rolled up his shirt sleeves, and the veins pop in his arms. Oh, yeah, I forgot to mention that the arrogant prick has very well-defined forearms with sculpted muscles covered with tanned skin and a peppering of dark hair. My fingers tingle.

How would it be to trail my fingers over them and feel the scrape of those rough strands against my skin? How would it be to have his blunt fingertips trail up my arm, over my shoulder down the curve of my breasts and—why am I thinking along these lines? Sure, Hunter Whittington has the sort of features that wouldn't look out of place on the cover of GQ, his build resembles that of a Hollywood action hero, and his broad shoulders invite me to snuggle into his chest. He makes my knees go weak, makes my throat dry, makes a pulse flare to life between my thighs… None of which negates the fact that he stands for the kinds of values I've always hated. He's an egotistical wanker who was born into one of the richest families in the country. The kind of family with bloodlines related to royalty. The kind who'd never have to work for a day in his life if he didn't want to. The kind who had everything handed to him on a silver platter. The kind who is the exact opposite of how I grew up. Plus, I hated him on sight.

The first time I met him was at 7A Club, an outfit run by JJ Kane and Sinclair Sterling, two of the most powerful men in the country, and founders of the club intended to help identify talent and invest in them. They invited me to be a founding member, and I was the only woman at the table. Given the career I've chosen, that's not unusual. What threw me, though, was the visceral reaction I had to this man. How I took an instant dislike to him and he toward me. How we barely managed to be civil to each other in that first meeting. It was only exacerbated when we met at work.

He filed his candidacy to run for the position of Prime Minister, and I'm the fixer. A well-known PR spin-doctor who the country's tastemakers—from influencers to politicians—come to when they need to salvage their reputations. Which makes things messy, to say the least. Because, no way, can I personally be involved in a scandal.

His ride to Downing Street depends on his track record being free of scandal. And my job depends on my not becoming the scandal. I need to always be seen as an impartial party by the media. My ability to manipulate the news depends on that. Which means, I can't let my association with him be seen as anything but professional; i.e. I need to be courteous toward him when we meet in person.

If the media gets wind of just how much we hate each other, it will only become the topic of debate. Not to mention, hating someone at a personal level never bodes well. It would only encourage people to see me as someone who can't be objective when it came to those in the news, and I can't afford that. I've built my career as someone who is never pulled into media clashes, and I need to stay that way. Which means, I need all of my wits about me. Ergo, I need to defuse this… situation between Hunter and me that's becoming increasingly untenable.

It's why, when he asked me to dinner so we could try to come to some kind of an understanding, I agreed. It's not like I had a choice, either. When my instinct was to turn him down, he challenged me by saying, perhaps I was too scared to spend time with him one-on-one, that I might find I actually like him. I knew I was being played, that he was appealing to my competitive spirit. And yet, I couldn't say no. That's my weakness. I never can resist a confrontation.

So here I am, in the car that he's parked in front of a building set back from the road.

Behind us, the security car—with his security detail—that has been following us, comes to a stop. Another pulls ahead and parks in front. I gather my things and reach for the handle on my door, but Hunter has already walked around to hold it open. My stomach folds in on itself. A stutter swirls about my chest. So annoying that he has to shove his good manners in my face.

I slide out, then straighten. "You didn't have to do that. I can open my own doors." I scowl.

"My mother taught me better."

I sniff, brush past him and head up the path leading to the restaurant without waiting for him. Footsteps follow as his long legs eat up the distance. He walks past me and is holding the door to the restaurant open by the time I reach it. I scowl up at him, then step through the entrance and up the short hallway. I reach the restaurant and pause. The lighting is dim, and the walls are painted a pale ivory. Both sides of the restaurant are glass walls. To my right, past the glass wall, is what seems to be a forest of bamboo trees. And beyond the glass wall on my left is a manmade fountain. The entire effect is soothing, like being in a Zen space. Strangely, all of the tables are empty.

"Where is everyone?"

"Everyone who matters is here." He takes my coat, hands it over to a maître d' who materializes out of nowhere, then shrugs off his own jacket and gives it to the same man. He guides me to the table in the center of the room—to the only table set with silverware and candles. He holds out my chair and I slide in. There's a third chair set on one side of the table between us.

"Is there someone else joining us?" I frown.

"That's for your bag."

Eh? I blink, then lower my eyebrows. "Care to explain?"

"I'm aware of how much you love your accessories, especially your shoes and purses. And I know you'd never place your bag on the floor. And putting it on the table is simply gauche, so—" He raises a shoulder.

"So, you arranged for an extra chair for my Birkin?"

"Was I wrong?"

"You were..." I hesitate. I don't want to admit he's right. That he correctly anticipated that I do take great care of my shoes and my handbags. They're an extension of me. They project who I am to the world. They are more than a brand statement; they are a declaration of how much I value myself. Somehow, I hadn't expected this...uppity, almost-royalty twat to understand that. But in one fell swoop, he's done that and more. Probably just a lucky guess. Maybe I'm reading too much into it. I place my handbag on the chair and tip up my chin. "Thanks," I murmur.

"You're welcome." He inclines his head.

I glance about the restaurant again. "So, we're the only ones here?"

"And the bodyguards."

In my peripheral vision, I spot my security detail positioning themselves at strategic points in corners around the room and standing by the entrance. It's dim enough that their black suits blend with the shadows. Only, I can't forget they're there, of course. It's a necessary evil I've lived with since I took on this position.

"You know I don't mean them, either."

"There's also the service staff." He waves a hand in the air, and as if by magic, a waiter materializes next to him with a bottle of champagne.

"Are we celebrating something?" I scowl.

"You agreed to have dinner with me—"

"I agreed to give you two hours to convince me why I shouldn't hate the idea of you" —he begins to speak, and I raise a finger— "of which, you now have eighty minutes left."

He curls his lips. "Are you always this...blinkered?"

"Are you always this...carefree?" I snap.

His grin widens. "Appearances can be deceptive."

"You don't say."

He arches an eyebrow at the waiter who pops the cork on the champagne. The sound ricochets about the space, emphasizing, again, that we are the only ones here.

"You still didn't tell me where everyone else is," I murmur.

The waiter pours the bubbly into my glass, then Hunter's. He places the bottle in the ice bucket perched on a stand next to the table that I only now notice. Then he fades away into the darkness.

"Given the potential speculation seeing the two of us together could cause, naturally, I had to find a solution to take you out to dinner in a public space while ensuring we had privacy."

"Ergo, you used your money and influence to buy out the place?"

"I simply asked the owner, who happens to be a friend, if he could accommodate us. And he did."

"Is it always this easy for you? To wave your hand and have all of your needs met? To incline your head and have minions jump to do your bidding? To ask and always receive?"

"Except with you."

He narrows his blue-green gaze on me from across the expanse of the table. The candlelight highlights the golden-brown specks in the depths of his eyes and haloes his dark hair, turning it almost blue. The hollows under his cheekbones seem more pronounced, the dip in his chin seems more delicious.

I try to tear my gaze from his, but it's as if he holds me in a tractor beam. Awareness tugs on and stretches the air between us. My heart begins to race. This is ridiculous. So, he's good-looking. I knew that already. What I hadn't realized is that hidden behind that polished mask he presents to the world is an untamed animal. A beast lying in wait to unleash that darkness inside of him. An edginess, a sharp wickedness that I never would've guessed he'd be capable of, but which I sense now lapping at the restraints that he's placed on himself.

I curl my fingers around the stem of my champagne glass. "I didn't say I wanted champagne."

"You love champagne. It's your drink of choice," he declares.

My eyebrows shoot up. "And you guessed this, how?"

"Nothing a little bit of research didn't reveal."

I stiffen. "You had me investigated?"

"Something you already knew about." He continues, "As you did me."

I blink, then surprise myself when laughter tumbles out from between my lips. "Touché." I raise my glass.

He seems taken aback, himself. Then his lips curve up in a smile that's so open, so real that something flutters deep inside. It's probably ripples of hunger, that's all. I had very little for lunch and no breakfast. That's the reason my stomach seems to be bottoming out.

"Also, your acting skills need leveling up."

"Excuse me?"

"You knew you were being followed, considering you gave my investigator the slip a few times."

I raise a shoulder. "So, get a better investigator."

This time it's he who barks out a laugh. "Keep up this banter, and I'll begin to think it's our brand of foreplay."

"You wish," I scoff.

His grin widens. "Of course, the fact that you evaded the detective I had on you makes me wonder what you have to hide."

The blood drains from my features, then I tip up my chin. "Maybe I have a lover."

"No, you don't."

I pull back my shoulders. "You seem awfully confident about that, Minister."

He stares at me. "Why is that so sexy coming from you?"

Heat flushes my skin, and my mouth dries. Why is it so hot to hear him say that particular four-letter word? Why is the thought of this man talking filthy to me such a turn on? I toss my hair over my shoulder, then tip up my chin. "Hold your horses. I only called you, Minister, not *Prime Minister*, which you're not—"

"—yet," he adds smoothly, then narrows his gaze. "You can't belong to anyone else."

"Oh?"

He nods. "You're mine, Zara, and I'll do everything in my power to make you accept that."

My belly quivers. My pussy clenches. I feel the tickling sensation between my legs that tells me I'm getting turned on, and I squeeze my thighs together in an attempt to soothe away the itch between them. Why is his declaration of intent so erotic? Why is the focus in his eyes as he fixes his gaze on me, and only me, make me feel like I won the lottery by becoming the cynosure of his attention?

I square my shoulders and grip the stem of my flute glass tighter. "And if you can't?" I tip up my chin. "

"I've never lost... And I don't intend to start now." He touches his glass to mine. "To us."

"There is no us," I scoff.

"Not yet."

"Excuse me?" I widen my gaze. "I'm not sure I heard you correctly."

"Oh, you did. You just don't want to admit it."

He brings the flute to his lips and takes a sip of his champagne. The tendons of his throat move as he swallows. My pulse rate speeds up.

Stupid. This is stupid—really stupid. I underestimated him. I thought I hated him. Oh, subconsciously, I'd noticed how my body reacted to his nearness, but I'd simply set that to one side. I'm not the kind who will allow my desires to lead me. Not after I've worked so hard my entire life to get to where I am. To break stereotypes. To make a difference to my community and to my country. This is what I've always wanted. This is why I studied so hard, why I got a scholarship to study law, then started my own PR firm. Why I've been so focused on my goals, to the exclusion of everything else. Why I accepted his challenge to spend time with him. I was confident I'd come out on top of our encounter. But now, I'm not so sure. And one thing I'm not is stupid. I know when to stage a strategic retreat. "Excuse me, but I have to leave."

I place my glass of champagne on the table and begin to rise to my feet, but he swoops out his hand and grabs my hand. Electricity shoots out from the point of contact. My breath catches in my chest. I look at where his fingers are wrapped about my wrist, then glance up to find his gaze locked on my face. Some of the color seems to have drained from his features. He releases me, and I sit back down. We stare at each other. The silence stretches.

Then the waiter wheels in a cart of food. What the—? He ordered ahead and decided to order for me, as well? Overbearing wanker. The waiter places a dish in front of me, then another in front of Hunter before, once more, retreating. All this time, we haven't taken our gazes off of each other. My throat closes. My pulse thuds at my temples.

Moisture pools between my legs, and I clench my pussy and wriggle around in my seat.

"That..." He inclines his head and smirks. "That is what I'm talking about."

"What?" I laugh, or at least try to, but all that emerges is a thready sound.

"You sensed it, same as I did. This chemistry that sizzles between us."

"We've only met a few times in person."

"And yet, every time I enter a room with you in it, my gaze instantly finds you."

Heat flushes my cheeks, but I manage to school my features into an expression of nonchalance. "Not my fault." I raise a shoulder.

"Don't shrug it off. If we don't address this" —he points to the space between us— "it's only going to build and become so monumental, it'll hurt something or someone. Possibly, both of us."

I pretend to yawn; except when I pat my mouth, my fingers are shaking. "I have no idea what you mean."

His eyebrows draw down, and for a second, he looks disappointed. "Funny, I had you pegged as the kind of woman who wouldn't hesitate to speak the truth, no matter how difficult."

"I'm also someone who knows when I'm better off ignoring the obvious."

"So, you'd rather lie to yourself than face the fact that the chemistry between us is explosive?"

"You said it; not me." I bite the inside of my cheek.

"I have a better idea. A way in which we can both be truthful to ourselves and walk away from this with our careers intact."

"Oh, so you do understand how dangerous it is for the two of us to even be seen together, let alone having dinner?"

"Which is why I've ensured privacy." He waves his hand at our surroundings. "And I have absolute trust in the restaurant staff, as well as my security detail. Additionally, I had my security detail ensure you weren't followed here by anyone else."

I stare at him. "I'm not sure if I should be impressed by your thoroughness or creeped out by how rigorous you've been in thinking through the possibilities."

"One thing you should realize about me... I'm always one step ahead of the obvious," he murmurs.

"One thing you should realize..." I lean forward in my seat. "I'm always thinking ten steps ahead of my rival."

This time, he's the one who laughs. "Am I your rival?"

"Aren't you?"

"When it comes to our jobs, yes, we don't see eye to eye. But I do believe we can use this intense hostility we feel toward each other to our advantage, when it comes to our personal lives."

I tip up my chin. "My personal life is my own business."

"Not anymore. Not since you caught my eye. Not since you can't stop tracking me with your gaze when we're in the same space and stalking me online when we're not."

"I don't stalk you—" I firm my lips.

He smirks. "That's what I thought. You're as obsessed with me as I am with you."

I open my mouth to protest, but he holds up his finger. "Don't even try to deny it. You and I both know, the fact that we never seem to get along when we meet is more than because we belong to opposing sides. It's because we are both aware of the other to an extent which is unhealthy."

"I am not going to dignify that statement with a response."

"All you need to do is accept my offer."

"Which is?"

"Let's fuck it out."

# 2

Hunter

"You're kidding me... aren't you?" Twin spots of color burn high on her cheeks. Her features wear an expression of surprise and shock, but her pupils are dilated, the black bleeding out until only a thin circle of gold can be seen around the circumference. Her chest rises and falls. She's flushed and angry, and also, turned on. I didn't think it was possible to shock her, but clearly, I have. Which is what I'd hoped for, of course. Except, I hadn't thought I'd be able to achieve it.

Since the moment I first laid eyes on Zara Chopra, she's fascinated me and also surprised me. Truth be told, I'm not even sure I like her. For one, she's curvy, with the kind of hourglass figure I didn't think I found alluring, until her. My previous girlfriends have been slimmer; mostly models and actresses, or those who've earned a living through their looks.

Zara, on the other hand, has striking features and is clearly more than a pretty face. In fact, she's the exact opposite of the kind of woman I normally date. Not only have we fought each time we've met, but she's also made it clear the dislike is mutual. Which I admit, is a blow to my ego. I've never met a woman who has been able to resist me. Until her. Perhaps, that's why I made that offer to her. Perhaps, the fact that we don't see eye-to-eye makes her the kind of challenge I relish.

I didn't bring her here with the intention of doing so, but when she sat opposite me and seemed unmoved by my presence, I had to test her. I wanted to catch her off guard—which I did. And perhaps, also, myself. For until I heard my own words, I didn't realize just how much I mean it. How much I want to bend her over this table right now and explore what it means to have her writhing under me, impaled on my cock, as I bring her to orgasm over and over again.

"Do I look like the kind of man who'd say anything I don't mean?"

"You're a politician," she scoffs.

"And you aren't?"

She firms her lips. "I'm a fixer, I solve problems. I am not the one who makes them, I leave that to you politicians."

"Spoken like a true salesperson."

She blows out a breath. "I didn't come here to be insulted."

"That wasn't an insult. Salespeople are some of the most persuasive, some of the cleverest people I've met."

"You'll forgive me if I don't agree with you. You ask me to dinner, then tell me you had me investigated, then order my favorite drink and" —she glances down at her plate, then back at me— "my favorite food."

"So, I did my homework." I raise my shoulder.

"Then" —she raises her forefinger— "you tell me you want to fuck me."

"I said we should fuck each other."

"No, thank you."

I lean forward in my seat. "You scared you'll like it too much?"

"I'm not going to answer that. I'm not falling for that again."

I survey her still-flushed features. "You are worried that you might be spoiled for anyone else after our encounter."

"Your ego knows no bounds."

"And your ego would never settle for anyone with balls smaller than mine."

She stares at me, then throws her head back and laughs. It's a full-bellied laugh that comes from the depths of her being. Her eyes are squeezed shut, and her mouth is open. It's not a pretty laugh; it's a wicked, full-of-life laugh. It's the laugh of a woman who knows how to enjoy life.

"Let's enjoy ourselves, Zara. One night. You and me. Let's find out why it is, that even though we can't stand each other, we also gravitate toward each other."

She lowers her head and fixes me with those glowing, tawny eyes of hers. The candlelight dances over her skin, highlighting her high cheekbones, her upturned nose, her stubborn chin. She's going to be a handful. She'll never give in without a fight. She'll resist me every step of the way, and fuck, if I don't find that thought exciting. Nobody has piqued my interest, or drawn my hackles, or made me want to both spank her and kiss her at the same time, as this woman has.

"What do you say? Twelve hours. Until the sun comes up, we explore why it is that we're so drawn to each other, even as we also hate the other's guts."

One side of her lips kicks up. She reaches for her champagne and takes a sip. "Very clever. You think by outlining all of the reasons this is going to make our relationship exciting, you'll tempt me?"

"So, you agree that we're going to have a relationship?"

A crease appears between her eyebrows. "That was a figure of speech."

"Or a Freudian slip."

"Or a slip of the tongue." She trails her finger around the rim of her champagne glass, and my balls tighten. Goddamn! Now she's teasing me, while she still continues to deny the attraction. Every little action of hers is calculated to tease me. She has the way of a seductress, a siren song on her lips, and the look of a huntress in her eyes. She's unharnessed, unbridled, a wildling come to turn my world upside-down. An untamed vixen who'll steal my heart and my soul, and whose name will be stamped into every cell of my body.

The hair on the back of my neck rises. Something like a forewarning ripples up my spine. Get away from her. Leave. Get out as soon as you can, before things get too complicated.

A-n-d the very fact that I have that thought, that for the first time in my life, I, Hunter Whittington, am thinking of leaving the battlefield without even trying to engage with my opponent, gives me pause. I'm not a coward. It takes balls to embark on a career in the public eye. It takes nerves of steel to decide to run for the highest office in this country. It takes courage of conviction and a special kind of crazy to embark on the journey I have. And I wouldn't have done it if I didn't love a challenge. If I didn't relish the opportunity to win a confrontation. If I didn't enjoy finding my way through obstacles. All of which she seems to personify. I drag my finger across my lower lip.

"I'd love to slip my tongue inside you," I murmur.

Her gaze widens. A pulse throbs to life at the base of her neck. She bites down on her lower lip, and I feel the tug all the way to the base of my cock.

I tighten my grip about my own glass of champagne. "You liked that, didn't you?"

She huffs. "I expected better than a cliché from you."

"Clichés exist because they're true."

"And I thought you were capable of more original thinking?"

"You don't want to know what I'm thinking right now."

She holds my gaze boldly. "Why don't you tell me?"

I release the hold on my flute, then lean forward and slide her glass from her grasp. I turn it to where the mark of her lips graces the rim and take a sip of the sparkling wine. "Are you sure you want to hear this?"

Her lips part, then she raises one brow. "Try me."

"I want to touch your curves and fondle the dips in your body. I want to hold you and kiss you and bite you and suck on you. I want to lick you, taste you, sink my fingers inside you. I want to take you to the edge over and over again, until your blood is coursing with pheromones; until you're so high from the experience, you'll be spoiled for anyone else; until all you can think of is me, all you can taste is me; until your every breath belongs to me; until" —I place my hand over hers— "I bring you to your knees and have you begging me to show you every depraved thing I can do to you; until I bring every secret, perverted dream of yours to life; until you're begging me to show you just how far I can push you; until you surprise even yourself."

Her breath hitches.

"I want to arouse you to the point you have no other thoughts but how it will be to have my cock buried in your pussy, my fingers in your arse, my tongue in your mouth, and how I'll take you to the edge until you beg me to come and even then, I won't let you—"

"Unless?" she breathes.

"Unless you submit to me."

# 3

---

Zara

His words are filthy and explicit, obscene and so damn hot. I shouldn't find them so hot. I shouldn't find his lack of filter in outlining exactly what he wants to do to me such a turn on. But it is. I enjoy sex. I enjoy men. I enjoy how it feels when my body is treated like it was made for another's pleasure. I want to find out how it feels to be dominated. But I'll never let anyone close enough for that.

It's why my persona is that of a confident woman who's aware of her sexuality and of the effect she has on men, most of whom are threatened by how I come across. A powerful career woman. It's why the kind of men I attract are more than happy for me to set the agenda in bed. It's something I both hate and relish, for then, I'm in control. And if I'm in control, I can't be threatened. It's what I'm comfortable with, and perhaps, it's why I prefer to bed the kind of men I can hold sway over.

This man, though, is nothing like anyone I've faced before. Not in my work life, and not in my personal life. He's not threatened by me, and each time I challenge him, it seems to make him determined to confront me right back. And it's invigorating, to say the least. It's also annoying. Because I don't want to like anything about this man. But the very fact that he can look me in the eye and lay out what he wants to do to me is exhilarating, but also makes me want to defy him. The hair on my forearms rises. My guts clench, and that's only because I'm angry with him. That's all it is.

"Submit to you, huh? If you think I'm going to give in to you, you can think again."

He holds my gaze for a few seconds, then smirks. The jerkface curls his lips. "Is that a challenge?"

*Oh, I'm so not walking into that one.* "I don't care how you take it. This conversation is over." I jump to my feet and snatch my handbag.

I turn to leave when— "So this is what happens when you come up against your match? You pivot and run?" he drawls.

I draw in a breath. *I will not lose my temper. Will not lose my temper.* I take another step forward, when he speaks again.

"I guess I was right. You're too chicken to find out how good things could be between us. Bet you're worried you'll be spoiled for anyone else, you—"

I spin around and stab a finger in his direction. "Please, don't make this about me. I'm leaving before I say or do something that will blow up into something neither of us will be able to handle."

His grin widens. "Oh, please. By all means, speak your mind. It's why I brought you here, so we could clear the air."

"By you propositioning me?"

"That's one route we could take. The most enjoyable route, too." He smirks.

"Are you listening to yourself?" I fume.

"Are you listening to yourself?" He leans back in his chair. "You're angry at me."

"Thanks for noticing, Captain Obvious."

"When was the last time you got angry at anyone?"

I scowl at him. "Is that a trick question?"

"Think about it, Zara. When was the last time someone pissed you off so much, you decided to leave a meal without even tasting the food?"

I glance at the dish sitting at my abandoned place. It has fish and chips, my favorite dish. And he ordered it for me.

"It's spicy and the fish is halibut." He refers to the lean white fish that's not easily available. The side dish is a salad with baby lettuce, rocket leaves, and pomegranate seeds. It's a combination I love, and one which is not available on most menus. I know because I made up the salad recipe myself.

I glower at him. "How did you know—"

"That you like this specific type of fish, and you prefer your fish and chips extra spicy? That the only time you eat your greens is when it's spiked with pomegranate seeds?" His lips curve up in a smile that's half-wicked, half-satisfied. "Did I surprise you?"

I sniff. "Probably just something else that came up in the reports you had ordered on me."

"Why don't you sit down and finish it, hmm?"

"I think not." I eye the fish and my stomach growls.

He must hear it because he laughs. "Come on, Zara. You have to admit, the interaction over the past half hour is the most stimulation you've had in conversation with another person in a while."

"Don't flatter yourself," I mutter. He's right, though. I've never felt more alive than in the time I've spent with him. It's a combination of nervousness and excitement, with breathless anticipation thrown in. A feeling I only get when I'm faced with a new challenge. Which intrigues me. Which is the only reason I am still here and haven't walked out on him. That, and this chemistry between us, which I can't understand. A problem I need to resolve. I'm a fixer, after all. Nothing engages me more than a puzzle that needs to be put together.

"Sit. Eat." He leans back in his seat. "I promise, I won't even point out that you still haven't answered my earlier question."

I shake my head. "Seriously, and I thought I had a big ego, but yours just might be more colossal."

"Not the only thing that's colossal." He smirks.

I make a gagging sound in my throat. "How very unoriginal of you."

"Have dinner with me, and I promise, I'll reveal more creative ripostes."

I take my seat and plant my bag on the adjacent chair, then reach for my knife and fork. I cut into the fish and place a small portion in my mouth. The delicate, almost flowery notes of its flesh melt on my tongue. That, combined with the sizzle of the spices in which it's been marinated, makes it seem like the two different parts of my heritage have coalesced on my palate. "Wow." I chew and swallow. "That's amazing."

"Right?" He digs into his own food. He's ordered a burger and fries —another surprise. I hadn't thought this man was capable of eating anything so ordinary. But then, I don't really know him at all, so guess I shouldn't be surprised. Maybe I shouldn't have been so hasty in judging him. And maybe that's the reason he's brought me here—so he can soften my opinion of him. Well, it's going to take more than a plate of fish and chips, even if it's possibly the best fish and chips I've ever had, to alter my viewpoint. So what, if he took the time to find out what my tastes run to and ordered accordingly? He still decided to do it without consulting me, thinking I'd fall in with his plans. It shows just how egotistical he is. How much he's taking me for granted. And I can't wait to show him that I know my own mind. I'm not one of those easily maneuverable bimbos he, no doubt, likes to hang out with.

He forks up a piece of the burger and holds it out to me. "Here, taste this."

"Umm" —I glance from the food on his fork to him— "you want to feed me?"

"Humor me." He half smiles, and it's a smile devoid of any agenda. Well, in as much as that's possible for a twathole like him. When I hesitate, he brings it closer to my mouth so the food brushes my lips. "Go on, you know you want to."

The scent of the burger is so aromatic, my mouth waters. *Oh, fuck this. It's only food.* Letting him feed me doesn't mean I'm submitting to him. I'm only pretending to play along with his agenda. I'm trying to lull him into a false sense of comfort, so he'll let down his walls and share a little more of himself with me.

*And he's trying to entice you to do the same.* Sure, he is, but I'm too smart to fall for his moves, no matter how smooth they are.

I open my mouth, and he feeds me the morsel. I close my lips and wipe the tines clean as he slides the fork back. The whole time, he holds my gaze. His blue-green eyes deepen until they are almost azure. My belly clenches, the pulse between my legs speeds up, and some-how, the simple task of feeding me has turned into a seduction. Damn, but he's good. Then the flavors overcome my senses. The meat is so tender, it seems to dissolve on my tongue, and the herbs woven through are so fresh, I can feel the wind in the trees and the slither of grass between my toes as I walk barefoot through a field somewhere far away from this city.

I flutter my eyelids open—when did I close them? —and stare at him in amazement.

"I know," he laughs. "James Hamilton is the most talented chef in the country."

I gape at him. "You called James Hamilton and had him shut down his restaurant for us?"

He arches his eyebrows. "Have I finally managed to impress you?"

"You got the most sought-after chef in, perhaps, the world to cook for us, so yeah, I'd say, yes."

"So, food is the way to get through your defenses, eh?"

"I never said that."

"You don't need to. The very fact that you're more relaxed after eating speaks for itself."

"Good food, good drink—" I raise my glass. "Despite present company, I admit, I'm not as wound up as I was. Let's just say I was hangry."

He chuckles. "Go on, you can complement me for my efforts. It's allowed."

"Fine, it wasn't a bad effort." I admit.

He smirks. "It's going to be interesting to up my ante with you."

"You don't have to up your anything with me, Hunter."

His grin widens, "I could up a lot of things, but in specific, one thing, when it comes to you, Zara."

I blink. The flesh between my legs clenches. *I did not find that hot. I did not. I did. OMG.* That was a cringe-worthy remark from him—not particularly original but damn, it seems to be working on me. *How am I going to live this down?* I raise my hand, palm facing him. "Don't try to distract me from what I'm going to say."

"Which is?"

"That we're different. We have nothing in common. And it's madness to even think we could sleep together and get away with it. But I got to taste James Hamilton's food, so it's not a completely wasted evening."

"Say that again." He studies me with a strange look in his eyes. Like he's realized something but is trying his best not to acknowledge it.

"Umm, that it's not a completely wasted evening?"

"No, before that."

"That we have nothing in common?"

"Prior to that."

"Huh?" I try to think back. "Prior to that I said.. That we're so different, and before that I said... Your name?"

"Say it again," he murmurs.

"This is madness." I place my fork back on my embarrassingly empty plate. "I really should leave."

"Zara," he lowers his voice to a hush, and a frisson of anticipation sizzles up my spine. My nerve endings seem to spark. My pulse rate shoots up. And all because he said my name in that tone… That very dominant tone of his.

I rise to my feet. He narrows his gaze. "Sit down, Zara."

My backside hits the chair, and I blink. What the—? Did I just follow his order? Did I obey him, without intending to? When was the last time that happened? When has that ever happened as an adult? No man has ever dared to command me to do his bidding. I've never followed someone else's orders. Not like this. Not in my personal life. Even worse, I don't feel guilty about it.

I feel queasy, like I've stepped off a cliff, and instead of falling, I'm being pulled higher in the air, and I'm waiting for my stomach to catch up with the rest of my body. My blood begins to pump harder through my veins. The pulse between my legs becomes thicker, harder, stronger. And all because he directed my actions. This…is…insane. I feel so out of my depth. Like someone has cut off the cords that ground me and now I'm floating…floating.

I draw in a deep breath, then another. Draw on an ember of anger low in my belly. I fan it until it spreads through my stomach, my blood, my arms. I reach for the glass of champagne and toss it in his face.

# 4

Hunter

One second, we're engaged in that now familiar battle of wills, where our gazes are clashing and holding, and neither of us is ready to back down. The thrill of the chase unfurls in my chest. My blood begins to thump through my veins. My vision narrows. Adrenaline laces my blood, but before I can act, she's thrown the champagne in my face. The liquid stings my eyes, drips down my cheeks, and I react on pure instinct. I jump to my feet, lean forward and grab her arm before she can withdraw it.

"Let me go," she snaps.

"No."

I tighten my grip on her wrist and the empty champagne flute slips from her fingers. It hits the table with a soft thud and rolls once, then stills.

"You shouldn't have done that," I say slowly.

"You deserved it," she spits at me.

"You're gorgeous."

She stills. "Excuse me?"

"You heard me. You're magnificent when you're angry. Your eyes flash fire. Your cheeks turn a gorgeous color that makes me want to close the distance between us and lick you up."

She shakes her head. "Am I dreaming? I must be dreaming that I'm in this restaurant with one of the people I hate the most holding my hand."

"Hate fuck. Think of how explosive it will be when we come together."

"Keep dreaming." She tosses her hair back from her face.

"It can be a reality, Z."

"Don't call me that."

"I feel like we've blown past the preliminary part of our relationship already."

She raises the forefinger of her left hand. "One. There is no relationship. And two" —she holds up her middle finger— "you can go fuck yourself." She lowers her forefinger and keeps only her middle finger upright.

"There she is. You turn me on when you get enraged."

"Didn't you listen to me?" She thrusts her middle finger forward. "I want nothing to do with you."

"And I want everything you can give me." I grab her free hand and pull so we're both stretched across the table with our faces so close our noses almost bump. I bring her outstretched middle finger to my mouth and close my lips around it.

She draws in a sharp breath and her pupils dilate. Those golden-brown sparks in her eyes glitter until they lighten to silver shards. I curl my tongue around her digit and suck harder.

A moan bleeds from her lips. The taste of her floods my mouth, sinks into my blood. My groin hardens. The crotch of my pants tightens. She lowers her gaze to my mouth and swallows. Her lips part. The scent of her, orange blossoms and vanilla with a hint of pepper, floods my senses.

She leans in closer, until our eyelashes tangle. She raises her gaze to mine, and lust flares in the depths of her eyes.

The blood beats in my ears, and goddamn, I want to kiss her. And I will... Just not yet. First, I need to tease her, taunt her, seduce her. Perhaps, court her. Coax her, so she comes willingly. Here, kitty, kitty.

"Maybe next time." I release her so suddenly, she falls back into her chair.

"What the—?" She gapes at me.

"You wanted to leave? This is your chance."

"After that…that…" She seems at a loss for words.

I mentally fist-pump. Rule number one in any negotiation is to catch your opponent off guard, and that's exactly what I've done. Question is, what's she going to do next?

She seems to get control of her emotions. "You're an asshole."

"Alphahole." I smirk.

Her gaze narrows. "Do you play chess?"

"Eh?" It's my turn to be surprised.

"Chess, Whittington. Do you play chess?"

"Do you wish to be beaten at your own game?"

She narrows her eyes. "You wish." She squares her shoulders. "Let's move our encounter to a more equal footing."

"Ah, so you're going to see me again?"

She firms her lips.

"You said it, not me," I remind her.

"I didn't mean to, but you got me so pissed-off, I didn't realize I was committing myself to seeing you again."

"Are you backing out?"

She tips up her chin. "I don't go back on my word."

"Neither do I."

"Good." She sniffs.

"Good." I widen my smile.

"Wipe that grin off of your face. You don't need to look so satisfied."

My phone pings a warning. "A-n-d, our two hours are up. Time sure goes by fast when you're having fun."

She makes a rude sound. "Whatever."

"Ah, the famous word that's the last resort when no other insults come to mind." I smirk.

She picks up her bag and slides it over her shoulder. "Goodbye, Whittington."

"Not so fast." I round the table and tuck her arm through mine. She trembles a little. Good. She's responding to my proximity. Which means, she'll miss me when I'm not around. Which will help build up anticipation for our next meeting.

When we reach the maître d's station by the entrance, he steps up with our coats. I hold hers up, and she slips her arms through the sleeves. I smooth it over her shoulders and lean in enough to sniff her hair. Orange blossoms and vanilla tease my senses. My cock lengthens at once. It's as if I'm hardwired to respond to her at every level. Which is…interesting, to say the least. When the chemistry between us finally explodes, it's going to be incendiary.

I step back and slide my arms through the sleeves of my jacket the maître d' holds out for me.

"Thank you, Charles."

"Pleasure, sir. Madam." He tips his head and melts back into the darkness.

Our security detail walks ahead, and I lead her to the door. By the time we step out of the restaurant, my Aston Martin is waiting for us. I open the door, and she slides in. I round the car, slip into the driver's seat, then ease the car forward.

We drive in silence for a few seconds, then I jerk my chin in the direction of the glove compartment. "Open it."

She glances at the built-in door in the dash, then back at me with a frown. "I'd rather not."

"I promise, it's not what you think," I coax.

The groove between her eyebrows furrows. "You have no idea what I'm thinking right now."

"You're thinking how much you'd like to slap me, then kiss me." I smirk.

Her jaw drops, then she laughs. "So damn cocky."

"With good reason."

"Not going there now," she warns.

"Go on, open the door and look inside, Alice."

She shoots me a glance from under those thick eyelashes, "Only because you referred to Alice in Wonderland."

"Do you know *The Matrix* was inspired by it?"

She blinks. "Was it?"

"Nah." I grin.

She scowls, then chuckles again. "You can be charming, if a little cringe-worthy, I'll give you that."

"And you want to open that door." I nod in the direction of the glove compartment again, "Go on, do it."

"Hmph." She leans over and presses the button on the panel, and it slides down. There in the middle of the space is a colorful rectangular packet. She reaches for it and draws it out, then holds it out to me.

"Haribo?" she asks in a dazed voice.

"They're your favorite," I say simply.

"You bought me Haribo gummy bears?" Her voice has a breathless quality to it now.

"Open it," I urge.

She tears open the small packet and pours out a few in the palm of her hand. "They are all the same color."

"Gold."

I say at the same time as her.

"They're your favorite," I add.

"You never get Haribo bears all in one color in one packet."

"I do."

She looks up at me, then back at the packet. "Not sure what to make of this." Her voice now has a touch of panic to it.

"It's only candy, Zara; don't read anything into the gesture."

"You're doing this to throw me off-kilter."

"Am I succeeding?"

She squares her shoulder. "Of course, not."

"Good, so why don't you eat one?"

She looks down at the splash of gold in her palm. "Maybe I will."

She pops one into her mouth, slides the rest back into the packet, except one. She drops the pack into her bag, then reaches over and holds it out in front of my mouth.

Without taking my eyes off the road, I open my mouth and she slides it in. I close my lips about her fingers and lick the gummy bear off her digits. The taste of her, more complex than the sweetness of the candy, goes straight to my groin.

I draw in a sharp breath; so does she.

She leans back, and out of the corner of my eye I watch as she brings the fingers to her mouth and sucks on them. A white flash of heat zings through my chest. I tighten my fingers about the steering wheel.

Her chest rises and falls, and I sense a ripple of something pulse through her body. The air between us grows heavy with lust, charged with the kind of lust that could detonate at any second. I knew the chemistry between us was explosive, but this is taking things to another level of combustion.

For a few seconds, neither of us says anything, then she reaches forward and touches the panel on the dash. The haunting strains of Mozart's "The Queen of the Night" flood the space. Some of the tension eases… Only because I'm going to let this go for now.

"Didn't take you for someone who listens to classical music," she murmurs.

"My mother loved listening to it. My fondest memories are of her knitting while listening to classical music, while my father worked on his papers in the study."

"That sounds like a very cozy scene."

"She was a home-body. She loved her husband and her sons." At least, until it all went to shite.

"You have a brother?" She turns to look at me.

I nod.

"Is he older than you?"

"Younger."

"I guess he's not in politics, or I'd have heard of him."

"He's not. He prefers not to be associated with the Whittingtons. He turned his back on his family and currently lives in Thailand, or at least, that's where he was when I last heard from him."

"Ah, so he's the rebel, and you're the obedient son?"

"Do I look like an obedient son?" I scoff.

"You look like no one can make you do anything you don't want to do."

"Very astute, Councilor." I shoot her a sideways glance before turning back to the road. "Why did a lawyer decide to get into the big bad world of PR?"

"You mean, the only professions worse than that of a lawyer are being a journalist or a spin-doctor, and I opted for the last?"

"You said it." I smirk.

"I got into law because my parents asked me to choose between becoming a doctor or a lawyer, and I knew I wasn't cut out to be a doctor, so—" She raises a shoulder.

"And PR?"

"I have the gift of gab and I've always been fascinated by media. Besides, I think becoming a lawyer prepared me for the cut-throat world of PR, don't you think?"

"As a politician, I'll be the first to admit that I loathe spin doctors while also knowing I can't do without them."

"You said it," she says lightly.

I laugh. "You're a breath of fresh air."

"You mean, as opposed to the models you normally date?"

"Was this a date?"

"You tell me."

I ease to a stop for a red light, then turn to her. "If this were a date, I'd have dismissed our security detail from the restaurant and told the staff to leave us undisturbed. Then, I'd have bent you over the table and fucked you so hard, you'd have felt the imprint of my cock for days."

Her breath hitches. Even in the dim light, I can see her pupils dilate.

"Does that excite you, Zara, hmm?"

"As propositions go, that wasn't very original."

"That wasn't a proposition. That was a statement of intent."

She laughs, then leans back in her seat. "I'm never sleeping with you, Whittington."

A familiar excitement zings through my blood. The hair on my forearms rises. My fingers tingle, and before I can change my mind, I reach forward, wrap my fingers about the nape of her neck, and pull her forward.

"Wait, what are you—"

I kiss her. I press my lips to hers and inhale her breath. For a few seconds, she remains stiff, either from surprise or because she's holding herself back. Tension vibrates off of her. Her entire body is one coiled mass of rigidity. I soften my mouth. I nip on her lower lip, and with a groan, she parts her lips. I sweep my tongue inside, tangle with hers. Suck on her, draw from her. Pull her as close as the seatbelts we're wearing will allow. I tilt my head and deepen the kiss. A moan bleeds from her. The blood in my body drains to my groin. The crotch of my pants tightens. A hot sensation wells in my chest. A shiver runs down my spine. All the cells in my body seem to come alive at once. Fuck, I need to get closer, need to be inside her, need to—

The blare of a horn cuts through the haze, and we break apart. Her pulse beats at the base of her throat; her glorious hair flows about her shoulders. Her lips are swollen, and she's staring at me with a dazed expression on her face. She's not the only one who's surprised. I hadn't thought it was possible for me to want a woman so much, so quickly. Especially a woman I had a strong reaction to on sight—something that doesn't happen often.

I thought I hated her. Turns out, my response to her is more complex than that. It's not black or white. It's more layered... More complicated. It's more… Everything. It's definitely unexpected. The car behind us honks again. I step on the accelerator, and the car moves forward. We drive in silence until I turn off the main road onto the side street leading to her apartment.

"If you think that kiss changed anything, *you're* mistaken."

"If you think that kiss *meant* anything, you're mistaken."

"Oh, trust me, I know exactly what it was. A chauvinistic way for you to shut me up. I told you I wasn't going to sleep with you, so of course, you took it as a challenge. You wanted to prove to yourself, and to me, that I want you, and I assure you, even if I did—which I don't—I'd get someone else to scratch the itch."

I brake so suddenly, we're thrown against our seat belts. I park the car, release my seatbelt, lean over, unlock hers, and once more, grip the nape of her neck and pull her across the partition between our seats.

"Wha—"

I don't let her complete the word. I close my mouth over hers and kiss her fiercely. She slaps her hand against my shoulder, then keeps it there, palm flattened against my jacket. I tighten my hold on her, bring my other hand up, and bury my fingers in her hair. I tug on it, and she shudders. I deepen the kiss, and with a groan, she grips the front of my shirt with her free arm and tugs me even closer. She bites down on my lower lip, and my cock jerks. My thighs harden. I thrust my tongue inside her mouth, dancing it over hers. Her chest rises and falls, her breasts crushed into my chest. The taste of her coats my mouth, the scent of her sinks into my skin, her curves melt into me, and my head spins. My breath comes in pants. A bead of sweat slides down my spine. My stomach muscles harden until it feels like I've been sucker-punched. I release her mouth and stare into her eyes. She holds my gaze, the look in hers dazed and angry. She moves, and I guess her intention, but I don't stop her as her palm connects with my cheek. My face snaps back with the momentum, but I don't look away.

She searches my features, with something resembling panic on her face. "Don't ever do that again," she spits out.

"Worried you won't be able to stop next time?"

"If I were you, I'd be worried about keeping my balls," she retorts.

"I told you we should have simply fucked it out."

"You're irredeemable." She raises her hand again, and this time, I catch her wrist. In a flash, I twist it behind her back so her breasts are thrust out. I take my time perusing her features, down the arch of her slender neck to where her tits are outlined against the coat she's wearing. By the time I raise my gaze, her face is flushed.

"I'm not going to apologize for what I did," I drawl.

"You're conforming to your image of being an inconsiderate twat," she snaps.

"Keep talking dirty, and I won't be responsible for what happens next."

She tries to pull away, but I tighten my grip on her.

"You may be physically stronger than me, but I promise you, I'll never give into you." She bares her teeth at me, and goddamn, all of my senses home in on her. I want nothing more than to throw her over my lap and spank her curvy behind before I take her so hard, we both see stars. Unfortunately, though, that will have to wait.

"That remains to be seen." I lift her back over to her seat, then straighten.

"You're an animal," she snaps.

"Only with you."

She blinks, then barks out a laugh. "That should sound trite, but somehow, coming from you, I almost believe it. Almost."

I rake my fingers through my hair, then drum my fingers on the wheel, "Believe it. I don't normally get this handsy on a first date—"

"Not a date."

"I took you to a restaurant, we ate, we kissed. Twice. It's a date."

She draws in a breath, and for a few seconds we sit there in silence. Then she murmurs, "You also bought me Haribos."

"I did."

"Thank you for that."

I tilt my head. "You're welcome."

"I suppose you're right." She straightens her spine, "It was a date, but believe me, it's never going to happen again."

We'll see.

She snatches her bag from where it's fallen on the floor. By the time she's shoved her door open, I've walked around the car. I hold it open for her as she steps out.

"You don't have to walk me to my door."

"On the contrary." I nod to my security detail who are poised on either side of the vehicle, then I walk her up the driveway. She uses her keycard to open the front door and I follow her in, up the wide staircase and to the door of her apartment.

"I'm not going to invite you in."

"I didn't expect you to."

She opens her door, then steps inside and turns to me. "I'm not going to thank you for tonight, either, except maybe for the champagne and the food which, I have to admit, were exceptional."

She goes to shut the door, and I plant my foot in the way. "See me again."

She laughs. "No fucking way."

"I'll get my way, one way or the other."

She sets her chin. "Not if I can help it."

"Don't underestimate me." I narrow my gaze. "When I want something, I go after it."

"Don't patronize me. Once I make up my mind, it's very difficult to change it."

A sizzle of excitement zips up my spine. Adrenaline laces my blood. Fucking hell, this thrust and parry of words, this matching of wits is as potent as foreplay.

"And what if I get you to come out with me again?"

She snorts. "Not gonna happen. But if it does, I promise you, next time, I'll be the one to initiate the kiss."

I hold out my hand. "Deal."

# 5

Zara

"So let me get this right. Cesar Underwood's car was caught speeding on camera, but he claims his car was stolen and it wasn't him?"

Steve, my right-hand person nods. "We suspect it's either because he was visiting someone he shouldn't or because his car really was stolen."

It's been three months since that dinner with Hunter. Two months in which I have seen Hunter's growing profile in the media. Clearly, he's being groomed by his party to take on the role of the next Prime Minister. The country will be going to the polls soon and rumor is the sitting Prime Minister is going to resign with Hunter tipped to take his place as the lead candidate. Keeping aside my personal issues with Hunter, I have to admit that he makes for a charismatic contestant.

His relative youth in comparison to his opponent, his presence, which the camera loves, the force of his personality, that comes through almost as strongly through any media platform as in real life, and the fact that when he speaks you are compelled to listen means his approval ratings in the polls have sky rocketed in the months since I met him. And all this time, there hasn't been a call or a text from him. Not that I had expected it. Okay, maybe I had...

A little. A man doesn't take you out to dinner then eye-fuck you the way Hunter did, only to back off because you turned him down. A man like that doesn't take no for an answer. If anything, my declining his overtures will only push him to be challenged. To find a way to come back at me faster and harder than ever, and in a way that will take me by surprise. Which is the only reason I've been following his media coverage. It's best to keep an eye on your opponent, track their every move, and not let them out of your sight. And trust me, I've been following his media appearances. Following his social media feeds, as well as the regular appearances he's been making at various industry shindigs, each time with a different woman on his arm. Not sure who's advising him, but that's the only glitch I could spot in his otherwise constant media presence. He's top-of-mind with the voters, all right, but not always for the right reasons. However, he doesn't seem to be worried about it. Entitled asshole that he is, he probably doesn't care how he comes across to the people. Or maybe he's confident he can smooth over any perceived mistakes with that blindingly bright smile of his.

Either way, I'm not his PR manager so I didn't need to worry about it. Right? Of course, given I am a crisis manager, a spin doctor, and a lawyer, all rolled into one, I'm the best in the business. The one sought after by celebrities, media personalities, and politicians in distress—like Cesar Underwood, who's one of the hottest actors on both sides of the pond right now. Second only to Declan Beauchamp, who I also happen to know personally.

I fold my arms across my chest and glance around the table in the conference room of my office. "Anyone believe Cesar is telling the truth?"

The team shake their heads.

"Anyone believe he was having an affair and was en route to see his mistress?"

The looks on the faces of my team give them away.

I blow out a breath. "That's what I thought."

"You'd think celebrities could, at least, try to be original when they come up with lies," Casey, my social media specialist murmurs without taking her gaze off of the device in her hand.

"I assume the media isn't buying it, and neither is the rest of the internet."

"No surprises there." She winces.

"That bad, huh?"

"Worse." She finally tips up her chin. "He cheated on everyone's sweetheart, who is pregnant at home with their first child. Her fans are baying for blood."

"He's in an impossible situation." Kate, my senior associate and crisis media manager, drums her fingers on the table. "Who'd want to cheat on his pregnant wife who is one of the biggest Hollywood stars and girl next door, within the first year of their marriage?"

"Someone who clearly doesn't know a good thing when he sees it." Casey rolls her eyes.

"Or someone who is running from something and didn't give a damn about being caught," Steve interjects.

"He's not that stupid." Kate sniffs.

"I don't know. When men are in love and trapped, they can go to great lengths to get a semblance of freedom." Steve murmurs.

Kate blinks. "You mean, he's feeling trapped by marriage to the kind of woman every man fantasizes about, which is why he's running out on her?"

Steve raises a shoulder. "Or maybe he just needed space to breathe. A monster hit in Hollywood, followed by marriage to someone the fans adore, with a child on the way, and all in under one year."

"You just listed all the reasons for him not getting an ounce of sympathy from the media or the fans." Kate sniffs.

Steve raises his hands. "So many changes can be an emotional burden for anybody. Then, try living it out in glare of the spotlight where the public scrutinizes your every move, and it's almost understandable why he jumped into his car and ran. If he hadn't been caught by a speed camera, he'd be free, and none of us would be the wiser."

"So why did he lie about it? Why not admit that it was him and pay the fine?" Kate raises her chin.

"Now, that's the big question." Steve touches his fingertips together.

"It's because he was under so much pressure that he decided to have an affair," Casey offers.

Both Kate and Steve look at her.

"What? I'm not making excuses for him, but if we go by what Steve said, it lays the case for him reaching the end of his tether and doing something crazy. Although, in the bigger scheme of things, it's not that crazy, compared to what others before him have done."

"I tend to agree with you," Steve says slowly.

"Whatever the reason may be, we can agree that he acted like a guilty person when he lied." Kate purses her lips.

"And that's the point. We're not here to judge our clients. We're here to solve their problems. It's why the wealthy and the powerful come to us." I slap my hands on my hips. "So, where's Cesar Underwood now?"

"I put him in the Zen meeting room," Mandy replies.

Now, it's my turn to wince. We only use that room when the client who comes in through the door is so stressed out that normal methods of calming them down don't work.

I square my shoulders, then turn and head out the room, Kate and Steve on my heels. I reach the door to the conference room and tap once before I push it open.

The soft sound of flutes and bird song piped in through the speakers fills the air. Underneath it, the tinkling of water from the small water-feature in the corner lends an air of peacefulness. Together with the simple wooden chaise pushed up against one wall, the deep-cushioned chairs opposite it, as well as a lava lamp in another corner and the bamboos growing from a pot near the window, the room manages to retain a semblance of tranquility. This, despite the waves of tension pouring off the man who's standing by the window. I step into the room, and he turns to face me.

"Zara!" He looks exactly like the face on the billboard I pass every day on my drive to work. Almost six foot three, broad shoulders, thick hair that flows back from his face in waves... With his square jaw and sharp cheekbones, he's handsome enough to have been called the most handsome man in the world, only he's nowhere near as charismatic as

Hunter. Huh, how weird I should think that. I'm certainly not saying Hunter's handsome—not at all. Okay maybe he is. From some angles. And why am I thinking of him right now?

"Cesar." I nod in his direction.

"You have to help me, Zara, please." He closes the distance to me in a few strides and grabs my hand.

"And I will, I promise, Cesar." I try to extricate my arm, but he holds onto it. "I didn't do anything wrong, Zara, I swear."

"Except you were at the wrong place at the wrong time," Kate mutters under her breath.

I shoot her a sideways scowl, and Kate wipes the disbelieving look off of her face. She's every inch the professional; it's why I hired her straight out of college six years ago. She's grown with the firm, and I know I can count on her loyalty and her discretion. As I can with all of the other members of my team. Now, she steps forward and pats his shoulder. At least, my team is impervious to his looks. Which is nothing more than I'd expect of them.

It should be difficult to resist the lure of fame and beauty. But when you see the price people pay to stay in the public eye; the dirty laundry that gets aired by the celebrities, media personalities and politicians who pass through these doors, you realize, behind each pretty face lies the seamier side of celebrity popularity. No matter how well-known or how gorgeous the person in front of the camera is. It's only confirmed my belief that those with access to money and power are normally the ones with the most to hide. And Hunter... What is he hiding, I wonder?

"Zara, did you hear what I said?" Cesar's voice cuts through my thoughts.

"Whether we believe you or not, is not the point. It doesn't matter what you did; we'll do our very best to spin it and ensure the media buys into it so you can walk away from this and to your wife—" I search his features. "—assuming that's what you want."

"Yes!" He shakes my hand—which he still hasn't let go of—up and down. "Yes, that's what I want."

There's a knock on the door, and I turn to find Mandy has popped her head through the door. "Uh, Brittney Ward is here."

"What?" Cesar's face pales at the mention of his wife's name. His knees seem to buckle, and now it's me who reaches over and grips his shoulder with my free arm to steady him.

"Cesar, you okay?"

"Yes! No!" He glances about the room with the whites of his eyes showing. "I'm not ready to see her."

I resist the urge to roll my eyes. Of course, he isn't. I turn to Steve, who's already backing out of the room. "I'll keep her occupied for a little while."

I nod with gratitude. I trained him well. Steve's a one-time commando, who defied his superiors when they asked him to open fire on a target in Afghanistan where the fatalities would have included women and children. He was court-martialed and tried. When I learned of his case, I intervened and helped him out, and defended him successfully. I got him off free and have had his unswerving loyalty ever since. He's happy to work for me, and happy to do what I ask him to do without asking questions.

The door snicks shut behind him.

"Why don't you have a seat?" I guide Cesar to the chaise. When I pull back my hand, he releases it. I sink down into one of the chairs opposite him. Kate pours him a glass of water and hands it over. He drains the glass, and when he lowers it, his arm trembles. Kate tops up his glass then shoots me a look before she sits down in the other chair.

Cesar swigs the second glass of water as if it's something stronger, then places it on the side table. He seems to have regained his composure, for when he looks at me, his features are calmer.

I lean forward in my seat and fix my gaze on him. "So, what's the real story?"

# 6

Hunter

"When do you plan to announce your candidacy for Prime Minister?" Declan Beauchamp, one of my closest friends and now a well-known film star, takes aim, then sinks his pool ball in the pocket. He straightens, walks around and takes aim again.

We're at the 7A Club in Piccadilly Circus. Sinclair Sterling and JJ Kane are the joint owners of the space with Sterling having paid enough to get the name of his company affixed to the club. When JJ Kane came up with the idea of a physical venue where he could encourage those who were contributing to the city in any form to be considered for membership, I wasn't sold on it. But in just a few months, it resulted in Liam Kincaid investing in a startup that was born in this very city and is now the toast of Silicon Valley; a startup that's going to earn him many times his original investment. Not only has it made Liam much richer, but it's also made the entrepreneur behind the idea the darling of the business circuit. So, perhaps he has an inkling of what he's doing.

Also, the club has proven to be one of the few places outside my own home where I will be undisturbed. And the moment I declare my candidacy, I can say goodbye to any semblance of quiet. I'll probably have to stop coming to the club, as well. Mainly because my every move will be scrutinized, and I don't necessarily want to draw attention to my friends. While each of them is well-off in their own way, I won't impose the kind of scrutiny I draw from the media on them. I tap my cue on the floor, then narrow my gaze on Declan.

"What's the hurry?" I drawl.

"Thought this was the dream of your lifetime?"

I incline my head and watch as he lines up his next shot.

A seemingly innocent statement but one which has haunted me, of late. Is becoming Prime Minister the dream of my lifetime? Or am I living someone else's dream? More specifically, that of my father. As the oldest son of the Whittingtons, it was assumed I'd walk in the footsteps of my old man, and his old man before him. Indeed, I've taken it as my inevitable future and embraced the certainty of it. I've never questioned it. Not until the last few months.

Maybe it's because I'm so close to achieving the dream I've spent so long pursuing. Maybe because, increasingly, I'm questioning how much I actually want it. Maybe it's because working late nights, focused on myself, and coming home to an empty house, one evening with a dark-haired, amber-eyed goddess made me realize I don't want to do it on my own. I want someone to share my thoughts with. Someone who'll match me word for word. Who'll challenge me, call me out on my bullshit. Someone who'll stimulate me in more ways than one. Someone whose features have haunted my dreams. Someone whose scent I carry, tucked away in my memory. Whose laugh I still hear when I close my eyes. Whose face I imagine waking up to, with my cock at full mast, and it's not just morning wood.

It's a painful, physical yearning that seems to come from a place deep inside. A place I've never acknowledged, and an intensity of sensation I've never expected. It's because of that, I decided not to call her. Not to approach her. Not to have anything to do with her... Not until I arrive at a decision about what to do with this new state of my emotions.

It's not that I like her more than I used to. I still consider Zara Chopra a hindrance in many ways. A distraction? Maybe. A diversion? Definitely. An interference in my well-planned life. A disturbance to my peace of mind.

Until a few months ago, I'd been confident about what I wanted, about where I was headed, about the kind of woman I wanted in my life. Then, I met her, and the sparks between us flew, and it confounded me. Like any sensible man, I proposed to her that we fuck it out of our systems. Which would have been the best course of action. For both of us.

But the fact is, she turned me down, and her memory is still an itch I carry with me, an itch no amount of jerking myself off has managed to scratch. An itch no other woman I've gone out with has come close to touching. An itch which has since grown to consume every cell in my body, every fiber of my being, every waking thought, every sleeping breath. An itch that, even now, makes me hard just thinking of her. And I'm nowhere near her. I hadn't seen her in three months. I haven't spoken to her. I've avoided any gathering of friends where she could have been present which, considering the number of people we have in common, is an achievement in itself.

Given that I'm entering an important phase of my career, I can't afford distractions. Now more than ever, I need to focus. I needed to plan, strategize, spend time analyzing my opponents and drawing up scenarios. I need to brainstorm with my party colleagues, schmooze them, and win them over. I've tried my best to stay centered, but despite my best efforts, I've found myself unable to harness the single-mindedness that's been my hallmark. It's the reason why, at only thirty-nine, I'm on track to become the youngest leader of this country. Assuming I win the election, which I have no doubt I can do. If I can simply keep my head in the game.

The cue ball cracks against the object ball, which slides into the pocket. "Yes!" Declan fist pumps. He walks around, positions the cue across the table and sinks another ball, and another. When he finally misses, I line up my shot... And miss.

Declan bursts out laughing. "Your concentration is shot."

"Don't sound so happy," I grumble as he positions his cue, and of course, sinks his last ball.

"Can't blame me for enjoying your misery. In all the years I've known you, I've never seen you this distracted."

He straightens and rests the head of his cue against the floor. "Want to play again?"

"Yes, do you want to play again?" A new voice asks.

I turn to find Zara leaning a hip against the doorway.

Heat flushes my skin. Awareness crackles across my nerve endings. I take in the dark locks that curl about her shoulders, the way she has her chin tipped up, the stubborn glint in those gorgeous sunbeam eyes, and my entire body seems to turn into a whirlpool of desire. Fuck, she looks even better than I remembered. She's wearing one of those skirts that clings to her hips and comes to just below her knees. It's supposed to look professional but hell, if it doesn't bring out the perfect guitar shape of her body. Teamed with a jacket that she's buttoned up with the red of her blouse peeking from under the neckline, she resembles a gift I can't wait to unwrap.

She pushes away from the door and glides toward us. When she reaches the table, she turns to Declan. "Good to see you again. You were amazing in your last movie."

"Why, thank you. And the pleasure is all mine." He flashes her a smile, then takes her hand in his and brings it toward his mouth. Or at least, that's what I think he's going to do. Before I can stop myself, I've stepped forward and between them, forcing him to drop her hand.

He arches an eyebrow in my direction and snickers. *Asshole.*

"What are you doing?" Zara snaps.

I jerk my head toward the exit.

Declan's grin widens. "It would seem my friend here would rather not have anyone monopolize your time."

"Out," I snap.

He laughs, then walks around us. "Good seeing you, Zara." He tosses his cue in her direction, and she snatches it neatly from the air. "Good reflexes." He jerks his head in my direction. "Can't say the same about you, wankface." He holds his middle finger over his shoulder and strolls out.

"Wankface?" Zara coughs.

"He can be creative when it comes to his insults," I admit.

"So do you wanna play?" She nods toward the pool table.

I peer into her face. "What are we playing for?"

"Whatever you want," she says lightly.

"Whatever it is, you're going to lose."

"You were the one losing when I walked in," she points out.

"I won't lose with you."

"Oh?" She tosses her cue from one hand to the other. "And why is that?"

"Because of the stakes I'm playing for."

# 7

---

Zara

"Stakes, huh?" I'm pleased my voice comes out in a low, modulated purr.

I'm one of the board members of the 7A Club. I'm also the only woman on the board; something I intend to rectify. Meanwhile, I decided to swing by to conduct a meeting with a prospective client. I completed the meeting and was on my way out when I heard Hunter's voice as I passed the billiards room. My instinctive response was to avoid him and keep walking, a response which annoyed the heck out of me. If it were anyone else, I'd pop in and say hi, so why am I treating him differently? Why am I so worried I'll give away just how much he affects me? He's only an arrogant twat. So what if he's sexy as hell? Surely, I've embellished our last encounter in my head. And that kiss... Oh, my god, that kiss. It can't be as good as I remember it, right?

There was only one way to find out. I had to walk into the room and face him. And that's exactly what I'd done. I entered the room and assumed my persona of the confident career woman, the one who'll never shrink from a challenge. It's a role I've perfected over the years. Only, I've always recognized when to back down. That's the reason I'm successful.

I know when to cede ground and when to push my advantage, and this entire situation is one where my instincts scream I need to get the hell out. Away from him, before I get in way over my head. But I've missed seeing him. Missed the high cut of his cheekbones, the meanness of his thin upper lip, offset by that puffy lower lip that seduces me to lean in and nip on it to find out if he tastes as dangerous as he appears. He's taken off his jacket and rolled up the sleeve of his button-down, and those veiny forearms—good god, they're enough to make my panties self-combust.

As it is, I'm aware of the throb between my thighs, the sweet ache in my lower belly that flared to life as soon as his gaze locked on mine. It's like a tractor beam pulled me toward him, and at the very last moment, I managed to tear my gaze from him and greet Declan. And then, Hunter stepped right in front of me. He blocked the other man from my line of sight, and for a second, I was shocked, and I hate to say it, but it also aroused me.

That's the move of an alpha staking his claim. A primal instinct he harnessed to make very clear to the other male that I'm out of bounds. It was both unnecessary—for I regard Declan as a friend and nothing more—and also, so primitive, so elemental in its rawness, it left me breathless.

My thighs clench, my core spasming in on itself with the keen awareness that I'm so empty inside. I've never felt like this before, not in relation to a man, and the sheer suddenness and strength of my reaction has left me unable to protest. Also, damn, but it's so good to see him. I didn't realize how much I've missed him until just now, while he's standing there, all power and grace and so much masculinity, I'm sure my ovaries are opening up and welcoming him to stamp his name on them.

Whoa! This is unexpected. I know I'm attracted to him, but to think of pursuing something with him is career suicide, to say the least. He's in the public eye, and if the chemistry between us were spotted by the tabloids, my reputation would take a nosedive. I'd be the woman the

Prime Ministerial candidate has a thing for. Forget what I've achieved on my own merit so far. It's a narrative I'm determined not to have thrust on me. It's why I'm going to come out on top of any encounter with him. It's why I'm going to win this game with him.

"Remember what you said the last time?" He leans forward on the balls of his feet. "If you come out with me again, you'll kiss me of your own accord."

"I'm aware," I murmur.

His lips curl. "If you lose this game, you come out with me on a second date."

"I won't lose."

He chuckles. "You're very confident of yourself."

"Is that a problem?"

He narrows his gaze. "The only problem is that the more I try to keep away from you, the more I can't stop thinking of you."

I blink. "Excuse me?"

His gaze intensifies. "You sound surprised," he drawls.

"I... I am. I wasn't expecting you to—"

"Say what's on my mind?"

I nod. "It's not the kind of candor I thought I'd hear from a man who comes from a privileged background."

The skin around his eyes creases. "There you go, passing judgment on me again."

I stiffen. "I'm not passing judgment."

"Aren't you?" He shoves his free hand in the pocket of his pants. "Since we've met, you've told me you hate my background, you don't trust my upbringing—"

"I didn't—"

"'You belong to the kind of entitled, snobbish, rich pricks who think the world owes them.'" He inclines his head.

Heat flushes my cheeks, but I don't look away. "You remember what I said word-for-word, eh?"

His lips twist. "I remember everything about you, Fire."

The heat spreads to my chest, and down to that traitorous core of me. My toes curl. I like his nickname for me. A little too much, maybe. I tip up my chin. "Don't call me that."

"You're fiery, stubborn and light up everything around you. You snipe at me, and I want to turn you over my lap and spank you. You scowl at me, and I want to kiss you. You challenge me and give no quarter, and that only turns me on more. You constantly try to—"

"Stop," I say through gritted teeth. "If you think you can sweet talk yourself into my pants—"

"I'm not just thinking; I know I'm going to fuck you."

"Oh?" I scoff.

"You can deny it as much as you want, but there's enough chemistry between us to light a bonfire without matches."

"A-n-d he's poetic, too." I tap my finger to my cheek. "But that's not going to make a difference."

"Hmm." He looks me up and down. "How about we play for it? You win the game, and I'll let you leave. I win the game and—"

"And?" I snap.

"And you kiss me, right here, right now."

"I thought you said, if I lose this game, I come out with you on a second date."

"Oh, that, too—" He smirks. "But first, you kiss me."

"Keep dreaming, buster. I'm not going to lose."

I toss my cue in his direction, and he snatches it.

I slide the button of my coat out of its eye, and his breath catches.

This is the true power I hold over him, and I am going to enjoy every single moment of his annihilation in this game.

I undo the next button, and his gaze follows my movement. I release the last button on my jacket, and the front falls open. I ease the jacket down my arms slowly, slowly, then hold it out to him. He transfers my cue to his other hand so he's holding both my cue and his in the same hand, then takes my jacket from me. He brings it up to his face and sniffs it. A hot sensation springs to life between my legs. It's not like he sniffed my panties, but oh, god, he might as well have. One side of his lips kicks up. He walks to the side and drapes it over the back of a chair. Before he's done, I'm walking over to the pool table. I rack the eight balls, then position my ball in apex position.

I straighten, turn and gasp, for he's standing next to me. And he's only holding one cue. Huh?

"Aren't you going to play?"

"I already am, baby." He lowers his voice to a hush, and my nerve endings crackle. A cloud of heat seems to spool off of him and smash into my chest. I draw in a sharp breath, and he smirks. *Jerk.* He probably knows exactly what his nearness is doing to me. He holds out my cue, and I take it from him; or at least, try to, for when I wrap my fingers about it and tug, he doesn't let go. For a second, both of our fingers are wrapped about the stick, his fingers mere centimeters from mine. He hasn't touched me, but the way he rakes his gaze over my face... Well, it doesn't bear contemplation. His scent is a deep, woodsy bouquet that teases and weaves its fingers through my hair, about my neck, down my spine. I tug on the cue, and this time, he releases it.

I spin around, then line up my shot. I bend over the table, knowing the skirt is pulling tight across my butt, knowing the hem has slid up the length of my thighs, knowing the cut at the side has pulled apart and bared an expanse of skin for his perusal. I sense him stiffen. I haven't moved my head, but I can feel the tension that radiates off of him. Good! Two can play this game, and if jerkwaffle here thinks I'm one of those girls who'll be taken in by his charm and a few words of flattery, he is sadly mistaken.

With a clack, my ball breaks the formation and I sink two of them. I straighten, turn in time to see him raise his gaze from where he'd fixed it previously—in other words, on my arse. I'm not Kim Kardashian, but I'm not being immodest when I say my rear end is almost as spectacular.

My figure bloomed as soon as I hit puberty. While I was self-conscious about it, I soon realized boys loved my behind. I'm not flat chested, either, but while my bust is what an ex called 'neat,' it's my butt that captures the imagination of men and keeps it there. And this asshole is no different.

I stretch a little, thrust my arse out, then walk around the table, making sure to put an extra swing into my hips. I twitch my backside, then bend over again, positioning my cue so that I am almost halfway across the table as I line up my next shot. I take my time, focusing on the ball. Once again, I sense his gaze track down my spine to my behind and lower to where my skirt has ridden up almost to my arse.

It's still decent; I'm sure my panties aren't showing or anything. I'm equally sure the material has pulled across my butt enough to show off the mounds of my arse-cheeks. I focus on my shot, then swipe my cue forward. My cue ball hits the one on the far side with a thwack, when thwack, a slap heats my backside. The shock zings up my spine. What the—!

I straighten and swing around with the cue stick raised. He shoots out his arm and grips my wrist, stopping me. The feel of his palm print seems to be etched into my behind. A snarl boils up my throat. I try to pull my hand away, but his grip tightens. My fingers loosen their grip on the cue stick which clatters to the floor. I raise my free arm, but he grabs it and twists it behind my back. He yanks me forward so my breasts are smashed into his chest. So I can feel the planes dig into my curves. I struggle to break free, and he hauls me even closer, until we're joined from chest to pelvis to thigh. Until the hot thick column at his crotch stabs into my lower belly. Until a shiver zigzags down my spine. Until my core clenches. Until wetness coats my lower lips and my toes curl.

"Let me go," I snap.

He curls his lips. "After you teased me like that?"

"I wasn't teasing you."

"What do you call laying across the pool table until you were all but making love to the play field?"

"That's called trying to get a competitive advantage." I bare my teeth.

His grin widens. "And this is called pushing my advantage."

# 8

Hunter

I lower my head to hers, slowly, slowly, giving her enough time to move her head. I'm holding her hands so she can't move, but I'm giving her the freedom to turn her face away from mine. I pause with my lips so close to hers that our breaths mingle. We're so close I can make out the golden flares that jump deep in her eyes.

"I'm going to kiss you now."

I'm not sure why I warn her. It's not like me to announce my intentions. I want something, I take it. But with her, somehow, it's different. I need her with me every step of the way. And maybe I say it aloud because I expect her to take advantage of the choice I'm giving her and turn away. Instead, she tips up her chin and rises up on tiptoe so her lips brush mine. A jolt of lust zips down my spine. My balls harden. She must feel it, for a groan slips from her mouth as she pulls back.

The next moment, we move toward each other. I open my mouth over hers. I suck on her lips. I hold her gaze as I deepen the kiss—as I swipe my tongue across the seam between her lips, as I nip on her mouth, as she thrusts her breasts further into my chest, as her hips cradle the column that throbs between my legs. The blood drains to my groin. Those golden sparks in her eyes lighten until they seem to resemble flickers of static. The hair on the back of my neck rises. I release her, only to grab handfuls off her butt cheeks. She moans, and the sound arrows straight to my cock. I squeeze the soft flesh and she yelps. Color flushes her face. Her eyes resemble pools of liquid gold, and fuck, if that isn't the hottest thing I've ever seen.

I hoist her up and onto the pool table. She winds her arms about my neck, and I plant my bulk between her knees, forcing her legs further apart.

"Wait, my skirt—"

There's a ripping sound, and suddenly, I'm standing between her thighs.

"My skirt—"

"Fuck the skirt." I close my mouth over hers and swallow whatever it is she's been about to say. She freezes for a second, and I take advantage of her temporary complacency. I sweep my tongue between her lips, and when she parts them, I swoop inside. I dance my tongue over hers, tilt my mouth and deepen the kiss. I suck from her, swallow her breath and knead my way up those gorgeous thighs of hers, the sight of which has been driving me crazy over the past fifteen minutes. I bring one hand up and wind my fingers about the nape of her neck. With the other, I coax her to wind those spectacular legs of hers about my waist. A shudder grips her. I nip on her bottom lip, and with a groan, she melts into me. She swings her legs up and locks them about my waist. I release my hold on her neck, only to cup the back of her head. I deepen the kiss and lean forward and into her. She resists for a second, then allows me to guide her onto her back on that damn pool table which I had been so jealous of earlier when she'd leaned over it. I ensure my palm cushions her head, then with my other hand pinch her chin to hold her in place. Still holding her gaze, I kiss her deeply. And she kisses me right back.

She digs her fingertips into my hair and tugs. My cock jumps. Her chest rises and falls, and she squeezes her thighs pulling me even closer into the valley between her legs. I'm so hard now, my dick is going to stab straight through my boxers and my pants. I release my hold on her chin and cup her breast. I squeeze, and her entire body jolts. I tug on her nipple, which stands to attention, outlined by the fabric of her silk shirt. I pinch her nipple, and she tightens her hold about my waist. And still, she hasn't closed her eyelids, but neither have I.

If we could talk without speaking, then surely, that's what is happening now. My body is communicating with hers, my eyes holding hers, my breath mingling with hers, my lips fused with hers, and my cock aching to be inside her. My heart stutters; that warning beat is back, pounding in my chest. For a second, I stay where I am with my palm cupping her breast, then I tear my mouth from hers.

We stare at each other, my blood pounding in my temples, my throat dry, a ball of emotion forming in my chest and growing until it seems to weigh me down. I step back and pull her up with me. She blinks and looks between my eyes, then lowers her legs. I hold her shoulder until I'm sure she's stable, before I move away from her.

"That shouldn't have happened. I'm sorry."

"Excuse me?" Her voice is soft, her expression open. The look in her eyes is one filled with lust. I feel myself leaning toward her and stop myself. I am doing the right thing.

"It was a mistake. A moment of weakness, which I allowed myself to be overcome with. It won't happen again."

"Wait, hold on—" She raises a hand. "You're calling what we just did a mistake?"

"Yes."

"You bastard." The lust clears from her gaze. Her features harden. Her eyes snap golden fire, and goddamn, she's a sight to behold.

She glances around, then snatches up a pool ball.

"What are you—"

She lobs it at me. It's thanks to my quick reflexes that I duck. The ball grazes past my cheek. I straighten in time to see her sling another one, and another. I weave to the left, then right. I close the distance to her and wrap my arms about her, holding her captive. "Let me go," she snarls.

"Not until you calm down."

"Calm down? I'll show you how calm I am." She straightens up and sinks her teeth in the side of my throat. Goddamn, my cock twitches. Pinpricks of heat radiate out from where she's bitten me. She leans back, and I spot the blood that coats her teeth.

"Fuck!" I bend my head and fix my mouth on hers. She struggles in my hold, tries to kick out, but I don't let go. I kiss her and keep kissing her, absorbing the taste of my blood from her mouth until she stops trying to escape. Muscle by muscle, she relaxes in my arms. I soften my kiss, draw on that drugging taste of hers that swirls on my palate. A groan wells up. I loosen my hold on her. The next second, she's pulled free. She pulls back, flattens her palms on my chest and pushes. She's not strong enough to move me, but I pause. We stare at each other. I see the same confusion in her gaze that I feel.

"I'm sorry, I didn't mean that." I murmur.

She opens her mouth as if to say something, and I press a finger to her lips. "Don't, baby."

She swallows, glances between my eyes, then flicks out her tongue and licks my digit. A flash of fire coils low in my belly. My thigh muscles bunch. "Jesus, Fire, this is crazy."

"You can say that again." Her voice comes out hoarse, and she clears her throat. I bring my finger to my mouth and suck on it. Her gaze intensifies.

"You're right, we shouldn't be doing this. It was a mistake." She swallows.

I nod. "A temporary insanity."

She glances away, then back at me. "It won't happen again."

"It can't," I agree.

We glance at each other, and the air between us grows thick. Sparks seem to shoot out from our joined gazes. The blood in my veins pumps harder. We move toward each other when— "Hunter, good to see you here." A voice I recognize as JJ Kane's calls out.

I jump back; she stiffens, then smooths down her skirt.

I stay where I am, hoping I've blocked her from the line of sight of the door. She brushes the hair back from her face, then smooths her features into what I've begun to realize is her 'media face.'

"If you know what's good for the both of us, you'll stay away from me." She turns and heads to where I've hung her coat over the back of the chair. The rip in her skirt is barely noticeable, and the confidence with which she walks deflects from the flaw in her outfit.

She shrugs into the coat, then turns to JJ. "I was just leaving."

He looks from her to me, then back to her. "It's nothing urgent, I can come back."

"No, really, we're done here." Without another look at me she marches toward the door. "Nice place you have here. Can't say the same about the members you've opened it up to though." She brushes past him and leaves.

"Ouch." JJ winces. "What did I interrupt?"

"Nothing." Everything. I bend and retrieve the fallen cue stick, then walk over to the case and stow it next to mine. At least our cues get to spend the night together. I shake my head. Did I actually think that? Clearly, I'm going out of my head. I need a change. Need to do something different. Maybe call one of the models I've been out with recently—and all of them were dull, boring, perfectly turned out, and completely vapid.

"Hunter?"

I shut the door to the case and pivot to face JJ. "You were saying?"

"That you need to unwind, you're wound too tight."

"Exactly what I'm thinking." I head past him when he speaks again.

"I thought I couldn't be with her, but then I realized the only thing stopping me was myself."

I pause and glance at him over my shoulder. "I assume you're speaking about you and your girlfriend?"

"Lena, she was my son's girlfriend before we got together."

I'd heard so but hadn't really concerned myself with the details.

"I thought we were all wrong for each other. I'm twenty-six years older than her, you know?"

"There a point to this conversation?" I scowl.

One side of JJ's lips kicks up. "Humor me." He slides two cigars out of his jacket pocket and offers me one. I hesitate, then walk back and accept it. He heads for the bar on the far side of the room and picks up a cigar cutter from the corner top. He snaps off the cap end of his cigar, turns and takes my cigar and does the same before handing it back to me. He picks up a lighter, leans over and lights my cigar, then his own. We puff for a few seconds. Then he raises his cigar in my direction. "I tried to give her up. God knows, I did, but each time I tried to leave her behind, it's as if a part of me shriveled up and died. I realized then, the most important part of me was her. Living without her was like living without air…or water…or any of those things that are life-critical. Know what I mean?"

"If you mean you seem to have a romantic core that, I admit, surprises me, then yes."

He chuckles. "You remind me of myself when I thought sharing my emotions was a sign of weakness. I didn't realize how ballsy it was to share what was on my mind with her. I didn't realize how life-changing it would be to go after her. The moment I stopped fighting my instincts and embraced my reality, everything flipped on its head. I knew I was going to find a way to be with her, no matter what it took."

"You didn't have the media spotlight on you. You weren't going to embark on a campaign for the top leadership spot in the country."

"You're right, I didn't." He places the cigar between his lips and takes a puff, then blows out a cloud of smoke. "I only had the relationship with my son at stake. She and Isaac were living under my roof. Of course, they were already having problems, but still… She was, technically, his girlfriend. I was also her boss. The relationship was forbidden on so many levels. Of course, she found out later that he'd cheated on her, but still…" He glances at the tip of his cigar. "All the external signs indicated even thinking of having anything to do with her was so wrong."

"But you couldn't stop yourself."

He barks out a laugh. "Everything within me insisted she was it for me. That I couldn't let her go. That I was going to fight for her any which way, even if I had to play dirty."

"With your own son?"

"There was that. I'd been estranged from him. A possible relationship with Lena meant I might lose him…" He winces. "But that didn't happen."

"It didn't?"

He glances up at me. "Turns out, we found our way through it, after all. Isaac and I are far from the best of friends, but at least he stays in touch with me. It's more than I could say about the state of our relationship before. I wouldn't have found my woman, and gotten my son back, if I hadn't put aside my doubts and focused on what my heart said was right for me."

I take a drag of my own cigar, and the sweet cherry-laced scent reminds me of Zara. Hell, everything reminds me of her. Which is crazy. We don't have a future together. I'm going to become the Prime Minister of this country. That's where I need to focus my attention. Nothing can come between me and the goal I've held for so long. Even if it wasn't my dream to begin with, somewhere along the way, I adopted it for myself. I've internalized it enough that it's a part of me. One I can't cast off. And if I have to bury thoughts of her deep inside to fulfill my ambitions, so be it. I place my cigar on the lip of the ashtray and straighten. "Good talk." I turn and head for the door.

"Hunter?" JJ calls after me. "Sometimes, you only get one chance at finding real happiness. Don't screw it up."

# 9

Zara

"What if this is my one chance at true happiness and I blow it?" My friend Solene's face fills my phone screen. She's an up-and-coming pop star whose last song hit number one on the charts. When that happened, it seemed like her life changed overnight, and she's still coming to grips with it. Especially the impact it's had on her personal life.

I met Solene through my other friend, Isla, who's a wedding planner. I met Isla via a work gig a few years ago and we hit it off right away. I met Lena through her as well, and the four of us ended up hanging out a lot. Then, after Lena met JJ and moved in with him, Solene, Isla and I gravitated toward each other.

Now Isla, too, is married—which really leaves me and Solene as the last singletons standing in our social circle. Strike that. Solene has a boyfriend—who also happens to be one of the hottest stars in Hollywood. And clearly, while both of their careers are taking off, it's not all smooth sailing in their relationship, as evidenced by her pinched features.

"What if I've already blown it?" She hunches her shoulders.

"Why, because you decided to go off on your tour rather than stay home with your boyfriend?" I scoff.

"We've only been together for six months; it's still early in our relationship," she says softly.

"Six months is not that young a relationship. And if the two of you love each other, then it shouldn't matter how far apart you are, right?"

She places her phone on the side of her dressing table and begins to apply her make-up. "I guess so."

I narrow my gaze. "What does that mean?"

She pats the foundation onto her cheeks as she answers, "It's just, sometimes I'm not quite sure what we feel for each other."

"Umm. You either love each other or you don't. There's no gray area here, is there?" Not that I'm the one to give relationship advice, considering I have no idea what the hell that last encounter with Hunter was all about. I walked in there intending to prove to him—and myself—that I was impervious to his efforts. I spectacularly failed. Sure, I flaunted my body at him, and I expected him to react, but I was also confident I'd be able to resist him. Boy, was I wrong. Did I say that already? Well, it's true. And I just can't stop thinking about it. I'm so mad at myself.

The moment his lips touched mine, the moment his breath mingled with mine and his scent teased my senses, it's like I descended into a fugue state. My body insisted I lean into his and absorb his taste, and his touch, and the indentation of his hard muscles into my skin. I came undone, my panties soaking wet as he leaned into the space between my legs.

That was two months ago, and I still haven't forgotten how that thick, fat column in his pants stabbed into the softest part of me. How his fingers felt wrapped about the nape of my neck, around my wrist. How it thrilled me when he grabbed greedy handfuls of my butt and squeezed and—

"Zara? You there?"

"Eh?" I glance at the screen. "Of course, I'm here."

"Hmm..." Solene looks at me closely. "Seems to me like you're distracted."

I laugh. "Moi? Distracted? You know that's not possible."

She picks up her eyeliner wand and scans my features. "I don't know. For a second, it seemed like you drifted off."

"I'm very much here."

She continues to survey my features. "You have dark circles under your eyes. Have you been sleeping okay?"

"I've been sleeping just fine," I lie. No, I *haven't, actually.* The twathole is haunting my waking thoughts. I tossed and turned last night, and when I finally fell asleep, I dreamed of Olly. Something I haven't done in a while. I thought I finally put his passing behind me, but maybe something like that never truly leaves you. Maybe all that happens is that the grief settles somewhere deep inside you where you can't see it, only to unfurl when you're feeling more vulnerable. Which I am now, thanks to Hunter-knobhead-Whittington.

"You sure? Is there something you want to talk to me about?"

"Not right now." I mean, what am I going to say? That I have a huge crush on the one man I need to steer clear of? That the more I try to not think about him, the more it seems my body is unable to forget how it feels to be around him? Nah. Best to pretend nothing happened. And nothing *did* happen. We had dinner. *And you let him all but fuck you on the pool table in a place where anyone could have walked in on the two of you, and damn, but that had been hot.* Not only how he made me respond, but also the fact that he didn't give a damn that we could have been discovered at any moment. And somehow, his confidence, his not giving a damn about what that could do to his reputation, and the fact that the entire situation is so forbidden... It only turned me on even more. Ha, even thinking about it makes it all seem insane. "I'm good, really." I paste a smile on my face.

Her lips curve. "Not fooling me, but fine. If you're not ready to talk about it, I'll let it go."

"Thanks. I promise, I'll tell you more when there's something to tell, okay?"

"Hmph." With a last look at me, she turns to her mirror and begins to outline her eyelids. "We haven't really gotten around to declaring our feelings for each other."

"That's normal, right?"

"Is it?" She completes one eye, then turns to the other. "When my sister Olivia got together with Massimo, they declared their feelings for each other within weeks."

She's referring to Massimo, who was once part of the notorious Cosa Nostra. However, in the past few months, he and his brothers have gone legit. They funneled their assets into the formation of CN Enterprises and Massimo's the CFO.

"By all accounts, coming clean about your feelings and marrying each other within weeks of meeting is the exception, rather than the rule," I point out.

"I know." She sets down her eyeliner, then reaches for her mascara. "Guess their relationship raised my expectations. I keep thinking Declan will announce his feelings for me, but so far, there's been nothing."

"The two of you did take to each other right away though. You left for the US with him within days of meeting him, didn't you?"

I wait while she finishes applying mascara. "I was bowled over by him. Once I saw him, nothing else existed."

"So, what changed?"

She picks up a lipstick and puckers her lips. "Both of us becoming so successful so quickly. He was already on the rise when I met him, and now, with his second big hit, he's a hot Hollywood property. He needs to capitalize on his success and sign the best offers he can get his hands on. And then my big hit—which was completely unexpected..."

"So, the two of you have had to focus on your careers? It happens, right?"

"I always knew it would be challenging when both of us have such demanding careers. What's complicating it is being in the media eye."

"You mean #solan?" I chuckle.

She pauses to smear the color over her lips, then when she's done, sets down the tube. "We've barely had the chance to get to know each other, and now the media's all over us. The paparazzi are everywhere. We can't step out of our house in LA without being snapped. I don't mean to sound ungrateful. This is why I moved to LA, to make a name for myself. And Declan is so talented, too—"

"So are you."

"Thank you." She lowers her mascara wand and turns to me. "It just hasn't been easy. And now, he's shooting in London, and I'm about to embark on my tour."

"Which has already been getting amazing reviews, by the way."

"It's been better received than I expected."

"Don't sound so surprised. You're amazingly talented, and that video of your song with the both of you is adorable."

She blushes. "Thanks. It feels so good to hear it from you and—"

My phone vibrates. I glance at the message that pops up on screen. "Oh, my god, the baby's coming."

"The baby? Whose? Summer's, or Karma's, or—"

"Summer's."

My phone vibrates again. I read the second message from Lena.

"And Karma's," I murmur.

"What? Both of them?" Solene screeches.

I hold the phone away from my face. "Yes, apparently. Gotta go, babe."

"Message me and keep me posted."

"I will." I blow her a kiss and disconnect the call, then grab my bag and run out the door.

---

I burst into the waiting room of St George's Hospital and come to a stop. The room is crowded. Summer's husband Sinclair has close knit friendships with the rest of the Seven of 7A Investments, and Karma's husband Michael is one of seven Sovrano brothers, and the former Don of the Cosa Nostra.

The wives of the Seven have become friends with those of the Sovranos. And...given the fact that Summer and Karma are sisters, it means there are a lot of people invested in the arrival of these two babies. Still, I hadn't expected quite so many of them to be here.

It's through Isla that I met the rest of the Seven and the Sovranos.

Summer has included me in various get-togethers. While I initially turned her down, she was persistent that I attend—that's Summer for you, as I've discovered—and eventually, I gave in.

Now I take in the familiar faces of Arpad, who is one of the Seven, and his wife Karina, as well as Weston's wife Amelie who's talking to Karina. Then there's JJ and Lena, who jumps up from her seat as soon as she spots me. I walk over to her, and we embrace each other.

"You came!" she gushes.

"Of course, I came." I lean back and gaze into her face. "How much longer do you expect it's going to be?"

"We don't know. These are babies, remember? They set their own schedules." Amelie reaches us, and while I'm not one for group hugs, this occasion definitely calls for one. I wrap my arms about the other two women.

"Isla, did you—"

"I messaged her, and told her not to rush back from her fourth, or is that fifth, honeymoon?" Lena laughs.

Liam and Isla got married six months ago on Liam's island near Venice. Since then, the couple has split their time between the island and London. It seems like they rush back to the island every chance they get.

"And Karma? How's she doing?" I glance between Lena and Amelie. "I thought there were a few more weeks to go before she gave birth."

"The baby's premature. But hopefully, everything will be fine," Lena says in a soft voice.

"Weston is with her now, along with Michael," Amelie adds.

Karma suffers from a heart condition that was exacerbated by her pregnancy. Michael has been very worried about her, all through the pregnancy. It's why they moved from Sicily to London—so Karma could be close to Summer, and the sisters could support each other through their pregnancies. Weston, who's a heart specialist, has been monitoring Karma through the last few months.

"I'm sure she's going to be okay." I pat Amelie's shoulder.

"Oh, I hope so," Lena says and lowers her chin to her chest.

"She's a fighter. I'm sure her baby is going to be running circles around us very soon," I say firmly.

"I agree." Karina joins us. "Medical science has advanced so much, and the baby is only a few weeks early. She is in safe hands."

I shoot her a grateful look. Normally, in situations like this, it falls to me to be the strong person in the group. It's my default setting—to bury my doubts and be the person everyone else can lean on. And I sense a kindred spirit in Karina. Her background, too, is slightly different from the others. She comes from a Russian family, and her brothers form the Bratva. She also runs a top-notch security firm that the Seven and the Sovranos have turned to when they need additional safety measures in place. She nods in my direction, then wraps her arm about Amelie's shoulders.

The door bursts open, and the hair on the nape of my neck stands to attention.

# 10

Hunter

I burst through the doorway of the waiting room, and the first person I see is her. She's standing in the circle of women, with her gorgeous dark hair flowing down her back. She's wearing a dress this time—a dark blue number that clings to the dip of her waist and stretches across the lushness of her behind before it outlines her strong thighs and comes to below the back of her knees. She's also wearing stockings — netted stockings, with a seam running up the back before it disappears under her dress. The blood instantly drains to my groin. The fuck? Oh, and I almost forgot, she's wearing four-inch heels which make her legs appear even longer, accentuate the muscular lines of her calves, and push out that spectacular butt of hers so I can't take my gaze off of it. I am here to lend support for the delivery of my friends' wives' children. Instead, I seem to have sprouted a boner that most assuredly tents the crotch of my pants. I stalk inside and she turns toward me. Those amber eyes of hers gleam. For a second, something like happiness flashes across her face. Her gaze widens. Her lips part. She takes a step toward me, then stops herself.

I cross the floor until I come to a stop in front of her. Even with those fuck-me heels, she only comes up to my shoulders. She's not short, by any means, but she's also not a tall woman. She's five feet, seven inches, at the most. The perfect height for me to lift her up and coax her to wrap her legs about my waist as I bury myself inside her hot softness... As if she's reading my mind, she tilts up her chin. Those amber eyes turn molten gold. Sparks of silver flash in them. But her breathing is erratic, and her chest rises and falls. Her orange blossom and vanilla scent teases my nostrils, and my heart thuds against my rib cage. I raise a hand to touch her cheek when—

"Hunter, you're here!" Arpad draws abreast and slaps me on my back. "Where's Declan?"

"I messaged him. He's on his way."

"Don't you have a campaign to run?" Zara scoffs. The earlier delight I glimpsed on her face is replaced by that haughty aloofness I now recognize as her mask.

"I have two months to go before I file my nomination," I say mildly.

"Well, don't you have to do whatever it is rich pricks like you do in the run up to the nomination?" She flips her hair over her shoulder.

"Does it bother you that I'm here?"

She seems taken aback, then laughs. "Of course, not."

"You sure?" I scan her features. "Because you seem to be rattled to see me."

"That's your ego speaking. Not everything in this world revolves around you."

"Except that—"

Arpad clears his throat. "Umm, guys, maybe you want to take this outside?"

"No need," I say at the same time as Zara. I narrow my gaze on her, and she scowls back at me.

"We're done here." She turns to leave, when I shoot out my arm and circle my fingers about her wrist. Pinpricks of heat shoot out from the point of contact. She must have the same reaction for she stiffens.

"Actually, I think we do need to speak."

She scowls at me over her shoulder, and I drop her hand at once.

"We have nothing to say to each other," she snaps.

"On the contrary. I think we need to discuss our last meeting."

"Our last meeting?" She scowls.

"Unless you prefer to talk about it here?" I glance about the assembled group of people, all of whom are now watching our interaction.

She follows my line of sight, and her lips tighten. She scowls at her friends, but it doesn't seem to have any impact. Amelie smiles sweetly at her. Lena leans an arm on Amelie's shoulder and grins. Karina has a wicked smile on her face.

"I don't think it's right to leave. What if the babies come while we're away?"

"I'll text you if I hear anything," Amelie says brightly.

"Hmm." She blows out a breath and turns to me. "Fine, let's go, but I'll choose the space."

---

"This is where you want to speak?" I glance around the bustling cafeteria located on the ground floor of the hospital. Many tables are occupied by doctors in scrubs; others by nurses in uniform. Still other tables have people in street clothes. Either staff, or people who have come to visit patients. The buzz of voices fills the air.

"You have a problem?" she retorts.

"I know what you're trying to do."

"Oh, so now you're trying to read my mind?"

"You think it's safer to have this conversation in a public setting. That's why you brought me here, didn't you?"

"I brought you here because I heard the coffee here is good."

I shoot her a disbelieving look. "At a hospital cafeteria?"

"Don't mock it until you try it." She walks over to the buffet counter and places a salad on her tray. I pick up my own tray, then select a plate of pasta. By the time we reach the payments counter, I've added some fruit and a slab of chocolate cake.

"That all you're having?" I glance at her tray which still has only the salad on it, in addition to two cups of coffee.

She gives me a withering look. "You have a problem with it?" She reaches for her handbag, but I lean over and tap my card on the machine on the counter.

"I can pay for my own food," she says in a hard voice.

"Too late." I smile at the cashier, who smiles back at me.

"You look familiar." She scans my features.

"It happens sometimes. I have the kind of face that people seem to think they've seen before."

She continues to stare at me as I watch the machine process the charge, then her face lights up. "Oh, I know who you are: Hunter Whittington." Her smile widens. "You were so good on Newsnight last night on the BBC."

"Thank you."

The machine spits out the receipt which she hands over to me. I turn to leave, but she pulls a strip of blank paper from the register, grabs a pen, rounds the counter, and thrusts them at me. "Please, can I have an autograph? It's for my son."

"Your son knows who I am?" I frown.

"No, but you're famous, aren't you?"

Next to me, Zara snorts. A reluctant smile tugs at my lips. I place my tray on the counter and take the pen and paper napkin from the woman.

"I'll grab us a seat." Zara turns and walks away. I can't take my gaze off of the sway of her hips.

"Are you two dating?" the woman asks.

"Can I pay for my food please?" An irate voice pipes up behind me.

"So sorry for holding you up." I quickly dash off my signature and hand the paper and pen back to the woman.

"Excuse me." The woman opens her mouth to speak, but I grab my tray, then spin around on my heels and head toward where Zara is seated. I slide into the seat opposite her, facing away from the crowd, and once again, glance at my full tray and the lone salad bowl on hers.

"You sure you don't want to share some of my food?"

She slides a cup of coffee in my direction. "Very sure."

I glance at the coffee then back at her. "Really?"

She inclines her head. "Don't you trust me?"

I hold her gaze. "I do." I reach for the coffee and, without breaking my gaze from hers, take a sip. An intense aroma fills my mouth, followed by a sweet flavor tinged with just the right edge of bitterness, all coated with richness that makes me groan.

I blink. "Whoa!"

"Told you."

I place my cup back on the table. "Question is, do you?"

"Do I what?"

"Do you trust me, Zara?"

She lowers her gaze, then stabs her fork into the salad and spears some leaves. "Not on your bloody life."

I blink, then bark out a laugh. "Jesus, woman, can you be any more perfect?"

She shoots me a glance laced with disbelief. "Umm, did you hear what I just said?"

"Did you hear what I said?" I smirk.

"Do you always have to answer my question with a question?"

"Do you always have to pretend you don't enjoy our verbal sparring?"

Her lips twitch, then she schools her features into an expression of haughty indifference. "What did you want to talk to me about?" She lifts the leaves to her mouth and closes her lips around the tines of the fork. I watch in fascination as she licks some of the dressing off her lips. The sight of her pink tongue sends a shiver of lust down my spine. My pants grow tighter at the crotch. Fuck, this is so not the time. I really should tear my gaze off of her mouth, instead of imagining how much I'd like those lips wrapped about my cock. A-n-d my balls tighten. If my dick grows any thicker, I'm risking an embarrassing accident the likes of which haven't happened since I was sixteen.

"Hunter?" Her lips form my name and warmth pulses through my veins.

"Once more," I order.

"Excuse me?"

"Call me by my name again," I murmur.

"Are you serious?" The edge in her voice cuts through my thoughts. I raise my gaze to find her glowering at me.

"Very. I haven't been able to forget what happened between us, Zara."

She scoffs. "I have no idea what you're talking about."

"You mean to say you haven't thought about what would have happened if we hadn't been interrupted by JJ that day at the club?"

She holds my gaze for a second, then glances away. "What happened that day was a mistake."

"Look at me and say that."

She swallows, inhales, then turns to hold my gaze. "It was a mistake."

I look between her eyes, but the mask she wears for the world is back in place. She's almost as good at hiding her feelings as I am. She's just as much of a professional who can play the media. We're so evenly matched, I couldn't have found a woman more in tune with my needs than her.

"Zara—" I reach over and place my hand over hers. "You don't mean it."

Once again, a zing of electricity shoots out from the point of contact. My throat closes. A weightless feeling flutters in my chest. And all I'm doing is holding hands with her in a crowded cafeteria. The noise fades away. The rest of the people disappear. It's as if we are cocooned in a world of our own where all that exists is her and I. And this…jolting awareness that joins us.

She must feel the same sensations, for color suffuses her cheeks. "You haven't called me once in the two months since that day," she says in a low voice.

"Two months and fifteen hours, to be precise," I murmur.

Her gaze widens. "How did you…" Her voice trails off. She scans my features and her lips firm. "Why didn't you call me, Hunter? Once again, we meet, and then I don't see you for two friggin' months. It's as if you're committed to only running into me after long intervals of time."

"I was traveling. Also, if I recall correctly, you're the one who told me to stay away from you."

"I know what I said, and that's beside the point. You didn't even message me."

"You could have called or messaged, too," I point out.

"Why would I do that?" She begins to pull back her hand, but I grip her wrist and hold on. "Don't do that, Zara. Don't shut down on me."

"This won't work, Hunter. We both have too much to lose."

"I, more than you."

She firms her lips. "Oh, you're going there, are you? Because you're the man in this relationship—"

"The man who's standing for elections to be the leader of this country."

"And I've built my career as a crisis manager. Someone who can be relied on to defuse tricky media situations for my clients. Imagine if it got out that I was involved with you."

"We'll cross that bridge when we come to it."

"Easy for you to say that. You're not the one whose competence will be questioned."

"Because you're dating me?"

"Who said anything about dating?" She tugs on her hand again, and this time, I release her.

"I'm saying it. Now. I want to try and see how it would go if we were to formally date."

# 11

Zara

"Date? Did you just ask me out on a date?"

"It would seem that way, yes," His lips twist, and damn, but that smirk of his is so hot. As is the invisible print of his fingers around my wrist that I can still feel. He forgets about me for months on end… Again. And when we run into each other, he thinks he can pick up from where we left off?

"No," I snap.

He blinks. An expression of surprise forms on his features before he smooths it away. "Okay." He picks up his fork and digs into the bowl of pasta.

"That's it? Okay?"

He licks the pasta sauce from his fork, and my core clenches. How would it feel to have him stab that tongue inside my cunt. *Oh god, you did not just think that. Did not.* I stab my fork into my salad and shovel some of the cheese into my mouth.

"You don't want to date me. I can respect that."

"Hmm." I fork more leaves between my lips, watch as he digs into the pasta with gusto. He chews and the tendons of his throat flex as he swallows. My stomach stutters, and moisture pools between my thighs. Damn it, I should be impervious to him. Especially after how he ignored me for the past few months. In fact, come to think of it, there's a strange pattern to our meetings. We run into each other, apparently by accident, and the attraction flares. I end up doing something crazy, like kissing him, or he fingers me, or I get a sense of what he's packing between his legs… And then, he's gone. Poof. Just like that. It's almost like he's showing me how it could be between us, then vanishing so that I'm left wanting. And then I have to stop myself from stalking him online. Except for the headlines he makes when he attends some social event or another with his models. Something which I'm sure he wants me to see so he can make me jealous. I push away the salad.

"Not hungry?"

"Nope."

He finishes off his pasta—which he seems to have inhaled, by the way—and reaches for his chocolate cake. He scoops up a spoonful of the icing and slides it between his lips. He licks the spoon and my core clenches. My toes curl.

I reach for the coffee and take a sip. The bitterness of the brew laced with a tinge of nutty sweetness sinks into my palate. "Mmm." I close my eyes to savor the liquid, letting the warmth envelop me.

When I open my eyelids, he's watching me with those blue-green eyes of his, which now resemble a stormy sea. His nostrils flare. His jaw is tight. He seems to be trying his best to get control of himself.

Good. Two can play this game, and it's not one I intend to lose. I take another sip of the coffee, and he draws in a breath. I swallow and his gaze narrows.

Then he scoops up a sliver of the chocolate and offers it to me.

"You're going to feed me here?"

"No one's watching us."

"There's always someone watching. You should know that."

"Indeed. But I'm willing to take the risk. Question is, are you?"

My heart flutters in my chest like the wings of a dragonfly. Am I willing to take the risk? Am I? That's the big question. One for which I don't have an answer. I glance about us and find, sure enough, no one is paying us any attention. Also, our table is set to one side in an alcove, so we're somewhat hidden from the rest of the room.

"Where's your security personnel?"

"They're around."

Once again, I scan the people at the other tables but don't see anyone who resembles his security team.

"They're good at their job," he drawls.

"Indeed. How about you? Are you good at what you do?" Shit, hadn't meant for that to come out quite that suggestive. My subconscious is getting ahead of me.

His lips kick up and he gives me a full, blinding smile that lights up his features and positions me at the receiving end of all of his charisma. Even though I know exactly what he's doing, it doesn't stop my pulse from drumming at my wrists, at the base of my throat, between my legs. He is potent. All he has to do is turn on his charm and few would be able to resist him.

He looks at the spoon of chocolate he's holding out, then back at my face.

I scowl.

"Zara." He lowers his voice to a hush and a thrill of anticipation grips me. No one, no man so far, has been able to command me, to tell me what to do. Yet this man, with simply an intonation of his voice, has me salivating to fulfill his every demand. He's good, I'll give him that. Am I going to give in to him. Am I?

He holds my gaze, and the air between us grows thick, charged with everything unsaid, tinged with the lust that has colored our every encounter. A cloud of heat seems to plume off his body and slam into my chest. I gasp. He leans forward and slides the spoon between my lips.

The creamy dessert melts on my tongue. The acrid taste of cocoa combined with the sweetness of sugar coats my taste buds. I swallow, and it slides down my throat, and seems to head straight for my core. He has a direct line to the most intimate parts of me, and I'm not even sure how that happened.

He brings the spoon to his mouth and sucks on it. A million fires seem to erupt under my skin. I grip the edge of the table, my breathing erratic. I need to look away from him, now. I try to tear my gaze away from his, but it's like we're connected, entwined, linked, affixed together. It's as if some part of him has hooked into me and is now reeling me in.

I lean forward; so does he. He places the spoon down, leans across the table. Closer, closer. I can see the fine lines that radiate out from the edges of his eyes, the flashes of gold deep in his irises, as if he's drawing on that secret fire power that lights him up from inside. That haloes him and attracts people to him. I am but a helpless insect caught in his web and he's reeling me in. We're so close, his breath grazes my cheek. I glance down at his mouth, part my lips.

My phone buzzes. I ignore it and flutter down my eyelids. His phone rings, and I sense him hesitate. I snap my eyes open to find he's looking at me with so much longing that my breath catches. His phone continues to ring. My phone buzzes again.

"The babies!" I exclaim at the same time as him.

---

"He's so cute." I touch the tiny fingers of the baby that Summer is holding. Twelve hours of contractions, followed by five hours of labor in the hospital, and the baby finally burst into the world. Weighing in at nearly nine pounds, he's also bigger than expected.

"I can't believe you pushed him out without an epidural." I wince.

Karma's baby was born a few minutes after Summer's, but he was nearly four weeks premature, so they rushed him to the neo-natal unit. Karma's still sleeping off the emergency cesarean. Michael opted to stay with her. We were told that we can see her tomorrow. Both sisters gave birth to boys.

Summer had a natural birth, with both her and the baby in good shape. She bounced back quickly after the birth and was eager to show off her son to the rest of us. Now, I watch as she kisses her son's forehead. "I confess, it's the hardest thing I've ever done. But it's worth it."

"He is," I say softly. I draw my fingertip over his tiny knuckles. "He's perfect."

"He is." Summer sniffs.

Sinclair, who's sitting next to her, kisses her forehead. "You did well, baby. I'm not sure I could have gone through what you did." His voice is tinged with awe.

I glance up at him and realize, under his tan, he's pale. Summer, on the other hand, is glowing. There's an ethereal light in her eyes that tells me she still hasn't come down from whatever endorphins flooded her system during the birth.

"I hope you're giving her a 'push gift' that makes up for everything she went through." I narrow my gaze on him.

Summer laughs. "This" —she glances at the baby— "is enough of a gift. I don't need anything else."

Sinclair rubs his cheek on her hair. "You know I'd pluck the moon from the sky and place it at your feet if I could, baby. You showed me what it means to feel. Without you, I was lurching from one disaster in life to the next. Then you came along and taught me what it is to belong. I love you, Summer."

"Aww," Summer raises her head for a kiss.

I look away and my gaze clashes with Hunter, who's been standing on the opposite side of the bed.

All of the others came by and saw the baby in pairs, so as not to crowd the newborn, until it was only Hunter and me. When we were ushered in together, I didn't protest. It seemed silly to say I'd go in separately. But being here with him, and watching Summer and Sinclair cuddle as they enjoy their first few moments as a family with the baby is, somehow, more difficult than I expected.

"Do you want to hold him?" Summer's voice interrupts my thoughts.

"But he's just been born." I blink.

Summer laughs and holds him in my direction. My stomach coils in on itself. I glance blindly in Hunter's direction.

He must sense my panic, for he steps forward. "I'll take him." He scoops up the little bundle from Summer and cuddles the baby close to his chest. The sight of the tiny infant against his big broad chest as he holds him carefully is unexpectedly poignant and hot. So hot. I've never found the sight of men carrying babies sexy, until now. For that matter, I've never consciously gravitated toward babies.

I have friends who've been obsessed with their biological clock and swore they needed to have children to feel complete, but I've never been like that. Maybe it's because I had to be the strong one in my family, and was used to taking on responsibility from a very young age. Or it's because my father always encouraged me to be independent. Because I wanted to break stereotypes from the time I was little. Because I had to protect my twin brother and be strong for him. Because I was so focused on my career.

Either way, having children has never been a priority for me. So why am I so shaken at seeing Hunter with a baby? Why is my mouth dry, my stomach churning, and my heart pumping so hard, I'm sure it's going to break through my ribcage? "Excuse me." I rise to my feet and stumble toward the door.

# 12

Hunter

"Zara, wait!" I hand the baby over to Summer and follow Zara out of the hospital room. One second she was fine. The next, she jumped to her feet and bolted for the door. I'm not sure what upset her, but I plan to get to the bottom of it.

She hustles down the corridor and toward the waiting room at the far end. By the time I enter the space, she's standing by the window looking out.

"What's wrong?" I draw abreast with her, but she refuses to look at me. "Zara, why are you upset?"

"I'm not upset," she says in a hard voice. But when I try to peer into her face, she looks away.

"You are definitely upset." I step around her, and she instantly looks the other way again.

"Zara... Fire."

"Stop already with your silly nicknames. Especially when you don't mean it," she bursts out.

"How do you know I don't mean it?"

"If you did, you wouldn't have just disappeared after the last time we met. Not a message, not a phone call, not even a goddamn dick pic."

I stifle a chuckle. "Do you want me to send you a dick pic?"

"No. I don't want anything to do with you. Can't you get that through your thick skull?"

"And yet, you're pissed off at me because I wasn't in touch with you."

"I'm not angry at you. I'm angry at myself." She locks her hands together in front of herself.

"And I'm trying to figure out why that is."

"I don't need to tell you anything." She pulls out a handkerchief from her handbag and dabs under her eyes.

"Zara, baby, don't cry. Please." I grip her shoulder and turn her to face me, but she averts her gaze. "Please, tell me what set you off. Please?"

"You don't get to ask that question—"

"—Because I wasn't in touch with you for the last few months?"

"I know, I'm the one who told you to stay away, and I was right. So I'm not really sure why I'm upset right now."

She tries to pull away from me, but I don't let go.

"Is it because of the baby?" I scan her features.

"What?" She stiffens. "What makes you say that?"

"Because I thought we came to some kind of agreement in the cafeteria. I thought you agreed to date me."

She tips up her chin. "You're the one who said you want to date me. I didn't agree to anything."

"So are you saying you don't want to date me?" I peer into her features. "Are you, Zara?"

She tips up her chin. "I'm saying, anything between us is impossible. I've worked too hard to get to where I am. I can't throw it all away by getting involved with you. I don't want to be seen as someone who sleeps her way to the top of her profession."

"I'm not even a client, Zara."

"But your party is. I've done work for them in the past. I've built my career on being someone who is a problem solver, someone who can defuse the trickiest media situations. I am a fixer. I am the expert media personalities, including pop stars and politicians, go to when they need help. I'm good at what I do."

"I know that."

"And I'm effective."

"What are you trying to say?" I frown.

"That my reputation rests on the fact that, while I've helped others with their PR campaigns, I, myself, have always stayed away from any scandal. I've kept my reputation intact by steering clear of any kind of involvement, with anyone or any situation. It's why the media has never found anything on me. It's why I am respected. It's why I am able to influence the influencers. It's why journalists and celebrities alike agree to be steered by me. The position I occupy in the minds of the media is my currency. I can't fritter it away."

"You're likening what's between us to the makings of a scandal?"

She looks between my eyes, then nods.

"But what if it didn't have to be that way?" I lean in closer to her. "What if we give this—whatever this connection is between us—at least, a chance?"

"It will have to come out at some point. You're going to be standing for elections. I've worked with other members of your party. At some point, people will connect the dots and know what's happening."

"Why don't we cross that bridge when we come to it?"

She laughs. "Typical. Of course, someone who comes from a wealthy background doesn't need to plan out. Maybe you can do things on the fly, but I'm not that way. I couldn't have gotten to where I am without having planned every step of my career. And that did not include—"

"Someone like me."

She swallows, then nods. "That's right. I didn't plan for someone like you coming along. I can't afford to have someone like you in my life on a personal level. You're a distraction I don't intend to dwell on for too long. We're too different, you and I, and there's no common meeting ground for us."

I tighten my hold on her shoulders. "Are you sure about this? Is there nothing I can do to change your mind?"

She looks between my eyes, then nods. "There is one thing you can do."

"Anything."

"Forget you ever met me."

A hot sensation stabs my chest. My stomach muscles clench. It shouldn't be so difficult to walk away from her. We barely know each other. So why does it feel like I am cutting off a part of myself I didn't even know belonged to me?

"Zara—"

She shakes her head. "There's nothing more to say Hunter." She pulls back, and I release her. She secures her bag over her shoulder, then pivots and heads for the doorway.

"Zara!" I call out after her.

She pauses.

"This isn't over."

———

"The coffee actually is quite good here." I slide the paper cup in Michael's direction. We're seated at a table which has been pushed up in the corner of the waiting room of the hospital.

"I think I should be with Karma." His gaze remains focused on the doorway. His shirt is crumpled, and for the first time since I met him, he's not wearing a jacket or a tie. His hair is mussed, his chin shadowed with whiskers with hints of gray peeking through. There are dark circles under his eyes and hollows under his cheekbones. He looks like someone who's wife has given birth by emergency cesarean to a four week early premature baby.

He insisted on sitting by Karma's side, his fingers entwined with hers as she slept. It took the combined efforts of Sinclair and me to get him out of her room. He only agreed when Zara, who dropped by to see her, insisted that she'd stay with her. A Zara who refused to even acknowledge my presence, much to my annoyance. Not that I expected anything more, given how we parted yesterday. I left the hospital soon after and returned this morning to check in on Karma and Michael.

I found the waiting room, once again, full—this time, with Michael's brothers who had taken to keeping watch outside Karma's room and the nursery. Not that there's any danger to Karma from anyone, given the Sovranos have made peace with most of their enemies—and, rumor has it, neutralized those who didn't accept their offer to end any clan wars.

Still, given the newborn is Michael's heir, the first in the next generation of Sovranos, they feel duty-bound to stay alert and ensure no one gets through to mother and child. The hospital didn't protest about their presence, which isn't a surprise, considering the kind of weight the Sovranos carry with those in power. And while I'm confident that same influence extends to keeping their presence out of the media, I don't particularly want to tempt fate by being seen with them in public. But Michael's my friend, and I want to be here for him and Sinclair. Which is why I grabbed a couple of coffees on my way in and insisted he join us for coffee in the waiting room. Now, I train my gaze on him.

"She's in good hands," I reassure him.

"Weston is the best in his field." Sinclair leans forward in his chair. "Along with the Chief Consultant of Obstetrics from the hospital, they won't leave any stone unturned when it comes to her safety."

Michael drags his fingers through his hair. "The doctors have been wonderful, and the baby is going to be fine. I just worry what impact going through the delivery has had on Karma."

"The challenging part is over, and she has a new baby to look forward to. She's going to be back on her feet and healthy very soon." Sinclair takes a sip of his coffee, and an expression of shock skims his feature. "What the—" He glances at the coffee, then back at me.

"Told you." I try not to recall sitting here with Zara when she said the same thing to me just yesterday. Yesterday... When she reiterated that I shouldn't try to keep in touch with her, while her actions conveyed the opposite. She was upset that I hadn't messaged her or called her since the time we last met. Yet, she was as insistent that nothing could develop between us. She's not even willing to give us a chance, which is bloody frustrating.

"Did you hear me, Hunter?" Sinclair's voice cuts through my thoughts.

"It's Zara who introduced me to the coffee." I roll my shoulders, trying to dispel the niggling ache that has settled there.

"Zara, huh?" Michael seems to grow alert and narrows his gaze on me. "So, you and Zara—"

"Me and Zara, nothing," I add quickly.

"I think he's protesting too much. Don't you think he's protesting too much?" Sinclair turns to Michael.

"I think he's protesting too much," Michael agrees.

I scoff. "Since when did the ex-criminal and his victim begin to see eye-to-eye?"

Both of them stiffen. "Tread carefully, Whittington. Spouting bullshit to your constituents seems to have loosened your tongue," Michael says in a low voice.

I raise my hands. "You're right. I'm sorry. I crossed a line there." I glance between them. "Still, you have to admit the two of you sitting across the table from each other and ganging up on me is a far cry from when you two were essentially on opposite sides."

The two of them exchange glances. Something passes between them, then Sinclair cracks his neck. "It's true that Michael's family was behind the incident when the rest of the Seven and I were kidnapped. But now that I'm a father, I've realized no child should pay for the sins of the father. I haven't exactly lived a blemish-free life, myself… And it's true what was done to us changed the course of our lives forever. It left us emotionally crippled, and if we hadn't met the women who've given each of us the courage to allow ourselves to feel again, things would have looked very different. But we did meet them, they did change us, and here we are today, with both of our wives having delivered newborns next to each other in the same hospital ward."

"Also, our wives are sisters." Michael rolls his shoulders.

"Summer would never forgive me if I held a grudge against her sister's husband," Sinclair admits.

"And I am deeply apologetic for what happened to the Seven."

I glance between them. "I assume this apology also had a monetary aspect to it."

"It did cross my mind that an offer of investing in Sinclair's company would help ease the pain of what had happened, but then Karma told me to put myself in Sinclair's shoes. She asked me how I'd feel if I had been the one who'd been kidnapped and emotionally tortured as a child, and then had my perpetrator's family tell me they'd make it up to me with money." He winces. "Rest assured, that put things in perspective."

Sinclair inclines his head. "And Summer asked me how it would feel if someone held a grudge against my child because of something I did." He raises a shoulder. "It's time to move forward. Our sons are cousins."

"I don't want any child of mine to be tainted by my past," Michael agrees.

"And I don't want any of my children to carry on the quest for revenge that dogged most of my life," Sinclair confirms.

I rub my chin. "If only politicians could see eye-to-eye on important policies." I draw in a breath. "I say that because I'm one of them. Sometimes, it's difficult for me to see things from the opposition's point of view. And hearing the two of you, my instinct says it's best for my country if I try to find common ground, rather than take issue with them."

"Perhaps that might not be a savvy move though. It would dilute your message," Michael points out.

"Perhaps," I reply, and tap my fingers on the table, "but the only reason I went into public service is so I can make a difference to the community and my country."

"You having second thoughts about running?" Sinclair narrows his gaze on me.

"Maybe."

"Does it have anything to do with a certain dark-haired woman who's been able to stand up to you and who clearly takes no bullshit from you?" Michael drawls.

"Possibly." I glance at the cup in front of him. "Also, have you tasted the coffee yet?"

He glances at it, then lifts the cup to his mouth and takes a sip. He blinks, then does a double take. "And that came from the hospital cafeteria?"

"Good, right?" I smirk.

"Almost as good as the espresso in Italy, and far superior to the swill they serve at most coffee shops in this country." He takes another sip, and the muscles of his shoulders seem to unwind. "Give my thanks to Zara for introducing you to this brew."

"On that..." I rest my elbows on the table and place the tips of my fingers together. "I need your help with something."

# 13

Zara

"How are you feeling now?" I take Karma's hand in mine.

Her lips curve slightly. "I do feel like I've run a marathon, or many marathons, but it's all worth it."

I squeeze her fingers. "Spoken like a true mama. You are so damn brave, Karma."

"Because I gave birth?" she asks a tad dryly.

"Not only, and you know what I mean."

She glances to the side, then at me. "It was stupid of me not to have mentioned my heart condition to Michael."

"Maybe. But you wanted the baby, and I can understand why you didn't want to worry Michael about your heart condition complicating things further."

She blinks. "You do?"

I chuckle. "Don't sound so surprised. Granted, I'm not the most maternal person around, but I respect how important being a mother is to you."

"You're wrong, you know." She scans my features, "You are maternal."

"I'm not," I scoff.

"You helped Isla through the ups and downs leading up to her wedding with Liam. You're the first to stand up for the underdog. As soon as you heard about Summer and me, you dropped what you were doing and raced to the hospital. If that isn't being empathetic—which is really what a mother is—then I don't know what is."

Heat flushes my cheeks. "I did what any good friend would have done."

"You went beyond the scope of friendship. You're here holding my hand so my husband can take a break."

I dip my chin so my hair covers my features. "It's not a big deal. Anyone else would've done the same."

"You have an incredibly busy life, an agency to run, and some very tricky PR disasters to mitigate, as we speak. In fact, if I asked you to pull out your phone, I bet I'd see innumerable missed calls, text messages, and an overflowing email inbox, and yet, you're here sitting with me instead. Not once, have you glanced at your phone in all the time you've been talking to me. And I've heard it buzz."

I laugh. "I'm here because I wanted to see you. Of course, I'm not going to look at my phone while I'm talking to you. It would be disrespectful to do so, not to mention, discourteous."

She stares at me.

"What?" I scowl back.

"How many people do you think would say what you said just now?"

"I don't know about anyone else. This is just my mindset, you know."

"Precisely." Her smile widens.

"Now what? Spit it out, woman. Clearly, you've spent some time thinking about this. Whatever it is." I resist the urge to roll my eyes.

"Actually, no, but you're easy to read, at least, for me."

"Oh?" I incline my head.

"You hold your feelings in check, and think showing them is a sign of weakness."

"Isn't it?" I shuffle my feet.

"See?" She jerks her chin in my direction. "That's what I mean. Bet you have a gamut of emotions running through you right now, but to look at you, one would think you're the very epitome of grace and beauty and sophistication. Which you are, of course—"

"Of course," I deadpan.

"It's just… You don't like showing your feelings to the outside world. Maybe not even to your close friends."

I shrug. And yet, I revealed more of myself to him than I intended.

"Hmm." She purses her lips.

"Now what?" I tug on my arm, and she releases it.

"It's just—" She surveys my features.

"Just what?" I squirm a little, trying to find a more comfortable position. I would've never guessed Karma's this insightful or this intuitive when it comes to sussing out the feelings of others.

"Just… When you meet the right man, you're going to fall really hard." Her lips kick up, once more, in that smug smile. You know the kind—where someone who is married and has a baby smiles, hinting that they know a secret, something to which you're not yet privy.

But even she doesn't know exactly how much Hunter occupies my thoughts, and I plan to keep it that way. I wave my hand in the air. "That person does not exist."

"So they all say. I—" She winces.

I stiffen. "Are you okay? Do you need something? Should I call the doctor?"

"Stop, now you're acting like my husband. It was just a twinge from the stitches."

I grimace.

She chuckles. "I bet, when it's your turn, you'll be the one to deliver without an epidural."

"God forbid I ever get pregnant," I exclaim in horror.

"And, I bet you'll be back on your feet the next day."

"Umm… I'm not Superwoman."

"You sure?" she says smugly.

"Wait." I blink. "Was that a trap? I feel like I walked into a trap."

"I'm not sure what you mean." She releases my hand and lays back against the pillow with a sigh.

"You sure you're okay? I can call the nurse if you want more painkillers—"

"You need more painkillers? Why do you need more painkillers?" Michael strides into the room. He rounds the bed and drops into a chair next to Karma. "You okay, Beauty?" He takes her hand in his, then leans forward and surveys her features. "Are you in pain?"

"No, I'm not, Capo," she says softly.

His chest rises and falls, and he seems to be controlling his emotions with great difficulty.

"Are you sure? If there's anything else I can do to make you more comfortable..."

She shakes her head. "I'm fine. Have you seen him yet?"

He holds her gaze. "I'm looking at you now."

A shadow crosses over her features. "He looks so much like you."

He swallows. "I almost lost you."

"But you didn't. I'm not going anywhere, Capo. I plan to live to a ripe old age, and have more kids with you, and nag you so much you'll wish you'd have never married me."

"There's not a single day that goes by when I don't thank God for bringing you to me. As for more kids—"

She lifts her fingers to his mouth. "Let's not argue about that yet."

He seems like he's going to argue, then shakes his head. "Fine, we won't talk about that now. But Karma, you have to realize, I can't let anything happen to you. If anything had happened to you—"

"Kiss me, Capo," she murmurs.

A-n-d that's my cue. I pick up my bag, rise from my seat, and head toward the exit. I spot Hunter talking with another of the Sovrano brothers. It's Luca. I know who he is because Karma introduced us earlier.

All of the brothers I've met so far are tall, dark and good-looking in that swarthy, slightly exotic way that Sicilian men seem to possess. They're also stone-faced. And while Luca comes across as testy as them, he also possesses a streak of wickedness that marks him out as more unpredictable than the others.

Hunter is as tall as Luca, and on the face of it, more easy-going, but I'm coming to realize that's a fallacy. His brand of charisma is more lethal, for he can hypnotize you into thinking you're making your own decisions while, in actuality, you're following his lead. Hunter's brand of dominance is more dangerous, in that sense. You think you have a choice in the actions you take, but actually, it's him influencing you to do what he wants, without you having an inkling of what he's doing.

In a way, it's similar to how I operate. Which is why I recognize his technique. We're more similar than I realized; it's what makes him such a dangerous adversary. I can anticipate his moves, as he, no doubt, can mine... I have a sense of how he thinks. And while he may often be two paces ahead of me when it comes to planning his move, I'm going to do my best to outwit him.

"Excuse me." I jut out my chin.

Luca steps aside at once. Hunter, on the other hand, stays where he is.

I glower at him.

He shoots me a lazy smile.

My blood pressure spikes. "May I pass through?" I say through gritted teeth.

"Not stopping you," he drawls.

"This isn't the time, Hunter."

"On the contrary" —he slides a hand into the pocket of his slacks— "I'll take any time I meet you as the best time to try to convince you to date me."

"That ship has sailed," I snap.

"You're still standing here, aren't you?"

I pull back my shoulders. "Let me go, or I'm going to kick you in the balls."

Luca chortles.

Both Hunter and I glare at him.

He glances between us, then backs up a step. He turns and engages one of his brothers in conversation, keeping his voice so low I can only make out the odd word in Italian.

Hunter turns back to me. "You won't knee me, Fire." His lips twist. "You have a vested interest in my balls, remember?"

A chuckle bubbles up, and I bat it away. "Ha! Keep dreaming."

He looks between my eyes. "And my dreams are always of you."

My heart jumps in my chest. My stomach flip-flops. Stupid, stupid, school girl crush that I have on this guy. I'm acting like I'm sixteen again. Strike that, I've never had such a crush on anyone, not even when I was sixteen. I was too busy laughing at boys who'd fall for me and ask me out, and then I'd turn them down. Like I did with him. Only this time, I can't stop thinking of him. All the more reason to put this madness behind me and move on with whatever is next on my agenda and in my planned career trajectory.

"Hunter," I say in a low smooth voice. "Let me through."

"Nope." His smirk widens.

"If you don't, I'll—"

"You'll—?"

"I'll, uh, have to go through you."

"Please." He leans forward until the heat of his body envelops me. I shiver. My blood pressure elevates, until I can hear my heart pounding in my ears. Sweat beads my palms, but my mouth is annoyingly dry. To hell with this. I turn sideways, then ease myself through the gap between the door frame and his heavily muscled arm.

# 14

Hunter

She brushes past me, and for a moment, I want to turn and pin her in place against the door frame. And perhaps, she expects it, too, for she glowers at me. It turns into a look of surprise as I step back, then follow her down the corridor to the elevator doors. She stabs the elevator button, then turns on me. "What are you doing?" she hisses.

"What do you think I'm doing?"

Her gaze narrows. "Don't do that."

"Do what?"

"Don't think you can change my mind about our dating."

I tilt up my lips. "Wouldn't dream of it."

"So, why are you standing here with me?"

"Why, I'm waiting for the elevator, of course."

She tightens her lips. "You—" she begins to speak but the elevator dings. The doors open to reveal an empty cab.

I clap my hand on the doors to hold them open, then jerk my chin toward the cab.

She opens her mouth as if to protest, then changes her mind and walks through. I follow her in and press the button for the ground floor. The doors close and the elevator begins to descend.

We stand in silence for a few seconds, watching the numbers count down. The orange blossom, vanilla scent of her seems to intensify. I curl my fingers into fists at my sides. Do not do this, do not. You're going to stand for elections; you're on track to become the Prime Minister of this country! You don't need to screw everything up by risking your reputation. And what choice do I have? If I let her go now... I may never see her again. And then I'll have lost the opportunity I had to feel her, hold her, touch her, kiss her.... Kiss her.

I swing my arm out and slam the stop button. The elevator jerks to a stop.

"What are you doing? Are you crazy?"

She reaches for the control panel, but I grab her shoulders and push her up and into the wall of the cage. Her jaw drops. "Have you lost it completely?"

"Would you blame me if I had?" I flatten my palm on the wall next to her face. "Do you have any idea what being in close proximity to you does to me, Zara? Do you know just how much I need to feel my skin against yours, my lips on yours, my breath mingling with yours, my hands cupping, squeezing, kneading your curves as I bury myself in your hot, tight pussy?"

Color flushes her cheeks. Her chest rises and falls. She opens her mouth, then raises her gaze over my shoulder and at the camera in the far corner of the cage.

"It's not working."

"Eh?" She swivels her head in my direction. "How do you know that?"

"I have my means," I assure her.

Her gaze widens. "You mean to tell me that you knew how to get to that camera, in this lift, at precisely the time we are here and ensure the camera is out of order?"

I thrust out my chest, hold her gaze.

She draws in a sharp breath. "So this is how you use your power—"

"—And my connections." *Thank you Michael.*

"—To make sure you get what you want?"

"Only when it comes to you." I glance between her eyes. "I'd use any means possible to make you see the fallacy of your ways."

"And that includes accepting help from the Mafia to shut off the camera in this lift?" she snaps.

Very good. She's smarter than I gave her credit for, but a part of me already knew that. She and I, together? We'd be unbeatable. But first, I need to tame my Fire. Not that fire can be tamed; contained maybe, temporarily. And I certainly don't want to douse my Fire, but won't that battle of wills be thrilling? A flush of anticipation pulses through my veins. My balls tighten. I widen my stance to accommodate the column that throbs between my legs, then incline my head. "If needed."

She seems taken aback, then squares her shoulders. "While I have to credit you on your ingenuity, I must warn you, you'll never succeed in changing my mind."

"Is that a challenge, Fire?"

"It's reality, Hunter." She tips up her chin. "Your background gives you the confidence to walk on the morally gray side, with the blind faith that you'll get away with it, knowing that you are risking your career… And for what?"

"For you."

Her gaze widens. She reads my features, and she must see something there that gets the message home. She swallows. "Hunter, don't make this more difficult for both of us."

"It's very simple, Zara. We'll be good together—more than good, we'll have the kind of sex that comes along once in a lifetime—and you know it."

"Excuse me, are you hearing yourself?"

"Are you, Fire?" I search her features.

"I'm not sleeping with you, Hunter." She firms her lips.

"You will."

A shudder grips her shoulders, and her pupils dilate. Oh, she feels the certainty that has every part of me thrall. She senses the truth in my words. Her subconscious does, even if her rational mind is unwilling to accept it.

She tips up her chin. "No." The pulse at the base of her throat beats faster.

"Yes," I murmur.

She leans her head back against the wall of the elevator car. "Not sure what you're high on—"

"The nearness of your body."

She chuckles, then rubs at her temple. "Jesus, can't believe I actually allowed myself to laugh at that. Hunter, you have to stop this. You can't keep—" She waves her hand in the air.

"Can't what?"

"You know—" She gestures between us.

"No, I don't."

"You're going to make me spell it out, aren't you? Fine, here it is. You can't go around making these sweeping statements like you mean it."

"I do mean it."

"No, no. Stop right there." She shuffles her feet. "Enough already with the cheesy platitudes."

"Nothing cheesy about the truth, Fire."

"Oh, my god." She squeezes her eyes shut. "Are you seriously hearing yourself? You sound delusional, obsessed—"

"I am, about you." I lean in closer until my chest brushes hers, until my breath raises the hair on her forehead, until her scent intensifies, and I draw it in and hold her essence deep in my lungs.

A trembling grips her. "Hunter, this is all wrong. I can't let you do this. I can't let you jeopardize your career...and mine."

I tuck a strand of hair behind her ear. "Or maybe, this is how we take the leap to finding a path that's different, but much more satisfying for the both of us."

One side of her lips twists. She opens her eyes, and in the depths of her gaze, I see pain and regret...and something else. Something that gives me hope and squeezes my heart at the same time. It's a kind of wistfulness, a forlorn yearning, a longing for something that is so within our grasp. Something that she is going to turn her back on. Again.

"Don't do it," I snap.

"It's already done." She lowers her gaze and, this time, when she raises her eyelids, there's only calm acceptance, and a steely resolve. One that makes the band around my chest tighten further. I tighten my hold on her, and she stiffens. "Let me go, Hunter."

"I can't."

"Oh?" Her lips thin.

"If I did, you'd hate me for not pushing my advantage when I had the chance."

"If you don't release me, I'll hate you more."

"I'll take my chances." I lean into her, and she begins to struggle. Every brush of the sweet cradle of her hips sends a thrill of piercing lust radiating out from the point of contact. I pin her with my hips, and she gasps. A flicker of heat bursts to life in the depths of her gaze. Finally, fuck.

What I wanted to do earlier? I only temporarily managed to control my impulses. But being with her alone in the enclosed space of the elevator car, combined with her stubbornness in not wanting to give us a chance, has pushed me over the edge. I have no regrets that I manipulated the situation to essentially trap her here with me. I have no compunction that I'm holding her against her will right now. I'll take every opportunity I can get to convince her to give us a chance.

I lower my head until our breaths mingle. I draw in her scent, pulling it deeply into my lungs, letting it sink into my cells, and allowing it to slide down to my cock, along with most of the blood in my middle section. My head spins. My muscles harden. I am so engrossed in her that it isn't until my head snaps back and pain slices across my cheek that I realize she slapped me.

Anger pulses through my veins. Lust streaks under my skin. I glare at her, and the pulse at the base of her neck skitters. Her breath comes in pants, her pupils dilate, and something seems to snap inside of her. Thank fuck. It's the same animal instinct I've tried to hold in check since I met her. We move at the same time.

# 15

Zara

He moves at the same time as me. Our mouths fuse. Our teeth clash. A growl rips up his chest. The next second, he grips me under my butt and lifts me up. I wrap my legs about his hips. There's a ripping sound, and I stiffen for a second. Then he pushes his pelvis forward, and the long, thick column in the crotch of his pants stabs into my core. My pussy clenches, my clit throbs, and my nipples are so hard, I'm sure they'll tear through my blouse and jacket.

I have too many clothes on. I throw my arms around his neck, plaster myself to him. Mold myself to his hard planes and angles and gradients, and that very manly chest of his, which is so wide, it never fails to make me feel dainty and utterly feminine. Which is a first. It's not that I haven't been attracted to other men. No one has been macho enough, strong enough, secure enough, dominant enough to not feel intimated by my personality. With Hunter, that has never been a problem. He's so masculine, so virile, so completely male. And I don't mean just the fact that he is six-foot-three with shoulders so broad, they never fail to make my breath flutter and my ovaries clench. It's his mindset, his gaze, the way he surveys the space around him with a confident manner that is downright sexy and potent and so...so... Hot. It makes me want to climb him...and lick him...and punch him...and slap him...and then kiss him... The way I am right now.

As if he senses the roiling emotions running through me, as if he feels the surrender from deep inside of me, as if he's aware of the slippery slope of my thoughts, he tilts his head, opens his mouth over mine and devours me. He nips on my lower lip, and when I moan, he thrusts his tongue over mine, draws on my breath, sucks from me, and it feels like he's consuming me completely. A whine slips from my lips, the sound so needy, so wanting that it turns me on even more. My panties are soaked, and I can smell the sweetness of my arousal in the air.

As I cling to him—with my ankles locked about his waist, and my arms locked around his neck, with his cock jabbing into my pussy in a gesture so demanding, I'm tempted to rip off my panties and take him inside—I know, for sure, I've met my match.

A shudder grips me. My stomach seems to bottom out. My entire body turns liquid, and he squeezes the flesh of my arse to hold me up. My breasts are crushed into his torso, and my mouth is full of his tongue. My head seems to have dissociated from the rest of me. I have an out-of-body moment when it's as if I'm looking down on the titillating image we present. Then he releases my mouth, only to whisper kisses up my jaw and down my throat. He brushes aside the neckline of my blouse, buries his nose in the curve of my shoulder and inhales deeply. The action is so salacious, so much more sexually explicit than anything else he has done to me so far that my eyes roll back in my head. My clit throbs, my core melts, and I begin to grind against the hardness at his crotch with abandon. Oh, god, I'm going to come. I'm going to... A ringing sound slices through the haze of sensations that grip my body. I stiffen; so does he.

What the—? I try to get my brain cells to form a coherent thought.

"Ignore it." He digs his teeth into the curve of my shoulder and my pussy clenches. Moisture pools between my legs. Heat surges out, from where he's bitten me, to my extremities. Every part of me is hard-wired to follow his command. To become his. *His. His. His.*

The ringing blares through the space, and I snap my eyes open. I take in the confines of the elevator car and a cold sensation clutches at my heart. I slap against his shoulder. "Let me go!"

He doesn't move.

"Hunter, let me the hell go!" I wriggle against him, and his cock lengthens; it grows even bigger. *Oh, my god.* My fingers tingle to hold that part of him, my mouth waters to taste him, my clit swells, and I push my pelvis up and into the tent at his crotch, yearning for release.

The ringing starts again, and Hunter swears. Without letting go of me, he reaches over and grabs the phone from the control panel of the elevator car. "What?" he barks.

He listens to the voice at the other end and draws in a breath. "No, we're good." He listens again. "Yes, Ms. Chopra is with me."

I stiffen. *Who is that? His security personnel? So now they know we've been trapped in the elevator for how long? Five minutes? Ten? More?* I struggle against him, and he leans more of his weight into me, rendering me immobile. *Asshole.* Still, he hasn't even broken a sweat, and he's holding me up with one arm—and his cock...umm, not quite, but you get the picture—while talking on the phone, and that is impressive.

"I'll see you on the ground floor." He slaps the phone back into the cradle, and the elevator car begins to move.

"Hunter, let me down!"

He scowls down at me. "You're the most annoying woman I've ever met."

"Ditto."

"And the most stubborn."

"Pot, meet kettle."

"And the most gorgeous."

"Same," I snap, then freeze. "You're a jerk."

"Yep."

"Let me go, you piece of—"

He moves back, and I hit the floor of the elevator, on my arse. *What the hell?* I shove the hair from my face and jump to my feet. "You let me fall? How could you let me fall, you—"

"You asked me to let you go."

Anger twists my guts. I take a step toward him, and he jerks his chin in the direction of the indicator above the door. We're on the second floor. *Shit!* I smooth down my skirt—my second ripped skirt, and this one is Chanel, argh! —then pat down my hair. I grab my Birkin from the floor and hook it over my shoulder. To think, I had been so caught up in our mutual lust that I hadn't realized I'd let it fall to the floor of the elevator... That's something. To be honest, a bomb could have gone off next to us and I wouldn't have noticed. That kind of distraction is epic, a once-in-a-lifetime occurrence and... Nope, not going there. It was a kiss; just a kiss. A mind-blowing, panty-melting, London Fashion Week kind of kiss... It was...something significant, all right.

This is so unfair. Why am I so attracted to him? Why is he so irresistible? And hot and sexy, not to mention charismatic, and he wants to do something for his community and his country. Yes, I've listened to some of his speeches in Parliament, and observed how he doesn't hesitate to raise tough issues with his opponents and doesn't think twice about questioning measures he doesn't agree with. He's known for taking risks, for speaking his mind, for challenging those whose outlook opposes his. He's seen as somewhat of a champion of the underdog—something which I find really attractive, too.

I hate to say it, but if there were a man powerful enough to hold his own against me, it's him. And he doesn't even need to try. It's both annoying and hugely seductive. That he could just be, and I'd gravitate to him; that he could reel me in without any protests on my side, and not much of an effort on his. It's frustrating and oh, so erotic. Tantalizing and completely exciting. And I can't afford to dwell on it.

I am going to put it behind me and move on. Stay focused. Stay centered. Keep moving forward. I draw in a deep breath, then another. When the elevator doors open, I hustle out, with Hunter on my heels. I brush past his security detail, then increase my pace. Of course, he keeps abreast. I reach the double doors leading out of the hospital and walk out, only for a flashbulb to go off in my face.

# 16

Hunter

"Mr. Whittington is Zara your girlfriend?"

"Zara, are you dating Mr. Whittington?"

More flashlights go off.

What the fuck? How did the paparazzi know I was here? Not that I'm trying to hide my movements, but it's not like I broadcasted to the world that I'd be here today. Perhaps, someone spotted me entering earlier?

My security detail brackets us in, one to my right and another on the other side of Zara.

"This way," David, one of my bodyguards says, and leads us through the throng of news people. One of the paps steps in our path and aims his camera in our faces. I reach out to cover the lens. "No photos."

"How about a comment then?" He lowers his camera. "Are you two dating?"

"Ian, isn't it?" I smile and hold out my hand. "How are you today?"

Ian hesitates, then takes my hand. "You still haven't answered the question. Is she your girlfriend?"

"She is a...friend."

"Was that a hesitation I sensed there?" Ian's gaze narrows.

"Have I ever lied to you before?"

He slowly shakes his head.

"We are here to see a mutual friend, and you caught us leaving together."

"Hmm." He doesn't look convinced.

"When I do have a girlfriend, if I ever have a girlfriend, I'll be sure to let you know."

He releases my hand. "I'll hold you to that."

I nod, then brush past him and reach for Zara's hand, both to guide her forward, and because I want to protect her from the pack, but she shakes it off. She flounces past me, a smile pasted firmly on her features. Her gaze is calm, certainly calmer than what I'm feeling now.

We reach my car, and I hold my door open.

"I am not leaving in the same car as you."

"Get in, Zara."

"They're still watching us," she hisses.

"And I'm giving my 'friend' a lift."

"I have my own car."

"David will follow us with it."

She scowls. I glare at her. "Fire, do this, please."

Maybe it's because I say please, or because she can't wait to get out of there, but she pulls out her key fob and slaps it into my outstretched hand. I hand it over to David. She slides inside the car, and I follow her. One of my security detail gets in the front seat next to the driver and we're off.

"We'll drop Ms. Chopra off at her apartment first."

My chauffeur nods, and I raise the barrier between the front and back seats.

She arches an eyebrow. "Fancy."

"Have I impressed the hard-nosed Ms. Chopra?"

She raises a shoulder. "Never seen a Range Rover with one of these." She nods toward the now raised divider.

"It's custom built."

She shoots me a sideways glance. "I assume it's also armored."

"And has a self-contained oxygen supply."

"Should you be telling me all this?"

"It's not a secret; you can look it up on Wikipedia. But even if it wasn't there, I'd share it with you."

She shakes her head. "Don't do that."

"Do what?"

"You know what. You're trying to pretend we have a future together and we don't."

"But we could."

She squeezes the bridge of her nose. "You're not listening to me."

"I am, but I don't agree with you."

"We were in that hospital together and you saw what happened. Already the newshounds are circling."

"And you and I are veterans at playing the media," I point out.

"Which is why I can't believe I allowed myself to be caught coming out of there with you."

"You couldn't have known that they'd have sniffed a story so fast."

"There's no story." She lowers her hand and locks her fingers together in her lap.

"Not yet."

She tips up her chin. "Never will be."

"You're stubborn."

"And you're a pain in the wrong place."

"I can do a lot to alleviate any pain in any part of your body, baby."

She groans. "Ugh, that was terribly corny."

"So, why are you smiling?"

Her lips twitch. "Am not."

"You are, too."

She covers her mouth with her palm.

"That's cheating."

The skin around her eyes crinkles.

I smirk. "Now you really are smiling."

She drops her hand and folds her arms across her waist. "You're good at distracting from the topic at hand. A born politician."

"And you do a fantastic job with your PR agency."

"You sound surprised."

"It was a genuine compliment." I raise my hands. "Honest."

"Hmph." She finally turns to scan my features. "Apparently, you do mean it," she finally says.

"Of course, I mean it. I've always admired your work ethic, your focus, and how you've defused the trickiest of media situations for your clients, including how you handled yourself back there." I jab my thumb over my shoulder.

"I'm a PR consultant." She angles her head. "Though I admit, being in the eye of the camera, rather than the person pulling the strings, has a very different feel to it. It's a good lesson to take away. I often demand a lot of my clients when they come to me with their problems. I've forgotten how you have to think on your feet while you are caught in the crosshairs of the paparazzi."

"You are inherently empathetic—"

"No, I'm not," she bursts out.

"—however you may try to hide it," I finish my sentence.

"Stop trying to find good traits in my character," she mumbles.

"Stop putting yourself down so much."

We stare at each, and a reluctant smile pulls at her lips again. "You're persistent."

"I am."

The moment stretches, the space between us, once again, charged with that connection that's shimmered between us from the moment we met. I reach over and rub the edge of her lips. She pulls away from me.

"Your lipstick; it's smudged."

"Oh, god, and that's how the photographers saw me?" She dips into her ever-present bag—now placed on the seat between us—and pulls out her lipstick and compact. She paints her lips with the color, and heat tightens my groin. She smacks her lips together, and fuck me, I almost come in my pants. I guess I make a sound, for she shoots me a sideways glance. "You okay?" she asks in an innocent voice.

"Don't push it, Fire."

She tilts her head. "Should I call you Brimstone then?"

"You may call me yours."

Her features harden. "Don't do this, Hunter."

"Now that you've refreshed your make-up, I think it's time."

"Time for what?"

"This." I reach over, clamp my fingers about the nape of her neck, and pull her close.

Her gaze widens. Her chest rises and falls. She swallows, but doesn't pull away.

"Do you want this, Zara?"

She doesn't answer.

"Tell me you don't want my lips on yours. Tell me you don't want to feel my breath entwined with yours, my fingers squeezing your arse, my cock in your pussy as I pound into you and take you to the edge but don't let you come... Not until I've pulled out and taken your arse; and even then, when you beg me, I won't let you orgasm—not until you agree that you belong to me and then—"

"Then?" she whispers.

"I still won't let you orgasm—not until I've shown you how explosive it is when you're in my arms. Until I've convinced you how good we are together. Until I've taken every hole in your body and shown you the kind of pleasure you've never felt before. Until every part of your body belongs to me. Until your curves cry out for my ministrations, your flesh yearns for my touch, your mind can no longer resist me, and your emotions and senses are honed in on me. Not until you acknowledge you are mine."

Her pupils dilate. The gold in them lightens until they seem almost silver in color. She lowers her gaze to my lips, and the pulse at the base of her throat speeds up.

I tighten my grasp about the nape of her neck. "Tell me to stop, Zara, and I will."

"Hunter, I... I can't." She raises her gaze to mine. "But if you kiss me, I'll never forgive you."


Zara

That's the last thing I said to him. In the back of his car, with the shaded glass of the windows hiding us from the outside world. He held my gaze for a second longer, his hold on the nape of my neck seemed to tighten almost imperceptibly, and then he loosened his fingers. He pulled back his arm, turned his head away, and it was as if a physical wall came down between us. He rolled down the screen that had hidden us from his chauffeur and bodyguard in the front seat, and for the rest of the journey he didn't look at me or acknowledge me again. He pulled out his phone and began to scroll through his messages. A first.

He never did that before. He always focused one-hundred percent of his attention on me, and now that I don't have it, I miss it. A few seconds earlier, he had his hands on me, his gaze locked with mine. And now, it's as if he's withdrawn from me. Completely. Of course, he did. The horrible, sinking sensation in the pit of my stomach tells me I've lost him. Irrevocably. I told him I'd never forgive him; it never occurred to me he might not forgive me.

I pushed him away once too often, and now, he's never going to look at me the same way again. It's really over, and he's never going to pop up in my life the way he'd been doing. The fact that it's been more than three months since that incident confirms it.

I glance through my office window and see the throng of shoppers on the streets of Soho. The Christmas lights were lit a few weeks ago. Christmas decorations began appearing in shop windows a few months ago. When autumn turned into winter, with the temperature plunging and warnings of early snowfall, I had no idea. I buried myself in work after that last run in with Hunter.

A new client—another impossible media disaster—a well-known politician turned down claims from a woman who insisted she was his illegitimate daughter. This time, I not only helped him navigate the barrage of negative publicity that followed his daughter's interviews with the press, but I also brokered a meeting between the two. I banked on the fact that when he came face-to-face with her he'd accept her, and sure enough, that's what happened. He even agreed to appear on her social media feed and publicly apologize for the emotional distress he'd caused her. He also publicly embraced her as his daughter, and the two hugged in a very touching moment on screen. Now that, I count as a win.

And perhaps, a few months ago I wouldn't have been so insistent that he meet with his daughter. Perhaps, I'd have focused only on the job he'd engaged me for, which was to redeem his reputation—which, by the way, I delivered in spades. But I knew I could make a difference, so I insisted he meet his daughter. In fact, the public claiming of his daughter helped to soften his reputation and make him more popular. It all worked out, and it wasn't all planned by me.

I'm...softening? Thawing? I can feel myself wanting to do better, to do good where I could. Oh, make no mistake, I'm still a cut-throat career woman, but somehow, something inside me insists I do more. The part of me I denied since my younger brother died... That emotional core of me came alive. And maybe, I have Hunter to thank for it.

I'm not going to admit that I miss his presence in my life, sporadic as it may have been. But I've been counting on him making an appearance two months to the day I lost him. In fact, I ensured I met up with Summer and Karma and their friends in the hope that I'd see him... And also, so I could test myself. Did I actually miss him? Or was it my ego, bruised because he no longer seemed to want to pursue me? Maybe the fact that he'd been so insistent, and not taken no for an answer was more than a little flattering. It was the first time a man had been so persistent, and I enjoyed it. So now that he backed off, it was sobering. I felt a little deflated.

Or maybe it was the Christmas season which I admit is not the most favorite of times for me. It reminded me of how much I missed my younger brother. I was going to meet my parents and my twin of course, but this season is always a reminder of another year that Olly was no longer in our lives.

My phone vibrates. I turn to my table, look at the name of the caller in surprise. I raise the phone to my ear. "Lord Alan, what can I do for you today?"

"Zara, how are you?" My mentor's plummy voice fills the airwaves.

He comes across as a crusty, old English gentleman, but his views have always been ahead of the times. No doubt, that's why he saw the potential in me and in my company, and hired me for my first project —to salvage the reputation of a bad boy rockstar after he trashed his hotel room and was caught urinating out of his window. A picture the paparazzi had a field day with. I not only helped turn around his reputation, but I also introduced him to a few charities which he supports to this day. Another win.

"I'm very good. How is Heather?" I ask after his wife.

"The same. She wants me to work less, but you know me. I'll rest when I'm dead."

"And not be around to trouble the rest of us? I can't see that happening anytime soon."

"Very true," he laughs, then quietens. I sense him gather his words and wait for a few seconds. Sure enough, he clears his throats then says, "I do have a very interesting project for you… Something which, if you deliver on it, will establish you as the go-to person when it comes to media management."

"Sounds intriguing," I narrow my gaze on a young couple walking arm in arm down the sidewalk. They stop to admire a window showcase. The girl leans her head into the man's shoulder, and his arm tightens about her. It's no different than hundreds of couples I've seen before but somehow, the way her dark hair flows down her back, as well the man's confident stance, the way he pulls her even closer as if he wants to hide her from the sight of the world, reminds me of Hunter and myself.

"Zara, are you there?" Lord Alan asks.

"Yes, of course." I turn away from the window and begin to pace my office. "So, it's a confidential project, and you can't tell me who the client is?"

"Not until the day you start."

I chew on the inside of my cheek. "Isn't that highly unusual?"

"Not in situations like this where we can't afford any information leaking."

"Hmm." I walk over to the couch in the corner of the room and lower myself onto it. "Of course, it's related to something political?"

He stays quiet.

"Is the top leadership of one of the political parties in trouble?"

"I didn't say it was political." His voice is cautious.

"You didn't have to. When Lord Alan, who's been retired from the industry and public life, calls me, I know it has to be about something more than a celebrity being caught with his pants down or a sportsman caught having an affair with a reality TV host."

"You did enjoy managing the positive spin campaign on that one though," he chuckles. He's referring to one of my previous successes, where I brokered an understanding between said sportsman and his estranged wife, so she didn't open up to the media about his other kinks. True story.

"That was one of the more satisfying campaigns I've worked on. The wife walked away with a massive settlement, and he later married his mistress, so everyone was happy."

"And if you take on this campaign and deliver on it, you'll consolidate your position as Kingmaker within the UK media circuit, a position which I know you're aiming for."

"So it definitely has to do with politics," I state.

"I can neither confirm nor deny that, Councilor," he laughs.

"So that's a yes."

"I never said that."

"Right." If there's one thing Lord Alan is good at, it's evading an issue. He can't be drawn into an argument at all. Not unless he intends to put forth his point of view which, at the moment, he is not in a mood to do. It's from him, I learned how to steer a conversation so it benefits me.

"So you'll do it?"

I blow out a breath. "You know I'd never turn you down."

"I know. And perhaps it's wrong of me to ask this of you, but I think, in the end, you'll thank me."

"Is there nothing else you can tell me about it?"

"Graham!" I hear a woman's voice call out his name over the phone.

"I'll call you when the details have been hammered out, my dear. Give my regards to your brother." He signs off.

I lower my phone to the table. My brother who's been overseas the last three months playing cricket matches and shows no sign of coming home, *that* brother? The last time I'd heard from Cade, was a rushed call before he'd left the locker room to get on the pitch. I doubt I'll hear from him again before the new year, if that.

Of course, I could go spend Christmas with my parents. But they still run the corner shop in a little corner of Leicester, so they'll likely be working through the holidays. Not even on Christmas, will they take time off. I've often told them they could afford to employ people to cover for them, but they won't even consider it. It's an unbroken tradition of forty years that the shop has stayed open. The only times they shut it was the day my father had a heart attack—not that he slowed down after that. And he insisted my mother open the shop the next day, which she had, reluctantly, leaving him in the hospital. And the other time was when the Queen passed away. They are staunch royalists, my parents. They admired the Queen for her work ethic, tenacity, and dedication, values they tried to instill in the three of us. And which my brother and I rebelled against, in our own ways.

My father's parents immigrated to the UK from the Indian subcontinent. My mother is English, but having married my dad, she seemed to have converted completely to his style of thinking and living, which equals embracing the need to equate your worth with your work. Despite my best efforts to rebel, some of their mindset must have sunk in because obviously, I inherited my workaholic tendencies from them.

Why else would I be at my desk in my office, at four p.m. on Christmas Eve? I definitely do need to get out of here.

I reach for my bag, when my phone rings again. Amelie's name lights up the screen.

"Hey you!" I say by way of greeting.

"Are you still in the office?" Amelie's wide-eyed gaze stares back at me from the rectangle of my phone.

"I was just leaving."

"Oh, are you coming over to our place for our Christmas Eve party?"

I wince. "Umm, I wasn't planning to, if I am being honest."

"Aww, Z!" Amelie pouts. "Everyone is here, including Karma and Summer." Karma's son had been kept in the neo-natal unit for nearly a month before being discharged. Since she brought him home, the boy has thrived and seems to grow bigger every time I see him.

As for Summer's kid, he looks exactly like a mix between her and Sinclair, and is the sweetest little boy I've ever seen.

"Victoria and Saint will be here with their new baby too," she adds.

She's referring to Saint, who's one of the Seven, and his wife Victoria, who had her baby at home. I love hanging out with them, but right now, I just need some time alone.

"I'm thinking of leaving London for a bit over Christmas."

"Really?" She tilts her head.

"Yeah." I rub the back of my neck. "I'm exhausted, and I think I could do with some down time."

"You've been working so hard lately," she says as she scans my features. "I understand why you want to get away, though I do wish you could come here. It would be nice to have you over. Why, even Hunter Whittington has promised to come by."

"He has?"

"Yep. Haven't seen him, either, since the day he arrived in the hospital after Summer's delivery."

"Oh?" I murmur, schooling my features into what I hope is an expression of disinterest.

"He hasn't announced his candidacy for Prime Minister. I wonder why that is?"

*I do, too.* And it's not because I've been following his appearances in the media or on his social media. Not at all. It's only because he's a newsmaker and my team keeps me briefed on all of the goings on when it comes to key figures in UK entertainment and politics, that's all. "I have no idea."

"You sure you don't want to come?"

"Nope." And especially not since what's-his-face is going to be there. I've been so good thus far. Coming face-to-face with him will only tempt me, and I can do without that. "I think it's best I get away for a bit. Re-energize, clear my head and all that, you know?"

"So where are you planning to go?"

"Umm... I... To be honest, I haven't thought it through. I only, just now, came up with the idea."

"Hmm." She looks at me speculatively.

"What?" I scowl back. "Do I have something on my face."

"No, but I may have something for you."

I tilt my head.

"I know the perfect getaway place for you."

"You do?"

"Uh, it's a little cottage just two hours out of London. Set in a beautiful little village which is right out of *The Holiday.*"

"You're referring to the Kate Winslet and Cameron Diaz movie?"

"Yep. The cottage is also where Weston and I hooked up for the first time last Christmas."

"Really?" I laugh. "Now this is a story I have to hear."

"I'll tell you more another time. If you go now, you'll have enough time to get there before it's too late."

"Umm okay." She seems awfully keen to get me to go. Maybe she can see how tired I am. "Are you sure it's okay? Who does the place belong to?"

"Oh, it's jointly used by all the Seven. It's been refurbished recently. They have a caretaking service that keeps it in readiness, in case any of them wants to pop over for a weekend away. In fact," —her features brighten— "we keep it fully stocked. The caretaker is scheduled to go there this afternoon to add some fresh items. Text me a list of some of your favorite foods and we'll make sure they're included. You'll be able to cook something special for Christmas."

I laugh. "Me and cook?"

"Or not." She raises a shoulder. "There should be enough in the kitchen that you could whip up a something simple to eat, if you prefer."

"It sounds ideal," I admit.

"It's a gorgeous space. You'll love it."

"Hmm." I chew on my lower lip. "And no one's going over there this weekend?"

"Everyone's here for Christmas. Unlike someone I know, who'd prefer to be on her own."

I hunch my shoulders. "I know, and I don't mean to go all Scrooge on you. It's just, since Isla and Liam decided to move to the island near Venice…"

"You miss her, huh?"

I rub the back of my neck. I miss Isla more than I realized I would. I hadn't realized how close a friendship I built up with her and Solene. And with Solene on tour and rarely able to call me, I became dependent on Isla for female camaraderie. But with her married now, and also in a different country, I guess I'm feeling a little more lost than I thought. Normally, I'd be working. It's when I'm out of the office and need to unwind that I feel a gap in my life. That's when thoughts of Hunter occupy my mind, which I hate to say, happens more often than I'd like. Which is why this getaway is going to do me good.

"I do miss her, but she deserves her happiness."

"So do you," Amelie murmurs gently.

"And I'll find it with a nice bottle of wine tonight."

"And a hot tub."

"A hot tub?" I stare at her. "This place has a hot tub?"

"On the back porch. It's covered, and you can enjoy the view of the fields stretching out in front of you." Her gaze turns dreamy. "It's so… Rejuvenating."

Did her tone turn tongue-in-cheek there? I gaze at her closely, but her features remain open, even if she does look a little flushed.

"Is it really as picture-postcard perfect you make it out to be?"

"More than you can imagine. If I could, I'd love to go back there, but we've already committed to hosting this party, so…" She raises a shoulder.

Someone calls out her name. She turns and waves at someone over her shoulder, then glances back at me. "If you don't want it then—"

"You convinced me. Where is this place, how do I get there and, more importantly, don't I need keys to get in?"

# 17

Hunter

I ease the car up the short driveway of the cottage and into the garage at the back. I noticed a garage in the front of the house, but Weston mentioned it was being used for storage at the moment. I switch off the engine and quiet descends. The kind where it's not just silent, but the type of silence where you can hear yourself breathe, sense the tension slide off of your shoulders, feel the lack of vibrations brought on by traffic, overhead flights and traffic helicopters, and the sound of eight million souls drawing breath in the metropolis called London.

A city I grew up in. A city I love, despite the ups and downs I've faced there, in a life which, admittedly, has been more up than down so far. Some would say a privileged life. One where I was groomed for the top position in this country. The one my dad occupied at one point, and which I'd known with certainty, I would one day, too. I never questioned that belief, was content with my choices—or the choices made for me by default, and which I adopted as my own—until I met her.

She told me she'd never forgive me if I kissed her that day in the elevator car, but I'd done it anyway. After all, the last time she'd asked me to stay away, I had, and she'd been pissed off at me. So it made sense to push aside her objections and kiss her... Or so I'd thought.

But then, I held her gaze and sensed the struggle inside her. Sensed, also, that she was going to use that kiss as an excuse to walk away from me. And that's something I'm not going to allow. I'd kissed her to show her what she was missing out on. And I'd been right. It had been mind-blowing, earth-shaking, pulse-pounding, a balls-tightening kind of kiss. And she'd felt it too. And if I had continued kissing her I'd have taken right there in that damned elevator car. Which is the only reason I had let her go. Not because it wouldn't have filled that dark yearning inside of me to take her right there, in a place where both of us could have been compromised any moment; for I didn't give a damn about being discovered. But she clearly did. And I couldn't risk hurting her like that. Indeed left to myself I'd have fucked her right there and then and walked out and told the journalists outside that she was mine... only that'd have pissed her off no-end, and while the make-up sex with Zara would be every bit as explosive as the hate-sex we're no doubt going to indulge in soon—fact is I want her to want to be with me.

When we come together, and we will, it will be because she needs it as much as me. Because she admits to yearning for it as much as I do, and decides to throw caution to the wind and be adult enough to own up to this insane chemistry between us.

Only, it's more than simple chemistry. It's the kind of connection that one rarely finds with another person. That click inside that signals once you've been with this person, it will spoil you for anyone else.

She knew it. I knew it. But she refused to accept it. And while patience isn't my strongest virtue, this time, I had no choice but to sit back and bide my time. And trust me, that is so against my personality, so against my natural instinct of chasing after her, that it's been far more stressful than preparing to launch my campaign to become Prime Minister. Something I can't put off forever, either. But I have a plan for it, and hopefully, it should all come together very soon.

Meanwhile, I needed to get out of London. I arrived at Amelie and

Weston's place to find it was packed with friends and pets and kids. And it was nice to hang out with them, and shoot the breeze with the Seven and the Sovrano brothers, and play with the babies, but seeing the waves of domestic contentment wafting off of them had made me realize, for the first time, what I was missing. And the very fact I was thinking that surprised me.

Perhaps, I was more tired than I'd realized. Perhaps, I definitely did need a break. I mentioned it to Weston, who told me he knew of the ideal place where I could unwind undisturbed. He gave me directions to the cottage a few hours outside of London, where he first hooked up with Amelie last Christmas. I was unsure about it, but he told me about the packed bar, the fact that it was stocked up so I wouldn't have to worry about provisions, and then he mentioned the hot tub on the back deck. And that settled it.

I took the directions and the passcode to the front door, which they put in recently, then headed home to pack my bag, fielded calls from my parents, who were disappointed I wasn't coming home for Christmas, and headed over.

Now, I push open the door of my Jaguar—my preferred make of car when I'm driving—and step out. I managed to give my security personnel the slip on my way here. It may not be my smartest move, but I needed a little time with no one breathing down my neck. Just an evening to unwind; I'm sure they'll track me down by tomorrow. Meanwhile, I'm on my own, with my thoughts—and with thoughts of her, of course— and an entire evening, and if I'm lucky, the entire day tomorrow, with no calls, no disturbances, and no intrusions. I open the back door, reach for my duffel bag, then lock the car. I head up the steps, key in the passcode to the door, and it clicks open. I step in, switch on the lights and glance about the place.

Weston wasn't exaggerating when he said it was renovated recently and has every convenience under one roof. The starlight pours in through the windows on the right to illuminate the space. A fireplace in the center, that dominates the space, is not yet lit. To my right, is a sectional couch. On the opposite side, is a wet bar. All the fixtures are gleaming.

I walk into the room, and my booted feet sink into plush carpeting.

I reach the fireplace and throw the switch on the wall next to it. The flames instantly ignite. I round the fireplace, then head through the door and down a short hallway that leads to the kitchen. To my right, a door opens into what I assume is the bedroom. I head through, drop my bag on the carpeted floor and stretch. A drink, and then a long soak in the hot tub, sounds perfect. I strip off my tie and shirt, then kick off my shoes and socks, my pants and my boxers. I grab a towel and wrap it around my middle before I head back to the bar. I reach over to grab the bottle of whiskey—Macallan 24-year-old; the Seven wouldn't stint on their alcohol, of course—and pour myself a drink. There's also a cigar box. I flip it open, snip a cigar and light it, then clamp it between my teeth. I grab the glass and head back through the hallway and past the kitchen to the back porch and the hot tub.

I move toward the sliding doors at the back when the strains of music reach me. Huh? Also the glass is fogged over. Which is why I hadn't noticed the flicker of light that gleams through. I take a step forward, and the notes grow louder. I reach the doors and ease them open.

The music resolves itself into the chords of a song that sounds familiar, but which I can't place. I can, however, place who the person in the sunken hot tub is. Her back is to me and she has piled her dark hair on her head in a messy bun. Tendrils have escaped to stick to the slim line of her neck. Her shoulders are bare and she has an arm spread out over the edge of the tub. As I watch, she wraps the fingers of that hand around the stem of a wine glass and brings the glass up. She turns her head at the same time, so I can see the curve of her eyelashes, her upturned nose, and those lush lips as she wraps them around the rim of the glass and takes a sip.

The blood drains to my groin. I don't need to look down to know that I'm already hard. Her throat moves as she swallows, and I wonder how it would feel to have it move around my cock. The light from the candles she's lit about the place lends an ethereal, dreamy feel to the tableau.

The woman's voice coming through the speaker she's placed on the platform near the tub warbles about getting lost in translation, about asking for too much, and generally, clearly, blaming herself for the inevitable breakup that so many pop-stars seem to sing about. Still, I'll admit, the tune is haunting.

I take a drag of my cigar and blow out smoke a second before I realize she'll probably smell it and realize I'm here. Not that I was planning to spy on her like a creeper. Although, being able to watch her without her knowing I'm watching her is a treat. And perhaps, I'm beginning to sound like one of those pop songs I despise.

She leans her head back, and though I can't see the rest of her, I can sense how relaxed she is. How she's communing with herself in the moment, and how I hope she's imagining me in whatever scenes she's playing out in her head. I take a sip of my whiskey, and the liquor burns its way down my gullet, setting off a pleasant warmth in its wake. None of which will compare to the heat of her pussy when she clenches about my shaft. I almost groan aloud at the throb of lust that tightens my groin.

I leave the city to escape thoughts of her...and run straight into the object of my obsession.

I came so close to taking Michael's suggestion, planting cameras on her phone and computer so I could track where she was. And if I'd done that, I'd've known she was here, and perhaps, not have accepted Weston's invitation. Of course, it would've taken me from being in the zone of 'morally gray' to straight up 'black,' not that I have any illusions about myself. I've always had that streak of darkness in my center, hidden carefully from the world; and it would have stayed that way, but for the fact I met her.

She brings out that primal, animalistic side of me that I've tried to deny even existed, but something about her makes me want to share it with her, if only to test her response. To see if it'll make her hate me further, or if I guess correctly, brings out a different side of her. The one I've sensed, but never seen unleashed in full. That sadistic, needy part of her that resonates with me, that pushes me to make her submit to me.

I blow out another puff from my cigar, then walk around the tub, drop my towel, and take the steps leading down into the hot tub. I lower myself into the bubbling water and place my glass of whiskey on the rim next to me. "Hello, Fire."

# 18

Zara

One second, Taylor Swift is warbling about her lost love with Jake Gyllenhaal, and how he called her up again just to break her heart; the next, a familiar, hard voice that has haunted my dreams, and if I'm honest, almost my every waking moment, reaches me.

I snap my eyes open, and he's there, in the hot tub, the light from the candle flames highlighting the hollows of his cheeks and turning his skin into a golden, candied surface that I'd like to lick and suck on. He has a cigar clamped between his teeth, a tendril of smoke wafting up from the lit end like the forked tail of a devil. And damn, if the tufts of hair standing up on his head don't resemble horns. His torso is bare... The carved planes of his chest and those broad shoulders make the hot tub, which had felt too big for one person, now too small for the both of us.

Both of us? What the hell is he doing here? I thought I smelled the sweet, cherry scent of cigar smoke, but had dismissed it as my imagination. Except, it hadn't been. The jerkhole who's haunted my dreams is sitting opposite me in the hot tub. He plucks the cigar from between his lips and holds it out and away from the water. With his other arm he reaches for his glass of whiskey and holds it in my direction.

"Salut, Fire."

I curl my fingers into fists. Yep, no doubt about it. He's really here. I am not dreaming. Not that I doubted it earlier—for I'm not given to flights of fancy, where my mind conjures up illusions which seem too real—but until he spoke, a part of me wondered if I'd thought about him for so long and with so much intensity that, perhaps, the images in my head had come to life. At least, now I know I'm not at fault. He's here and—I lower my gaze to his chest again—he's not wearing clothes. At least, not on the top part of his gorgeous, shapely, muscle-bound body.

The steam condenses on his chest. The droplets glisten like dewdrops on leaves in the early morning. Maybe I should say like the spots on a leopard because, sprawled there, with his eyes half-closed, as if he's waiting for the inevitable explosion of anger from me, he resembles a predator...a beast...a sleek feline...a sexy specimen of masculinity who's at rest and yet, ready to pounce at the least provocation.

Also, did I mention he's not wearing anything on his torso? I swallow. One side of his lips ticks up. His eyes gleam. Bastard's enjoying this. No doubt, he thinks I'm going to throw a fit and act all pissed-off —which I am—but damn, if I'm going to let him have that satisfaction. I reach for my glass of wine and raise it. "Cheers, Brimstone."

He seems taken aback for a second, then he chuckles. The sound grates over my already sensitized nerve endings and seems to travel straight to my core. A hot, heavy sensation thickens between my legs. My toes curl. Jesus Christ, and all this because the wankface chuckled?

Maybe it's not such a good idea to pretend I'm cool with his sudden appearance. Maybe I'd be better off throwing a fit. This is supposed to be my getaway. Why is he here? Either way, it's clear I can't stay here, now that he's here. Time to get out of here. Why are all of my sentences ending with here?

I clap my half-filled glass onto the platform of the hot tub with enough force that wine spills over the sides. Then I begin to rise to my feet, but his arm whips out and he locks his fingers about my wrist. A flash of electricity zips out from his touch. A-n-d here we go again.

Apparently, nothing has changed over the last few months. If anything, my body is even more responsive to his touch. If anything, the throbbing pulse between my legs has grown bigger, wider, stronger... Until my entire body seems to be weighed down with an overwhelming heaviness, even as my head feels lighter, like I am floating above my body and watching this bizarre situation unfold.

I glance at his grasp on my arm, then back at him, but he doesn't let go. "Stay," his voice rumbles across the distance. His gaze is intense, his blue-green eyes lightened to an impossible shade I can only describe as colorless? It's as if all of his emotions have been swallowed up and are churning inside, ready to be hurled back at me in a ball of sensation so intense, I won't stand a chance. I clear my throat, but still, it comes out as a croak. "Hunter—"

"No, don't speak. Let's just enjoy what's left of the evening, okay?"

I glance between his eyes, then nod. "Okay."

"Okay." His grip loosens, and he seems to release me with great reluctance. I sink back in my corner, reach for my glass of wine, and take a sip. I place the glass back on the rim of the tub, then lean back again. With nothing to do with my hands, I place them in my lap. His gaze follows the movement, and his eyes flash. I'm wearing my skimpiest bikini, which barely covers my nipples, and the bottom is a string thong. To be honest, I wouldn't even have worn that, since I thought I was on my own. It's just... I'd changed into my swimsuit and already immersed myself in the tub before I realized I needn't have bothered with wearing a suit, at all. By then, I was too lazy to change. Thank god... Or maybe not. Maybe I would've enjoyed shocking him if I hadn't worn anything—not that he'd have been shocked. He's probably been with enough women. A hot sensation stabs at my chest, and whoa... What's that about? I don't have a claim on him. Though I could have one. If I want to.

"I can hear you thinking," he drawls.

"And I wish I didn't have to hear your voice, at all."

His lips curl. "I can't wait to hear your voice when you finally scream my name as you come."

That hot sensation in my chest balloons into this massive explosion of lava that travels to my extremities. My arms and legs tremble. A shudder grips me, and I have to fight to not squeeze my legs together. Oh, my god, Hunter talking dirty is... The stuff my dreams are made of. And I'll be honest, I've groaned his name many times in all of my sordid fantasies where he's done exactly that to me.

"Let me guess, you had no idea that I was here?" I murmur.

"If I had known you were here... I'd have—" He searches my features. "I still would've come. For the record, I didn't see your car outside. I had no idea there was anyone inside the house."

"I parked my car in the garage." I firm my lips.

"Which would explain why I didn't see it. Guess we're stuck here for the night." His eyes gleam.

My gaze widens in horror. *No, no, no. I can't spend the night with him. I can't.* If I do, there's no way I'll be able to resist the pull between us. "You have to leave, now." I burst out.

"Have you looked outside lately?" He glances to the sky beyond the enclosed patio. I follow his gaze to find soft flakes of snow floating down.

"You're kidding me."

"There's a storm on the way, heard it on the weather forecast on the way here."

"You sure you didn't arrange for it just so we both had to spend the night together?" I scowl.

"Are we spending the night together?" He tilts his head.

My thighs clench. Every cell in my body seems to go on alert. Every pore on my skin seems to open in anticipation. I am so fucked. Well, maybe not yet. But let's be honest, I will be.

"Zara?" His voice is low and soft, and yet, there's a hard edge to it. A tension coils under his tone. It reaches out to me and lights the ball of heat that's taken up residence in my belly. Flickers of awareness sizzle through my blood. My toes curl.

"Fire?" he murmurs, and this time, the question in his voice is tinted with desperation. The skin around his eyes tightens. His stance is relaxed, but every muscle in his body is wound tight. The muscles of his shoulders are rigid and defined and oh, god... I want to reach out and trace their shape and feel their dimensions. I want to rub myself against him and lick off the droplets of sweat that roll down his temple and... I want to lower myself onto his thick, long, large cock and get myself off, then clench down on him until he abandons all control and fucks me so hard I can't think any further—

"You're killing me," he growls, and something snaps inside of me.

I surge to my feet.

# 19

Hunter

The water pours off of her shoulders and slides off of her hips. She stands there for a second, a cross between a mermaid and Artemis the huntress. That slip of fabric she's wearing barely covers her nipples, which are peaked and outlined through the top of her bikini. Her waist is tiny, her hips wide enough to form that classic hourglass figure that's driven me crazy since I first laid eyes on her. Her thighs are thick and strong. My fingers tingle, my palms ache and... I want to squeeze her flesh and mark her so every time she looks at it, she'll know who she belongs to.

She covers the short distance between us, then stands in front of me. I tilt my head back and watch as she reaches over and takes the cigar from my fingers. She brings it to her lips and closes her mouth around it, and goddam, my cock stands to attention at once. Who am I kidding? It was already standing at attention, but now it's... More so? She draws on the cigar, blows out a puff of smoke.

"You're playing with fire, Fire," I growl.

"What if it's because I want to be burned tonight?"

"Do you want to be burned?"

She searches my features. "Only if you burn with me."

I reach up, pluck the cigar from her fingers, and brush mine over hers. She shivers, and a fierce sensation tightens my chest. Without breaking the connection of our gazes, I place the cigar between my lips. The taste of her—something spicy and pungent and so fucking familiar—crowds my senses. I glare at her, but she doesn't flinch. Fucking hell, I am going to enjoy taming her.

"There is one thing, though," she murmurs.

"Oh?" I move the cigar to the corner of my mouth. "Are we negotiating?"

"Maybe." For the first time, she looks unsure. My heart stutters. Goddamn, what insanity is this that the very thought of her not being at ease is making me want to soothe away her uncertainties?

"What is it?" I snap, my voice coming out harsher than intended.

Her forehead furrows. "It's only for one night."

"Eh?"

"You. Me. We fuck. But it's only for tonight. Tomorrow, we go our separate ways."

"Weather permitting." I nod toward the snow that's begun to come down harder.

"Weather permitting," she agrees.

"And if it's still snowing tomorrow, the deal continues."

Her eyebrows knit. "I have to get back tomorrow."

"So do I. But if it's too dangerous to drive..." I raise a shoulder.

"Then I leave when the snow clears, no matter what time it is."

"Only if you let me drive you."

"I have a car—"

"I'll arrange for it to be dropped back," I retort.

She firms her lips, then nods. "Fine."

I look her up and down. "Of course, you'll let me do anything I want to you tonight."

She blinks. "What does that mean?"

"You'll let me do what I want to do to you, when I want to do it to you, and you do everything I tell you to do—"

"Within reason."

"Choose a safe word," I order.

"Excuse me?" She snaps back her shoulders. "I'm not into S&M."

"I am."

"Ah…" She opens and shuts her mouth. "What if I don't like it?"

"Oh you will," I smirk.

She flushes. Her eyes spark, and I almost jump to my feet and throw her over my shoulder and walk inside and to the bedroom, but… Patience. Patience. Wouldn't do to spook the tigress.

She bites the inside of her lip and sweat pops on my brow. This waiting and enticing game is not one I normally play with women. But when you're wooing a magnificent goddess, you do what it takes.

"What kind of S&M are you talking about?" she finally asks.

"It can be anything." I blow out a cloud of smoke. " You'll have a safe word, and the moment you use it, I stop."

"Just like that?" She scowls.

"Just like that. But remember, the moment you use it, the night is over."

"Huh." She purses her lips. "So I use the word, and that's it, no more sex."

"Something like that."

"You have a lot of confidence in your ability to turn off your libido."

My grin widens. "You won't want me to stop; this, I promise you."

She scoffs. "Don't make promises you can't keep."

"Do we have a deal?"

She narrows her gaze.

"Do you know, when you're thinking through all the pros and cons, you get a divot in the corner of your lips?"

"I do?" She rubs the left corner of her mouth.

I crook my finger at her. "Come 'ere and I'll show you."

She leans over slowly, slowly, until her face is just above mine. I reach up and rub my thumb into the other side of her mouth. She swallows but doesn't move away.

I drag my thumb across her lower lip, and a moan bleeds from her lips.

"Say yes," I murmur.

"And if I don't?"

"You will."

She shakes her head. "That goddamn cocky attitude of yours. I hope you have the equipment to back it up."

"Is that a yes?"

"Yes," she whispers.

"Choose a safe word."

"Do I need to?"

"You agreed, Fire."

She glances into my eyes, then nods.

"Did you settle on a word?"

"Pomegranate."

I tilt my head. "The symbol of fertility and abundance. The seeds that led to Persephone being tied to Hades."

"Didn't ask for a lesson in mythology," she scoffs.

I lower my hand, then jerk my chin toward her side of the tub. "Go back to your corner."

"Excuse me?" Her jaw drops. And fuck me, but the expression on her face is worth every bit of clash of wills that's going to follow. I am going to win her over, I have no doubt. And I'm going to make sure she enjoys every second of our time together. And if she hates me during the process, it's only going to make our inevitable union so much more satisfying.

"You heard me." I reach for my glass of whiskey and drain it. "Also, I need a drink."

She looks at me blankly, so I repeat myself, enunciating each word, "I. Need. A. Drink."

She rolls her eyes. "I heard you the first time, wankhole. If you need a drink, you can damn well get it yourself."

I glare at her, and she scowls back at me.

I tilt my head, and she slaps her hands on her hips, which only has the effect of making her breasts, barely covered in that itty-bitty bikini, jiggle. Her nipples are outlined against the fabric, while droplets of water cling to her chest and in the valley between her tits. My cock thickens further, and if I glance down, I bet it's going to be emulating submarine action. Not that I have anything to hide right now, but I'd prefer to pretend to have the upper hand. For the moment, anyway.

"Fire," I lower my voice to a hush and she swallows.

A shudder grips her and she throws up her hands. "Fine, I'll do it, and only because I don't go back on my word."

"I'm counting on it."

She reaches for my glass of whiskey, then turns and steps out of the hot tub. For a second, she's poised there with her curvy figure silhouetted against the flickering candlelight. That arse of hers? Fuck, it's the most phenomenal, jaw-dropping butt I've ever noticed and damn, if I don't want to sink my teeth into that ripe peach of a behind right now.

"You're staring," she murmurs without turning around.

"Are you complaining?"

"You're the one delaying gratification with this stupid exercise in trying to put me in my place."

"It helps to increase erotic arousal, baby."

"Why don't you admit that you're doing it to have control over me?"

"Or maybe I'm simply into self-torture."

She pauses, then turns to glance at me over her shoulder. "Are you always this...honest?"

"Did you think I was going to deny the obvious? When it comes to you and me, I aim to give you the truth... Unless there's a specific reason to hold back something."

She narrows her gaze. "So you're holding something back from me?"

"The sooner you get the whiskey, the sooner you'll find out."

"And just when the wordplay between us was heating up," she scoffs.

"Not the only thing that's heating up, baby."

She lowers her gaze to my crotch, and her gaze widens. Color flushes her cheeks.

I can't stop the smirk that twists my lips. "Does that answer your earlier question about my endowments?"

"How you use it remains to be seen, Brimstone." She picks up her own glass then flounces off in the direction of the door; but not before infusing an extra twitch into her arse. Heat flushes my skin, and sweat beads my shoulders. At this rate, I'm the one who'll give in to my needs before I've made any headway in getting her to submit. And no way, am I going to let that happen. I need her to open herself up to me, to become vulnerable enough to sense what I feel for her.

She disappears through the doorway into the house, only to appear a few seconds later, with both my glass and hers. She walks down the steps and into the bubbling water, which rises to her waist by the time she reaches me. She holds out my glass. I take it from her, once more allowing my fingers to brush against hers. Her breath hitches. The pulse at the base of her throat flutters like the wings of a butterfly.

"You okay, Fire?"

"Why wouldn't I be?"

I widen the space between my thighs, then jerk my chin toward it.

"You want me to sit...there?"

"You have a problem with that?"

"Of course, not." She turns around, then places her glass on the rim of the tub. Naturally, she has to bend over, which means that magnificent arse of hers is squarely in my face. My fingers itch, my thigh muscles grow rigid, and every brain cell in my head temporarily short circuit. Jesus H. Christ, I'd give anything to bury my teeth in that luscious behind—a reaction she, no doubt, expects me to have; which is why she's flaunting her asset at me. But I am not going to give her the satisfaction. Still, I must have made a noise, for she peers around with a gloating look on her face. "You alright back there?"

A-n-d that's the last straw. Two can play this game. And I don't intend to lose. Not this round. I plant my hands on her hips, then lean in and bury my face in her lower cleavage.

# 20

Zara

"Oh, my god." The glass of wine topples, but I manage to catch it at the last moment. His face. He's got his tongue between my arse cheeks. Heat flushes my cheeks. My *other* cheeks. I try to wriggle away, but his grip on my waist pins me in place. I'm not a prude; not by a long shot. I'm a strong, independent woman who has always believed that the right guy is an illusion, that the only person I can rely on is myself. That the person who'll appreciate me 'as is' has yet to be born. It's something I have believed in firmly, and no one I've ever met has made me revisit this assumption. But the way this man is worshiping my body by licking that very intimate, very forbidden part of me is making me question every one of my beliefs. And it's not only because of how my body is responding to his attention, how my heart is thudding against my ribcage like my favorite vibrator on its highest setting, how my nipples harden and my thigh muscles quiver, how I can't stop myself from clenching down and pushing back into his face, and holy hell, that's not what I want to do. I don't want him to realize how turned on I am because he's eating my arse. "Hunter, stop," I gasp.

It only spurs him on to drag his hands down to my cheeks and squeeze them apart even further. He pushes aside my bikini bottoms, then swipes his tongue over my puckered hole and my eyes roll back in my head. He twists his tongue inside my back channel, and I shudder. Pleasure contracts my lower belly, and my thighs squeeze together. My eyes roll into the back of my head, and I'm going to come. Oh, god, I'm going to—

He pulls out his tongue. "Don't you dare come, Fire." I hear his voice as if from far away. And he's stopped torturing me with that magic tongue of his. I push my butt back, trying to chase that sensation that brought me to the edge, and he laughs.

The twatwaffle snickers, and the lust recedes from my thoughts. I pull away—and this time, he lets me. I pivot around, straighten my bikini bottoms then raise my hand; but he catches it. Then he wipes the back of his free hand across his mouth. The gesture is so erotic, so salacious, that my pussy clenches. The shudder of lust that had retreated rushes forward in a wave again. My knees knock together, and I'd sink down into the water if it wasn't for the fact he has a tight grip on my wrist.

He scans my features. "You okay?"

"No, I'm not. Why did you stop?"

"Told you I wasn't going to let you come. Not that easily, anyway."

*Jerkhole.* I try to pull away from him again, but he tightens his hold on my wrist.

"Let me go."

"When you're no longer angry."

"You can't tell me how to feel," I snarl.

"Wanna bet?"

"Fuck you." I shouldn't allow him to see how much he's unnerved me, but damn it, I'm allowed, aren't I? First, finding him here, under the same roof, in the same hot tub as me, when I'd been thinking rather randy thoughts about him. Then, having him come through on said randy thoughts in the randiest way possible...was not what I'd expected of him. To be honest, I'm not sure what I expected, but it wasn't quite that. Definitely not Hunter Whittington squeezing my arse like it belongs to him. Not Mr. Stick-in-the-mud, stabbing his tongue inside my forbidden place and bringing me to the edge, only to not let me orgasm.

"I will, just not yet." He smirks.

"Go to hell."

"Only if you come with me, baby."

"Aargh." I squeeze my eyes shut. It's not like me to lose my cool when I'm dealing with a man. Definitely not Mr. Douchekabob, who denied me my climax. "Do you always have to have a ready comeback?"

"Only with you, Fire."

Something in the tone of his voice, a gentleness at odds with the ruthless restraint with which he pulled me back from the throes of a mother of a summit I came so close to peaking, has me opening my eyes.

He's looking up at me with a strange light in his eyes. A possessive-ness? A hunger, perhaps. More like a proprietorial look that, combined with his dominating presence, has me going weak in the knees. *Shit, shit, shit.* I knew I shouldn't have agreed to this one-night stand arrangement with him. He's manipulated his way into making me agree. Doesn't mean I have to go through with it. I take a step back, and he rises to his feet.

Just like that, he unfolds himself and straightens. The water cascades off of his shoulders like he's the model from the Old Spice commercial I watched growing up. No, he's more like Chris Hemsworth in *Thor: Love & Thunder*, or Chris Pine in that nude scene in *Outlaw Knight*. Ooh, la, la, and now, I'm resorting to French in my thoughts. That's it, I am truly flustered...but, in my defense, he's standing in front of me and he isn't wearing a stitch of clothing.

Those carved-out-of-rock chest planes extend to a lean waist, flat stomach—no, concave stomach—which, in turn, dips down to meet a humongous, monstrous, enormous, gargantuan, colossal, massive—you get the idea—appendage that points straight up toward his belly button. And ladies, I wish I could say it was grotesque, or hideous, or repellant, but the truth is, it's the most gorgeous, most beautiful, most immense cock I've ever seen.

My knees buckle all over again. I stumble forward, and he stops me with his other hand on my shoulder before I can fall against that wall of goodness—otherwise known as his chest. Before I can feel the hardness of all that male virility in that column he carries between his legs. And his balls, oh, his balls are a work of art.

They should have their own installation at the Tate Modern, along with the upthrust of his dick between them. A sculpture I'd call Hunter's Pillar, or a phallic representation of what it is like to be hunted by the owner of said appendage. Right, I've officially gone into meltdown then, and all because I saw his penis? Again, in my defense, I've seen the male member before, but none as prodigious as his.

The heat that had retreated toward my core turbo charges forward, until it seems to have flooded every part of me. My nipples tighten until it feels like they're ready to torpedo out of my bikini. As for my pussy...? It's in pussy heaven, with threads of moisture lubricating my cunt, readying itself for an imminent penetration—which I'm not going to let happen. Not yet.

I twist my arm and tug. This time, he releases me. I stumble back, right myself, then tip up my chin. "I'm going to take a shower."

# 21

Hunter

She scampers up and out of the tub and disappears through the doorway before I can call out to her. I saw her gaze lower to my groin, knew she saw the evidence of my aroused state. Then, her gaze widened, the color surged through her face, and still, she continued to stare hungrily at my cock, which grew even more erect under her perusal. Well, at least, now she knows I have the apparatus to back up my ego.

What I hadn't expected was for her to make that quick retreat. Apparently, she hadn't expected to see me naked. It had the effect I was hoping for. I took her mind off of the thoughts buzzing through her head. I'm almost certain she was going to call off our deal for the night, and no way, would I accept that from her. So, I opted to distract her instead, and by the looks of it, I succeeded... Maybe too well.

I sink down into the hot tub, then duck my head under completely, before coming up again. I do want to give her time to cool off. On the other hand, if I give her too much time, she's likely to develop cold feet, which I'm not going to allow.

I rise to my feet, step out, then walk through the doorway. My wet feet slap on the wooden beams as I walk past the kitchen, down the hallway, and into the bedroom. I notice the luggage stowed away inside the walk-in closet at the far end, something I missed the first time I walked in.

I push open the door of the bathroom and enter. The shower is running, and through the steamed-up wall of the cubicle, I can make out her figure. I head toward the sink, brush my teeth, rinse out my mouth, then head toward the cubicle. I push it open and walk in. She stiffens but doesn't turn around. Instead, she tips up her chin so the water pours over her face and down her hair, which sticks to her back in long twisty coils.

I walk over to her, take the shampoo, and pour it into my palm. I begin to massage it into her hair. Her shoulder muscles grow rigid, but she doesn't stop me. I dig my fingers into her scalp and knead it in circular motions. A moan spills from her lips. She leans back into my touch as if she can't help herself. I continue to massage her scalp and she slumps back further. I lean into her so her back is flush against my chest. Her eyes are closed, those long eyelashes spiky with moisture. I drag my fingers through her hair, then down to her shoulders. I dig my knuckles into her shoulders, and she groans. The sound is so sexy, so hot, my groin tightens. My balls harden, and my cock jerks from where it's nestled between her arse cheeks. Her muscles clench, and I press down on her shoulders. "Relax, baby."

She draws in a breath, then bit by bit, her muscles loosen. I continue to squeeze her shoulder muscles, working my way down her biceps, then back up. I drag my knuckles down either side of her spine and she groans again. "That feels so good." Her voice is relaxed, the words almost slurring together. I tilt her head so the shampoo suds slither down her back. She leans her head into my shoulder, and I bend and kiss the curve of her shoulder.

She wraps her arm about my neck, and I drag my chin up the side of her neck. She shivers. I cup her breasts and squeeze, and she arches further into me. Her eyes are closed, her breathing shallow. I glance down the slope of her waist to the hollow between her legs. I reach down and strum her pussy lips, and she gasps. I stuff two fingers inside her, and she rises up to the tips of her toes. She turns her face in my direction, and I close my lips over hers. I lick her mouth, and she parts her lips at once. I slide my tongue over hers, suck on her lower lip, and her pussy clenches around my fingers. My shaft throbs, my balls grow heavier. Fuck, I need to be inside of her. I release her lips, then reach for the conditioner. I step back and pour it between her butt cheeks.

"What are you—"

"Shh." I kiss her again and she opens up completely. She moves into me and I position my cock against her back opening.

She begins to protest, but I deepen the kiss and absorb her words. I work my fingers in and out of her until she widens her legs, allowing me to add a third finger inside her cunt. I fuck her even harder with my fingers, and her entire body trembles. That's when I thrust my hips forward and breach her puckered hole. She's so relaxed that I slip inside her and through her resisting ring of muscles in one smooth thrust. She gasps into my mouth, and I feel her shudder. I continue to kiss her as I allow her to adjust to my size. When she relaxes again, I soften my kiss. I press little pecks to her mouth, then up her jawline and to her ear. I lick inside her ear and she moans. "Hunter, please."

"Tell me what you want, baby."

"You're so big," she groans.

"All the better to fill you up, Fire."

"It hurts." She scowls up at me.

"Good."

"What the hell? How dare you—"

"Relax darling, it's only going to get better."

"Easy for you to say, you're not the one with a monster cock stuck up her backside."

"You mean this?" I pull out a little, then slip back inside her, and her entire body jolts. I pinch her clit, and she gasps.

"Oh, god. Oh, Jesus."

"You mean oh, Hunter, don't you?"

"You're so fucking smug, you twatarse."

I chuckle. "I'm the one inside your arse, baby." I pull back, then propel my hips forward again, sinking deeper inside. At the same time, I slide my fingers in and out of her pussy, and her head rolls forward. I ease her forward, then coax her hands out from behind my neck and place them flat on the wall. "Hold on, baby."

I grip her hip with one hand. With the other, I continue to finger-fuck her. Then, I begin to fuck her arse in earnest. Each time I sink deeper, she moans. When I pull back, she follows me, chasing the feeling of fullness that she's already adjusted to. I stay there for a few seconds, and she scowls over her shoulder. "You better finish what you started this time."

"You mean like this?" I propel my hips forward with enough force that my balls slap against her butt. She slaps the wall with her palm, then spreads her legs even wider, taking even more of my length. "Oh, god. Oh, god. Oh, god," she chants.

I tilt my hips and pound into her. This time, I sink all the way inside of her. I bottom out, and the tension at the base of my spine coils into a ball of tightness. Her entire body trembles. Her knees seem to give way again. I squeeze my hold on her hip, holding her upright, then tilt my hips and begin to fuck her in earnest. She clenches down on my cock, and I see black spots. Fuck, I'm so close. I grind the heel of my palm into her clit, and she cries out.

I lower my head until my cheek is pressed to hers. "Come with me, right now."

# 22

Zara

Barely are the words out of his mouth when that tension inside me explodes. The vibrations zip up my spine and crash between my ears. "Oh, my god, Hunter!" I'm aware of clenching down on his cock, while my pussy clamps down on his fingers, and I shatter. I hear his muted growl and he follows me over the edge. I slump forward, but he wraps his arm around my waist and pulls me in for an embrace. I sense him throb inside me and when he pulls away, I can't stop my moan of protest. He reaches over and shuts off the shower, then scoops me up in his arms. "What are you doing?"

"I'm taking care of you, baby."

I scowl up at him. "I can take care of myself."

"I have no doubt but humor me."

I glower at him, and he chuckles. "You're fucking cute, you know that?" He leans down and kisses my nose, and it's such a tender gesture that I gape at him.

"You don't need to look so surprised. You are eminently endearing when you forget to be prickly and put on that tough as nails mask that you like to show the world."

"I am as tough as nails," I insist, then yawn and spoil the effect.

"Of course, you are." He carries me out of the shower cubicle, then lowers me down next to the bathtub. He reaches for one of the folded towels and wraps it over my head. He dries my hair quickly, then my body with brisk strokes. He rubs the same towel down his body, then tosses it aside. Why is it so intimate that he used the same towel on his body as he used on me? It's just a towel. Doesn't mean anything. He scoops me up in his arms and walks over to the bed. He lowers me to the ground, yanks the covers up, then jerks his head in the direction of the mattress.

I slide in and scoot over, turning over on my side. He pulls the sheet over me. The bed dips, and the next moment, the heat from his body envelops me. He slides his arm under my neck, wraps his other arm about my waist, and pulls me close. Then he spoons me. He freakin' spoons and, OMG, it's the most incredible sensation in the world. I can feel his hard body embracing every inch of my back, his cock—still semi-rigid—lays in the valley between my arse-cheeks, his thighs cradle mine, and his feet, oh his feet are so warm. I tuck my own freezing toes between his feet, and he chuckles. "Woman, your feet are like ice, and you just got out of the bath."

"So are my hands." I place my palm over his, and it feels so right. It's just for one night. Doesn't mean anything. Heat cocoons me and sinks into my blood. My muscles are so relaxed. My head feels so light. Clearly, the sex helped me relieve a lot of the tension I've been carrying. My eyelids flutter down, then I snap them open. "We didn't use a condom," I exclaim.

There's silence, then. "I'm clean. I can show you the paperwork tomorrow."

"I'm clean, too," I say slowly.

The silence stretches, then, "It's not that I didn't remember that we needed to use a condom, but I didn't want to," he finally admits.

I stare at snow falling outside the window. "You didn't want to use a condom?"

I sense him shake his head.

Then, "Are you okay if we don't use a condom when I fuck you next?" He asks.

"What if I want you to use a condom?" I swallow.

"Do *you* want me to use a condom?" he parries.

Of course, I anticipated he'd answer my question with a question. Only, I hadn't wanted to answer his question because... I don't want him to use a condom. And damn, if that doesn't surprise me.

I turn in his arms and glance up at him. "I've never allowed anyone to fuck me without a condom."

"I've never fucked a woman without a condom," he replies.

We glance at each other. His blue-green eyes are a dark blue in this light. He holds my gaze, then bends and kisses my nose again. "Don't think too much about it. It's you and me, baby, in this cottage. There's no one else. Forget the outside world for the next few hours. It's just us. You can be yourself. I promise, I won't tell anyone."

I half smile. "As long as you'll be yourself, too."

His gaze grows earnest as he replies, "Always, and only with you."

Why does that seem like a promise? Nah, it's my imagination. Probably because I'm tired from the day.

"Okay." I nod.

"Okay." He kisses me on the lips, then tucks my head under his chin. "Sleep, so I can wake you up in the sexiest of ways."

My eyelids flutter down.

The images seem to flit over my mind almost as soon as I close my eyes. I know I'm dreaming, but I'm powerless to stop it. It's always the same thing. Me chasing after Olly, who's giggling and laughing as he runs from me. He steps on the road. I yell at him. He stops in the middle of the road and turns as a car bears down on him. He turns to see the car, and his gaze widens. "ZaraDi!" He yells my name with the honorific 'Di' added on at the end to symbolize his respect for me. Because I'm his bigger sister. Someone who should have been watching out for him. Someone who should have never let him escape my hold and stopped him before he stepped in the path of the car. Olly, my little squishy, smooshy Olly. Gone in the blink of an eye.

"Zara, open your eyes."

I snap my eyes open to find Hunter scowling down at me. His

features are pale underneath his tan or maybe it's just the moonlight that's turning his face into an effigy carved out of marble? So smooth, yet so hard, and soft on the inside. He scans my features. "You were dreaming," he murmurs.

I swallow.

"I'll get you some water."

He begins to pull away, but I grasp his arm. "No, don't leave me."

He looks between my eyes, then nods. "Want to tell me about it?"

I shake my head.

Hurt flashes across his features, and my chest tightens. A burning sensation coils behind my ribcage. "I will, just not yet." I bite the inside of my cheek. "Please, can you trust me on that?"

He draws in a breath then lowers his head and brushes his lips over mine. "Anything you want, baby."

Tears prick the backs of my eyes. It's not like me to cry—not in front of another, and definitely, not in the bed of a man I let fuck me. But then, there have already been so many firsts with Hunter, I'm beginning to lose count. Is that good or bad? Or maybe, here under this roof, and with him, as we are snowed in over Christmas, it doesn't matter?

As if he senses the train of my thoughts, he cups my cheek and says, "I'll do anything to make you feel better, Fire."

"Anything?" I tilt my head.

# 23

Hunter

"Anything," I murmur.

She blinks away the brightness in her eyes, then offers me a slight smile. "There was this one thing."

"Oh?"

She releases her hold on my wrist, only to trail her fingers up my forearm. Goosebumps pop on my skin. My shoulder muscles tighten.

"I have this burning sensation in my center," she murmurs.

"Was that here?" I kiss the tip of her nose.

"Not the center of my nose." Her lips tip up.

"Is it here, perhaps?" I lower my head and kiss the hollow at the base of her neck. Her scent—that blend of orange blossoms and vanilla, with a tang of pepper, instantly goes to my head. My cock thickens. "Or maybe here?" I press tiny kisses down to the space between her breasts.

Her breath hitches. She grips my shoulders, and I can't stop the rumble of satisfaction that wells up my throat. I continue to kiss my way down to her belly button. "Was it here, you think?"

"No," her voice trembles.

"Or maybe here?" I drag my chin down her lower belly to the flesh just above her clit.

She writhes under me, then digs her fingers into my hair.

"Not there." Impatience threads her voice, and I chuckle.

She tugs on my hair, and pinpricks of heat zip down my spine. My balls tighten.

I press a kiss into her inner thigh, and she moans. I nibble on the skin over her thigh and she pushes up her core, chasing my tongue.

I laugh and she makes a noise at the back of her throat. "Are you teasing me, Whittington?"

"Always, Fire."

She rears up, but I flatten my palm in the center of her chest and hold her in place. "Patience, Fire."

"Fuck patience," she snaps.

"Now, where's the fun in that, hmm?"

"I'm beginning to wonder if you can even find my cli—" She gasps as I swipe my tongue up her pussy lips. I wrap my tongue around the swollen nub hidden there, and she yanks on my hair. "Oh, god, Hunter."

*Finally, fuck.* "If I knew this is what it took for you to say my name, I'd have gone down on you as soon as I met you."

"As if I'd have allowed it."

I ease my tongue inside her channel, and she groans.

"You were saying?"

She pants. "I was saying that—" She yells, for I've slid my palms under her butt and squeezed the flesh. At the same time, I bite down on her clit.

She thrashes her head from left to right, yanks on my hair with such force, I'm sure she's pulled out tufts of strands. "Ohmigod, ohmigod!" She pushes her pelvis into my face as I continue to fuck her with my tongue.

Her entire body shudders.

I pull back for a moment, only to throw her legs over my shoulders. I cup her arse cheeks and position her so when I stab my tongue inside her next, she groans. Color smears her neck, her cheeks. Her eyelids are squeezed shut. Her mouth is open and she pants. Her entire body is an arc of desire, a bow of lust, and I'm the arrow that's going to slot into her center and make her come so hard, she's not going to be able to see straight for days. I continue to eat her out, and when she squeezes her legs about my neck in a vice-like grip, while her pussy clenches down on my tongue, I know she's close. I apply pressure on her thighs, so she parts them enough for me to rise up and crawl up over her. "Open your eyes," I order.

She flutters open her eyelids and her pupils are so expanded, there's only a circle of gold around the black. I sit up on my knees and she frowns.

I position myself over her so my hips are over her face and her pussy is directly below mine.

"Open your mouth."

She instantly complies.

"You okay with this, baby?" I look between her eyes.

She holds my gaze, then wraps her fingers around the base of my cock and slides it between her lips. No hesitation, she takes me down the column of her throat, holding my hip with her other hand. A groan rips out of me. I grit my teeth to stop myself from fucking her mouth. I dig my elbows into where I have them positioned on either side of her thighs, then force myself to open my eyelids.

"Do you remember your safe word?"

She nods.

"Anytime you need me to stop, tap my thigh."

Her gaze widens. Then she pulls back, allowing my cock to slip to the edge of her mouth, before she tips up her chin and takes it down her throat again

"Oh, fuck." I watch as, without breaking the connection with my gaze, she pulls back again and rolls her tongue up my length.

"You're fucking gorgeous, you know that?"

She merely swallows me down her throat, then gags. Saliva slides down the edges of her mouth, and maybe that's when I fall in love with her a little. So, I'm a cliché, but goddamn, if she isn't the most perfect woman in the world right now, as she massages my balls while swallowing my cock, like she was born for it.

I lower my face to her pussy, then squeeze her thighs apart and begin to eat her out in earnest.

She stutters. Her hold on my hip tightens. She's even more aroused than a few seconds ago. Fat drops of cum pool between her legs, and I lick them up. So fucking sweet. She tastes like honey and cloves. An amalgamation of tastes I'm never going to forget. I tilt my head, glide my tongue inside her, then out, then in, out, in. As I find my rhythm, her entire body jolts. Her movements become frantic, and she stuffs me down her throat, then out. And again. The blood rushes to my groin. Sweat beads my shoulders. I rub my whiskered chin down her clit, and she gasps. She arches up so my cock slides impossibly deep down her throat. The ball of tension at the base of my spine tightens and my entire body shudders. Fuck, I'm too close. Too fast. And this time I'm coming inside of her. I pull out of her, then flip around. I settle between her legs.

"You ready for this, baby?"

She nods.

I wrap her hands around the headboard, then throw her legs over my shoulders. "Hold on."

# 24

Zara

Maybe I should have asked him to use a condom. But I don't want him to use a condom. If this is the only night I get with him, I want to feel all of him. With nothing separating us. So, I've never felt this way before, and that makes this entire situation dangerous, but... It's only one night. I'll walk away tomorrow. I'll make sure our paths don't cross—it will be difficult with all the friends we have in common, but that's fine, I can manage it. I can.

That's when he brackets me with those massive arms, and positions himself at my entrance. He holds my gaze, propels his hips forward and breaches me. I know he's big, I've taken him in what is a smaller channel, not to mention, I just had him down my throat, but this...

Oh god, he feels so huge. So massive. So enormous. So damn good. A groan wells up, and he closes his mouth over mine and swallows the sound. He pulls back, then rams into me with such force the entire bed moves forward. The headstand smashes into the wall, and something crashes to the ground. Then he begins to pound into me.

He still hasn't released my mouth, and his gaze, locked with mine, is intense. His blue-green eyes, now a startling color that resembles the stormy seas, bore into mine. His shoulders are so huge, his body so large, so solid, the heat from his chest pins me in place, and it feels like I'm being consumed by him. The next time he pulls out of me, he releases my mouth and stares between my eyes. "You feel so fucking good, Fire. I'll never get enough of you."

I want to agree with him. I do. I open my mouth, but all that comes out is a groan. One side of his lips kicks up. He wraps his hand over my hip, then lunges forward. He tilts his hips and bottoms out inside me. He touches a part of me deep inside. One that sets off a series of reverberations that zip up my spine. My head spins. Sweat clings to my shoulders. I dig my heels into his back, curl my fingers into the headboard. "Hunter," I gasp. Not sure what else to say. What else can I say?

He seems to understand, though, for he lowers his head until his eyelashes brush mine. "Come with me, Zara." He thrusts into me once more, hitting that same spot. "Come right now."

I orgasm instantly. The climax slams into me, and I cry out. Sparks sweep across my vision, and as I black out, I hear his hoarse cry.

When I come to, I'm curled on his chest, his arms about me. His heart beats at an elevated rate against my cheek, and the heat from his body surrounds us like our own personal patch of beach in the sun.

I turn my face into his chest and lick up a bead of sweat.

"Did you just lick me?" he rumbles.

"I want to do more than lick you." I turn over to rest my chin on his chest. He folds his arms behind his neck and the movement makes his biceps bulge.

"For someone who spends most of his time in Parliament, defending your government's policies, you sure are built."

"I also spend time on the road with my constituents. And I work out most mornings."

"Let me guess. Up at five a.m. to work out, while listening to the morning news—"

"Four-thirty a.m., and also, the stock markets," he corrects me.

"Then run five miles on your treadmill."

"Ten miles, and normally outside." He smirks.

"And you eat political arguments for breakfast."

"I'd rather eat you."

I blink. "You have a one-track mind."

"You and public service. Nothing else has intrigued me as much in my entire life."

"Hunter, don't." I begin to pull away, but he flips me over and leans over me.

"Why is it that you don't like to talk about us?"

"It's only one night."

"Are you sure?"

"What do you mean?" I scowl.

He jerks his head in the direction of the window. I turn to find the gray light of dawn filtering through the window. Also, it's snowing, the flakes coming down so hard that it forms a sheet of white past the windowpane.

"Oh, no."

"Oh, yes."

I turn to find an expression of satisfaction on his face. "You knew this would happen. You knew we'd be snowed in today."

"I'd hoped for it, yes."

"So technically, our one night stand was never going to happen."

"Technically, today is a continuation of our one night stand, if you never leave the bed." His smirk widens.

"I think your logic is faulty."

"I think it's time you stop thinking." He lowers his weight onto me, and the thick column between his legs nestles against my pussy.

"Oh." I swallow.

"Indeed." He leans down and kisses my nose.

"I wish you wouldn't do that."

"Do what?"

"Go all tender and sweet."

"You don't want me to be tender?" His eyebrows draw down.

"I'd rather you fuck me hard."

He tilts his head. "So you don't have time to formulate your arguments on why we shouldn't be together? So you can put the blame of your agreeing to be fucked by me on me?"

When he says that, it feels so wrong. Like I'm putting the onus of our being together like this on him, and somehow, it's not fair to him. But neither is the fact that I'm pulled so strongly toward him, and after how we fucked, I know it's not going to be easy to forget about him. Maybe impossible. So, I don't deny what he says. But I don't agree to it, either.

The seconds stretch, then he tucks a strand of hair behind my ear. "You know what I think we should do?"

"What?"

"Have breakfast."

---

He places the breakfast tray on the bed between us. He insisted I stay in bed and snooze while he cooked breakfast. I protested half-heartedly, but when he'd reminded me that it was a one night stand, which was valid only as long as I didn't leave the bed, I agreed. Also, I love sleeping in, and I never allow myself to do so. All those years of my parents waking me up, along with my twin brother Cade, to study in the mornings because it was the best time to practice our math before we went to school, instilled a sense of discipline in me I've never been able to shake off. Trapped in this room and this bed, with the storm raging outside, it feels like I've found a liminal space that doesn't belong to my normal life. A space and time where no rules apply. Besides, getting thoroughly fucked last night relaxed me to the extent that when I cuddled into his pillow and drew in his scent, it instantly made me close my eyes and drift off. I awoke when he placed the breakfast tray in the center of the bed.

Now, I sit up, tuck the sheets under my arms, and eye the monstrosity of a breakfast. On the tray is a plate piled with two eggs over easy, bacon, baked beans, sausages, hash browns, and toast. There's butter in a bowl on the side, a glass of orange juice and a cup of coffee.

"That's a lot for one person," I murmur.

"It's for both of us."

He slides onto the bed. At some point, he pulled on a pair of gray sweats. But that glorious chest is shirtless. A-n-d I'll never get used to seeing that ripped torso, those eight pack abs, that trim waist with the trail of hair that arrows down to that very distinctive part of him. The one that I had my fingers around not very long ago. The one I had taken down my throat, and felt thicken and fill my mouth—and earned me that compliment from him.

"Men are suckers for blow jobs, huh?"

"You mean, you don't like it when I go down on you?" He smirks.

My belly clenches. What is it about this man talking dirty that touches something primal inside me? Still, I manage to meet his gaze without blushing, "Feel free to eat me out anytime." I reach for a piece of toast, but he gets there first.

"Let me." He butters the toast, holds it out, and I crunch down on it. Then he feeds me some of the baked beans, followed by hash browns, and finally, the crunchy bacon.

"Mmm." I lick my lips. "You can cook, apparently."

"Surprised that the entitled, poshhole can get his hands dirty?"

This time, I can't stop myself from blushing. "Poshhole, I like that." I reach for my cup of coffee, and once more, he gets there first.

"Now, now, no cheating, Fire." He raises the cup of coffee to my lips. I sip from it, and his eyes flare. He brings the cup to his mouth and sips from the same spot I did. When did the action of drinking from a cup become so pornographic? He places the cup down, then feeds me more of the hash browns. "You like your potatoes, eh?"

"What's not to like? It's my fave vegetable. I can have it in any form. Fries and crisps are my downfall."

He feeds me more of the hash browns, and the shredded potato pieces melt in my mouth. I've had hash browns before, and let me tell you, that's gourmet level cooking right there.

"Did you study cooking?"

"That obvious, huh?" He cuts up a piece of the sausage and offers it to me. I chew on it, and once more, the intense green of chives, with the bite of peppercorns, combines with the chewy texture of the meat and fills my mouth.

"I'm not a great cook, to be honest. But this food could come from a very fine restaurant." I lick my lips.

His gaze is fixed to my mouth, and he feeds me more of the sausage. "I could spend all day watching you eat."

I redden. I'm good with accepting compliments; I really am. So why is it that these remarks from him make me blush?

"I briefly entertained the thought of becoming a chef." He picks up a piece of the sausage and chews on it.

"You? A chef?"

"That's how I met James," he adds.

"You mean James Hamilton, the chef?"

He nods. "I even went to culinary school with him. But then, my father had a heart attack. I came home to find him weak and almost at death's door. He told me his one wish was for me to follow in his footsteps."

"And you did," I point out.

"I always knew I was going to go into public service eventually; the cooking was a hobby I enjoyed. I loved experimenting with ingredients almost as much as I enjoy putting the right people together to create a group that will draw on the strengths of the individuals and make the combined team much more than the sum of the parts."

He glances up, then tilts his head. "That's a very thoughtful look you have there."

"My father was very demanding of me and my brother. He never treated me as a girl, actually. He always told me, anything my brother could do, I could do better. I found the weight of his expectations both crushing and exhilarating. And maybe, I felt more compelled to rise to the challenge. Maybe I felt I had to deliver on his dreams for me."

"Hence, you became a lawyer?"

"I did." I tuck the sheet firmly under my arms. "And then, I started my own PR firm."

"A gamble, maybe?"

"No more than you going into public life."

"I'll be the first to admit that following in the footsteps of my father, and his father before that, opened doors for me that otherwise might have remained closed. It also invited comparisons with my father and grandfather, which I was prepared for. I took it as a compliment that people contrasted my style to theirs. I knew I had to focus on my strengths, that with time my style would shine through, and I'd develop my own approach, my own modus operandi."

"Your own brand appeal," I murmur.

"Indeed. As have you, Councilor. You're one heck of a ballsy, fearless negotiator, who'll go to any lengths to ensure your client is protected. You have single-handedly steered tough journalists into writing stories from the angles that benefit your principals."

"Why, thank you," I dip my head. "And you have a strong brand, Minister. Not only are you charismatic, but your confidence comes across as a self-assuredness which is very attractive."

"Is it now?" He smirks.

"Clearly, it's going to swell your already oversized head, but since I've opened this particular line of thought, I may as well tell you that you also speak sense. Which is more than I can say of many of your colleagues."

He laughs—a full belly laugh that wells up from deep inside, rumbles up his chest, and brightens his features. With his tousled hair and days-old growth on his jaw, not to mention, those gray sweatpants and bare chest, he could well be a sex god. Correction, he is a sex god, who not only has the equipment but also delivers on the promise.

He lowers his chin and watches me with a speculative look.

"You haven't eaten much breakfast." I gesture to the half-full plate.

"That's because I'm saving my appetite for something else."

# 25

Hunter

Her eyes flash and her breathing grows rough. She moves restlessly under the covers, which dip down between her breasts. I slide my legs off the bed, take the tray and stow it on the side-table. Then I quirk my finger. "Come 'ere."

Her color heightens. For a second, she stays still, then she shakes her head.

"Zara," I lower my voice to a hush, and she shivers. But she still doesn't move.

"If you don't do as I say, I'll have to interpret that as a sign of battle lines being drawn."

"Oh, good." She rises to her knees, then shuffles toward the edge of the bed, and I click my tongue.

"Remember what I said? You can't leave the bed."

"I have to use the bathroom." She protests.

"I'll take you."

She scowls at me over her shoulder. "I'm not an invalid."

"And you agreed to a one night stand, an agreement which *is* invalid the moment your feet touch the floor outside the bed."

"I'll have to touch the floor of the bathroom," she points out.

"That's allowed."

She scoffs. "Who makes these stupid rules anyway?"

"I do, babe, you should know that by now."

"Doesn't mean I have to follow them." She puts out a leg to jump off the bed, and I throw myself across the length of the mattress. I grab her around her waist, and she yells as I pull her to the bed and clamber on top of her.

"Let me go." She begins to struggle under me, and each time she moves, her thigh brushes against the hardening column between my legs. She must feel it, for she freezes. Her color is high, and her entire body vibrates with a nervous energy that tells me she's both afraid of what I'm going to do next, and excited about it.

"You're being bratty, hmm?"

"You're being all dominating, hmm?" She tips up her chin.

"It's who I am, baby, and you find it appealing"

"Do not."

I lower my head and run my nose up the side of her throat; she shudders.

"You can try to deny it as much as you want, but your body responds to my every touch."

"Doesn't mean much when my mind's not in it, does it?"

I stiffen, then pull back. "Are you saying you don't want me to touch you, Zara?"

She holds my gaze.

"All you have to do is use your safe word, and I'll stop."

She swallows.

"Well, what's it gonna be Zara?"

She firms her lips. "I'm not using my safe word, am I?"

A hot sensation stabs my chest. A flush of triumph sweeps under my skin. *Huh? Was I so afraid that she'd use her safe word? And would I have allowed her to leave if she had? Would I have gone back on my word?* Good thing I don't have to answer that question. I search between her eyes, then roll off the bed. Once on my feet, I scoop her up in my arms.

"What are you doing?"

"I'm taking care of your needs." I pivot, head for the ensuite, then deposit her next to the toilet bowl. She makes a twirling motion with her finger. I simply fold my arms across my chest.

"Why aren't you turning around?"

"You don't get to ask the questions, Fire."

She flushes. "You can't coerce me into doing anything I don't want to."

"But I can seduce you into it."

She blinks, then chuckles. "You have me there. And why is it that every time I want to stay angry at you, you say or do something that makes me laugh instead?"

"Maybe it's because we're on the same wavelength."

"Not bloody likely. Also" —she turns around and sits on the commode— "if you think I am shy about peeing in front of you, think again."

She holds my gaze, and then the tinkle of a stream of water hitting the pot fills the air. Color sweeps up her throat and her cheeks, but she doesn't look away. This woman has nerves of steel.

If there's anyone who can stand by me through the upcoming campaign I'm embarking on to become the Prime Minister of this country, it's her. Question is, how do I convince her of it? Do I want to convince her of it? Am I really thinking of binding myself to someone after years of never wanting to be tied down? I'm well aware of the optics related to a Prime Ministerial campaign. Having my woman by my side will send the message that I'm grounded and reliable. A serious person who's ready to settle down. But that's not why I want her. It's because it feels right to be with her. To have her by my side feels like the completion of a journey I hadn't even been aware I was on. I set out to tame her, but somewhere along the way, she began to tame me, and I wasn't even aware it was happening.

The sound of the water being flushed pulls me out of my reverie. She walks over to the sink and washes her hands. I close the distance to her, wrap my arm about her waist, and tuck her head under my chin. She dries her hands, then glances up. Our gazes catch. The contrast between us couldn't be starker. She's not tiny, but not too tall, either. She comes up to the level of my heart, and fits into me like she was made for me.

Her skin is flushed, and I know it's soft to the touch. Her eyes sparkle with intelligence, with that awareness of her own self that I've always found so appealing. There's something about her confidence that turns me on. It makes me want to own her, possess her. To pit my wits against her, and to celebrate her when she wins an argument, too. A-n-d whoa, that's a first. I've always been confident about my ability to win, but to acknowledge another person's intellect, to recognize their strengths, to own their successes as mine? That's definitely a first.

She turns around in my arms, then reaches up and straightens out the fold between my eyebrows.

"Whatever it is you're thinking has you disturbed," she murmurs.

I tighten my hold on her. "Only because my thoughts have gone down paths never traversed before."

She tips up her chin. "Is that a confession?"

"It's an observation."

"Oh." She bites down on her lower lip, and my cock twitches. I reach over and slide her lip out from between her teeth. "No one can hurt you, Fire. No one except me."

She scoffs. "Have you any idea how you sound?"

"Like a demented, possessive bastard who can't get enough of his woman?"

"I'm not your woman." She tips up her chin.

"You are for one more night."

"Only you could define a one night stand as one that extends over two nights."

"Whatever it takes to keep you with me, baby." I smirk.

"You're so full of yourself."

"And you like me for that."

She glances between my eyes. "It's true. It's not that I like you, and yet I can't keep away from you."

"It's not that I like you... No... My emotions are too strong to be called like," I parry.

She laughs. "Neither one of us can win a war of the words."

"Only because I'm letting you get away with it."

"Oh, yeah? You're letting me get away with it, you—" She gasps in surprise as I lift her up and throw her over my shoulder.

"What are you doing?"

"I'm making the most of the time we have left."

"You're using brute force to win the argument." She wriggles in my hold, and I place my arm over her waist to hold her in place.

"Let me go."

"You know better than to say that, Fire."

"And don't call me by that nickname," she snaps.

"I'll call you what I want, when I want, and you'll answer to it, *Fire*."

She groans in annoyance. "And if I don't?"

"Are you sure you want to find out?"

# 26

Zara

"Do your worst, you twathole."

No sooner have the words left my lips than a white jolt of heat screams up my spine. I yell, "You spanked me, you…you…jerkass."

"You're beginning to repeat your insults," he observes, right after which he brings his palm down on my other arsecheek.

I scream, wriggle about over his shoulder. He simply swings around, heads for the bedroom, then toward the bed.

"Let me go, Hunter. Right now."

"If that's what you want." He throws me down on the bed, and before I've even completed my first bounce, he shoves off his sweat-pants—no briefs—and follows me down. He covers my body with his, digs his elbows into either side of my head, and presses his hips into mine so there's no mistaking just how turned on he is. The thick pole between his legs nestles into the valley between mine. His weight pins me down, and he lowers his chest to mine, the carved planes digging into the softness of my breasts. The heat of his body slams into mine, and it's like I'm in a sauna.

Goosebumps pop on my skin. Moisture pools between my thighs. He stays there, holding my gaze, not moving, simply allowing me to feel every inch of his hard body against mine. Letting the rightness of us being together in this moment sink in. My nipples peak, and my clit throbs. That emptiness in my belly unfurls and grows. All of the cells in my body seem to open and ready themselves to be invaded by him. He's all around me, enveloping me. I've never felt this fragile, this intensely conscious of just how much bigger than me he is.

Our bodies seem to communicate without words. Our gazes lock. The thickness at my core grows even more prominent.

"Do you remember your safe word?"

His voice is hard; there's a meanness to it that reaches that part of me deep inside I've never wanted to acknowledge. The part that yearns for a male strong enough to overpower me. A man who is as determined as me; someone intelligent enough to pit his wits against mine, quick-witted enough to trade words with me, dominant enough to command me, skilled enough to manipulate my body, and considerate enough to bring me to orgasm every single time—an area in which all of my previous lovers have failed.

"Zara, do you?" He peers into my eyes.

I nod.

"Say it aloud."

"I remember my safe word." My voice sounds like it's coming from far away. My mind seems to have detached from my body, floating somewhere above while I watch this entire scene unfold. I shouldn't find it so hot—oh, god—but I do. I push up my chest so my nipples stab into his unforgiving chest planes.

His lips twist. "Good girl."

I shudder. Pleasure sweeps through my veins, and I almost orgasm. And all because he praised me? Jesus, what's he doing to me?

He pushes away from the bed and stabs his finger at me. "Stay right there."

I couldn't move if I tried. The primitive part of my brain has acknowledged he's the master. And I'm his to do with as he wants… For now. All of my senses are focused on him, on how his powerful thighs ripple as he stalks over to his bag in the corner and rummages around before turning to face me. A few strips of silk dangle from his hand.

"What's that?"

"Relax, Fire, I promise you're going to enjoy this."

"That's what you said when you fucked me in the arse… For our very first time together."

He reaches the bed then glares down at me. "Did it hurt?

"What do you think?" I scowl.

"That you screamed my name as you came so hard that you could barely move afterward. And now, you're embarrassed about it."

"I'm not embarrassed about anything."

"Then why is your face so red?"

"It's not—" I firm my lips. "Fine, I didn't expect to enjoy it so much. Also, I definitely didn't think that the first time we fucked you'd enter the wrong way."

He chuckles. "That's a quaint way of referring to anal."

"I believe in social, political and economic equality of the genders; doesn't mean I'm not well-mannered," I say primly.

"Seems to me you also believe in the anal quality of pleasure."

I laugh. I can't help it. Here I am, trying to make him feel guilty for jumping right into having anal with me. I've never allowed any of my partners to take that liberty with me. Not even my longest relationship, which lasted all of three months. And Hunter here, hunted me down and boldly went where no one had dared to before.

"Hold on a second." He scrutinizes my features. "Was that your first time?"

My cheeks heat. "What? Don't be ridiculous."

"It was your first time with anal."

My face is so hot now, I'm sure there are flames leaping up from it. "Can we stop this discussion?"

"Is it because four letter words are an issue for you?" he asks slowly.

"Fuck, no." I tilt up my chin. "But I do have an issue with your having opened your innings with anal."

"Not to worry, baby. I'm a believer in marathons and five-day long cricket matches." He places a knee on the bed.

"Personally, I prefer working in short quick bursts." I choke out.

"And I prefer to keep my stamina, when it comes to both the campaign trail and my sexual performance."

"Did you just compare politics to sex?" I gasp.

"There's a similar high when you win over a particularly stubborn opponent in both, wouldn't you say?"

I widen my gaze. "And now you're comparing me to a political rival?"

"You're, by far, the most beautiful, most vital, most intelligent adversary I've ever taken on."

"So, we've covered cricket, politics, and sex in the space of a few sentences." Three things I am passionate about. "That's a—"

"First," he says at the same time as me.

The air between us thickens and swirls with unsaid words. The kind you don't dare blurt out for fear of where they might lead. And yet, you also can't ignore it. When was the last time my pillow talk with a man covered such a large spectrum of interests?

"I don't know of many women who're familiar with cricketing analogies," he says as if he's read my mind. And it's no surprise I am. Cricket is the one game that we watched as a family when I was growing up. It's the one time my father allowed my brother and me to slack off our studies—when there was a cricket match on the TV. Also, my brother now plays cricket for England, something I don't publicize much.

"My brother plays cricket for England," I say, then squeeze my eyes shut. Did I say that aloud? I said that. Not even my closest friends know about Cade.

It's not that I have anything to hide. It's more to do with the fact that, given the kind of job I do—being a fixer, that is—it's simpler to keep my family out of the limelight. Also, Cade attracts his share of attention, given the high-profile nature of his sponsorships. So, it's simpler not to draw the media's attention to our relationship. I've even managed to keep it off of my Wikipedia page. And now, I shared it with this man. This man, who I've known for barely a few days...

Okay, more than that. But the sum total of time we've spent together amounts to a couple of days or less. Although it will be more than that by the time this interlude is over.

"Zara, you okay?"

I nod, still keeping my eyes shut.

"What are you afraid of?"

I snap my eyelids open. "Who said anything about being afraid?"

"Why are you upset?"

"I prefer not to tell people about my family. It's how I protect them."

"Understandable, given the nature of your job. But it doesn't explain why you're so pissed off with yourself."

"I'm not—" He tilts his head and I firm my lips. "You're right, I am upset with myself." I glance away then back at him. "That was my first time."

His eyebrows shoot up. "Your first time with anal sex?"

My cheeks heat further, if that were even possible. "Why don't you yell it out so the neighbors can hear you?"

His lips kick up. "Our nearest neighbor is miles away. And you have nothing to be embarrassed about enjoying it, baby." He scans my features. "Do you know how it makes me feel to find out that I had one of your firsts?"

Did I hear him correctly? It shouldn't mean anything to me, what he just said, and yet my body insists otherwise. My thighs quiver, and my knees threaten to turn to noodles. My toes curl and I have to reach deep inside myself to find the strength to stay standing. "H...how does it make you feel?" I finally manage.

"It makes me want to fuck you for days so you'll not be able to walk straight. In fact—" He bends his knees and peers into my eyes. "I promise, before I'm done with you, you're going to come at least ten more times."

"In the space of eighteen hours?" I scoff.

"Fine, so eighteen, then."

"An orgasm an hour?" I throw my head back and laugh. "Not even you can deliver on that."

"Make sure you keep count, baby."

He holds out his hand. I look at his outstretched palm, then at his face. "What are you going to do?"

"Don't pretend you don't know what I'm going to do," he retorts.

"Can you give me a straight reply, for once?"

"Can you honestly say you don't know what's coming next?" He glares at me, and the threat in his tone slithers down my spine. He's right about one thing—there's a special thrill in pushing him, in being bratty and getting him to act all dominant with me. It fulfills that masochistic streak in me. Hold on, masochistic? Did I just label myself as masochistic? Did I just agree that I want him to be a sadist with me?

I'm not a prude when it comes to sex, honestly. But something inside of me stopped me from exploring S&M and everything it has to offer. And it wasn't my strict upbringing, either.

My parents were very strict and did not allow me to date as long as I was under their roof. What they didn't know about was the boys I smuggled into my room when they were away at the shop. My brother, too, had his share of girls parading through the house. By mutual consent, we never spoke about it. Then, when I was sixteen Olly was born, and all that stopped.

Once I left for university, I celebrated my freedom by hooking up with a variety of boys, and one of them was into S&M. I made it very clear I wanted nothing to do with that. And he never pushed the point, something that told me our relationship was going to be short-lived. He's the guy with whom my relationship lasted for three months. I was the one to break up, as was normally the case. All of the men I've been with have respected my wishes. Not one of them pushed me to re-evaluate my boundaries, like Hunter has.

"What if I say I'd rather be surprised?"

"Do you want to be surprised, Fire?"

I hold his gaze, then place my hand in his.

# 27

Hunter

"Good girl."

A shiver streaks down her body. Her pupils dilate. Oh yeah, she loves being praised, and I am only too happy to oblige her on that. Of course, she'll have to earn it, as she's already realizing, but that should only make the praise, when she receives it, so much more satisfying.

I twist her arm over her head, then loop the scarf about her wrist and tie it to the headboard.

When I hold out my other hand, she places hers in mine without hesitation. I tie her hand to the headboard, then slide off the bed. I walk around to the foot, then circle her ankle with my fingers.

She tries to pull her leg away, but I hold on. "You remember your safe word, don't you?"

She nods.

"Are you going to use it?"

She shakes her head.

"Then let me do this for you, Zara. I promise you're going to love it... Eventually."

"That wasn't very reassuring."

"You're doing so well, baby, just put yourself in my hands."

She swallows, then nods.

"That's my girl."

This time, a moan bleeds from her lips. The scent of her arousal fills the air. My groin tightens, and I bend and tie first one leg, then the other, to the footboard. I straighten, then fold my arms over my chest. I take my time perusing her—from her flushed features to her upturned breasts, her narrow waist, and the flare of those gorgeous hips, she's a vision I'm going to carry in my head long after today.

"You're so beautiful, baby," I murmur.

She swallows, and goosebumps pop on her skin.

"Have you ever been told just how gorgeous you are? How spectacular your body is? How incredible you look laid out there for my delectation?"

I wrap my fingers about my cock and squeeze. Her body jerks. She writhes, tugs on her bindings, and that only tightens her restraints further.

"Untie me, so I can touch you," she pants.

"Not yet."

I massage my dick from base to crown, and her pupils dilate. Her gaze is fixed on my crotch, her lips parted.

"Do you want to taste me, baby?"

She nods.

"Do you want my shaft down your throat?"

"Yes." She licks her lips.

"Are you going to swallow every last drop and then lick me off?"

She tugs on her ties again, then scowls. "Why are you torturing me?"

"Because you love it."

"I didn't sign up to be taunted."

"Oh?" I continue to swipe myself from base to crown, and again. Her thigh muscles clench. She's trying to squeeze her legs together, but of course, she's unable to pull free of her bonds.

"Hunter," she snarls.

I laugh.

Her frown deepens. She still hasn't taken her gaze off of my throbbing and very erect cock.

"You want this, don't you, Fire? You want me to fuck your face, then your pussy, and your arse… Or preferably, have me fill all of your holes at the same time, don't you?"

"Fuck you, Hunter," she snaps.

"If that's how you feel, then..." I turn as if to leave, and she gives out an angry cry.

"Fine! You plonkface, you jerkass, you prathole, fine. You win."

"I love it when you speak dirty, baby."

She draws in a breath and lets it out. "I told you, you win."

"Not the words I was looking for."

"What do you want me to say, you…you…wanker?"

I arch an eyebrow. "You know what."

"I'm not a mind reader," she snaps.

I raise a shoulder. "But you have an IQ of 160. I'm sure you can figure it out."

"Too bad I can't say the same about your EQ. You…you…"

"Charismatic, attractive, magnetic man. Isn't that what you were trying to say?" I smirk.

"You wish," she spits out.

"Okay, then." I turn and head toward the doorway.

I've almost reached it before she calls out, "Fine, fine. Yes, that's what I was going to say."

"What was it? I didn't quite hear you."

She blows out a breath. "I said you're an intelligent, intuitive, charming man," she finally says.

I turn to glance at her. "Do you mean that?"

"You know, I do."

"Then prove it." I walk over to the bed and straddle her. "Take my cock like a good little slut and suck me off."

The pulse at the base of her throat accelerates. Her chest rises and falls. Her hair crackles about her face like a medieval goddess. She's so fucking magnificent, I almost undo her ties and pull her to me, but that won't help; I want every orgasm she has to be better than the previous one. I want the endorphins to fill her blood. I want her to be so drunk on the happy hormones that she remembers this time for the rest of her life. I want her to feel this connection between us as intensely as I do. I want her to experience just how connected we are, how in tune our thoughts are, how on the same wavelength our emotions are, how good it is when we both open up to each other, how there's nothing like the sensations our fucking evokes in both of us. I want all of her. I want…

I crawl up her body, then position myself over her face.

"Open your mouth, baby."

She does.

I drag the crown of my weeping cock over her lips, and she licks them. My balls tighten, and I squeeze the base of my shaft to stop myself from coming right then.

"Remember to tap my hand if you want me to pull out."

She nods.

"You have the most perfect mouth, you know that? The first time I saw you, all I could think was that I wanted to have those beautiful lips around my shaft."

"We're even then. The first time I saw you, I knew I wanted to sit on your face and pull your hair."

I blink, then bark out a laugh. "And you will, I promise. I'm going to give you so much pleasure you'll forget everything else but my name."

"Promises, promises—"

Her words cut out because I've slid my dick between her lips. "Open wider still," I order.

She extends her jaw, and I glide my cock inside and down her throat. She breathes through her nose as tears squeeze out from the corners of her eyes. Then she breathes through her mouth, and I pull out until, once more, my cock is balanced between her lips.

"You okay to continue?"

She jerks her chin.

"You sure you don't want to stop?"

She scowls at me, then tips up her chin and drags her tongue up my dick. She closes her mouth about the head, and heat squeezes my chest. She begins to pull back, and I dig my fingers into her hair to hold her in place. She moans around my cock, and my balls throb. I ease the head back until I'm positioned between her lips, then once more, I slip my cock over her tongue. She draws in a breath, and my head spins. I wrap my fingers about her throat, and goddamn, the feel of my cock moving down her gullet is the most erotic thing I've ever experienced.

Her golden gaze widens; her eyes blaze with a combination of lust and heat, and that edge of defiance that draws me to her over and over again. This queen of a woman agreed to suck me off, and fuck, if that isn't both humbling and titillating. She has me by my balls, literally. I'd do anything she asked. It's good that she doesn't know that... Yet.

"I'm going to fuck your face, baby."

She swallows, and the suction around my shaft drives me a little out of my head. I grit my teeth, forcing myself to slow down. To focus on the pleasure. Just enough pain to make sure she's on edge. Enough friction to get her all hot and bothered, so she can't stop thinking how it'd feel to have my dick inside her hot, melting pussy.

"If I feel between your legs, I bet you're going to be so fucking moist. One strong tug of your clit, and you're going to detonate, aren't you, Fire?"

She groans, and the vibrations travel up the column of my cock. Sweat beads my forehead. My balls draw up. I increase the intensity of my back-forth-back motions. Inside her mouth, down her throat, and out, and again, and again. Her entire body shudders, and I know she's close, so close. I pull out of her, then slide down her body. I bury my face between her legs, and she screams.

I slide my hands under her butt and squeeze as I stab my tongue inside her slit. I draw her clit into my mouth and suck on it, and she shatters. She throws back her head and yells as she climaxes. I lick up her cum, then crawl up and position myself over her face.

"You ready for me, baby?" She cracks open her eyelids, and the drugged, contented look in her eyes cuts me to the core. So, this is how it feels to put someone else's pleasure ahead of my own. It's the most fulfilling, most sexy feeling, almost as good as shooting my load. Almost.

I ease my cock between her lips and hold her gaze as I pull her hair behind and over her head so I can watch my dick disappear into her mouth. I pull out, then slide back in, again and again. She closes her mouth about my girth, and the suction shudders up my cock, squeezes down on my balls, and I empty myself down her throat.

Her eyelids flutter down and her body slumps. I reach over, untie the bonds from around her wrists, then release the restraints around her ankles. I lay back, pull her on top of me, and hold her until her breathing quietens. Finally, she tips up her chin and raises those gorgeous eyes to mine.

"Wh...what was that?"

# 28

Zara

"I do believe that was your first of eighteen orgasms. And I'm only getting started."

"I came...again." My voice is awed, as if I just discovered sex. Which, in a way, I have. Sex with someone you have this connection with is a completely different ball game—pun intended.

"That you did, Fire." He tucks my hair behind my ear. "How do you feel?"

"A little light-headed, like someone shot me out of a cannon and I'm floating down to earth." I yawn.

"You're tired."

"Just sated." I try to keep my eyelids open, but they seem to be too weighed down. "Maybe I'll nap just for a few minutes." I press my cheek into his chest.

When I open my eyes, I'm alone in bed, and the light outside has that gray-blue which hints at it being late afternoon. Did I sleep the morning away?

I yawn, then sit up and gasp when I find him sitting at the foot of the bed.

"Sorry, didn't mean to scare you." He reaches up and cups my cheek. "Did you sleep well?"

I nod, unable to speak. The words seem to dissolve within me... My brain cells don't seem to be able to put the words together to form a sentence. Heat flushes my cheeks, and he watches my face with interest.

"Did you just blush?"

"I don't blush," I protest.

"Hate to say it, but I've seen your face turn all shades of red in the last few hours."

"Only because you're a filthy, dirty, man." I try to pull up the sheet but am unable to budge it because he's sitting on it.

"Don't cover yourself up. I love your body."

I lower my hands to my sides and take in the T-shirt he's pulled on over the same gray sweatpants he was wearing earlier. What a pity I can't see those chiseled abs. On the other hand, Hunter in a worn, black T-shirt that clings to his shoulders, and hair mussed about his face, is both sexy and adorable, and so endearing.

"Come 'ere." I crook my finger at him.

His lips quirk, but he obliges. He leans forward, and I dig my fingers into his hair, pull him even closer, then brush my lips over his. I mean it to be just a quick kiss, but Hunter being Hunter, deepens the kiss until it feels like he's sucking my breath from my body. When he finally releases me, my heart is pumping, my blood thudding in my ears, and the heat between my thighs threatens to streak up my spine. "Wow." I swallow.

"Indeed," he says with a smirk. "You didn't think I was going to let you off that easily now?" He rubs his nose against mine. "You hungry?"

"I could eat," I concede.

"Good." He straightens, then walks to the closet in the corner of the room. When he returns, he's holding a silk bathrobe.

"I think I'd prefer to get dressed."

"I think you should wear this." He holds it out to me.

"You're not going to take no for an answer, are you?"

He smirks, and it's so sexy, I can't stop my heart from doing that little flip-flop in my chest. "Fine, but only this time."

He places the robe around my shoulders, and I shrug into it. Barely have I finished tying the knot around my waist, when he scoops me up in his arms.

"I really can walk." I try to sound angry, but my words come out in a giggle. Multiple orgasms can do that to a woman, I suppose. Also, the dick providing the orgasms is memorable. And as for the man attached to said dick? He's proving himself to be irreplaceable. I'm reluctant to admit it, but always being the person in charge, and the one who makes the decisions at work... Well, it's refreshing to lean on someone else for a change. I'll probably question my train of thought later, but for now, I hold onto his shoulders as he strides into the kitchen. There are pots and pans in the sink, and going by the various open bottles of spices, the chopping board, the bags of half-used vegetables he's been cooking. I sniff and draw in the heavenly scents of cooking. "You've been cooking again," I murmur.

"Indeed, I have."

He lowers me into a chair. A crisp white cloth is spread on the dining table. On it are plates, cutlery, two lit candles, as well as a bucket of ice with a cooling bottle of champagne. "And you laid the table?"

"You have to stop sounding so surprised." He laughs.

"You are Hunter Whittington. London's most notorious bachelor, alphahole extraordinaire, GQ's man of the year and one of Time's most influential people of the year. Not to mention, the person tipped to take the leadership role in this country. To find you cooking and laying the table is—"

"Just another aspect of me. One I don't show to the world—" He straightens.

"But which you are showing to me."

"But which I am showing to you," he agrees.

"Why are you doing this, Hunter?" I tilt my head back, and further back, to meet his gaze.

"Why am I cooking for you?"

"Yes, why do all this?" I beckon to the beautifully laid out table.

"Because I want to. Because it's Christmas, and I'm happy to be spending it with you."

I blink. "Oh shit, it's Christmas."

"Indeed, it is." He moves around to the bucket, places a white linen napkin over his arm, then uses his other to lift the bottle of champagne. Moet et Chandon Brut. He pops the cork, and the cheerful sound thuds through my veins. He pours the fizz into my glass, then his own. He places the bottle back in the bucket, then lifts his glass. "To us."

"Is there an us?" I narrow my gaze.

"You know there is..." More softly, he adds, "For this moment."

Okay, guess I can live with that. And maybe it would be churlish of me to point that out when he's gone to such lengths to cook a late lunch for the both of us. But if I agree to it without pointing that out, it could raise expectations—for both of us—and that wouldn't be fair to either of us. It seems even more important to remind the both of us that this—whatever this is between us—is temporary, fleeting, just two people who found themselves double-booked for the holiday in a cottage, with one bed between them. I wince. A-n-d that sounds like a cliché. One of those situations that the hero and heroine of a romance novel find themselves in. And of course, they end up together.

Unlike us. We're going our separate ways, come the morning. But for now... In this moment... Yeah, there's an us. And seventeen more orgasms to go. I raise my flute. "Salut."

"Salut." He takes a sip without breaking the connection of our gazes, and it's as if he's dipped his tongue back into the cleft between my thighs.

One side of his lips quirks, but he refrains from remarking. Instead, he bends, presses a hard kiss to my mouth, then straightens and stalks off to the counter. He pulls on a pair of oven mitts and slides out a tray from the oven. He walks over and places it in front of me. The tangy scent of spices wafts up from the dish.

"Roast turkey flavored with cumin, ginger, garlic and five spices, with orange and rosemary sprigs," he declares with a flourish. "And that's only the main course."

"There's more?" I exclaim, but he's walking over to the second oven in the corner of the kitchen, which I only now notice. He pulls out another tray then walks over and slides it over.

"Beetroot & red onion tarte Tatin."

"Wait, hold on." I glance between the dishes. A tickling sensation teases my nostrils. My head feels too light for the rest of my body. "You knew that I like spicy food, so you flavored the turkey accordingly; and beetroot is my favorite vegetable, after potatoes, that is, but how did you—" I glance up at him. "How did you—"

"Know it was your second favorite vegetable? Told you, I have my sources. And really, it wasn't anything to flavor the turkey to your taste."

"Still." I look back at the dishes. I texted the names of my favorite foods to Amelie. But for Hunter to not only know what I like but to also use that knowledge to cook the dishes accordingly? That shows attention to detail. It shows he cares. It shows he's been paying attention to my likes and dislikes. It shows that he wanted to do something special for me. And I can't remember the last time someone did anything like this for me.

"Zara, baby, hey!" He places his glass on the table, then hunkers down next to my chair. "Are you crying?"

"Of course, not." I sniff.

"You're crying."

"It's just dust in my eyes," I lie without looking at him.

"Hey, Fire, don't cry, please." He notches his knuckles under my chin and turns it, so I have no choice but to hold his gaze.

"I still can't believe you cooked all of this."

"I told you, I love to cook."

"And I was fast asleep. I didn't even help you." More tears run down my cheeks, and he wipes them away with his thumb.

"I looked in on you a few times, but you were so adorable with your eyes closed and burrowed under the covers, I didn't have the heart to wake you up."

"I don't even have a gift for you."

"You're here. That's my gift, Fire."

"A-n-d you also know the right thing to say." I throw up my hands. "You can't be this perfect. You can't."

He leans back on his haunches. "So, you're upset because I'm perfect?"

"It's not fair. I'm trying to resist you, and you go and do all of these things that make it impossible to resist you."

He laughs. "And I haven't even gotten through the rest of the orgasms."

"Don't remind me." Clearly, I don't stand a chance. By the time he's done with me, I'll have no resistance left in my body. I'll be a pile of mush—gooeyness without the ability to think straight. I'll have become his sex slave, not to mention a slave to his cooking.

"You're thinking so hard, you're giving me a headache." He takes my glass of champagne and hands it to me. "Have your drink and enjoy. I promise, you're not going to regret agreeing to stay here with me."

I know for a fact he's right, and that pisses me off even more. It wasn't supposed to be like this. It wasn't supposed to feel this good with him. It wasn't supposed to feel like I'm going to miss him when we leave. And he cooked for me. Jesus, he cooked for me. A warmth sweeps through me. It's almost as pleasurable a feeling as the orgasms he's given me. Almost.

I lift my glass and finally take a sip. The bubbles burst on my tongue. Flavors of peach and cherry, citrus and almond, cream and buttery toast. The notes merge, and the confluence of it all sinks into my palate. My head spins, and a burst of happiness sizzles through my veins.

"This is exquisite."

"No more than you, baby."

I chuckle. "You sweet-talker, you."

"Glad you're feeling better."

"I'm actually really hungry." Maybe I was hangry, or *horngry*? That could explain the tears. Yep, I'm sure that's all it was.

He peers into my face, then nods before he rises to his feet and takes his seat again. He carves out a piece of the turkey and places it on my plate. At the same time, I carefully slice a piece of the pie and place it on his.

He tops up our champagne, then grins. "Shall we eat?"

# 29

Hunter

"That was really, really good." She leans back with a sigh.

Her eyes are glazed over with what I recognize as the classic signs of food coma. A warm sensation floods my chest. My heart feels like it's expanding until it fills my ribcage. Satisfaction—that's what it is. A feeling of contentment so different from anything I've experienced before, it takes me a little time to understand the root of it. I may not have hunted down the food for my woman, but I cooked it and made sure she enjoyed it. It's the single most significant thing I've accomplished, except for when I made her come. It's more rewarding than winning the election in my constituency, more enjoyable than anything I've done for myself in the past. And all I did was make sure she was well fed. What is it about this woman that makes me want to take care of her every need?

"You did say that you trained to be a chef, but this was exceptional." She tilts her head back.

"I'm pleased you liked it." I polish off the rest of the food on my plate, then reach for the champagne bottle. I top her off, then myself.

"Are you trying to get me drunk, Minister?" She peers at me from under her eyelashes.

"Am I succeeding?"

"And I thought I was the lawyer." She chuckles.

"Oh, you know us politicians. We have to be part entertainer, part statesman, part every other profession that needs to be people-facing. And in my case, it's woven through with the need to do good for the country."

"Where does it come from? This need to do good for the country?"

"That's a good question." I look into the depths of my flute. "When I first decided to stand for elections in my constituency, I did so because it was expected of me. My father held down the seat, and my grandfather before that, so it was expected of me. I'd been preparing for it my entire life, yet when I got elected, no one was more surprised than me."

"I'd have been surprised if you hadn't been elected to the parliament," she murmurs.

"Two compliments in the space of two minutes, I do believe you may be thawing, Councilor," I drawl.

She raises a shoulder. "I may not always see eye to eye with you, but I'll be the first to admit that of all the politicians on the scene today, you stand out as being the most well-intentioned."

"Why, thank you, Fire."

She flushes, and goddamn, that's adorable. She might come across as a hard-headed career woman, but I can see the woman she really is —soft-hearted, generous, loyal. I know her better than she realizes.

"I'm not saying anything the critics haven't pointed out already." She scoffs.

"But it's you saying it; that means a lot."

She places her glass of champagne on the table with a clink. "Don't, please."

"Don't pay you a compliment?"

She nods.

"So, you can pay me a compliment, but I can't return the favor?"

She locks her fingers together, a sure sign that she's flustered. "I don't want you to get any ideas."

"Ideas, hmm?" It's my turn to place the glass of champagne on the table. "I wonder what you think these ideas may be?"

"You know. Me, you" —she flutters her hand in the space between us— "this thing between us."

"What thing?"

"You know this...this attraction, chemistry, lust, whatever you want to call it."

"And if I say it's more than that?"

She stiffens. "It's not more than that."

"You sure, baby? Because whatever we did last night touched the both of us, and I don't think that's happened to either of us before."

"It was just sex."

"I see." I drag my finger below my lower lip, and her gaze drops to my mouth. Her pupils darken, until the black bleeds out into the iris and there's only a circle of gold around the circumference. She swallows. The pulse at the base of her throat flutters like the wings of a hummingbird. "Just sex, hmm?"

She blinks, then glances away. "Just sex." She reaches for her glass of champagne and knocks it back, then slides it in my direction. "More."

"I live to fulfill every one of your wishes, Fire." I rise to my feet and her gaze widens. "Where are you going?"

"To get dessert."

"Dessert?" She frowns.

I head toward the counter and whip off the cover of a dish that I'd left to cool.

"You made dessert?" Her voice rises in pitch.

"Made would be a stretch. I merely pulled off the wrapper and slid it into the oven to warm up."

"And actually remembered to pull it out, counts as a win."

"You don't cook at all, I take it?" I scoop out the dessert onto two plates.

"Nope, much to my mother's chagrin." She pushes her hair back from her face. "My mum works side-by-side with my father, but she always finds time to cook for her family. It's just not something that interests me, I admit."

I place the dish on the table, then half bow. "Voila."

"Is that Christmas pudding?" She gasps.

"Cranberry and chocolate Christmas pudding."

She pales a little. "That's my favorite."

"I know." I scoop out some of the pudding and hold it out. "Open," I say in a hard voice.

She pales, looks like she's about to protest, then complies. *Thank fuck.* I slide the spoon of pudding between her lips. She closes her mouth around the spoon and wipes it clean. A dab of cream sticks to her lower lips. I reach over, wipe it off with my thumb, and bring it to my mouth. When I suck on my thumb, her breath hitches.

I scoop up more of the pudding and, once more, offer it to her. Again, she leans forward, closes her mouth around the spoon, and licks up the dessert. She swipes the tip of her tongue across her lower lip, and the blood drains to my cock.

I put the spoon aside, then drag my finger through the pudding and pick up a dab of the pudding. I lean over and spread it across her lips, before dragging my finger down her chin, her throat, to the valley between her breasts.

"What are you doing?" Her voice sounds breathless.

"I think I'd prefer to eat this dessert off your skin."

"You're crazy."

"And you agreed to do everything I asked." I raise my gaze to hers. "Unless you want to use your safe word?"

She stays silent for a second or two, then shakes her head again.

"Good girl."

Her features flush. She licks off some of the pudding from her lower lip, and I click my tongue. "I didn't give you permission to do that."

She scoffs. "Seriously?"

"Don't defy me, baby."

She tilts her head. A considering look comes into her eyes, then she reaches over, swipes up the pudding, and brings her finger to her mouth. She sucks on her digit and flutters her eyelashes at me. "Oops."

My heart begins to race. Adrenaline dumps into my bloodstream. "You've done it now, Fire. I'm giving you until I count to five."

"Eh?" She lowers her hand and blinks. "What do you mean?"

"Run, baby. If I catch you, I'm not letting go of you—not until I make you come the remaining sixteen times."

"Seventeen, actually." Her lips kick up.

"So, you were keeping count?"

"I take my orgasms very seriously."

"So do I." I rise to my feet; so does she.

"If you want a head start, I suggest you run, now." I jerk my chin in the direction of the door.

"Ooh, I'm so scared." She mock shivers.

"You should be."

"Five."

"What are you doing?"

"Counting down." I smirk. "Four."

She narrows her gaze. "Thought you didn't want me to touch the floor of the house with my feet?"

"Change of rules. Three." I roll my neck, and her entire body stiffens.

She looks at the doorway, then back at me. "Are you being serious about this?"

"I'm always serious with you, Fire. Two." I crack my knuckles.

She gulps, shuffles her feet. "I think this entire thing is stupid. You seem to change the rules at any time, and with very little warning."

"My rules. I change them as they suit my needs. Except for one thing. Are you going to use your safe word?"

She shakes her head slowly from side to side.

"Good girl."

A tremor shakes her shoulders.

"Your time just ran out, Fire. One." I lean over the table.

# 30

Zara

My heart somersaults into my throat. I push away from the table so fast, my chair crashes to the floor, and even then, his fingers brush against my bathrobe. I scream, then jump and race toward the door. Footsteps sound behind me, and I know he's on my heels. How can he move that quickly? He warned me he was going to chase me, but I didn't take him seriously. I thought he was joking... I underestimated him.

Surely, this is some kind of a twisted game for him—one which I don't intend to lose. I increase my speed and reach the doorway. Almost there, almost... If I can only get out of the kitchen and get to the bedroom, I can shut the door behind me, and then— Something latches onto the belt I tied around my bathrobe. I yell and pull away, leaving the bathrobe behind. Cool air touches my skin. *Shit, shit, shit.* And now, I'm naked, to boot. Footsteps thud behind me, and my pulse raps against my temples. Sweat pools under my armpits. My knees tremble, but I keep going.

I reach the bedroom and thrust one foot over the doorway when his fingers lock around my upper arm. I yell and try to wriggle away. The next second, the world turns upside down. Huh? Where the hell am I? What the—? My hair flows down my ears—or is it up? I don't know. I'm upside-down. Down is up and up is down—and over my face—not under. That would make me inside-out. And why the hell am I having these nonsensical thoughts? What is wrong with me? Clearly, I'm delirious.

I stare at his backside—his very spectacular arse hidden by those sweatpants.

"The fuck! What are you doing?"

"I caught you, fair and square, Fire. Now you're mine." His voice rumbles from somewhere above me; the vibrations travel down his back, and my chest, which is pressed up against his spine. I wriggle and writhe. He places his arm across the back of my thighs.

"Let me go, Hunter," I snap.

"Not a chance, baby." He strides away from the bedroom and through to the kitchen. He approaches the dining table with the over-turned chair next to it and comes to a halt.

"What are you doing?"

"I haven't had my dessert yet."

"Excuse me?" I squeeze my thighs together. He can't mean… Surely, not. "Hunter, don't you dare," I yell.

"Don't challenge me, darlin'." He lowers me down onto the table. I spring up at once, but he presses his palm into the center of my chest. "I love it when you stand up to me. And when you defy me, it fucking turns me on, you know that?"

I glance at the tent in his crotch and then up at him. "I can tell." I push into his palm and he steps forward until his knees brush against mine.

"Part your legs for me."

"No."

His eyes gleam. "Fuck, if that doesn't turn me on even more."

"You're a psychopath, you know that?" I snarl.

He tilts his head as if considering my statement. "Only when it comes to you. Although right now, what I am is really fucking horny. Also, I think the word you were looking for is sadist."

I swallow. That part of me that yearns to have him handle my body as he sees fit, that hidden side of me that can't wait for him to do to me as he wishes, that submissive woman inside who wants to open her thighs for his tongue, his fingers, his cock—ideally, each and every one of those parts, in different holes of my body, at the same time— rises to the fore. He must sense it, for he bends his knees and peers into my eyes.

"Open. Your. Thighs."

I widen the gap between my legs.

"Good girl."

He plants himself in the space between my thighs, and my core clenches. He reaches past me and his neck brushes against my nose. I draw in a breath—only because I have to breathe—and my lungs fill with Hunter. My head spins. I hear the sounds of the dishes being pushed to the side, then he pushes down on my chest. I lay back until the back of my head meets the table.

"Jesus, look at you." His voice is harsh, the tone gravelly, as he rakes his gaze from my face to my stomach to the space between my legs. "Fuck, you're aroused, aren't you, baby?"

"I'm not."

He laughs, then shoves two fingers inside me. I groan as my core clenches down on his fingers. He pulls out his glistening fingers, then brings them to my lips. "Suck it off."

I scowl at him.

"Now," he commands.

And I don't want to do it; I don't. But that feminine core of me, the one that yearns to be his, the one that's riding me hard, takes over. I open my mouth, and he places his fingers on my tongue. I lock my lips about his digits, and he slides them out. I pop my lips together, taste myself and...and him.

"How do you taste?"

"Like you."

His eyes darken until they seem like the depths of the sea. I can see it clearly. I'm going to dive in, and when I surface, I'll be changed. My stomach knots. My chest hurts. *Am I really going to go through with this?* "Hunter, I—"

"Shh, baby, let me take care of you."

He looks into my eyes, and in his, I see lust and need and something else. Something more intense. That emotion he's been hinting at over the last day. That...sensation that's bound us together from the moment I laid eyes on him. The connection I've been trying to deny, knowing it's going to take root in me. The one that's already tying me to him. No matter how much I deny it, he's crawled under my skin, and when I leave here, I'm going to feel empty. I'm going to miss him... But for now, I have him, and I intend to make the most of the time we have.

I force my muscles to relax, one by one, not taking my gaze from his.

He nods, as if he senses my submission and accepts it as his right. Then he reaches behind and pulls off his T-shirt displaying those perfect chest planes. He throws it aside, and before I can say anything else, he leans over, scoops up the pudding, and smears it across my chest.

# 31

Hunter

I glance at the sticky pudding that smothers her breasts, except for her nipples, which peek through the gooey mess. They're like blackcurrants, enticing me to close my mouth around them. The next second, I do just that. I squeeze one nipple and nip at the other one. A moan spills from her.

"Hunter," she gasps and winds her arms about my neck. I lick the dessert up from her breast, the complex sweetness of raisins and almonds mixed with the salty taste of her skin is a perfect blend of opposing flavors. I lick the last of the sauce from one breast, then turn my attention to the other. I eat my way through the pudding before I lick her nipple, which hardens further. I drag my teeth over the bud, and she shudders.

"You're so damn responsive." I raise my head and stare into her eyes. "I want to eat you up."

"Thought you were already doing that."

"I haven't even started."

She chuckles. "It shouldn't feel this right, Hunter. Why does it feel so right?"

"Because it is."

"But it can't be. You and me… It'll never work."

"Trust me." I press a hard kiss to her lips. She opens her mouth, and I suck on her tongue. The taste of her is deeper than chocolate, more complex than nutmeg, more flavorful than citrus, and as contradictory as politics can sometimes seem on the surface. She pushes up and into me so our skin sticks together. She digs her fingers into the hair at the nape of my neck and tugs on it. Goosebumps pepper my skin. I manage to lift my head and gaze into her face. Her eyelids flutter open.

"Eyes on me, baby. I want you to see me as I eat you out."

Her gaze widens. She opens her mouth, but I've already slid down until my face is above her pussy. I blow on her lower lips, and her hold on my hair tightens. I sink to my knees and bury my mouth in her cunt, and she groans. "Hunter, please, please, please—"

She cuts out with a gasp when I stab my tongue inside her soaking wet channel. I twist my tongue inside her, and she screams as she orgasms. Her cum soaks my tongue and runs down my chin. I glance up to find her eyelids fluttering down. I squeeze her thigh. "Eyes on me, baby."

She raises her eyelids and glances down as I lick her pussy lips. I circle the swollen nub of her clit, then tease it with my teeth. Her entire body jolts.

I straighten, then grip her arms and twist them over her head. I lock them around the edge of the table. "Hold on."

I take a handful of the pudding, slap it over her pussy, and her gaze widens. She bites down on her lower lip as I sink back to my knees. I throw her legs over my shoulders, then bend my head and swipe my tongue from her puckered hole to her clit.

She writhes under me, locks her thighs about my neck, and I begin to eat her out in earnest. I nibble on her clit, lick her pussy lips, then stab my tongue inside her slit. I close my mouth over her cunt and her eyes roll back in her head.

"I can't come; not again."

"You can."

I fit two fingers inside her pussy and scissor them in and out of her. I suck on her clit, add a third finger inside her, and her entire body jolts. I curl my fingers inside her, and she shudders.

"Ohgodohgodohgod," she chants.

I tease her puckered hole and she cries out. Her entire body jolts as she orgasms. I lick up the cum from her slit, from the crease between her pussy and her inner thigh, then surge to my feet. Her chest rises and falls, and her eyes have drifted closed. I press her thighs further apart, position her legs so she can lock her ankles about my waist, then shove down my sweats. I fit my cock into her slit, and she flutters open her eyelids.

Her golden eyes are almost colorless, her features are flushed, and her hair flows about her face like the halo of a goddess.

"Again?" She draws in a breath and lets out a sigh.

"And again." I plant my hand next to her head, then thrust my hips forward. Her gaze widens, and in one smooth move, I bury myself inside her. She parts her lips, and I close my mouth over hers. I absorb her scream, then thrust into her with enough force that the entire table moves forward. Cutlery falls to the floor, and one of the plates hits the wooden floor and rolls away. She jerks, but I don't release her. I deepen the kiss as I pound into her, again and again. I slide my palms under her hips, angling her just right, then slam into her. My balls slap against her inner thighs. I tear my mouth from hers and check her face. "Open your eyes."

When our gazes clash, I pull out of her, then plunge forward again. I slide my hand between us, then grind the heel of my hand into her clit. "Come with me," I order.

She opens her mouth, and with a silent cry, she shatters. I thrust into her once, twice, thrice, then follow her over the edge.

---

"Umm, what was that?" She rubs her cheek against my chest.

After she came with me, I carried her to the bathroom, where we showered. And I went down on her and made her come again, then turned her into the shower wall and fucked her in the arse, and she came. Twice.

"That, baby, was me warming up."

She laughs, then groans. "Shut up, you egoistical monster."

"It's true. I'm only now finding my stride."

"Right." She turns her face into my chest and inhales deeply.

"How do I smell?"

"Like sex and mint and lust and something sweet. You smell like us."

I lock my arms about her and pull her closer. She melts into me.

"How many, baby?"

"How many what?" Her voice is muffled. Her muscles relaxed. Her still wet hair lies in long coiled strands about her shoulders.

"You know what."

"No, I don't." She clears her throat.

"It's the reason why you've been screaming my name over the past few hours."

"That's because you like it when I call your name."

"Which I do, of course. Guess you've forgotten why you did it though. Maybe I need to remind you?"

I begin to turn, and she slaps my shoulder. "Fine, fine, you asshole. Fine. That was because you made me orgasm."

I make a circular motion with my fingers, indicating she should keep speaking.

She huffs. "That was five orgasms—"

"Six—" I smirk.

She throws up her hands. "Fine. It's six so far, are you satisfied?"

"Not until I make you come another twelve times."

---

I made her come another three times, back-to-back, after which we both napped for a few hours. I woke up with a raging hard-on a few minutes ago and reached for her, only to find she, too, was awake. I reached over and kissed her deeply. She wrapped her arms about my shoulders and pulled me even closer. Now, I position myself between her legs, and she draws in a breath.

"I can't, Hunter. I can't," she whimpers.

"You can, baby. Lift your hips; let me in."

She obliges, and inch by inch, I slide inside her.

"Oh god, you're stretching me, you're so damn big," she groans.

Even after I've buried myself inside her again and again, it still feels like it's the first time. I plant my elbows on either side of her head and peer into her eyes. I hold her gaze, tilt my hips, and sink further inside. Her gaze widens.

Strands of hair are stuck to her forehead. Her face is flushed, and her eyes, those gorgeous golden eyes, had turned silver and now, they're a shimmering, translucent gray. The purple smudges under her eyes cause my heart to stutter. "I should let you sleep." I begin to pull out, but she locks her ankles about me.

"Not so fast, buster. You owe me another nine orgasms."

I rub my thumb over her cheekbone. "You could always take a rain check on it."

Her face pales. She looks away, then back at me. "I'd prefer to cash that check in now."

It was worth a try. I hoped to seduce her into agreeing to meet me again, but maybe it's too early to get that commitment from her.

I brush my mouth over hers. "You sure, baby? You look tired."

Oh? She flutters her eyelashes at me. "Or maybe it's you who's tired."

"Oh?" I rotate my hips so my hardening cock slides even deeper inside. Her breath stutters. My lips kick up. "Does that feel tired to you?"

"That feels...so good." She wraps her arms about my shoulders. "Why does it feel like it's the first time every time you fuck me?"

Her words echo my thoughts from earlier. I run my nose up her jawline, and she shivers. I curl my tongue around the shell of her ear, and she moans. "Hunter, please."

"What do you want, baby?" I nibble little kisses down her cheek to the edge of her mouth. "Tell me."

"You know what I want," she whines.

"Not unless you tell me, I don't."

"I want you to fuc—" She gasps as I pull out and thrust back into her with enough force that her entire body moves up the bed. I lunge forward again, then bottom out inside her. Her back curves, her body stretched so tight, her muscles vibrate with tension. She's close, so close.

I pull back, then peer into her eyes. "What are you thinking of now?"

"You."

"Who are you going to dream about, Fire?"

She swallows. "You, Hunter."

"Whose cock are you going to fall apart around?"

Her features flush, and her lips part. "Yours, Hunter, only yours." I lower my face to the curve of where her neck meets her shoulder, then bite down.

She moans, "Hunter, oh god, I'm going to—"

"Come with me, baby."

# 32

Zara

I drift on a cloud of warmth. My muscles are so relaxed. I try to move, but my arms and legs feel weighed down. My thigh muscles ache, and my shoulders hurt. There's a pleasant thrum under my skin, like I've spent the night plugged into a low-key electricity generator. Or had a rather large, monster cock plugged into me, shooting me up with cum. *Ugh, I didn't just think that. Did I think that? Of course, I did. It's not as if there's someone else controlling my thoughts.*

I turn on my back, and my entire body protests. My core clenches down on the emptiness, then protests at the movement. I'm alone in bed and already, I miss him. And I'm sure there's no way I can bear to come again. Not after how he fucked me in every position I can imagine—as much as the bed, and the table, and the shower would allow, that is.

Of course, he's not going to allow my feet to touch the floor of the bedroom. Another of his rules—-which he could change at will. The man makes them up at the drop of a hat, and leaves me breathless and unable to keep up which is… Another first.

Every time I think I have him pinned down, Hunter Whittington surprises me. It's what makes my interactions with him so interesting. For a cynical media whore who spends so much of her time interacting with people for whom appearance is everything, and who assumed that Hunter was one of them… Well, he's definitely proved me wrong. For one, he's more caring than he comes across. More humane. And he can cook. God, the man can cook. And he knows how to use his cock, and his fingers, and his tongue, and he's focused on my pleasure. Indeed, he didn't stop until he made me come over and over again.

I'd have lost count, except after each one, he asks me how many orgasms I've had, and I have to recount the tally to him. And each orgasm has been delivered creatively. On my back, on my front, on my hands and knees, me on my side and him standing behind me, him kneeling and me balanced on his thighs, pretzel style, flatiron style, me with my legs thrown over his shoulders G-whiz style, me riding him, me riding him reverse-cowgirl style, and then the wheelbarrow style, where he made me balance on my arms as he planted his feet on the floor, positioned himself between my thighs and took me from behind… And…then there was the magic mountain pose. Oh, my god. I've read about it, but never tried that one before. He positioned me leaning back on my arms, with my legs bent, then mirrored my pose and inched toward me, then slid his dick into me.

And then, the most memorable one. The eighteenth one was just as the dawn light filtered through the windows. That time, he held my gaze and spooned me, but from the front, so we could maintain eye contact. And that made it so much hotter, so much more intense. He caressed my butt, then squeezed the back of my thigh, and encouraged me to slide my leg between his. He took his time as he buried himself, inch by inch, inside of me and penetrated me while maintaining the connection of our gazes. The position allowed him to thrust into me so that he hit that spot inside of me every single time. Then he pulled me close enough for my clit to grind against his pelvis, and it set off a long, slow, deep orgasm. A shiver snakes down my spine at the recollection. Oh, god, that had been incredible. I came and came and then I must have blacked out for when I awoke I was in bed alone.

My stomach grumbles. The activities of last night, clearly, gave me an appetite. The only thing that would make things even better is having pancakes for breakfast.

I should move, should swing my legs over the bed and get dressed and leave. This one night stand is well and truly over. I try to force my body to respond, but it seems to have developed a mind of its own.

Everything you hear about body memory is true. I can still feel the touch of his fingertips on my skin, of his breath on my cheek, the sound of his breathing speeding up as he buries himself in me, the vibrations of his heart thundering against his ribcage, and into my chest as he thrusts into me, the echo of his groan as he empties himself inside me...

I rub my cheek against the soft cotton of the pillow. The remnants of sleep tug at my eyelids, and I try to sink back into my dream. If I do, I won't have to face the future...

A day when I won't be with him. When I have to go back to my world, my career—the one I spent so long building. A world I love, but where there's no space for love. No room for someone like him. He only makes me weak. He makes me want to lean on him. He makes me want to abandon the rules I created so long ago for success. He makes me want to redefine the idea of success and—

Whoa, I can't do that. I can't let a man change my mindset, my reason for living. I can't let the future Prime Ministerial candidate of this country transform me into exactly the kind of woman I swore not to become. A woman like my mother, who allowed her life to be defined by her husband. That isn't me.

I owe it to myself to rise above the events of the past few days. To keep it where it belongs—in my thoughts, in my deepest memories. To never be looked at again. A hot sensation knifes my ribcage. My guts churn. A tell-tale pressure stings the backs of my eyes. Nope, I'm not crying, not now. Not when I didn't allow myself to become weak when Olly was diagnosed as having autism spectrum disorder. I didn't shed a tear then, and I certainly won't now.

I'm a strong, independent woman. I know what I want. I know

what makes me happy, and Hunter makes me...feel at odds with myself. He brings out the hidden, vulnerable parts of me that I never even knew existed. And that will only prevent me from doing my job well. So no, there's no space for him in my life. I had my fun with him, and now it's time to move on. I push back the sheets and sit up. That's when the door opens and the object of my thoughts strides in.

# 33

Hunter

One look at the furrow between her eyebrows, at the downward tilt of her lips, at those eyelids still weighed down by the weight of the pleasure I wrought from her body, even as those golden eyes flicker with awareness of what passed between us the last two nights—and I know she's come to a decision about us.

"Don't do this." I stalk over to her.

She begins to swing her legs over, but I push her back into the bed and cover her body with mine.

"Hunter," she half-laughs, half-tries to push me off of her. "What are you doing?"

"What do you think I'm doing?"

"Do you always have to answer every question with a question?'

"Do you?" I lean enough of my weight into her, and she stops struggling.

She glances between my eyes, then tips up her chin. "It's over."

"It's not over until we say it is." I growl.

"It was a one night stand that stretched to two," she murmurs. "And now the sun has come out."

As if to mark her words, a ray of sunlight beams through the window and across our faces. It picks out the flickers of silver in the depths of her eyes. The ones that captivated me from the moment I first spotted them. The ones that tell me her emotions are nowhere as settled as she'd like me to believe.

I cup her cheek, and she blinks. "Hunter, please."

"You know I'm not going to be able to let you go." I hold her gaze.

She looks away then back at me. "That was the deal. We had this time together, and now it's time to leave."

"Not before you promise it's not over between us."

"I can't." She swallows. "We can't be seen together. It will only get people talking."

"So let them."

"We've been over this. I can't afford to be linked with you."

"Why not?"

"You know why." She firms her lips.

"I'm not sure why."

"You're the Prime Ministerial candidate—"

"And you'd be the woman I'm seeing."

"There, that's what I mean. You'll be the leader, the man in charge, the one in power and—"

"You'd be my equal. In public, I may be the future Prime Minister. In private, I'd be the man who makes you orgasm so hard you can't have a coherent thought for days."

She laughs, and her features light up. She looks so goddamn beautiful, I lean in and press my mouth to hers. She parts her lips, and I deepen the kiss. By the time I raise my head, we're both breathing hard. I press the tent between my legs into her. "See what you do to me, Fire? How do you expect me to not pursue you after this?"

"Because your career is important to you—"

"Not more than the woman I want by my side."

"What?" Her gaze widens. "What did you say?" There's a thread of panic in her voice. *Fuck, I shouldn't have said that. Why is it that when I'm with her all my careful planning goes to pieces?*

"You heard me. I want you to be with me on the campaign trail."

"No. That's not going to happen. I can't allow anything to tie the two of us together. I won't allow my personal life to become the fodder of gossip blogs and political commentators."

"Why not? What are you so scared of? Why do you always want to stay behind the scenes, Zara? Why is it you never want to face the issue that's standing right in front of you? What are you hiding?"

She pales, then shoves at me again. "Let me go."

"No."

"Let me go, Hunter." Her voice is so cold, it stabs through my heart like a bloody knife. I'm going to lose her. I'm going to lose her. That's when the phone in my back pocket vibrates. Fuck, I shouldn't have switched it on earlier, but I thought I could get through some of my work while she was still sleeping. I hoped to buy myself a little time before the inevitable demands of the campaign pulled me away. The very fact that I didn't switch on my phone for the last forty-eight hours, no doubt, sent the rest of my team into a panic. No matter that it was Christmas and the day after, which is also a public holiday in this country. There's no time off when you're running to be Prime Minister. Something I knew and pushed aside because I wanted to spend time with her.

"You need to answer that," she points out.

"I don't need to do anything I don't want to."

The doorbell rings, I swear aloud. She tilts her head. No way, am I going to move. If I do, I'll lose her. And if I don't? She'll hate me anyway, for keeping her here against her will.

My phone vibrates, and the doorbell rings again. The sound of someone pounding on the door reaches us. My phone pings with an incoming message.

"I think that must be your security team?"

"Fuck that," I growl.

"I think we've done enough of that, don't you think?"

"When it comes to you, it's never enough."

She draws in a sharp breath. Her pupils dilate. I lower my head and my phone vibrates again and doesn't stop. At the same time, the doorbell rings, a series of long bursts of noise that tear through the liminal space we created.

"This isn't over yet, Zara." I press a hard kiss to her mouth, then roll off her and off the bed.

She begins to rise, and I stab a finger in her direction. "Make sure you're dressed properly before you come out there."

Turning, I stride out.

---

"I strongly advise that you not attempt to lose us again, sir. We are only doing our jobs in trying to protect you, and if you leave without telling us, and then disengage the tracking device on your phone, you put yourself at risk and—" Ralph, the head of my security team breaks off halfway through his tirade as Zara sweeps into the living room where I've been talking with them for the past forty-five minutes.

I told her to get dressed properly, and I have no doubt she hated the fact I ordered her to do so. It wouldn't have hurt to tack on a please at the end of my statement, but had I done so? Of course, not. I was pissed with myself that I hadn't found a way to get her to agree to see me again. At least, when I had her under me, I used my cock to seduce her into submitting to me, but with the length of the room between us, all I can do is watch as she looks away from me.

"Zara Chopra," she says, and holds out her hand as she approaches us.

"Ralph Sanders, Mr. Whittington's Head of Security." Ralph reaches to shake her hand, and I stiffen.

Before I can stop myself, I step in between them, forcing him to retreat. I cut off his view of Zara and glare at him. "Shouldn't you be out doing a search of the perimeter?"

"Already done," Ralph replies.

Behind me, Zara tries to peer around my back, but I shift my position.

"And checking my car to make sure it's safe to drive back," I snap.

Ralph's eyebrows draw down. "My men are on it."

"Ms. Chopra's car..."

"Is parked in the front garage." She shoves at my arm, but I don't move.

"You're parked in the front garage, huh?"

"So?" She frowns.

"I'm parked in the one at the back."

"Your point being?"

"Weston told me, specifically, to use the garage at the back," I murmur.

"Huh." She purses her lips. "Amelie texted me to say that I should use the garage at the front."

"Jesus." I roll my shoulders, "You don't think—"

The creases in her forehead clear. "I do think."

Our gazes meet, hold.

"I can't believe they did this," she says finally.

"I guess I owe Weston one." I allow my lips to curve.

Ralph clears his throat.

I stiffen, then turn my gaze on him. "Once you're done checking our cars, could you wait outside?"

"Of course, sir; ma'am." He walks out the front door, and Zara punches my arm.

"The hell is wrong with you?"

"What are you talking about?" I strive for what I hope is an innocent tone.

She stomps around to stand toe-to-toe with me. "You were acting like a Neanderthal. You planted your ugly arse—"

"Didn't hear you calling it that when you had your fingers squeezing down on that part of my body last night," I murmur.

"—in between us. You forced that man back. You didn't let him see my face while I spoke to him."

"Trust me, if I could control myself around you, I would, but apparently, I'm not ready to allow the outside world to look at you."

"Deal with it." She throws up her hands. "Have you heard yourself? You sound deranged. Like an over-the-top, overprotective, dominant, possessive, wankhead."

"All true, except that last descriptor. Not sure I agree with that."

"This is no laughing matter, Hunter."

"Do you see me laughing?"

She glowers at me. "You're smirking; that's close enough."

"Fine, I accept maybe my behavior was a little extreme." I raise a shoulder.

"A little extreme?" She snaps her shoulders back. "And you told him we were having a discussion. A discussion!"

"Isn't that what we're having now?" I incline my head.

"This is not a discussion. This is our—"

"First argument as a couple?'

"We're not a couple."

"Strange, that's not what it seemed like to me last night."

"One night—okay, two nights of sex, no matter how mind-blowing, how out of this world, orgasmic, how—"

"So, you admit it was mind-blowing and out of this world?" I ask.

"Of course, it was, you numbskull. And you don't need me to confirm that to you, and oh, you keep interrupting me." She tucks her elbows into her sides. "Hunter, what are we doing?"

"We" —I place my hands on her shoulders— "are going to leave here, have breakfast somewhere nice, and then drive back to London."

# 34

Zara

I glance down at the stack of pancakes on my plate, then toward his plate, which holds a pile of waffles dripping with syrup and ice cream on top.

"You found the only diner in the UK that serves American-style breakfast dishes?" I ask. We're seated at a table at the far end by the window. A table where he pulled up a third chair for my Birkin. In that moment, I felt something inside me melt all over again. I opened my mouth to tell him that maybe I would see him again, after all, when the waitress arrived to take our orders.

Hunter's back is to the door, and he's big enough and broad enough that I'm hidden by the width of his shoulders. Also, he's wearing a cap and had on a scarf and sunglasses, which he took off once we were seated. Not that he was trying to disguise himself. He's well-known among the media, but perhaps, not as much with the general public, though that will change once he hits the campaign trail.

The waitress didn't recognize him, either. If she did, she didn't let on. And the place is charming. I glance around the wooden fixtures, the large fireplace, the wooden tabletops with the gleaming cutlery, the bar at the other end where, despite it being Boxing Day morning, there are still a few people—clearly regulars—seated. It has a homey feeling, and the food looks amazing.

"You should know by now; I'll always find a way to fulfill your heart's desires." Hunter lowers his chin.

"I never told you I wanted to have pancakes for—" I cut off my words because he fixes me with an all-knowing glance.

"How did you know I wanted pancakes for breakfast?" I scowl.

"A lucky guess."

"Don't bullshit me, Whittington. Did you find out my tastes from having me investigated?

He merely shoots me a look. I guess that's a yes, then. He cuts off a big chunk of the waffles and shoves them into his mouth. Some of the ice cream sticks to the side of his mouth.

"Umm, you have a—" I nod my chin in his direction.

"What?"

I lean over, scoop up the dab of ice cream, bring it to my mouth and lick it off. "There, you're fine now."

"Am I, though?" His eyes turn a stormy shade of green. Like there are emotions roiling around inside him, and he's not sure how to give them words.

"You have to be. I have to be. Don't you see that?"

His gaze intensifies, and a dull ache gnaws behind my breastbone. I tear my gaze away from him and pick up my knife and fork. I cut off a small portion of the pancakes and pop it in my mouth. It melts on my tongue. "Mmm, this tastes even better than it looks."

"So do you."

I cough, then reach for my glass of water and wash down the food.

"Hunter, seriously, stop doing this. You really have to stop."

"Give me one reason why," he shoots back.

"Because there's somewhere I need to be."

"Right now?'

I glance at my phone, then back at him. "Someone's waiting for me."

His lips firm. "Someone more important than whatever it is between the two of us?"

"Definitely more important. Also..." I set down my cutlery and fold my arms across my chest. "Let's not forget, you said one night. I gave you two."

"You gave me two? As if you didn't get anything out of it? Besides, you stayed a second night because of the storm," he points out.

I glance away, oddly ashamed. "Agreed, and now we have to go back to our daily lives."

He looks between my eyes. "Is that your final decision on the matter?"

I swallow, force myself to meet his gaze. "Yes." I clear my throat. "Yes, it is."

He stays silent for a few seconds, then nods. "Okay." He pulls out his phone and begins to scroll the screen.

I blink. "Did you say okay?"

"I don't repeat myself, Zara."

*Zara, not Fire.* He called me Zara earlier, but not like this. Not with his attention focused on something other than me. Not with his jaw hard. Not with an invisible barrier he seems to have pulled down between us. What happened? Did I finally succeed in pushing him away? It's what I want. It's what I've been trying to achieve since I met him. I succeeded and now, I already miss him. He's sitting in front of me, but it's as if he's not with me anymore. This is how it feels to not be the cynosure of Hunter Whittington's attention. It feels like all the warmth in the room has drained out. Like an avalanche has dumped ice all over me, and now I'm frozen, unable to feel my limbs, while my heart flutters in my chest like a caged bird.

He glances up from his phone suddenly, and our gazes connect. And his eyes? Oh, god, his eyes are a cold blue, a glacial frostiness in them that I've only seen reserved for others. And now, he's aiming that aloof politeness at me.

"Don't you want the rest of your breakfast?" He glances at my plate, then at me.

"Not hungry," I murmur.

He seems like he's about to protest, then catches himself. "Fine." He rises to his feet and brushes past the table.

My jaw drops. I watch as he stalks out the door of the pub without waiting for me. He didn't wait for me to finish. So, I told him I wasn't hungry, but he could have, at least, asked me if I really meant it. Is this how it's going to be from now on? Isn't this how I want it to be from now on?

I jump to my feet, grab my bag, and march through the doorway. I walk outside and into the parking lot to find him talking to Ralph. When I reach them, Ralph nods at Hunter. "I'll follow you back to the office, Sir." He nods at me and says, "Ms. Chopra," then walks toward one of the two black SUVs parked next to the car Hunter drove us in.

"You're heading to the office?" I turn to Hunter, who slides my car's key fob from his pocket and holds it out.

I take it, and he retrieves his hand before our fingers touch... And why do I feel so deprived?

"Goodbye, Zara." He takes a step back.

I want to jump forward and grab his sleeve but stop myself. "It doesn't have to be like this, Hunter."

"Like what?"

"Like... Like this..." I point between us.

"I don't know what you're talking about."

"If you're going to be so immature about this—"

"I'm merely giving you want you wanted. You don't want us to have a relationship? You don't want to be seen with me? This is how it looks."

"Can't we be friends?"

"Friends?" For the first time since he took his phone out in the restaurant, his eyes turn more green than blue. "With what I feel for you, we can never be friends."

# 35

Zara

"That's what he said? That the two of you can never be friends?" Solene asks from the screen of my phone.

"That's what he said." I pour myself a cup of coffee and carry it to the window of my office.

It's been three weeks since Hunter threw those words at me and took off in his car. He left one of his security detail behind, who insisted on following me on the drive back to London. They ensured I was safely inside my house before they left. I felt protected by Hunter's gesture, that despite the fact we parted on what were not the friendliest of terms, he insisted on making sure I got home safely.

At the same time, it's not like he asked me if his team could escort me home. He simply assumed I'd be fine with it and ordered his team to to it. I could hardly tell the team not to do so when they approached me. To do so would have made me appear churlish. Besides, I was glad they were following me home, given how treacherous the roads still were after the snow last night. So, I accepted their offer.

Which meant, ultimately, he won, even though he agreed to walk away from me, just as I asked him to do. And he did. And now, I feel his loss so deeply, I feel like the biggest loser of all. Instead of feeling joyful to have escaped his clutches, I feel empty inside. Like I had a chance and wasted it away. Like all that's remaining in my life now is empty evenings and nights in a bed that feels too big and too cold, like... I've lost a part of me, a part I could have had but refused.

"Zara, you there?"

"Eh?" I turn to my phone. "What did you say?"

"It's not like you to be so pissed off over a man's words."

Only, he's not just any man. He's Hunter. He's the man who I can't stop going toe-to-toe with, the man who I was sure I didn't like; the man who gave me the most memorable night—okay, nights—of my life.

This is what happens when orgasms addle your brain. You can't think straight. Not that it seems to have affected the day-to-day life of the jerkhole. He's been in the news almost every week, spotted at openings and galas, each time, with a new woman on his arm. And he hasn't called me. Not once. Nor texted. But neither have I.

"It must have been some weekend break with him. The sex must have been phenomenal."

I flush. Her jaw drops. "OMG, did you just blush, Zara?"

"So what?" I flip my hair over my shoulder, trying to school my features into an expression which I hope is casual.

"So what? I've never seen you blush."

"I blush." *Especially when I'm in the presence of the poshhole.*

"Not when it comes to talking about sex, you don't."

I raise a shoulder. "Yeah, so I have a liberated view about sex, in general."

"And a rather low opinion of men, in particular," she points out.

"I did—" I admit.

"So, not anymore?"

"I mean, I still do," I say hastily.

"Umm, I think not." She chuckles.

"Can we change the topic?" I scowl.

"No way. In fact, I'm going to dial in Isla."

"No, wait! Don't. What are you—"

My screen changes view, and a third window pops up with Isla's eager face. "What's happening? What did I miss?"

"Hello to you, too. I assume you are finally back from honeymoon number five?" I ask in a droll tone.

"It was our sixth, actually. Although, since we decided to move to the island, every day with Liam feels like a honeymoon," she says in a dreamy voice.

Solene and I exchange glances. It's almost funny how much Isla is in love with her husband. Truth is, he seems just as crazy about her. And the few times I've seen them since they got married, they couldn't keep their hands and their gazes off of each other.

"Anyhoo" —Isla beams at both of us— "I didn't jump on the call to talk about myself. Tell us about your latest man."

I look down my nose at her. "Why does it have to be about my man?"

"Because I'm married, and Solene is, more or less, in a relationship." Isla's referring to Solene dating Hollywood heartthrob Declan Beauchamp.

"I'm not," Solene butts in.

"Okay, so she's not, at the moment, but given we know their ups and downs last until one of them misses the other and they get back together—"

"Or not," Solene chimes in again.

"Or not, which I don't believe for a moment. Either way, it's not as if she's interested in anyone else. You though" —Isla's smile grows broader— "you are Zara Chopra, Ms. Shark herself—"

"I'm a tough negotiator." I shrug off the title the media seems to have thrust upon me.

"Indeed. And you are not easy to please. So, if you have a new man in your life—"

"I don't," I snap.

Both women look at me.

"Okay, fine. So, I may have had a dirty one night stand," I finally admit.

"I knew it." Solene does a mock fist pump.

"It's Hunter, isn't it?" Isla bursts out.

When I don't reply, Solene chimes in, "It is Hunter. Also, he told her they could never be friends."

"And when has that bothered you?" Isla asks.

"It doesn't bother me."

She scans my features. "Hmm."

"What's that hmm for?" I glance at my coffee. It's only four p.m. If only, I could have something stronger. Only it's dry January, and I'm trying to detox. And not just when it comes to alcohol, apparently, because since that night with Hunter, I haven't wanted to sleep with anyone else. Or been attracted to anyone else, for that matter. In fact, I haven't been able to stop thinking about Hunter, which is, honestly, not great.

"Just hmm," Isla's voice has a sly tone to it.

"What's going on in that head of yours?"

"Me? Nothing." She widens her gaze and I sigh.

"'Fess up, will you."

"Oh, I'm just thinking that the two of you make a good couple. Of course, not that you are together or anything, but if you were, then you could help him with his leadership campaign."

"It would be a disaster. The two of us would not be able to agree on anything. He wants someone who's more submissive, and I'm not someone who likes to be told what to do." Except in bed, and only by him, apparently.

Isla blinks. "Umm, are we talking sex, or are we talking about getting on the campaign trail here?"

"Both," I shoot back.

There's silence, then Solene presses a finger to her cheek. "I think it's the fact that the two of you challenge each other that makes you both so well-suited for the other. In fact, I think you are exactly the kind of person he needs to help him during his candidature."

"What do you mean?"

"Ever since my track went viral, the number of people who've crawled out of the woodwork and want to become part of my entourage has multiplied. In fact, the only people it hasn't affected are the two of you—"

"And Declan," Isla points out.

"And Declan," Solene agrees, but her tone is hesitant.

I narrow my gaze. "Is it all the publicity surrounding your success that's made it difficult for the two of you to be together?"

"One of us being in the public eye is difficult enough," she replies and blows out a breath. "But add in the fact that Declan's last film was a big hit, and the media speculation on our every move, can make things challenging, to say the least."

"Oh, honey, I'm so sorry," Isla says in a soft voice.

"Media intrusion is never easy. The trick, though, is not to give any weight to what they write. Don't respond to them, don't engage with them. And never, ever google yourself," I add.

"It's not easy, though, when you are in the eye of the storm—"

"You find the calm," I murmur.

"Wise words." Solene chuckles. "But again, we're not talking about me, and neither Isla nor I are letting you off that easily." She waggles a finger at me. "So, going back to sex and the hot Prime Ministerial candidate to-be, you were saying—"

"Not much. I don't have anything to do with his campaign, or with the man himself."

"Is that why you're moping?" Solene tips down her chin.

"I'm not moping."

"You refused to come out and meet any of us on New Year's Eve."

"I was busy." I fold my arms across my chest.

She firms her lips. "How many New Year's Eves have you spent on your own at home before this?"

This was the first one. It really is not like me to be a shrinking violet. To prefer my own company to that of my friends, or indeed, a roomful of strangers I could socialize with. But I've been feeling so tired and under the weather, nothing has felt as good as watching the News at ten on BBC, then crawling into bed. On my own. Jeez, am I growing old before my time? My face falls.

Solene's features soften. "Didn't say that to make you feel bad. It's just that you have dark circles under your eyes. Also, I think maybe you've lost weight."

"Gee thanks," I drawl.

"Solene's right." Isla's gaze narrows on my face. "You do look a little peaked. Are you coming down with something?"

"I'm fine." I bring my cup of coffee to my mouth and my stomach churns. Ugh, nothing worse than coffee gone lukewarm. I pivot, head back to my table and place the coffee on it.

"So, when do I see the two of you again?"

"I'll be in London in a few weeks. Liam's board meeting is coming up, and he needs to be there. Also, I have a few new wedding planning clients I'd like to meet in person." The scene behind Isla changes. She climbs up the stairs at the mansion on the island she and Liam now call home.

"I'll try to stop over on my days off between gigs," Solene chimes in.

My phone buzzes again with an incoming call. I recognize the caller ID and frown. "Can't wait to see the both of you. So sorry guys, I have a call coming which I can't not take."

"See you soon."

"Can't wait."

Both women disconnect. I switch to the other call. "Lord Alan?"

"Zara my dear, how are you this very fine morning?" His familiar voice reverberates over the phone.

"I am well, sir, and you?"

"Never been better." There's a pause, then, "Remember our last call? I now have more details regarding the project I spoke to you about. I assume you're up for it?"

# 36

Hunter

"So, you're launching your campaign bid?" Sinclair leans back in his chair.

"I am," I confirm.

"About fucking time." JJ Kane smacks the table in front of him.

"The question I have is, why did it take you so long to make up your mind?" Michael places his fingertips together. This is the first I'm seeing him since Karma's delivery. He's spent the last few months at home with her and the new baby. Given Karma's delicate health and the baby being born prematurely, he was, understandably, very stressed about them, but both mother and child are doing well, which is why he agreed to meet the three of us for a meeting at my office.

"Politics is all about timing and" —I glance about their faces— "about who you have in your corner."

"And other than the three of us, I assume there's one more person who's support you need to put your best foot forward?" Sinclair drawls.

I lean back on my heels. "You could say that."

"And does this ace up your sleeve happen to be the shrewdest fixer this side of the pond?" Michael smirks.

"And does she happen to be a dark-haired spit-fire who's known for defusing scandals related to well-known personalities?" JJ Kane's grin widens.

"It's no secret that Zara and I ah…have a connection, and it's true that I've been waiting to ensure I had her on my team before I declared my candidacy."

"And is that wise?" Declan's voice interrupts from the phone.

I turn to where the device is balanced against my glass of water on the table.

"It would have been unwise to not have included her. I need her insights to plan my roadmap to the foremost leadership position of this country."

"But does she know that?" Declan retorts.

I rub the back of my neck. "Not yet."

"And when were you planning to tell her?" He scowls.

"At the right time?"

"I suggest you not delay that, not if you truly want her working with you," JJ murmurs.

I raise my hands. "Point taken, chaps. Though, that's not why I asked you here today."

"Could there be anything more important than figuring out your personal life and how it's going to impact your professional life?" Sinclair drums his fingers on the table.

"My personal life is my own. I take all of your advice and consider it, but ultimately, it's my decision how I decide to take things forward."

"Yours and hers," JJ reminds me.

"The callousness of the man who's lost his heart but is not yet aware of it." Sinclair scoffs.

"Hold on. I have feelings for her. That doesn't mean I've lost my heart, thank you very much."

The three men look at each other, then burst out laughing.

"Wait, what did I miss?" I scowl.

The three continue laughing, and I turn to Declan. "Do you know what they're laughing about?"

He rubs his hand across his face. "I'm not married, mate, and at the rate things are falling apart around me, I won't be for a while."

I pause, then pick up the phone and peer into Declan's features. His eyes are bloodshot, his hair mussed, and he's sporting days' old growth on his chin. "You all right, ol' chap?"

"No, but I will be. Fame is a double-edged sword, isn't it? You spend your career pursuing it. You think you want it. Then when you have it, it bites you in the arse."

"Anything you want to talk about?" JJ calls out.

I place the phone back in position on the table so the rest of the men can see the screen.

"Not that we're the best source of advice, considering we're scrambling to get our heads out of our arses after the birth of our kids." Sinclair yawns. "Sorry, the boy kept fussing last night, and it was my turn to feed him the bottle. So, as I was saying—" He looks around the table with a puzzled expression. "What was I saying?"

"That you're not the best source of advice." Declan chuckles. "Right now, you seem more tired than I feel."

"It's losing sleep at night that's wrecking me. You'd think raising a child would be a cakewalk. Everyone does it, after all, but after the fifth consecutive night of lost sleep, I swear, I'd give anything to find a way to put him to sleep so I can hit the sack by ten p.m."

"Ten p.m.?" I smirk. "Is this the same Sinclair Sterling who partied 'til dawn with the rest of the Seven?"

"Most of whom are probably spending an evening at home cuddled on the sofa watching Netflix and ordering a curry with their wives." He points out.

"Yep, I'd do anything for a good curry." Michael nods slowly.

"Man, I'm all for a good curry. The spicier, the better." JJ smirks.

I look at the three of them. "I'm definitely missing something aren't I?"

"Of course, not. You'll know when it's time for an exceptional curry. Nothing like getting your own recipe right for it, too." JJ's grin widens.

"What are you guys talking—"

The door opens and Lord Alan walks in. "Gentlemen, Minister." He nods his head in the direction of the assembled men.

JJ, Michael and Sinclair exchange glances, then as one, rise to their feet. "We were on our way out." Sinclair yawns, then shakes his head as if to clear it. He looks like he's about to keel over any moment.

JJ walks over and shakes Lord Alan's hand. "Good seeing you here. I'll leave the Minister in your capable hands."

He heads toward the door, when it opens again and Zara steps in. Her gaze arrows straight to mine, and her face pales. She opens her mouth, then shakes her head. She glances at Lord Alan, then at me, and understanding dawns on her features.

JJ dips his chin in Zara's direction, then walks out. Sinclair and Michael, too, shake Lord Alan's hand. They nod toward Zara before they follow JJ out.

"Good chat, Hunter, keep me posted how things develop." Declan signs off.

Lord Alan waddles over and lowers his bulk into one of the seats facing me. He waves his hand in Zara's direction, "I do believe the two of you have met?"

Zara's gaze narrows. "I believe we may have met on one or two occasions." She squares her shoulders and walks into the room.

"Ms. Chopra, a pleasure." I tilt my head.

She pauses next to the empty chair opposite me and next to Lord Alan. "Mr. Whittington." She jerks her chin.

"Please take a seat."

"I'm not sure I'll be here long enough for that."

"Oh?" I cross my arms over my chest.

"I plan to be out of here as soon I have a word with Lord Alan." She turns to the older man. "I'm not sure I'm the right person for this project."

Lord Alan places his elbows on the arms of his seat, then locks his palms under his chin. "So, you're going to let your ego get in the way of managing a campaign that's going to put a breakthrough candidate in Downing Street?"

She swallows. "I'm not right for this role."

Lord Alan barks out a laugh. "I don't mentor fools, nor losers. And you are neither of the two. You're not the type to give up without a fight, Zara, so what's making you do so now?"

"I'm not giving up," Zara splutters.

"Aren't you?" Lord Alan lowers his arms to his sides.

"Of course, not. It's just, I don't want to work with him." She stabs her thumb in my direction.

I drag my thumb under my lower lip. "I'm afraid, I have to admit, the two of us are incompatible."

"Or maybe you haven't dug deep enough to find common ground." Lord Alan glowers in my direction. "We need you in number ten, Whittington. And you" —he jerks his chin in Zara's direction— "we need your brains, madam, and your spin doctor skills, not to mention your acumen in getting the media to dance to your tune."

Zara flushes. "You give me too much credit, Lord Alan."

"Oh, take the praise when it's due."

She draws herself up to her full height. "You're right. I'm damn good at what I do. There's no one better placed than me to run the Minister's PR campaign. Without me, he may as well give up any hope he has of closing in on the leadership position."

"Now, hold on a second—"

"No, you hold on a second." Lord Alan glowers at me, "This woman is all that's standing between a good campaign and a brilliant campaign that'll put the wind under your wings and sail you right into number ten."

I raise my hands. "I defer to your wiser counsel, sir." I allow my lips to quirk. "Of course, if Ms. Chopra doesn't want this opportunity—"

"Ms. Chopra would relish this opportunity, but I have a few conditions."

"Oh, good, I can leave the two of you to sort out the details then?" Lord Alan pushes up to standing, then glances between us with a thoughtful look on his face. "Of course, I don't have to warn the two of you that anything beyond the lines of what is proper could be damaging to not only the two of you, but also the party?"

I blink. Lord Alan is the chairperson of the party, and as such, it's within his right to ensure that all of us toe the line. Indeed, anything that could harm the Party's image comes under his purview. But to hint at the possibility of anything that isn't within the margins of being 'proper' is surprising, to say the least.

I exchange glances with Zara, who has a similar confounded look on her face. I signal to her with my eyes that we need to agree and that we can sort out what he meant later. She nods subtly. "Of course, Sir Alan, nothing I say or do will hurt my client's image."

"And you know me, Sir Alan, I'll only ever do what is in the interests of the Party."

"Good." He raps on my table. "I'll take my weary bones out of here and let you two thrash out the rest of your agreement."

He brushes past Zara, and the door snicks shut. For a few seconds, we look at each other. The silence stretches. Then she places her bag on the chair closest to her, reaches for a book on my table and hefts it in her hand. "So, you had no idea this was coming, did you?"

I glance at the book, then at her. "You mean about Lord Alan asking you to join as Communications Manager for my campaign? Of course, not."

"Liar." She raises her arm and pitches the book at me.

# 37

Zara

He ducks, and the book flies past him. Anger churns my guts. "You think I'm going to believe you when you say you didn't know Lord Alan was going to ask me to become your PR manager?" I shoot out my arm and grab the paperweight. Who keeps a paperweight on a desk anymore? This stuck up, privileged prick does, and isn't that helpful? I pitch the paperweight at him. He moves so fast, he's almost a blur. The paperweight misses him and crashes to the wooden floor and rolls away.

"Zara!" he growls.

"Don't even start." I reach out blindly. My fingers encounter a ceramic mug which he must have drunk coffee from earlier. "You knew he'd ask me, and that I wouldn't be able to refuse. You told him to keep your name out of it so I wouldn't know it was you he was talking about; not until I walked into this office and saw you." I launch the cup at him. This time, he swoops out his hand, catches it, and places it on the table.

The slow burn of anger erupts into flames of rage. The blood pounds at my temples, and my heart catapults into my throat. I grab a book from the table and chuck it at him. Then snatch up a pencil, a pen, a stapler, and throw them at him, one after the other. He easily evades them and slaps his hands on the table. "Zara, stop that. You're acting unreasonable."

"You think this is unreasonable? You haven't seen anything yet." I reach for his phone, and he rushes around the table. I raise my hand, but he reaches up and circles my wrist with his fingers.

"Let me go."

"You need to calm down first."

"Don't tell me to calm down, you twatworm!" I burst out.

He chuckles. "Where do you pick up your gutter language, baby?" He grabs my other arm, then twists both of my hands behind my back.

"Don't you dare 'baby' me, you conniving piece of shit." I try to pull free, but his hold on me tightens. He squeezes my wrist just enough that I loosen my fingers. The phone slips from my hand. He releases my wrist and catches the phone before he places it on the table. At the same time, he draws me flush against him so I can feel all of him from chest to groin to thighs.

"Hunter, don't you dare."

"You know I can't stop myself from rising to a challenge." He thrusts forward, and the unmistakable bulge in his crotch stabs into my arse.

"Fuck you," I spit out.

"I will, but only if you ask me nicely." He leans his weight into me so I'm pushed up against his desk. Then he circles my wrists with the fingers of his one hand; the other, he plants in between my shoulder blades. He applies pressure, and I find myself folded over his table, my arse jutting out and flush against the column in his pants. He's even more aroused than a few seconds ago, if that were possible. Heat spurts in my lower belly. A shudder of need ladders up my spine. He must notice, for he pulls the hair back from my face and drapes it over one shoulder. Then he bends and nips on my exposed earlobe.

I shiver. "Hunter, stop."

"Do you remember your safe word?"

I swallow.

"Do you, Fire?"

I nod.

"Unless you use it I'm going to keep going."

I draw in a ragged breath. My heart is beating so fast, I can feel the pulse between my legs, behind my knees, at my ankles, my temples, even behind my eyelids.

"Do you want to use your safe word?" he growls.

I hesitate.

His entire body goes solid. I feel the tension flow off of him. His muscles are so hard, I can feel every individual chest plane outlined against my back. His heart canters against my back, the speed so fast it echoes my own.

"Do you, Zara?" He releases me and steps back. "If you want me to stop use your safe word, now."

I squeeze my eyes shut. My knees feel like they're going to turn to jelly. He's giving me a choice, and that makes it so much worse. Because what I'm going to do now is only going to show me how reckless I am. How totally seduced I am by his touch, the feel of his skin on mine, his eyelashes brushing my cheek, the feel of his hard thighs gripping mine. The length of his cock stretching me, while his fingers probe that forbidden place between my arse cheeks.

"Zara, do you want me to stop?"

I shake my head.

"I need you to say it aloud, baby."

"I don't want you to stop."

"Open your eyes and say it like you mean it."

*Jerkhole.* I snap open my eyelids and glower up at him from the corner of my eyes. "I want you to fuck me, you bastar—"

He's on me so fast, I gasp. He rolls up my skirt so it's over my hips, then tears off my panties. A moan falls my lips. My pulse rate is so fast, it's as if I'm competing in a sprint. "What if someone walks in?" I manage to get out.

He lowers his head until his gaze is on level with mine. "You'll just have to come fast enough so they won't catch us."

A tremor of heat coils in my underbelly. My pussy clenches, and my thigh muscles quiver.

"That turns you on, doesn't it?" he growls.

"Of course, not."

"Oh?" He straightens, then kicks my legs apart. He shoves his fingers inside me—rough and hard and with no consideration for me, just how I like it. He pulls out his fingers and holds them in front of my face. The unmistakable white liquid stretching between his digits reveals just how turned on I am. "Your body never lies to me, baby." He thrusts them in my mouth. "Lick them clean for me."

I don't need a second urging. I am a slut for punishment. That's who I am at my most basic. God help me. I lick myself off his fingers, and a tremor grips his body. Apparently, I'm not the only one who's excited. A calm descends, and my normal heart rhythm resumes. This is going to happen. I'm going to let this happen because I want it. Because he wants it, too. Because when we're together, we're as combustible as dry wood and fire.

He lowers his fingers. I hear the jingle of his belt, and another spurt of heat pumps through my veins. Then the blunt head of his cock teases my slit.

"I'm going to scream," I warn.

"I'm counting on it."

"Won't be so good if the rest of your office listens to it."

"It's soundproofed, baby."

I scowl. "How many women have you fucked in here before?"

He stills, then lowers his head again so he's on eye level with me. "Jealous?"

"Not at all."

"Liar." He tucks a strand of hair behind my ear. "And you're the first woman I've taken on this desk."

My heart seems to open in my chest. A thrill of joy bursts through my veins. He straightens, grips my hips.

"The only woman I plan to fuck again and again on this surface."

"Wait, what? This is not happening agai—"

I gasp as he pistons his hips forward and impales me. Oh god, that familiar thickness, the way my pussy expands around his girth; it hurts and yet, it's also so very erotic.

He leans over and wraps my fingers about the edge of his desk. "Hold on."

He pistons his hips and sinks into me with such force that the entire table jolts. I slide forward and his hold on my hips tightens. He pulls back, then thrusts into me and his balls slap against my inner thighs. He reaches under and rubs on my clit, and the climax sweeps out from my core. He releases his hold on my hips only to slap his hand down next to my face. He's rolled up his shirtsleeves and the veins on his forearms flex. That, along with the smattering of dark hair on his arms, sends me over the edge. The next time he crams himself into me, my entire body jolts. He bends over, his wide chest covering me as he presses me into the table. Then he places his cheek next to mine and growls, "Come for me, Fire. Come right now."

A cry spills from my lips and I orgasm instantly. He fucks me through the aftershocks, then with a groan, empties himself inside me.

He stays that way with his weight pinning me down, with the heat of his body holding me captive, the cum running down my leg— a combination of both of us—and my head floating somewhere above my body. He pulls out, and I wince at the loss of his heat. I hear him walk away, and know I must move, but my legs seem to have lost the ability. Then I hear his footsteps, and something cool brushes between my legs. He pulls down my skirt, then pulls me up and turns me around in his arms. "Are you okay?"

# 38

Hunter

She raises those heavy eyelids, and her sated eyes hold my gaze. "This can't work."

"I thought that worked very well, actually."

"We can't work together. Not when every time we meet, you want to fuck me, and I can't stop you from fucking me."

She pulls away from me and begins to pace. I ball up the paper towel with which I wiped her and am about to toss it, then bring it up to my nose and sniff.

She turns just in time to catch me do so and her gaze widens. "You're an animal."

"Only when it comes to you."

"See?" She stabs a finger in my direction. "This is what I mean. We can't even have a normal conversation without it turning into this sexual gameplay."

"One which I enjoy."

"One which your team is going to notice," she retorts.

"Not if we're careful."

She plants her palms on her hips. "You really think they won't notice the chemistry between us?"

"No," I admit. "But that chemistry is precisely why it makes sense for you to be my PR manager. You know what I am, how I think. No one knows me better than you. And you can use that to your advantage."

"You're not going to budge on this one, are you?"

I shake my head.

She glances away, then back at me. "I can't do this, Hunter. I'm sorry. I'm putting myself and you at risk. I can't allow our relationship to become media fodder. It would remove every last bit of leverage I have with the news people."

She smooths her skirt down over her hips, pats her hair into place, then reaches for her bag. She turns and heads toward the door when I call out, "Where do you think you're going?"

"We can't work together, Hunter. Even though I owe this to Lord Alan, I'm sorry, but I can't deliver on it this time. Please give him my apologies."

I reach for my phone and swipe up the screen, then tap a button. The sound of her moans, and the unmistakable impact of flesh on flesh fills the room.

She pauses, then pivots to face me. "What's that?"

"Why don't you come and see for yourself?"

She heads toward the desk, then rounds it and stands next to me. On my computer the scene playing out shows a woman stretched out over a desk, with her entire body moving forward. The man's hand is in view, the rest of him is hidden. Her face, though, is in full view of the camera.

She spins around, arm raised, and I catch her hand before it can connect with my face. "Careful, Fire, there's a limit to how much leeway I grant you."

"Limit? And what about what you're doing?"

"That's self-preservation."

"You'd use it to blackmail me?"

"If it means you'll be working for me, then yes."

She firms her lips. "You're more despicable than I thought you were."

"Is that a yes?"

Her gaze narrows. "I'll never forgive you for this."

"You haven't answered my question yet."

"Goddamn you, yes. I'll work for you. Now, will you release me?"

"On one condition."

"You're a real piece of work, aren't you, Whittington?"

"Only when it comes to you."

"Stop saying that."

"But it's true. There's no limit to what I'd do to make you mine, Zara."

She looks between my eyes, then tips her chin. "There's no limits I'll go to avoid becoming yours."

I twist my lips. "We'll see."

"Okay."

"Okay."

The door swings open. "Oh, sorry Mr. Whittington, I didn't realize you were with someone."

I release her hand and step back.

"It's fine, Daniel, come on in. Meet Zara Chopra, my new PR manager. Zara, this is Daniel, my campaign manager."

---

"That went as expected." Zara pushes back from the conference room table and rolls her shoulders.

After the meeting with Daniel, I called a team meeting and introduced Zara to all of them. She, of course, was impressive, and within minutes of meeting everyone, began to draw up a PR strategy for the campaign.

"I thought that went better than expected."

"You mean at least one-fourth of your team doesn't resent me for having marched in here and redrawn half the campaign strategy?" She snatches up her notepad and pen, then her phone, and slides them into her bag.

"I mean, you cut through the clutter and came up with a coherent strategy. You did in an hour what my team and I have been trying to pull together for months."

She turns in her chair to face me. "Is that why you never launched your campaign? Because you weren't happy with the strategy so far?"

"Among other things."

"Why else would you hold back when every day you didn't declare you were running would make it tougher for you to win?"

"I'm still launching before the deadline."

"If you mean twenty-four hours before the final deadline, then you're barely squeaking through. As it is, you've lost so much time—"

"But I'll be off to a strong start and that's more impactful than simply announcing my campaign in order to be seen."

She tilts her head. "Sometimes, I'm forced to agree with you."

"As I recall it, when you were stretched out across my table earlier you were very vocally in agreement with me. In fact, I recall precisely you saying that you didn't want me to stop, that I should fu—"

"Shut up, Hunter." She glances around the room, then back at me. "How can you be so careless?"

"There's no one here. There are also no cameras or bugs in here."

"How can you be sure?" She frowns.

"I have the premises swept every morning."

"Except your office where you have cameras placed so you can film anyone who comes in to meet you," she says bitterly.

"I do have cameras in my room. It's a precaution, and only I have access to the footage."

"So you can blackmail people into doing what you want?"

"If need be."

She tips up her chin. "Are there any other indiscretions you need to tell me about? Anything I need to be prepared for as your PR manager?"

I close the distance to her, then grip the arms of her chair and bend until I'm eye level with her. "I've never used the filming to blackmail anyone else before."

"So only I'm subjected to your machinations then?"

"Not letting you go so easily, Fire."

"We're working together now; it's best to keep our relationship professional so I can do my job."

I hold her gaze, and she doesn't glance away. I see the hurt in the depths of her eyes, and damn, I already hate myself for what I did. But if it's the only way to have her close to me, then I'll take my chances. But I also know when not to push further.

"I won't touch you again; you have my word. Unless—"

She swallows "Unless?"

"Unless you ask me to."

"That'll be the day," she scoffs.

"Don't underestimate how much you enjoy being with me, in every way."

———

"You're underestimating how easy it is to piss off a woman. One wrong move, and they'll never forgive you. Not unless you grovel and go back to them with your hat in your hands, and sometimes, not even then." Liam leans forward in his chair. "And you've crossed the line here with what you did."

*Don't I know it?* "I had no other choice. She was going to walk out the door."

"And you should have let her."

"Eh?" I blink. "Did I just hear the man who's never backed down from a corporate takeover tell me that I should have given up without a fight?"

"In matters of the heart, the boardrooms don't apply."

I tap my fingers together. "If you mean I don't know when to back down—"

"What I mean is, the rules of engagement are different when it comes to affairs of the heart."

"We talking about Hunter's non-existent love life, then?" Declan prowls in. He collapses into the chair between us and kicks out his legs. He's wearing jeans torn at the knees, a hat on his head, and a sweatshirt with the hood pulled over the hat. He pulls off his sunglasses, revealing dark circles and hollowed cheekbones.

"You look like shite, mate," I offer.

"Fuck you very much." He reaches for the bottle of Macallan, lifts it to his mouth, and takes a swig.

"Last I checked, we're still civilized enough to drink out of a glass," Liam chides.

"You do the whole proper English gentleman thing. Right now, I need sustenance to get me through the rest of this shitty day." He raises the bottle of Macallan and chugs down more of the liquor.

"And I thought I was in the doldrums." I raise my cigar to my lips.

He lowers the bottle, wipes the back of his mouth with his hand, then places the bottle on the table. "Never fear. When it comes to lessons in how to ruin a relationship, you can consider me the fore-runner."

"Surely, it can't be that bad?" Liam leans back in his seat. Bastard looks all relaxed, with that happiness radiating off him that men who are settled in relationships seem to have. He's temporarily back from his sojourns in Italy, and clearly, living abroad suits him.

"No, it's worse." Declan lowers his arms between his legs. "But that's what happens when you're trying to juggle not one, but two careers, not to mention, a burgeoning relationship in the media limelight."

"Speaking of, should you even be here? Won't your adoring fans have surrounded the club by now?"

"Nah, it's a little better in London, as long as I keep my face hidden. I even took the tube over here."

"Impressive."

He reaches for the bottle again, and Liam moves it out of reach. He pours out a glass and slides it over to Declan who tosses it back. "Enough talk about me, anyway. How's it going with your spin doctor?"

"She's now the official PR manager for my campaign." I study the ash building up on the tip of my cigar.

Declan straightens in his seat. "That's good, right?"

"Not the way he got her to accept the role, it isn't," Liam interjects.

"Do I want to know?"

"No," Liam and I say simultaneously.

"O-k-a-y, but if it gets you time with her, perhaps it's worth it?"

"I sure hope so."

"So what are you doing here?"

I narrow my gaze on him. "What do you mean?"

"If you want her, you need to go after her. Why are you wasting your time here with us?"

"Our relationship is now professional." I take a puff on the cigar and blow out a cloud of smoke. "So, I can't exactly pop into her place without reason, the optics on that wouldn't be great."

"But a work meeting wouldn't attract the same scrutiny, would it?"

"Hmm." I place the cigar in the notch in the ashtray, then lean over and grab him by the scruff of his neck. Which, mind you, was easier when he was a skinny junior who always got ragged by the rest of the boys for being the scrawniest of the bunch. Now, he's six-foot-three, with shoulders like a quarterback, yet I can't get over the habit of treating him like a cheeky younger sibling.

"Hey, watch it, man." He grabs my neck back in return.

Yep, he's definitely grown up. Doesn't mean I'm going to stop behaving like a protective older sibling. "Sometimes you do have words of wisdom to offer."

Liam snaps his fingers. "The V&A Ball. That's the one you need to attend, and invite her to it, as well."

I glance between them. "I'll go on one condition."

# 39

Zara

"How do I look?" I pop out a hip and the light bounces off of the Swarovski crystals that decorate my shimmery-silver, one-shoulder dress. It clings to me like it was made for me, which it probably was, considering it arrived in a box by special delivery just a few hours ago. I almost turned it away, until I noticed the label on the box. Armani. Only a fool would turn away the chance to wear an Armani original, and a fool, I am not. Still, I hesitated when the courier handed over the second box. This one bore the Manolo Blahnik label. And if I had any doubt, the third box—this one sporting the Birkin brand—sealed the deal.

"Well?" I quirk an eyebrow at the phone which I've propped up against the mirror.

"You look gorgeous and that dress might as well be painted on," Solene replies from the screen.

"That's what I thought, too." I turn sideways, running a hand down my stomach.

"You look amazing, Z."

"It's the dress," I demur.

"It's the woman in the dress. Your confidence shines through."

"That's the glitter of the Swarovski crystals." I laugh weakly.

"The man knows your weakness." She chuckles.

"Doesn't he ever." If I had any remaining doubts about accepting the dress, they vanished as soon as I slid it on. Something about the gunmetal color, and the one-shouldered cut, lent a regal air to the outfit. As for the fit… It's clear he memorized my curves. There's no other way the dress could have fit without my having tried it on in advance. I thrust out a leg and the slit, which slashes almost up to my waist, parts to reveal the line of my thigh. As for the heels, the Manolo Blahnik's have a bondage-type strap that clings lovingly to my ankle.

"Those shoes alone are going to make the man combust."

"I hope so." I look at myself with a critical eye. I'm dressed to bring a man to his knees. And he must have known this would be the outcome when he sent me this specific combination of clothes to wear.

"You sure about this, though?" Solene's voice pulls me out of my reverie.

"You mean about wearing the clothes he sent me?"

"It's your favorite designers, and creations you couldn't possibly buy off the shelf, so I'm not surprised you didn't turn it away. It's just…won't he misinterpret your wearing the clothes he sent you for your encouraging him?"

"He might." I run my palms down the Swarovski studded fabric. "And if I had turned it away, he'd have won, and I can't allow that."

"This thing between the two of you isn't a game," she cautions.

"Sure could have fooled me," I murmur

"Just don't want you getting hurt, babe."

Might be a little too late for that. I turn to face her image on the phone screen. "I'll be careful, I promise."

"Good. You're a strong woman, Zara, but you have a heart that can be hurt easily."

Damn, when your friends see you so clearly, it's humbling. "You're a good friend, Solene."

"Because I'm looking out for you?" She laughs. "If our roles were reversed, you'd do the same. You know that."

"You bet I do."

The doorbell rings.

"That must be Liam and Isla." I blow a kiss at the phone. "I love you, babe; can't wait to see you in person."

"Same, and don't forget to tell me all about it."

"I promise" I disconnect the call, then drop the phone into my clutch with my lipstick and house keys. A last look at myself, and I grab my coat and head for the door. When I throw it open, he stands there with one hand against the doorframe.

I open and shut my mouth. "What are you doing here?"

"Liam and Isla are running late, so I offered to pick you up."

"I didn't hear anything from Isla." I scowl.

"Have you checked your messages?"

I pull out my phone, check my messages, and sure enough, there's one from Isla.

ISLA:

> So sorry babe. Liam's mom wasn't feeling well —she's fine now—but Liam wanted to look in on her before we went to the ball so we're running late. I hope you don't mind that Hunter's coming to pick you up. I know things are rough with you two, but you do work together now, and he offered. We won't be long, I promise. See you soon.

Guess in all the excitement of the new clothes and accessories, I missed her message. I pull up the app for the cab company, and he places his hand on mine. Tendrils of heat flicker out from the point of contact. Both of us pull back.

"What are you doing?"

"I'm ordering a cab."

"It's Friday evening; you're not going to get one in time."

"We'll see." I type out my destination, press the relevant buttons and the app stalls. "Damnit." I try again and again; each time the app crashes.

"I have a car waiting, Zara."

I ignore him and continue to try the app with the same result. "Bloody hell." I drop the phone back in my bag and scowl at him. "You planned it all, didn't you? Inviting me to the ball—"

"As my PR official; nothing personal about this."

"Then making sure, somehow, Liam and Isla couldn't pick me up."

"You think I orchestrated Liam's mother falling sick?" His gaze widens. "Not even I could pull that off."

"Hmph." I scan his features. He's combed back his hair and is wearing a tux which outlines his broad shoulders. His crisp white shirt stretches across his chest. His jaw is freshly shaven, the bowtie at his neck turning his entire look from sophisticated to positively deadly. Why does he have to look so edible? So hot? So sexy, so everything. I frown. He arches an eyebrow.

"Something wrong?"

"You have a—" I lean up and press my thumb to a dot of blood at the edge of his jawline. I show him the drop of scarlet, then bring the digit to my mouth and suck on it.

His nostrils flare. His blue-green eyes darken until they resemble pools of midnight blue. "I must have nicked myself shaving."

"Right." I swallow, glance away, then back at him. "If I'm to travel in the same car as you, we need rules."

"Rules?" He arches an eyebrow.

"No touching without permission."

"Goes both ways," he points out.

I flush, then draw myself up to my full height. "That was an instinctive reaction."

"So was mine."

I nod slowly. "Moving on, no looking at me like you want to—"

"Fuck you?" he interjects.

Heat sweeps up my back. "Exactly. You need to be on guard when we are together in the open."

"I'll have my game face on."

"No kissing."

"Not unless you ask me to."

"No moving into my space."

"You mean like this?" He moves in until the lapels of his jacket almost brush my dress. Until his breath kisses my cheek, until the heat from his body wraps around me, and his scent—that gorgeous spicy, testosterone-laden scent of his permeates my pores and my cells, sinks into my blood, and arrows straight to my core.

"You promised," I whisper.

"You set the rules; I didn't agree to anything," he says, his voice as hushed as mine.

"We can't, Hunter, please." I swallow.

He glances between my eyes, then nods, and to my relief, takes a step back. "Shall we?"

---

"You pulled out all the stops, didn't you?" I accept my flute of champagne and glance about the interior of the Jaguar. It's definitely custom-made, complete with the bar and the panel between the front and back seats, which is now currently up.

"No reason not to travel in style." He slides the bottle of Moet & Chandon Espirit du Siecle Brut into the ice bucket then raises his glass. "To the evening ahead."

I clink my glass with his and raise it to take a sip. The clean notes of citrus and pear, shot through with licorice, tickle my nostrils. My stomach churns. I raise the flute to my mouth and take a sip. That churning sensation grows stronger. I manage to swallow down the champagne without gagging, then place the glass back on the table.

"Good?" he asks.

"You know it is." I heave an internal sigh of relief as my stomach settles. I forgot to eat lunch. I should remember not to skip meals.

"Nothing like hearing the appreciation first-hand."

I chuckle. "You're smooth."

"As smooth as the champagne?"

"Smoother, and stop fishing for compliments."

He laughs, and his entire face lights up. That square jaw, that aristocratic nose, those high cheekbones, and in the designer suit he's wearing, he's the most gorgeous man I've ever met.

"You're staring, Zara."

I glance away. "My mind was a million miles away."

"Oh?" I hear the disbelief in his voice.

"An upcoming family reunion, which promises to be as stressful as the ones before." And that's the truth. Though I only brought it up as a means to divert attention away from that slip up. So, the man is sex-on-a-stick, but I already know that. So why am I so flustered being this close to him? Especially since I've been much closer to him in the past.

"I take it, you don't get along with your parents?"

"I do, until something sets one of us off, and then it all descends into pandemonium."

"You have a brother?"

I hesitate. "He's my fraternal twin, but you know that already."

Now, it's his turn to hesitate. "I do, but it's different hearing it from you than reading it in a folder."

I reach for my flute and take another sip. "My grandfather arrived from the Indian subcontinent when he was five years old. He met my grandmother, who's also Indian, here in the UK. My father was born here. My mother's English. She met my father at the grocery shop that his father established. It's the same place that she and my father now run. When my parents had us, they were determined we would make a mark."

"And both of you have."

I glance away, then back at him. "They weren't very happy when, after qualifying for the bar, I moved into this 'ungodly' profession." I make air quotes with my fingers.

"Parents normally come around when they see their children are happy."

"Oh, and let's not forget, I'm past my prime and not married. So, I've doubly failed them."

"How old are you?"

"Twenty-nine, but you know that—"

"Already, yes, but can we pretend I don't, for the purposes of this conversation?"

"A little tough, considering, as your PR manager, I have access to the most intimate details of your life."

His lips quirk. "Not all of them."

"No?"

"No." He taps his temple "Not the ones I carry here or" — he taps the place over his heart— "here."

I blink, then glance away.

He blows out a breath. "I didn't mean to say that. But when I'm with you, it seems, I can't stop myself."

"Well try harder, Hunter. You seem to forget, it's both of our careers on the line."

"And I promise, it'll be game-face out there."

I throw back the rest of the champagne, then place the glass back on the table.

"So your brother's going to be at this family reunion?"

"He will be, and he's the darling of my parents. As you know, he plays cricket for England. He's famous, and in their eyes, a success. And of course, they don't care that he's not married or doesn't have kids. It's the daughter who always bears the brunt of that particular line of thinking."

"I'm sure you'll persuade your parents otherwise."

"Oh, when I'm with them… All these PR skills? They go out the window. I seem to go back to being five and I'm unable to do much but listen to them rant." I begin to flick my hair over my shoulder, then remember I've put it up for the evening. I settle for locking my fingers together and looking out the window.

"It's because they care about you," he murmurs.

"You don't say."

"They seem like they were very hands-on parents."

"Too hands-on, when they were around. They were always trying to make up for the fact that they couldn't be there at all times since they were running the store." I snort.

"I'd have liked mine to be more hands-on."

I shoot him a sideways glance. He's looking into the depths of his champagne flute, a furrow on that perfect forehead.

"Your parents weren't around as much as you'd have liked them to be, I take it?"

"More like, not around at all." He glances up and holds my gaze.

"Yep, I'm the poster child for the poor little rich boy," he says in a self-deprecating voice.

"Did they also leave you *Home Alone*?"

He blinks, then barks out a laugh. "Very good, Chopra."

"Why do you call me by my surname when you think I'm being particularly witty?"

He raises a shoulder. "Shouldn't I?"

"It's like when I'm unexpectedly witty you, somehow, attribute my intelligence to the patriarchy."

His gaze widens. "And all this, because I referred to you by your surname?"

"Think about it. When you're turned on, you refer to me by my nickname, when you think I'm being bratty, you scold me by calling me by my name, and when I say something particularly witty, you refer to me by my surname."

"I still don't get it." He shakes his head.

"That's the problem. With all you private school educated, entitled prats, your background fosters emotional austerity and fierce clique loyalty, not to mention the misogyny that runs through you lot."

"You mean, I spent the formative years of my childhood in boarding schools being looked after by adults who didn't love me," he drawls.

"Are you trying to make a play for my sympathy?"

"I'm merely letting you know that you judge me and my lot" —he makes air quotes with his fingers— "too harshly."

My gaze narrows. "You think I need to re-evaluate my opinion on you and your lot who never grow up. You, who forever remain boys; who think they can do anything and get away without consequences."

"I think" —he tilts his head— "I think you need to see it from my point of view. I remember my childhood as long stretches of desolate homesickness, of having my attachments to home and family broken abruptly several times a year. I lost everything—parents, pets, toys, younger siblings… Of course, I could cry if I liked, but no one was going to help me."

He drags his thumb under his lower lip, and my nipples harden. I shove aside the traitorous reaction of my body and tip up my chin. "So you learnt to cultivate the stiff upper lip. You could either be yourself —homesick, vulnerable, lovelorn, and frightened—or you could perform being loyal, robust, and self-reliant. Wear a brave face and distance your feelings, growing the hardness of heart of the educated.

"And you chose the latter. You convinced yourselves early that you had no great need of love. You decided to act grownup, even when you were very young, for that meant you needed no one. In fact, your experiences toughened you enough that, later in life, when you saw other people cry, you felt no great need to go to their aid. That's what you're getting at, aren't you? That it's not your fault how you turned out. It was circumstances that made you what you are."

"Didn't your circumstances make you what you are today?" he counters.

"I hardly think our backgrounds have anything in common."

"On the contrary." He places the champagne flute on the small table and turns to me. "You understand me so well because you've been through the same experiences I have, albeit in a different milieu."

I scoff. "Are you contrasting my upbringing with that of your privileged lifestyle?"

He looks between my eyes. "We're both the products of over-ambitious parents who wanted their children to become over-achievers."

"And here we are," I murmur.

"Indeed. Both of us, high-performing goal-setters, never happy with the status quo. And" —his gaze grows intense— "I've never been happier than I am right now, sitting next to you."

I swallow, then set my lips. "You forgot to add, we're never meant to be."

"You're here now, aren't you?" His shoulders are relaxed, yet a nerve pops at his temple. His body is sprawled out against the rich leather seat, but his gaze is wary. This man is so full of contrasts, it makes my head spin. He's such a puzzle. It both energizes me and chips away at my reservations—all of the hurdles I've been throwing in my own path of why I can't be with him.

"You're so—"

"Clever, witty, erudite?" he drawls.

"—full of yourself," I snap.

"And soon, you'll be full of me."

I blink, then make a gagging sound. "I can't believe you just said that."

"Believe it. It was a good comeback, though, admit it." He smirks.

"You have a one-track mind."

"Don't tell me you aren't, right now, thinking of straddling me as I thrust up and into you."

My belly clenches. My pussy hums. I can feel the evidence of my arousal gnaw at my lower belly and...oh, god, my breasts hurt, my thighs feel so very heavy, and my core? It feels so empty, so aching, so yearning for that sensation when his beloved thickness has me impaled and stretched and skewered around his gorgeous cock. A-n-d, did I just think of his penis as 'his beloved thickness'? Why do his words turn me on so? Why am I so unable to resist him? I squeeze my thighs together, then pretend to frown at him.

"Hunter," I say in a warning tone.

He laughs and raises both of his hands. "Just kidding you, Fire."

"So now it's Fire, is it?"

"You set my world on fire."

I half-laugh, then turn away. I shake my head, try to gather myself, and I'm all too aware of his big body taking up so much of this small, enclosed space, of his dark scent that envelops me, the cloud of heat that spools off of his chest and pins me in place, the strength of his dominance which is a palpable presence, one that turns my throat dry, that wrings my insides into coils of tremulous anticipation, and oh, god, I'm losing myself. I'm going to hell for what I'm going to do next, but I can't fight this... Can't fight us anymore.

I square my shoulders. "So..." I turn to him. "That scenario you painted earlier, do you want to recreate it?"

# 40

Hunter

"Which one?" I take in her gleaming eyes, her thick hair put up in some intricate hairdo that I've been itching to get my fingers into, just so I can pull out the pins and see her hair down in thick strands about her face again. Clearly, she's been processing our conversation and come to some kind of conclusion in her head, the results of which I'm about to experience.

"This one." She rises to her feet. Then, in a move that has my breath catching, she hitches her dress above her hips, and straddles me.

My heart slams into my ribcage. My pulse rate shoots up until I can feel the blood thudding in my ears. I slide my palms up her thighs to squeeze her hips.

"Fuck, Zara, you don't have any panties on," I growl.

"Oh, so it's Zara, is it? Is that because you're trying to scold me for being impudent? I wonder."

"You're playing with fire, Fire."

"And maybe, this time, I need you to be brimstone. To allow both of us to burn in the time it takes us to reach the gala."

"Sir, Mr. Whittington, it's eight minutes until we reach our destination, sir." My chauffeur's voice comes through the speaker.

She frowns.

I raise my fingers to her forehead and smooth out the wrinkles in that beautiful brow.

"I told him to give me a warning when we were close."

"Because you expected us to be in this situation?"

"Maybe?"

"Oh, for fuck's sake, and just when I thought, perhaps, you weren't as much of a tosser as you made yourself out to be." She begins to slide off, but I hold her in place.

"Just kidding you again, baby. No. For once, my intentions in wanting you with me were purely so I could spend time with you in a legitimate fashion, on a professional basis."

"Being photographed arriving together is barely going to make it seem professional."

"You're with me as my PR specialist. Sure, you're my plus-one for the evening, but we're not hiding anything. If anything, being seen together openly will only make it even more obvious that there's nothing between us."

"Or maybe, people will pick up on the chemistry between us." She frowns.

"If you were that concerned, why didn't you say anything earlier?"

"It was the dress...and the shoes... And the bag." She glowers at me. "You blindsided me with my favorite brands. I'm a proud woman, but even I bow at the altar of Armani. Add Manolo Blahnik and Birkin to the mix, and you knew I was not going to return them." She stabs a finger into my chest. "Especially not, after I tried on this dress."

"I prefer you even more dressed in only the Blahnik's and nothing else." I wrap my fingers about her delectable arse cheeks and massage the rounded flesh.

It's her turn to groan.

I pull her even closer so her soft core grinds down into the tent over of my crotch.

This time, both of us exhale sharply.

"I'm going to leave a damp spot on your pants," she protests.

"Fuck that." I tilt my hips so the tent at my crotch stabs into the apex of her legs.

She moans; my balls tighten. "Baby, I need to be inside of you," I growl.

"You have less than eight minutes to make me come." Her voice breaks, but her gaze is alert. Her color is high, but anticipation radiates off of her. It sinks into my skin, ignites my own need.

"I'm going to make you come at least three times before we reach our destination." I wrap my fingers about the nape of her neck and pull her in. Our lips meet, teeth clash, tongues entwine. I kiss her, and she kisses me back. I lick into her mouth, and she bites down on my lower lip. My cock stabs into the fabric of my pants. I tear my mouth from hers. Holding her gaze, I reach between us, unfasten my belt, slide down my zipper, and take out my cock. I position her over the head of my shaft, then thrust up and into her. I breach her, and her gaze widens. Her mouth opens in a soundless gasp. Her golden eyes catch fire, and for a second, it's as if I'm gazing into my destiny. Into a future that belongs to the both of us. It's scary, and so fucking right, it turns me on even more.

"I'm going to fuck you, Fire."

She grips my shoulders and swallows. "Don't you dare spoil this dress."

"I'll buy you a hundred more."

"I prefer to buy them for myself," she says primly.

"And I prefer when your attention is solely on me."

"Aww, feeling left out, are you?" She flexes her inner muscles, and the reverberations seem to travel up my spine.

"You're so hot, so tight, so fucking wet for me, baby." I pump up and into her, hitting that spot deep inside of her that makes her cry out. She throws her head back, and I bite the curve of her breast. She moans, and the noise goes straight to my head. Something snaps inside of me.

"Look at me." I apply pressure to the nape of her neck, and she opens her eyes.

I hold her gaze, then slide my hand down between us. I pinch her clit, and she explodes. The orgasm seems to take her by surprise, for her entire body jolts. Moisture bathes my cock, and she shudders and places her forehead against mine.

"Oh, my god."

"You mean, 'Oh, Hunter,' don't you?"

"Why do I find your arrogance such a turn-on?"

"Because you like a man who's confident enough to dominate you, baby."

She opens her eyes and stares into mine. "Your ego is going to be your downfall."

"Right now, it's on the ascent, Fire." I piston my hips up, and my shaft drills up and into her.

She groans. "Ohgod, ohgod, ohgod."

"Hunter."

"What?" she whines.

"Say my name."

"No."

"Oh?" I pull her off my cock, and she glances down at where my dick stands up at attention between us.

"Why did you do that?" she wails.

"So I could do this." I pull her back further, then bring down my palm on her pussy.

"What the—" she howls. "What are you doing?"

"Making you say my name."

"Don't you dare, Whittington."

I spank her core again.

Her back arches. "Fuck you, Hunter."

"Just my name."

"No way."

I slap her on her clit, and again, and she orgasms.

# 41

Zara

Holy hell. I've never orgasmed simply by being spanked between my legs. But there you have it. Another first for me. The other being, I decided, of my own volition, to put my career at risk and agree to ride with him, and then, because that wasn't enough, I decided to fuck him enroute to the event. But I don't regret it. Not yet. Not when the added edge of the time running down to reaching the gala is clearly accelerating my ability to orgasm back-to-back. The climax punches through me, then dies away, just as suddenly. I begin to slump, but he holds me up.

"Eyes on me."

I open my eyelids, which must have fluttered down of their own accord, thanks to that last orgasm. Then, I'm gazing into his now midnight blue eyes, and all other thoughts vanish from my mind.

He releases his hold on the nape of my neck, only to squeeze my hips and position me, once more, over the swollen head of his cock. He nudges my opening and my legs tremble. My toes curl. A shiver squeezes my lower belly, and he's not even inside me yet.

"Hunter," I rasp.

His eyes flash. An expression of satisfaction sweeps over his features. He yanks me down and onto his cock. "You are" —thrust— "mine. You hear me?"

I can only gasp as, once again, that thickness… Oh, that incredible girth of his, which still feels like it's the first time, and yet, it's also so familiar how my channel struggles to adjust to his size. The sweet pain of his intrusion convulses up my spine, and it's so right. So hot, so everything, I can't stop myself from leaning in and placing my lips on his.

He instantly takes control. Of course, he does. He wraps his mouth around mine and sucks on me as if he's trying to absorb my very essence into himself. Then he fucks me. He tunnels up and into me with such force, the entire cabin of the car seems to shake. He drives up and crams himself fully inside of me, once more, hitting that spot. This time, the trembling begins somewhere at my toes and spirals up, up to my core. He pulls back, thrusts up and into me, and at the same time, he wraps his fingers about my throat. "Come with me, Zara," he orders.

I do. I orgasm right there, for the third time, and still holding my gaze, he empties himself inside of me. I begin to slump again, and this time, he rests his forehead against mine. For a few seconds, we stare at each other then— "Two minutes to arrival, Mr. Whittington, two minutes." The chauffeur's voice fills the space.

He kisses me hard. I nod. We haven't spoken, but the understanding between us is seamless, as I move, and he helps me to lower my legs onto the floor of the limo. I reach for the paper towels by the window but he curls his fingers around my wrist. "I want you to feel my cum dripping out of your cunt as you meet and greet people tonight."

I flush. "You're a filthy beast."

"And you love it."

I begin to protest, then stop myself. Unfortunately, he has a point.

Instead, I reach over, pull at his collar and bite the side of his neck. "Now, we're even."

I slide the dress down over my hips and take my seat next to him. He rubs his thumb across the reddening patch of flesh, then pulls off his bowtie and throws it aside.

I gape. "What are you doing?"

"Wearing your mark with pride, baby."

"B-but, that'll only raise speculation."

"I can live with it, if you can."

His gaze lowers to my chest. I glance down to find there's what can only be described as a twin reddening mark on the slope of my left breast. "Oh, hell." I glare at him. "You did that on purpose."

"No, you did this on purpose." He points to what now clearly looks like a hickey on his throat.

I reach up, pull out the pins from my hair, and the strands flow about my shoulders. I pull a couple down over my breasts. Hopefully, that will help deflect from the mark.

"Smart." He inclines his head. "You think on your feet, Councilor. A true PR pro."

"And you, sir, live dangerously. You need to be more careful, or your campaign will be over before it starts."

"Will it?" He smirks.

A-n-d there's that confidence I love and hate, and goddamn, I'm beginning to fear is going to be my downfall. There's something so seductive about a man who knows what he wants and who doesn't hesitate to go after it. In this case, it's me he's set his sights on, and the sinking sensation in my stomach tells me he's close to getting what he wants. Somehow, though, it doesn't feel like it's a loss for me, or a game between us, anymore. It's turned into so much more, without my even realizing it.

"You okay?" He reaches over and tucks a strand of hair behind my ear.

"I will be."

He holds my gaze, nods. The limo comes to a stop. He glances to the window, through which I can make out the shapes of the paparazzi lined up on either side of the red carpet.

"You ready?"

---

As it turned out, I needn't have worried about the paps because, apparently, being seen together and out in the open means they accepted his answer that I was there with him as his work colleague. This, despite the fact that when we left the hospital together, they instantly speculated that we were together 'together'. But now that we were formally attending an event together, we didn't have anything to hide, did we? The media truly is a fickle creature. You never can predict how they'll behave.

When they asked me why I was with him, I replied with, "You know me, guys. I'm the PR consultant, and he's my client, and I'm here simply to make sure Mr. Whittington gets a great start to the campaign."

After which, I stepped aside, despite Hunter indicating I should stay with him. I left him to the mercy of the cameras and reporters— he's good at talking his way out of any situation, politician that he is. Plus, he deserved to be sacrificed to the wolves for a little longer, after that stunt he pulled in the limo. Luckily, the collar of his shirt was high enough to cover the hickey I gave him, and if anything, not wearing a bowtie added to his rakish appeal.

And no one noticed the love-bite on my cleavage. If they had, I know for a fact, I wouldn't have gotten away with an easy explanation. I can moan about it as much as I want, but the fact is, the media, and the public, still view and judge women with a different lens than it does the men. The double-standard persists.

All I can do is try my best to correct the status quo and hope my daughters will have an easier time.

My footsteps slow and I almost stumble before I catch myself. My daughters. Did I just think about 'my daughters'? Why am I thinking about 'my daughters?' I've never thought about having a child or getting pregnant. Now I'm suddenly thinking of having offspring, and in plural? My head spins.

I manage to keep my wits about me as I check my phone at the entrance. That's right, the event is a phone-free zone. Given the profiles of the attendees, the organizers insisted this was the only way to allow guests to relax, and apparently, they wanted to maintain secrecy around the silent auction that came at the end of the event.

I head inside the massive ballroom. It's a beautiful room, but I barely manage a glance at the frescoes which decorate the ceiling. Instead, I glance around for a place to sit down for a bit, catch my breath, and get something to eat, perhaps. A waiter passes by with canapés. I beckon him over, relieve him of a few of them and— whoever is watching be damned— scarf down the hors d'oeuvres.

They're as insubstantial as party canapés are reputed to be. Why is it that the booze at such gatherings is top-notch, but when it comes to the food, the portions are miniscule? I glance around for another waiter to flag down, when a plate piled high with food—the non canapé variety, i.e. the real stuff—is thrust in front of me. "Looking for this?"

I follow the arm attached to the plate and turn to find familiar features beaming at me.

"Isla!" I exclaim.

"You seem starved," she says and grins at me.

I lean around the plate and hug her. "I missed you, babe." We've been talking via FaceTime a lot, but nothing beats seeing your friends in person. With Isla in Italy and Solene's career taking off, and the rest of the Sisterhood of the Seven—which is what the wives and girl-friends of the Seven call themselves—either pregnant or having given birth recently, as in the case of Karma and Summer, I didn't realize how lonely I had been. Tears prick the backs of my eyes, and I blink them away. How strange. First I think of my own kids for the first time in my life, then I get emotional when I see Isla. Things are getting weird.

"I missed you, too." Isla pats my shoulder.

I sniff. She stills. "Zara, you okay?"

"Of course." I step back and tip up my chin. "Let me see you." I scan her features. Glowing eyes, glowing skin; in short, glowing everything. She's the picture of contentment.

"Marriage suits you."

"I know, right." Her smile widens. "Liam is the absolute bestest husband ever. He waits on me hand and foot, takes care of me, refuses to let me out of his sight, and the sex—" Her gaze turns dreamy.

A stab of something... Jealousy? No, more like a want, a need to feel what she's feeling, to be in that slightly blissful state where it feels like you have someone in your corner, your partner, someone who has your back, no matter what... Someone like Hunter. The hell? Just because I have his cum running down my thigh doesn't mean I've developed 'feelings' for him. Especially not now, when he's my defacto boss. Who I fucked on the way over in his limo. Jesus, what a mess.

I must make a noise for Isla, once more, peers into my face. "You sure you're okay Zara?"

"Just hungry." On cue, my stomach growls. I reach for the plate of food, then glance around for a place to put it down.

"Over here." Isla guides me to one of those high-top tables which are at a perfect height to lean on, specifically, one that was pushed to the side behind a large potted plant.

I place the plate of food down on it, then reach for the knife and fork she placed on it, and tuck in. I shovel in the fried mozzarella sticks, then the goat cheese crostini—yum—followed by the glazed pecans, and the turkey avocado pinwheels.

I hail a passing waiter and grab a glass of apple juice from him.

"You're not having champagne?" she asks, surprised.

"My stomach's been a little funny with alcohol, of late. With coffee, too, come to think of it. I might have overdone it over Christmas."

"Christmas was nearly three weeks ago," she points out.

"Guess it's taking a while for my system to stabilize." I raise a shoulder.

"And how long have you had this upset stomach?"

I bite the inside of my cheek. "About a week?"

Silence.

I glance up to find Isla staring at me.

I swallow down the morsel in my mouth and frown. "What?"

"Your stomach seems to tolerate the food okay, though."

"Huh." I glance down at the almost empty plate in front of me. "You should have seen me after I tried to eat breakfast this morning. I couldn't keep anything down. Actually," —I place the now empty glass down on the table— "it's been that way this entire week."

"You've been sick in the mornings?"

I nod.

"And you haven't been able to tolerate coffee or alcohol?"

I shake my head slowly.

"Hmm."

I grip the edge of the table with clammy fingers. "Oh, no, no, no. It's not what you think it is."

"I never said anything," she murmurs.

My heart seems to stop beating for a second, before starting up again. "It can't be. It can't be." I glance about the quickly filling room, then back at her. "Can it?"

"You tell me, honey. I assume you've been careful with all the horizontal action you've indulged in with—"

"Don't say his name," I rasp.

She raises her hands. "Okay."

"I'm on birth control." I grip the table tighter. "I can't be, I really can't be…" I can't say the P word. If I do, it will all seem very real. Besides, I don't need to say it aloud. "I'm not…you know." I tilt up my chin.

"Didn't say you were. But maybe it's worth testing?"

"Testing?" I feel the blood drain from my face.

"A—that word that I should not speak right now— test?" she says gently.

"Right." My head feels like it's dissociated from my body. I'm having an out-of-body experience. That's the only explanation for this strange conversation I'm having.

"Zara, babe. It's going to be okay." She wraps her arm about my shoulder. "You're going to be okay."

"There you are." Liam materializes next to Isla, then glances between us. "Everything okay?"

"Of course," both of us say at the same time.

His forehead furrows, but he doesn't push it. "There's someone I want you to meet," he tells Isla.

"Oh, but I want to stay with Zara," she protests.

"Nonsense, I'm fine, you go with Liam." I insist.

"It's not urgent," he starts, but I wave him off.

"Please, take your pretty wife and go mingle. That's what this shindig is for, after all."

"But—" Isla starts.

I turn and hug her. "I'm fine, and if I need anything, I'll message you."

She hugs me back. "Promise?"

"I promise."

She steps back and squeezes my shoulder. "You let me know how everything goes, okay?"

I swallow, knowing she's referring to the thing-I-shall-not-call-by-name test. "Okay," I manage to say in a voice that sounds nothing like the little butterflies of nervousness that have taken wing in my stomach.

She nods, then Liam takes her hand, and they walk away.

I stand at the table for a few more seconds. This is so not like me, hiding in a corner. I need to follow my own advice and get into the thick of things and live up to my reputation as The Shark. The woman who loves to mingle and talk to people, and keep her ear to the ground and find out the latest gossip doing the rounds—which at the moment, is not me, yet. My stomach curls in on itself. No, no, no, I'm not going to be sick, not now. I drain my glass of juice. To my relief, my stomach rights itself. Okay, that's good.

I grab my little bag and walk toward the crowd. The orchestra has struck up a waltz, and some of the guests have taken to the dance floor. The chandeliers in the ceiling pick out the colors of the dresses worn by the women. Tiny lights strung up at intervals turn the entire space into a fairytale setting. The architecture of the building is in the style of the Italian Renaissance, and it lends a storybook feel to the event.

Someone steps up to me. "Would you like to dance?" a voice asks from somewhere above me.

I turn to face a man whose features are familiar. He's tall, with broad shoulders and dark hair. Dressed in the obligatory coat tails, he looks dashing. Of course, he's not Hunter. Maybe it's time I stop thinking of Hunter for a while.

I take his proffered hand. "Why not?"

# 42

Hunter

"You're doing well in the polls," JJ Kane says as he puts his arm around his girlfriend. His much younger girlfriend who, at one point, was his son's girlfriend. But to see how happy he and Lena are now, you'd never know the journey they went through to get here.

The younger woman looks up at him with adoring eyes, before turning to me. "You have my vote, Minister."

"Thank you." I tilt my head.

"Your strategy to launch your campaign a little later than the other candidates paid off."

"Thanks to the hard work put in by my team," I demur.

"They've done a stellar job in getting you off to a good start." Sinclair Sterling joins with his wife Summer. Lena and Summer embrace. Sinclair takes two glasses of juice from the hovering waiter and passes one to Summer.

"Thanks, darling." She takes a sip while Sinclair places his own glass on the table between us.

I glance at the glass, then back at him.

"Summer's nursing; I'm keeping her company." He raises a shoulder.

"I told Sinclair he can drink for the both of us, but he insists he'll start drinking once I wean off the baby completely." Summer laughs.

"He's right." I raise my glass in their direction. "Parenting is bloody hard work, not that I know anything about it. But hats off to you guys, you're doing an incredible job."

"Sinclair's been so helpful. He insists on waking up at night when the baby starts crying and is really good at putting him back to bed."

"Good on you." JJ, too, raises his glass in their direction.

"This is our first night out in" —Sinclair shakes his head— "in forever. Speaking of," —he takes his wife's hand in his— "I'm going to take my wife dancing."

"Go for it." I laugh and take a sip of my champagne.

Sinclair pulls away with Summer. JJ turns to Lena and asks, "Want to dance?"

She shakes her head, then wraps her arm about his waist. "I'm happy to watch."

He pulls her even closer. "And I'm happy to watch you."

They share a look, and it's such an intimate moment, I feel like I'm intruding. "I think I need to get around and press the flesh and all that." I shuffle my feet.

JJ and Lena look at me. "You sure, you—" He looks past me and his jaw firms.

"What is it?"

Lena follows the direction of his glance and her gaze widens.

I begin to turn, when JJ shakes his head. "Don't."

I arch an eyebrow. "Meaning, I really need to look at this."

I glance over my shoulder, and all of my muscles coil. The hair on my forearms rises. I curl my fingers so tightly around the stem of the glass that it cracks. "Fuck." I swipe out my other hand and catch the thin bowl of the flute before it can roll over the side. I place it back on the table upside down so it doesn't fall, then shake out the champagne that's fallen on my hand. Luckily, I didn't cut myself. I pull out the handkerchief from my pocket and dry my fingers before stuffing the cloth back in my pocket.

"Excuse me."

I turn to leave, when JJ grips my shoulder. "Don't do anything stupid."

I hesitate.

"The paps are salivating for gossip. Your enemies can't wait for you to take a wrong step. It's your career at stake."

I set my lips.

"And hers," he adds.

I draw in a breath and force my muscles to relax. When I nod, he releases me. At which point, I turn and stalk toward where she's dancing with someone else. I know she has to circulate among the guests. It's her job. It comes with the territory of being a fixer. Of keeping an ear to the ground and staying abreast of events. I get that. But this… This is where I draw the line. She came to the event with me and now she's dancing with another. How dare she dance with another man?

There's something familiar about his stance, his features, but I'm positive I've never met this man before. He's much taller than her—as tall as me—and in comparison, she looks tiny, fragile. His swarthy looks complement her delicate ones. With his head of full dark hair, and Zara's dark locks that flow behind her, they make a striking couple.

My chest seizes. My heart pumps so hard, the beats reverberate through my cells. The bastard has his hand around her tiny waist, the other holding her hand. As I watch, he releases her waist, only to twirl her out then back toward him. She laughs, that full-bodied, hearty laugh that arrows straight to my cock. He leans forward, until his face is close to hers, until his mouth is close to her ear, until it feels like his entire body is a hair's breadth from enveloping hers. That's when something inside me snaps.

I weave through the people standing around the edge, then past the other dancing couples, to stand beside them.

For a second, they don't notice me, so engrossed are they in each other, and that only fuels this burning sensation that's flared in my chest.

"Let her go." I hear my words, and only then, do I realize I've spoken.

Both of them turn to face me.

Her features pale. "Hunter, we were just dancing."

I glare at her, then back at the motherfucker who still has his hands on her.

"Let her the fuck go."

He looks between us. "Are you with him?"

"I'm not," she snaps at the same time that I growl, "She is."

He frowns. "Maybe it's best I step back."

"That would be best for all of us, motherfucker," I growl.

"No need to swear." The man's lips firm. "I'll leave once I make sure Zara's okay." He turns to her. "You all right, Z?"

"The fuck?" He called her by a nickname? How dare he call her by a nickname. No one gets to do that, except me.

I glare down at where the bastard still has his hand on her hip. "Let her the fuck go."

"And if I don't?"

I raise my fist and bury it in his face.

---

"Really? Really?" She paces back-forth-back in the small room up the corridor from the ballroom where the gala was being held. "What were you thinking, Hunter?" she snaps.

*I wasn't thinking.*

I saw his hands on her and I swung and connected with his face. The stranger took the hit, staggered back, only to recover and swing at me. I ducked, of course, and growled at Zara to step aside, which she did. When I was sure she was at a safe enough distance I swung at him again, and we both went tumbling to the ground.

"You were lucky that Michael Sovrano happened to be there and caused a diversion by pulling the fire alarm," she rages at me.

Which also opened up the sprinklers in the ceiling of the ball room, and water rained down on us. It hit me with the impact of a cold shower. Literally. I pulled back; so did the stranger. We stared at each other, chests heaving, breath coming in pants. Logic dictates that's when I should have apologized to him for starting the fight. Which I hadn't.

"'Stay away from what's mine'? You growled at him to 'Stay away from what's mine'?" She turns on me, eyes spitting golden sparks, her hair clinging in long damp tendrils to her shoulders, and that gorgeous dress showing off the curves of her spectacular hips. "Who says something so Neanderthalish?"

"Is that a word in the English language?" I ask in a mild tone.

Her already pink cheeks now flush red. "That's what you take away from what I said?"

"Not only."

"Oh?" She plants her palms on her hips.

I nod. "I also know now that I can't bear it if anyone else dares touch you. If any man dare look at you again, I'm going to kill him."

She throws up her hands. "You've declared you're going to run for the top leadership position in this country. You can't afford to lose your temper at such a trivial matter."

"Trivial matter?" Anger punches my guts with such force, specks of black dot my vision. I rise to my feet and prowl toward her. "He. Had. His. Hands. On. You." I stop in front of her and glare into her features. "He was dancing with you. You were laughing at something he said, you—"

"He's my brother, Hunter."

I still. "Eh?"

"He's. My. Brother. Cade Kingston."

"That was Cade Kingston, aka the King, the Captain of the English Cricket Team?"

She nods.

I shake my head. "He looks different from his pictures."

"He shaved off his beard and his hair."

Of course, I know Cade Kingston is her brother. And there was something familiar about him... But I was so consumed by anger, and he looked so different from his pictures, I never, in a million years, would have recognized him as her brother.

I rub the back of my neck. "Fuck, fuckity, fuck."

"Indeed." She folds her arms across her chest. "If you had paused to think for one minute, or better still, decided to think with something else other than your dick—"

"Which is very difficult for me to do where you're concerned."

"—you'd have noticed that he had his hands on me, not in a lover-like fashion, but in a brotherly manner."

I lower my hand to my side. "He still had his hands on you."

"Didn't you just hear what I said?" She scowls up at me. "He. Is. My. Brother."

"He was a man. He was someone other than me. And he was touching you."

She throws up her hands. "So?"

"So?" I bend my knees, peer into her eyes. "I will not tolerate you being with anyone else. I will set fire to the world before I let anyone else touch you, and that includes any sibling of yours."

"Jesus Christ, give me patience." She draws in a breath, then stabs her finger into my chest. "This passion of yours? This obsessive attention to what you want, this forgetting everything else except the one thing most important to you? This…this…all-consuming fervor is what you need to bring to the campaign trail."

I blink. "You're comparing what I feel for you to the emotions I need to bring to the campaign trail?"

"Absolutely."

I glare at her. She pales but doesn't look away.

"This fire inside of you, this need to go after what you want, this absolute focus that you have for me, it's the most flattering thing in the world.".

"It's how I feel about you," I growl.

"It's the true you." She flattens her palm against my chest. "The one you need to show to your constituents. To this country."

This woman, only she could take my words and turn them on me, and yet…a part of me wonders if she doesn't speak the truth. Is this what's been missing in the run up to my campaign? Why I haven't been able to galvanize my efforts behind this program? Why it felt empty, even to me, like something was missing? Why I feel alive only when I'm with her? Why I need her beside me to feel whole?

"You're right."

Now, it's her turn to look taken aback. "I am?"

I nod. "Since I met you, something inside of me, something I didn't even know I had, came to life. Until now, I'd been following the path that was expected of me. Well also, my instinct dictated this was right for me. That deep inside I do want to serve my country. But it's only when I'm with you that I feel inclined to follow my truth. Because you are my truth, Zara."

The color drains from her face. She pulls her hand back, but I curl my fingers about her wrist. "Don't. Don't deny what's between us."

"Hunter, but—"

"No buts. You saw me out there. You saw how I'm unable to control myself around you. And you're right. I need to bring that passion, that visceral feeling when you want something to the exclusion of every-thing else, that ruthless determination to succeed, that aggressive, tenacious urge for domination that I feel when I'm with you, that I sense only when I'm with you. I need to become it. I am all of this when you are with me, by my side. When I'm in your presence, I am alive. It's your proximity that fires me up. It's your look, your touch, the feel of your skin on mine, your breath entwined with mine, the thud of your heart echoing mine, the drumbeat of your pulse mirroring mine... It's always been you."

"Hunter, don't," she whispers.

She tries to pull away, but I hold onto her.

"I'm only truly me when I'm holding your hand, Zara."

I lower my gaze to where I clasp her wrist.

She follows my gaze.

I place my other palm on hers, enfolding her smaller one between both of mine, then I go down on bended knee.

# 43

Zara

"Wait, what? He proposed to you?" Solene screeches.

I hold the phone away from my ear and glance toward Isla, who's seated in the chair opposite mine. Isla raises a shoulder in a gesture that embodies the confusion I'm feeling right now.

"It would seem that way." I turn back to the screen.

"And what did you tell him?"

"Nothing."

Solene's gaze widens. "You didn't give him an answer?"

"Nope." Strictly speaking, I couldn't have given him an answer before, I was too busy gathering my jaw off the floor. He went down on one knee and asked me to marry him in this very room, and I was dumbstruck. A first. I stared at him for a few seconds, then pulled my hand from his. And this time, he let me. I backed away from him until the backs of my knees hit this very chair—where I'm still seated—and I sat down heavily.

Thankfully, I was saved from replying because Liam and Isla burst through the doorway immediately after.

Isla had one look at my face, walked over to me, and took my hand in hers, while I tried and failed to look anywhere but at Hunter's face. When I finally made eye contact, his blue-green eyes seemed almost colorless. His features, as if hewn from a material that gave no inkling of what his thoughts were.

"I'll be waiting for your answer," he bit out, then walked out of here, with Liam on his heels. I began to tell Isla what had happened, and she told me to stop and dialed in Solene so I could bring them up to speed on the soap opera that is currently my life.

My phone vibrates, then again. Yep, I have a second phone hidden away in the secret compartment of my bag. What? I'm a PR professional and the media is my lifeblood. You didn't think I was going to stay without my electronic lifeline for even a second, did you? Only this time, I haven't dared check my inbox, or my messages, or any of the social media channels…yet.

Given the crisis of Mount Everest proportions I walked out of earlier, I know things must be going crazy on the internet. But it's not going to help if I get drawn into the online speculation. Right after Hunter left, I called my team, briefed them, then told them to reach out to key influencers for damage control. If things were really bad, they'd call me, but considering fifteen minutes have passed and there've been no SOS calls to me…yet… Maybe we managed to nip this thing in the bud. I'm not holding my breath, though. While the hours and days after a slip-up like what happened earlier between Hunter and Cade is the stuff bloggers and social media users around the world are waiting to broadcast to their followers, the long-tail effect of it surfacing in the future at the most inopportune moment is nothing to be sneezed at.

"So, what are you going to tell Hunter?" Solene asks.

I exchange glances with Isla, then shake my head. "I don't have the foggiest."

"What does your instinct tell you to do?" Isla murmurs.

"To get the hell away from here. To refuse to be his PR manager. To cut all ties and move to another country and reinvent my life."

There's silence for a second, then Solene laughs. "You'd never do that. You're not the type to do a runner. You're the strongest woman I know, Zara. In fact, I've always aspired to be you when I grow up."

I flush a little. "Don't be daft, Sabatini, I'm hardly the poster child for how to live your life."

"You're doing a fabulous job of it so far, Zara."

"That's why I had a one night, which became a two night stand, with the possible Prime Minister to be of this country, and I might be pregnant with his child."

Silence descends on the room.

Isla looks at me with concern in her eyes. Solene stares at me with a shocked expression.

A woman clears her throat. "Umm, sorry, don't mind me. Cade sent me in to make sure you were okay. But uh, I'll just tell him you're fine."

I glance up to find a woman standing at the doorway. I scowl at her, and she raises her hands, palms face up. "The door was open."

*Fantastic.*

"Who're you again?" I manage to choke out.

"Uh, I'm Cade's friend's sister. Cade didn't have a date to the gala, that's the only reason he asked me to the ball and… Oh, god, I'm talking too much, aren't I? I swear, I didn't mean to barge in and listen to your secrets. And no, I didn't just hear you say that you're pregnant —I mean, possibly pregnant—with the child of the man who might be our next Prime Minister and… Hey, are you going to marry him?" She seems to run out of steam, finally, and glances between me and Isla. If Isla's face looks anything like mine, it's a combination of shock, horror, surprise, frustration, and maybe even a glimmer of humor—because, let's face it, there's a touch of absurdity to the proceedings.

Isla is the first to recover. She rises to her feet, marches to the door, shuts and locks it, then gestures to the sofa. "Take a seat please— what's your name again?"

"Abigail. My friends call me Abby... But you guys are not my friends... Yet... But I'd like you to be. You're Cade's sister, after all." She looks at me with big doe eyes that carry more than a touch of hero-worship in them. Oh, god, she has a crush on my brother, and it seems, by transference, on me.

"Umm, Abigail—"

"Call me Abby, please." She locks her fingers together in front of her in a gesture that hints at her nervousness.

"Abby, please do sit down." I nod toward the sofa.

"Of course." She heads for the sofa, sinks into it, then glances between the two of us again.

"So, you're Zara's brother's girlfriend?" Solene asks from the phone.

Abby presses a hand to her chest. "Oh, no, no, no, not his girl-friend." Her cheeks pink. "I'm, uh, his friend's sister."

"And you came with him to the ball," Isla murmurs before taking her seat again.

"Yes, and I saw what happened." Abby turns to me. "That was some fight, huh? They both held their own."

"Is Cade okay?" I ask.

"He has a shiner, but that only makes him look even more dashing." She bites the inside of her lip.

Isla and I exchange another glance.

"So, about what you heard when you walked in—"

"Oh, you don't have to worry." Abby waves her hand in the air. "It's been forgotten. I promise. In one ear, out the other. Nothing to it. Also, I know how to keep secrets." She mimes zipping her lips.

"Hmph." I look closely at her. Her gaze is open. Her expression indicates she has nothing to hide.

"No, really. I know when a person says that, you think the next thing they'll do is turn around and blab out the secret to everyone. But I understand how difficult it must be to conduct a relationship when all the media attention is on you. So, you can count on my discretion."

I press a finger to my cheek. Can I believe her? Should I believe her? More to the point, when did I become so cynical that I couldn't take a person at face value? Oh, wait, that's because I work in a cut-throat profession, where I'm trained to disbelieve the words of people, and normally, they deliver on my suspicions. Still, my instinct says Abby made an honest mistake, and she means it when she says she's not going to tell a soul. Doesn't mean I'm not going to find a way to ensure she sticks to her word. "So, Abby, what is it you said you do?"

"Uh, I'm interning at a communications agency."

"Oh?" I tilt my head. "And are you looking for a career change?"

# 44

Zara

"Smart thinking, offering her a job," Isla says after Abby has left.

Solene, too, signs off—after asking me to keep her posted on the results of the pregnancy test I promised I'm going to take as soon as I fire-fight the fall-out from the impromptu sparring session that my brother and my boss—who's also my lover—indulged in.

"That old adage about keeping your enemies where you can see them? It's a technique I've used more than once." Not that Abby is my enemy. Far from it. The girl almost fainted when I offered her a job as an executive in my agency. A step up from the unpaid intern position she's held for the past six months. She thanked me profusely and promised to do her best. I took her up on the offer by telling her to research all media mentions—if any—from the earlier incident. I lean back in my seat and place my hands over my stomach, which hasn't felt very steady over the past ten seconds.

Isla levels me with another look of concern. "Do you think you really are—"

"Pregnant?" I force myself to say the word. "I haven't taken the test yet, but my instincts are screaming that I am. Considering I'm already a week late."

"It might just be all the stress you're under."

"I thrive on stress. I've never had a day that hasn't brought with it new stress, and I've never been late."

"Hmm." She taps her fingers on the armrest. "Will you tell him?"

"I don't know," I say honestly.

"I suppose it's opportune that he proposed to you?"

I scowl at her. "I'm not going to marry him just because I'm pregnant."

"It's as good a reason as any."

"When—if—I marry, it will be because not only am I in love with the man, but I also see him as a partner in every way."

"And you don't with Hunter?"

I squeeze the bridge of my nose. "I don't know."

"I think you do know, but you don't want to accept it."

"Eh?" I lower my arm and stare at her. "What are you talking about?"

"You've been prejudiced against Hunter from the beginning. You've held his background against him."

"No, I haven't." I gape at her.

"Haven't you?" She half-smiles. "It's normal, though. You've worked hard to get to where you are, and a part of you resents that he seems to have gotten everything so easily."

I squirm in my seat. Is that true? Do I begrudge Hunter his success so far? Have I held him up to a standard of my own making and found him lacking? Just because he was born into money... Do I hold that against him? Is his success less credible because he, seemingly, didn't have to jump through the hoops to get to where he is, unlike me? I lower my chin to my chest. "Oh, god, Isla, do you think I've misjudged him? Do you think I'm holding him up to a standard that he could never match?"

"Zara, I—"

A knock on the door interrupts us. Then Liam pops his head through. "Everything okay in here?"

"Hey, babe," Isla beckons to him. Liam walks over to Isla and leans a hip against her armrest. The two of them kiss, and they've only been separated for half an hour. Gosh, they're so sweet together, it's almost too much.

I hear footsteps before Hunter enters the room, followed by my brother. Cade sports a shiner, which only adds to his good looks. The two of them stop halfway inside the room, then glower at each other. O-k-a-y, so apparently, whatever they were discussing didn't go down well.

Isla rises to her feet. "I think Liam and I are gonna leave now." She walks over to me and kisses my cheek. "Keep me posted on everything," she says in a low voice. I nod and hug her back. She steps back, then heads for my brother.

"I'm Isla, Zara's friend."

Cade's features break into a smile. "My pleasure." He brings her hand to his lips and kisses it.

Liam instantly closes the distance to them and wraps his arm about Isla. "Well played on your last innings. That was some record-breaking century you made." He's referring to the last cricket match, where my brother scored enough to win the tournament for his team.

"Thanks, man!" He releases Isla's hand, and nods in Liam's direction.

Liam holds out his hand, "Liam Kincaid."

"Cade Kingston."

The two men shake hands.

"Looking forward to seeing you play at Lord's next month." Liam refers to the upcoming match at the well-known cricket grounds.

"Can't wait to play there; it's my favorite venue," Cade acknowledges.

"We'll be off then." Liam heads toward the door with Isla in tow. He and Hunter exchange chin jerks in the manner of friends who know each other enough to say a lot to each other without saying anything. The door snicks shut.

I glance between the two men who are resolutely not looking at each other. Which means both of them are glowering at me. I blow out a breath. "Care to take a seat? Or do the two of you prefer to stand there and ignore each other?"

"Prefer to ignore each other," they reply at the same time.

A dull ache stabs behind my eyes. My stomach jumps in response. I rub at my temple and resist the urge to rub at my stomach. Oh, god, I can't really be preggers... And if I am? Best to wait until I have a positive test before I begin to panic, though truth be told, a part of me already knows.

"Zara, you okay?" Hunter's voice reaches me. I open my eyes, take in the concern on his features.

"What do you think? My boss beat up my brother, and you've probably made tabloid headlines with that asinine stunt."

My brother winces. "It's not pleasant to get on her bad side," he says in a conversational tone.

"So I'm learning." Hunter's lips twitch.

They finally look at each other, twin expressions of wariness on their features. Apparently, they're in agreement about something, and naturally, it involves their opinion of me. I make a sound at the back of my throat, and both men look at me in alarm.

"You sure you're okay, Z?" My brother—the clunkerhead asks.

"Don't keep asking me that as if I am an airhead who needs to be mollycoddled."

Cade raises both his hands. "Just brotherly concern, is all."

"And where were you all these months? You take off touring the world on your job, then show up at a gala. You could have told me you were going to attend."

"I didn't know you would be here," my brother protests.

"The biggest event of the season, with influencers, entertainers and politicians in attendance, and you didn't think my job would demand that I be all over it?"

My brother drags his fingers through his hair. "You're right. I should have thought it through. Should have reached out and checked how you were doing. I took the easy way out and stayed away so I wouldn't have to visit the folks. And calling you would have reminded me that I haven't been in touch with them, either." He raises a shoulder. "That was cowardly of me; I'm sorry."

I deflate a little. It's tough when your sibling is being all reasonable.

Hunter looks from Cade to me, then back to Cade. "How did I not spot the similarity?"

"Probably because you had your head stuck up your arse?" I retort.

Cade whistles. Hunter seems like he's having a difficult time controlling his mirth.

I glower at him. "You won't be laughing when your reputation is all over social media, and the two of you become a meme."

He leans forward on the balls of his feet. "No phones in the ballroom, remember?"

I scoff. "Do you think everyone in there followed the rules? There's bound to have been someone who had a phone stashed away. Someone who, at this very moment, is uploading footage from your faux pas to the internet, as we speak."

The knobhead grins. He actually grins. "You forget, I have the best PR manager in town who will, undoubtedly, stop anything like this from happening," he murmurs.

"You could have saved me the headache and simply used your grey cells—which I assume you have, considering you're vying for the topmost post in the country—and stopped yourself before landing that first punch," I snap.

Hunter draws himself to his full height. "I saw a stranger with his hands all over you. What the hell would you have me do?"

"You should have trusted me."

"I cannot look the other way when my—"

"Stop," I bark, darting my brother a glance. Thankfully, like most men, he's clueless enough about the undercurrents in the room. If anything, he looks uncomfortable.

"Uh, Abby's waiting for me outside. I think it's best I leave so the two of you can sort things out."

"No," I burst out.

"That would be a good idea." Hunter nods.

Hunter and I glare at each other for a few seconds.

This is when the penny drops for Cade, for he suddenly squares his shoulders. "Hold on, are you—" He glances at Hunter. "You're not—" He looks at me. "Are the two of you— Are you—"

"No," I snap.

"Yes." Hunter nods. "Your sister and I are in a relationship. In fact, I asked her to marry me."

# 45

Hunter

"You're marrying him?" Cade asks.

"I haven't answered him yet," Zara interjects at the same time.

"Right." Cade drags his fingers through his hair. "I guess I'd best let you two figure this out, but first…" He lowers his hand, and in a move I didn't see coming, he steps up to me and grabs me by my collar. "You hurt her, and you'll have me to contend with."

I curl my fingers into fists at my sides, more out of instinct than out of a need to avoid picking a fight with him again. Also, he's her brother. Of course, it's natural he'd threaten me. Especially, now that he realizes I'm not just a jealous boyfriend, but a potential husband.

"You hear me?" he growls.

"Crystal clear." I step forward so the toes of our boots collide. "You and I need to have a catch up, separately."

"No, you don't." Zara jumps to her feet.

"You bet," Cade says at the same time.

"Bloody hell." Zara seems to sway, then sinks back down in her chair.

I twist myself out of Cade's grasp and leap toward her. "Hey, Fire, you okay?" I squat down in front of her. "What's wrong? Are you dizzy? Is it because of the stress from what happened? I'm sorry it came to that. I promise, I'll never pick a fight again—not unless I absolutely have to." I take her hand between mine, and her fingers are cold.

"Fuck!" I turn to Cade. "Dr. Weston Kincaid—he's on my phone list. Call him; tell him he needs to get here pronto.

"No doctor," Zara says weakly.

"Save your strength, baby." I pull out my phone, unlock it, and toss it at Cade. He snatches it out of the air, then steps out of the room.

"Stop with the histrionics." She scowls. Her voice is stronger, but her color is still pale.

"I will not make any compromises when it comes to your health."

"Do you have any idea how cavemanlike you sound?" she murmurs. Her expression is far from being angry though. If anything, there's a softening around her eyes.

"I'm glad I'm living up to my reputation."

"Also,"—her brow furrows—"how do you have your phone with you?"

"How do you have yours with you?"

Her lips curve, and god, her smile is so beautiful, so bewitching, so everything. I bring her hand to my mouth and kiss her fingertips.

Her phone buzzes. She reaches for it, but I get to her bag first. I hold it up and out of her reach.

"Hey, gimme my phone."

"Not until the doc has checked you out and pronounced you okay."

"I really am okay, Hunter." She says softly.

"Let the doc give you a clean bill of health."

She looks between my eyes, then blows out a breath. "Fine, if he says I'm okay, then I walk out of here, on my own steam, and you don't follow me."

"No fucking way. You came with me, and I'll drop you back home."

"Let your chauffeur drop me off, but I'll ride alone. After all the speculation that is, no doubt, circulating amongst the guests, it's the least we can do to ensure no other gossip spreads."

"I don't fucking care what people say."

"But I do. I care about your campaign. I want to see you elected, Hunter."

I set my jaw, then take in the expression on her features. They mirror the stubbornness that is my hallmark, and which I'm recognizing is also second nature to her. "You're not budging on this, are you?"

---

"So, she's okay then?" JJ leans over and tops up my glass of whiskey. When he offers the bottle to Sinclair, he refuses. As does Michael. Both men are not drinking for the duration that their wives are still nursing.

"She seemed fine when I dropped her home, but I don't understand why she didn't allow me to be in the room when the doctor examined her." I peer into the depths of my glass.

Cade had reached Weston, who'd turned up in the next ten minutes. At which point, Zara insisted I leave. I refused and she grew increasingly agitated. Weston pulled me aside and told me it was best to respect her wishes. I didn't want her to get more stressed—her health is of paramount importance—so I removed myself from the room.

I paced outside for the half-hour it took for the doctor to complete the examination. Cade watched me with curiosity on his features, but he didn't ask me any further questions about my relationship with his sister. Thank fuck. Meanwhile, her phone vibrated non-stop, as did mine. I refused to look at either of the screens. Truth is, I wasn't able to focus on anything, until Weston finally came out of the room. He had a strange look on his face, and for a second, my stomach plummeted to my toes. Then he smiled and reassured me that she was fine. Maybe a little exhausted. Nothing that a good night's sleep wouldn't cure.

The tension drained out of my shoulders and I felt faint. Only then, did I realize how overwrought I'd been about her condition. Somewhat reassured, I thanked him and walked into the room to find her on her feet. Adamant woman insisted she was fine. She then told me I needed to tell my chauffeur to drop her home. I was having none of it.

No way, was I letting her be driven back on her own. Much to her consternation, I told her I was breaking my word and driving back with her. Cade supported me, and it was both of us against her, so she finally backed down.

I had the car come around to the back door so we could get in without any prying eyes. Then I took her to her apartment, insisted on seeing her up, and tucked her into bed. By then, she was so exhausted, she didn't protest. She fell asleep as soon as her head hit the pillow. I covered her up and placed her phone—after putting it on silent—next to her bed. I stayed there watching over her until the wee hours of this morning, then I came home and put in a full day's work, before arriving at the 7A Club. I walked into the private room which has become the unofficial meeting place for me and the rest of the Seven, as well as the Sovranos, and those known to us.

"You respected her privacy and left the room when the doctor examined her? I'm assuming you have eyes on her." Michael tips his chin in my direction.

"I'm running for office. I need to uphold the highest levels of ethics" —I glance between the faces of my friends— "but when it comes to her, there are no rules. I'll do anything to ensure she's safe. Even if it means protecting her from herself."

"So, you have eyes on her." Michael nods.

"On her phone, her laptop, in her house." And now, I'll finally find out why she kept evading the investigator I had on her. Y-e-p, that's me, wading out into the morally gray area.

While Zara slept, I called in Axel Sovrano and his security team. Axel is Michael's younger brother. An ex-cop, he now runs an agency and can be counted on for discretion. I explained what I needed, and he obliged. His team moved in within the hour and put the security measures in place.

After the team left, I brewed a fresh pot of coffee for Zara, and left a plate of breakfast for her. Woman needs to eat to keep up her strength, after all. Only then, did I leave.

"You do realize, this doesn't bode well for you? What you did is bound to come out, at some point. And when it does, she's going to be pissed." Sinclair drums his fingers on the arm of his chair.

"That's a bridge I'll have to cross when I get to it."

"I understand why you did it, but don't put off sharing what you did with her for too long. It's best to come clean."

"Shouldn't the leader to-be of this country keep his reputation clean at all costs?" A new voice announces.

I glance up, spot Cade at the door and groan. "The fuck you doing here?"

"I could ask the lot of you the same question." He glances about the table. The shiner around his eye is an interesting shade of purple. Not that I regret putting it there, in the first place.

Only, he's Zara's brother... Her twin...which means, I need to repair the relationship between us. That's the only reason I jerk my chin in his direction. "Have the rest of you met Cade?"

JJ is the first to beckon him in. "Great last inning at Lord's."

"Thanks." Cade walks over to JJ and holds out his hand. "Cade Kingston."

JJ shakes it. "JJ Kane."

"Sinclair Sterling."

"Michael Sovrano."

The men shake hands.

"Cade also happens to be Zara's brother," I interject.

The men glance at him, then at me.

"Ah." JJ lights up his cigar. "I can see the resemblance. Why do the two of you have different surnames though?"

"I took my mother's surname. Zara took my father's." He raises a shoulder. "Family dynamics can be complex."

"Tell me about it," JJ says in a self-deprecating tone. I have no doubt he's referring to the relationship between him and Lena, and his son. "These things have a way of working themselves out though," he offers.

"You haven't met my family." Cade shakes his head. "Speaking of...how's Zara?" He turns to me.

"She seemed fine, last I saw her." Which was through the camera app on my phone, which showed she was back at work in her office. She seemed fine, on the face of it, at least. Checking in on her, making sure she's okay, now that I could see her with the swipe of the screen, is getting to be a dangerous addiction. At least, I've managed to curb myself from doing so since arriving at the Club.

"And the fallout from the V&A Ball?"

"Seems to have been minimal." I also authorized Axel's team to track down anyone who got a hold of clips from the event and pay them to take them down. He'll be the front for all of the proceedings; my name will be kept out of it completely. Not that I don't trust Zara and her team to handle it, but if I can spare her the stress of finding any reference to the bout between Cade and me, then it could only be helpful for her, right?

"I assume that's where the shiner is from?" Sinclair jerks his chin in Cade's direction. I filled them in on what went down at the ball but left out the fact that Cade is Zara's brother. Now, all three men dart me knowing looks. Yeah, so it was stupid of me to swing without thinking, and I'm loathe to apologize for it. Except, he's Zara's brother. So…

I square my shoulders, "If it's any consolation, you got in a few good ones, too." I move my jaw from side to side.

"I should hope so." He flexes his fingers. The skin over his knuckles is raw.

"I owe you an apology." I hold out my hand.

He stares down at it, then at me. "This doesn't change anything. Zara may come across as strong, but she's fragile inside. She's one hell of a survivor, and you don't deserve her."

"In this, I am with you." I tilt my head.

His scowl deepens. "Hurt her, and I'll break your jaw next time."

"If I hurt her, I won't stop you," I concur.

He finally takes my hand. "For Zara's sake," he mutters.

We shake, then both of us pull our hands back. That's when my phone vibrates. I glance at the camera app, then rise to my feet.

"Good meeting you." I manage to infuse a note of sincerity in my voice, then turn to the others. "Later ol' chaps."

I head out of the club, then direct my chauffeur to take me to her place. Twenty minutes later, I'm pressing the doorbell to her apartment.

I hear movement behind the door before it swings open. "You?"

# 46

Zara

"Expecting someone else?" Hunter smirks from his position against my door frame.

"A grocery delivery, actually." I tip up my chin.

"Lying, Fire?" His smirk widens.

"You're the politician, not me, remember?"

He chuckles. "Touché, Councillor."

"Wish you wouldn't call me that. I'm not a practicing lawyer anymore."

"Your skills at verbal comebacks remain as sharp."

I widen my gaze. "Is that an honest-to-god compliment?"

"Not the only one I've given you." He lowers his voice, and his tone is so intimate, I can't stop the shiver that crawls up my spine.

"What are you doing here?"

"I've come to take you out."

"I don't recall agreeing to come out with you." I scoff.

"It's a last-minute...work thing." He schools his features into an expression of absolute innocence.

*Work thing, my arse.* "Is that what they're calling it nowadays?"

"Not my fault if your mind went to places it shouldn't."

I flush. "I'm not going anywhere with you."

"Are you saying you're refusing the candidate for whom you're running a PR campaign, and your defacto boss, to meet him on an important work situation?"

I blow out a breath. "The groceries—"

"Message them and delay the delivery to tomorrow," he orders.

"Oh, so now you're changing my grocery schedule to suit your needs?"

"Wouldn't you change your schedule to suit my needs?" he murmurs.

"Now who's mind is in the gutter?"

He raises his hands. "I'm simply asking you out to a business meeting, is all."

"If I postpone the grocery delivery, I won't have anything to eat tonight." My voice sounds whiny, even to me. Jesus, when did I become such a complaining little bitch?

"Which is why I'm taking you out to dinner."

---

"How did you pull this off?" I glance down at the blanket he's laid out on the floor of the House of Commons, in the Palace of Westminster. Yep, the same House of Commons which is covered so often on TV when the members of the ruling party face the opposition during Question Time, which takes place from Monday to Thursday during working hours. Today is a Friday. It's also after office hours, so the entire Parliamentary building is deserted.

"You should know better than to ask me that." He places the picnic basket at the edge of the blanket. He hauled it in from his car and up many steep flights of steps, all without breaking a sweat or getting out of breath, annoyingly.

I take a slow turn, taking in the galleries on either side of the floor.

The benches, as well as other furnishings in the chamber, are green in color, a custom which goes back 300 years. The adversarial layout—with benches facing each other is, in fact, a relic of the original use of the first permanent Commons Chamber on the site, St. Stephen's Chapel. There's so much history in this room. If I shut my eyes, I can almost hear the echoes of the voices of a debate between the ruling and opposition parties.

"You had a picnic basket in the trunk of your car when you came to my apartment?"

He straightens, then fixes me with that trademark Hunter look—raised eyebrow, smirk on his lips, and that part-innocent, part-wicked gleam in his eyes, which seem to imply all the world's a stage, he's a player, and everything is done in the spirit of good fun. Also, if he's done anything wrong, then he'll be happy to ask forgiveness... After the fact.

"You have quite the ego about you, don't you?"

"Which we have established many a time." He pulls out his phone and swipes his finger over the screen. The lights in the chamber dim.

"No way." I shake my head. "You arranged for mood lighting?"

"Not only." Another flick of his finger, and a melodic aria wafts from his phone speaker. He leans the phone against the basket, then straightens and holds out his hand.

When I hesitate, he chuckles. "I won't bite."

"Don't you?" I murmur.

His nostrils pulse. His blue-green eyes take on a midnight hue, a tell-tale sign he's aroused. A cloud of heat wafts off of his chest. It slams into me and seems to pin me in place. I gasp, unable to move, unable to do anything other than appreciate his sheer assuredness—this complete sense of rightness that fills me whenever we are together. He must sense some of the emotions running through me, for he closes the distance between us. He wraps his arm about my shoulders and pulls me in. I rest my forehead against his chest, then after a second, fold my own arms about his waist. We sway in place, as the haunting notes from the classical ditty fill the space.

"La fleur que tu m'avais jetée from Carmen, otherwise known as The Flower Song," he murmurs.

"It's beautiful." I close my eyes, and for the first time since I woke up in my bed and found him gone, my muscles relax. The stresses of the day fade away, and I lean closer. His arm tightens around me. He tucks my head under his chin. The thump-thump-thump of his heart is a reassuring vibration against my cheek. His dark scent is as familiar as my own. Some time, over the last few months, he crept under my skin, into my blood, and occupies my every thought and dirty fantasy. He's become a part of me, without my realizing it. Or maybe, I was very aware of it and did nothing to stop it. Either way, I can't deny the fact that I've come to depend on him. When I opened the door earlier and saw him, a flush of joy spread through my chest. Oh, I hid it behind the smart words I lobbed at him, but deep inside, I felt as if it were Christmas all over again. Pun intended. He rubs his palm over my back in slow circles, and a tingling grips my limbs.

Neither of us speak, and the notes of the aria replace any lingering stresses that may have hidden in my cells. The last strains fade away, and we continue dancing, slowly...slower...until we come to a stop, arms about each other. Neither of us seems to want to move. I wish I could capture this hushed silence, so full of everything in my heart, so I can take it out later when this moment is gone, as time inevitably does.

"Baby, I think we need to feed you." His voice rumbles under my cheek.

I shake my head, not wanting to pull away. Not wanting to separate from him yet.

Then my stomach grumbles.

"Definitely need to feed you." His eyes flash, and I wonder if what he's thinking of putting in my mouth is something more than what's in the basket.

I slide my hand between us and place it on the thickness between his thighs that made itself known a little earlier.

His nostrils flare. Then he leans down and presses a hard kiss to my lips. "First food, of the nourishing variety." He pulls back, then urges me to sink down onto the picnic blanket

"That was some spread." I pat my mouth with the paper towel that was packed into the basket. We ate from plates of the ceramic variety, with cutlery that wasn't plastic. He offered me champagne, and when I declined, he didn't push it. Or asked questions. He simply poured me some sparkling apple juice, which was delicious.

"I still can't believe you arranged for all of this." I place my now empty plate on the blanket and glance about the room.

"It had to mean something to you."

I narrow my gaze on him. "Am I that easy to read?"

"You trained to be a lawyer, then got into PR because of your love for the media. And you come into your element when trading arguments with me. You've also taken on some high-profile politicians as clients and prevented their names from being marred by scandals. It doesn't take a genius to realize you love politics."

I look away. How can he see me this clearly? When my own family, and perhaps, many of my friends have not.

"Hey, don't hide from me." He reaches over and tucks a strand of hair behind my ear. "Why didn't you get into politics yourself?"

I shoot him a startled glance.

"I'm sure the thought crossed your mind." He holds my gaze.

"I did think about it," I concede. "But the timing didn't feel quite right."

"When you marry me, you'll have the chance to set that right."

I place my glass on the blanket and scowl at him. "I haven't agreed to anything."

"You will."

"A-n-d there he is. Just when I thought we were getting along so well."

"Don't change the topic. You were born for a political career. With your communication skills, your intelligence, your background—"

"You mean my working-class credentials will complement your privileged one and portray a more holistic dimension to the voters."

He frowns. "I meant you are a product of modern British society. You stand for everything that is right with the system. You are a role model for so many young girls. Your being by my side will send a positive message across parties."

I shake my head. "It will never work."

"Why won't you give us a chance? Just once, why can't you open your mind to the possibility that this could work?"

"Because…" I shake my head. "Because I can't."

"If you mean Olly—"

"Don't mention Olly." I rise to my feet so quickly, my head spins. I must stumble, because the next second, he's gripping my arms and steadying me.

"You okay, Zara?"

I shake my head. "I'd like to go home now."

"Look at me." He takes me by my shoulders. "I'm sorry if I distressed you. That wasn't my intention at all."

I glance away.

"You don't give me much to go on. You don't share anything with me. It's why I keep trying to push you, even though I know it's wrong."

When I refuse to meet his eyes, he blows out his breath. "Zara, please, I really didn't mean to hurt you."

"And yet, you did." I turn and narrow my gaze on him. "Can we go back now, please?"

# 47

Hunter

"Are you sure she's okay?" I barked down the phone.

"Are you questioning my professional judgment?" Weston growls back.

I drag my fingers through my hair, then squeeze the bridge of my nose. "No, of course not. I'm sorry I woke you up so late."

There's a pause. "It comes with the territory," Weston finally says. "I can assure you that there's nothing wrong with Zara's health. As for the rest, it's up to her when she chooses to confide in you." He cuts the call.

I stare at my screen, then place my phone down on the table. So, she's all right. There's nothing wrong with her. Yet, she definitely seemed to pale when she rose to her feet too quickly earlier at our impromptu picnic. And then, she got upset when I mentioned Olly. Which was a tactical mistake. But she had to have known I'd have found out about her youngest sibling's death due to an accident when he was three years old.

She was only nineteen when he died, and she left home shortly after. I didn't mean to bring it up, but I wanted to reassure her that whatever's in her background that might be stopping her from considering a future with me, it doesn't matter. I didn't expect her to get so upset when I mentioned Olly. Which, I now realize, is understandable. Losing a sibling, especially one that young, would have been devastating for her. And I brought it up without any consideration for her feelings. After that faux pas on my part, we packed up the remnants of our picnic dinner. I dropped her off at home, made sure she locked her door behind her, and returned to my office, knowing there'd be no sleep for me tonight.

I lean back in my chair and stare at my blank computer screen. Something doesn't compute. Why is she so resistant to a relationship with me? Sure, she's my PR manager and part of my campaign team, but I want to be open about our relationship. Yes, it would bring a whole new level of scrutiny of us. It would mean changing the scope of her role from being only responsible for PR to weighing in on the bigger decisions, by my side. A warmth fills my chest at the thought. She would be perfect. She was made for that role. No, fact is, she was made for bigger things than being campaign manager. By my side, she could impact larger decisions. She could carve out a role for herself, one that complements my political career and which, no doubt, would be much more fulfilling than being a fixer. So, what's stopping her?

I squeeze the bridge of my nose, when my phone buzzes. At the same time, my computer screen springs to life with the ding of an email, then another, and another. My phone buzzes again, then rings. I pick it up, spot Zara's name and answer it at once.

"Everything okay?"

"They found us out, Hunter." Her face fills the screen. "We're all over social media," she cries.

"What?"

"Yes. There's a picture of us—"

"What picture?"

"I'll send you a link." She looks down into the screen, then my phone vibrates. I click through the link she sends me to the news in a tabloid. There's a picture of her and me, shot through a window. It's grainy, but clear enough. There's no mistaking the two faces in profile. Zara is reaching up to wipe something from the corner of my mouth. We're both laughing and looking at each other in a way that leaves no room for doubt. It's a picture of two people who have feelings for each other.

"It's from the breakfast at the diner," I murmur.

She nods grimly. "What are we going to do?"

I rise to my feet. "I'm coming to you."

"No—" she cries out. "I mean, there are already paparazzi pulling up outside my door."

"All the more reason that I be there."

"But—"

"No buts. You stay where you are and—"

"No, you listen to me. I'm the PR professional here—"

"And you're my—"

"My—?" She narrows her gaze. There's something like a dare in her voice.

"You're my everything, Zara. Whatever we have to do, we'll face it together."

Her face crumples. A tear slides down her cheek.

My heart stutters. "No, don't cry, baby. I promise, we'll come out of this."

She sniffs. "I know. I'm the PR professional here, remember?"

"It's okay to lean on me, baby."

She brushes away her tears. "Are you coming here, or are you going to waste time talking to me on the phone?"

I chuckle. "I'm on my way."

---

"Are you and Zara Chopra together, Minister?"

"What impact will this have on your candidacy?"

"Are you and Ms. Chopra getting married?"

"Minister, how long have you been seeing each other?"

The questions come thick and fast as I shoulder my way through the throngs of reporters. Just as I reach the main door of the apartment building, it slides open. Zara must have been tracking me from upstairs. I take the steps two at a time, then walk down the corridor to her apartment. Before I can press the doorbell, the door swings open.

"Hey." I peruse her features.

"Hey."

I follow her into the apartment; the door snicks shut behind me. She walks to the window and peers through the crack between the drapes. "There's more of them there than there were a few minutes ago."

"How are you holding up?"

She turns to face me. "I expected something like this to happen, just not so quickly."

I take in her pale features. "You look peaked."

"I'm fine," she says and slashes her hand through the air. "We're going to deny it, of course."

"Excuse me?"

She begins to pace. "We'll deny that there's anything going on between us."

"The picture suggests otherwise," I say gently.

"We could say we're friends."

"You're rubbing off a dab of something from the corner of my mouth. It's an intimate picture."

"Fuck." She halts, then locks her elbows at her sides. "Of course, it's an intimate picture. It looks like exactly what it is. The morning after a night spent fucking."

"Two nights, actually."

She turns on me. "Are you even taking this seriously?"

"I'm here, aren't I?"

She crosses the floor, then comes to a stop in front of me. "You don't seem put out by what's happened."

"Should I be?"

"Don't!" She throws up her hand. "Don't give me that. You know this means it ties you and me together. It means, it casts doubts on my talent, on my career, on everything I've worked to achieve."

"All that picture shows is that we are in a relationship. It doesn't take away from your talent because you've already built an outstanding profile as a fixer. You did this before we met. Of course, I'd want to hire you because of your abilities. You're not a newbie. This image doesn't take away from your abilities as a PR consultant at all."

She looks into my face. "This is what you wanted, isn't it? You wanted it to come out that we're together, so you could push me into making an announcement with you. So you could announce to the world that we're getting married. I can just see the headlines." She mimes a rectangle with her fingers. "The love story of the decade." She lowers her hands to her sides. "It's the kind of story that could propel you all the way to Downing Street."

"You have to admit, it's going to thaw the most cynical of hearts. Nothing like a marriage to give you a poll bounce," I admit.

"In fact," —she narrows her gaze— "I wouldn't be surprised if you're the one who leaked the picture."

I try to wipe all expression from my face, but I must be too slow. Her jaw drops. "Oh, my god, it was you. You slipped that picture to the media. And you did it to force my hand."

I shuffle my feet. I could deny it, of course, but it's not my style to hide behind lies. Besides, I don't regret doing it. If this is the only way to get her to marry me, then so be it. Once we're together, I can smooth over everything else. I can take care of her, ensure that she doesn't get too stressed, ensure that she has the kind of career she deserves—one beyond merely being the fixer to becoming the person who makes the news, who has a positive impact on society and the community. She has so much potential, this woman. All she needs is someone to help unlock it for her... And that's what I'm going to do, I'm—

"No." She takes a step back.

"Eh?"

"I'm not doing it. I'm not going to marry you. I'm not going to make a joint announcement with you. I will not be manipulated into a place where you make me feel like I have no options. I always have a choice, and I choose not to fall in line with your plan."

# 48

Zara

"Oh, my god, Zara, how are you holding up?" Solene's face wears an expression of absolute horror mixed with sympathy. She's the media darling, the upcoming music superstar. Of all my friends, she's the one most likely to understand what it means to be in the eye of a media shitstorm.

"Umm, I'm not sure, actually." I roll my shoulders, where a permanent ache seems to have taken up residence. "I've only ever been on the other side of the scandal. I'm the fixer. I'm not the one who's supposed to be in the eye of the storm."

I glance out the window of my apartment, where I've been holed up the last forty-eight hours. The crowd of paparazzi has only grown since that showdown I had with Hunter. After which, he left without making a statement, which only sent the journalists into a tizzy.

The speculation about our relationship has grown in an exponential fashion. From online blogs and social media, to tabloids, to the broadsheet newspapers, and today, the headlines of the leading financial daily. Everyone is asking if we're together, and if so, what we have to hide since we haven't bothered to address the rumors. One of them asked if I was pregnant. I read that article, then promptly rushed to the bathroom and got sick.

After that, I stopped checking the internet for the latest developments on the story. Instead, I have my team keeping track of the coverage. Abby keeps me up to date, shielding me from the details, but sharing highlights as they unfold, without going into the gory parts. She's only been on the job for a few days, but she's a fast learner. Kate and the rest of my team have warned me that every minute I delay only adds fuel to the conjecture around our relationship. As if I don't know that. It's PR 101 to address the postulations around a theory head on, in order to kill them. If you shut your ears to it and ignore the rumors, they rarely go away. More often than not, they take on a life of their own, which will snowball to affect other areas of our lives. As is happening to Hunter.

The speculation is affecting his ratings, as evidenced in the latest polls. His approval has dropped by five points since the picture of our being together broke. Of course, you could argue that he brought it down on himself. And yet... He did it because he wanted me enough to risk everything. He risked my ire, risked his career, risked so much... Just so he could coerce me into marrying him. Of course, he could have just asked... But when he did, I refused to give him an answer. I still haven't given him an answer. I can't give him an answer, not when there's so much unanswered in my own life.

I glance around my apartment. I need to get out of here. Need to go to the one place where I'll find some peace of mind so I can think. Which means, I need to leave without drawing the attention of the paps. I need a diversion.

I pick up my phone and make a few calls.

---

"You sure about this?" Isla asks.

"It'll work, won't it?" Abby shuffles her feet nervously.

Only Kate seems completely unruffled by what I proposed. The woman's cool in the face of pressure. Almost as collected as I normally am—when it's a situation that does not have me at the center of it. It's so much easier to take stock of a crisis when you're not the one in the eye of the storm. I'll never underestimate the courage of my clients after this.

I just need perspective on the situation. A chance to get my bearings and feel myself again, and then it will be fine. I trust myself to make the right decision. I simply need a little space to get to that point.

"It will work." I glance between them. "All you have to do is hold them off long enough for me and Isla to slip out the back."

"You sure you want to risk going, today of all days, when there's a good chance you'll be followed?" Isla interjects.

"I need to go there. I need to be there… Just for a little while."

"Okay." She nods.

"Okay." I blow out a breath, then turn to face Abby and Kate. "You guys ready?"

---

In the end, it worked fine. Kate and Abby went out onto the steps of my apartment building and gave a statement—full of sound and fury, signifying nothing. Essentially, it was a holding pattern statement that gave the press some words to embellish but did not cast any light on the situation. Which they knew. And they knew we knew. And the more astute of them weren't happy about it. But everyone went along with the charade, happy to have something with which to fill the pages and posts.

I pulled on a baseball hat and wore glasses, as well as the biggest pair of sweatpants—shudder—that Isla brought for me, along with a sweatshirt and trainers. It was a get-up very unlike what I'd normally wear. It did the trick, though, for we slipped by the lone, enterprising journo who was loitering around the backdoor exit to the building, but who let us pass without glancing. It was only when Isla pulled away in the car that I noticed him give us a second glance, but by then, we were well on our way.

Now, I glance at the squat, gray building she's stopped in front of. The sign on the gate said Presley Academy.

"You good?" she asks for the fifth time since we left home.

"I will be." I turn to her, then lean over and kiss her cheek. "Thanks, Isla."

"Anytime, babe." She shoots me a smile. "You sure you don't want me to wait?"

I shake my head. "I'll call for a ride home."

She scans my features. "So, this is it?"

I nod, then push the door open, and walk into the school.

"Hey Naz," I greet the man behind the reception counter.

"Hey, Zara. You made it!" He flashes me a huge smile.

"Of course, I did." I walk up the corridor, up the steps, and toward the gym on the first floor of the school.

"Zara, glad to see you." Debs, the session coordinator greets me. I place my bag in the classroom next to the gym, then join the rest of the volunteers in the gym.

"We'll be doing warmups, followed by basketball, then a spot of cricket, where we'll be dividing ourselves into two teams. If all goes well, we'll play Duck-Duck-Goose, finish off with the Hokey-Pokey, and then the Parachute Game. If, at any time, you need help in communicating with the athletes, you can use the visual support cards." Debs looks between us. "Remember, coaches, you are role models for the athletes. At the same time, make sure you have fun. Any questions?"

I shake my head, as do the rest. Then I pair up with Samira, my partner coach, and we begin the warmup exercises. Soon, the first child bursts into the gym.

"Jeremy, hello." One of the other coaches approaches the boy, along with his partner and they follow the child as he tears around the gym before making a beeline for the small playpen that's been erected in a corner of the gym with toys that the children can use to entertain themselves during the session.

Tracy, my athlete, soon arrives, and I spend the next hour-and-a-half, along with Samira, playing with her, letting her be when she needs space, coaxing her to join the group activities, which she finally does when we approach the last twenty minutes. Tracy loves Duck-Duck-Goose, and soon, we are all seated, and the children take turns walking around the circle, tapping each player on the head until they finally tap someone and say 'Goose.'

The hair on the back of my neck prickles. I glance up and am almost not surprised to see him standing by the door to the gym.

That's when one of the children decides I'm 'It.' I hurry after the child, but he takes my spot. I slow down, then walk forward until I tap one of the other athletes as 'It.' When I'm seated, I look toward the doors of the gym, which are now shut. He's no longer there. Huh, did I imagine that?

For the final ten minutes of the session, we play the Parachute Game, and the children sprawl on the floor as the adults float the large colorful cloth up and down over them. The kids stare up at the colors. Some have smiles on their faces. All of them are calmer than when their parents dropped them off earlier. Then we wrap up the game.

The doors to the gym open, and the parents trickle in. Tracy's mom arrives smiling. Tracy jumps up and races toward her. I head for the bench at the side of the gym, pick up Tracy's bag and jacket and hand them over to her mom.

"How was she today?" Tracy's mom asks me.

"She was gold."

"Thank you so much." Tracy's mum clutches at my hand. "What you volunteers do every weekend is a godsend. It gives me some much needed me time where I can catch my breath, knowing she is in good hands."

"Yes, this is the only place my Yacine can be himself and not be judged," another mom nearby agrees.

"It's all thanks to Debs and the team who founded this charity and have kept it going for ten years." I jerk my chin in Debs' direction.

The parents leave with their kids, and we head into the classroom next door.

"Don't forget to fill out the feedback forms before you leave. It helps us in tracking the progress of our athletes." Debs points toward the tablets on the table near the doorway. "Thanks everybody, that was a great session."

Samira and I fill out the feedback form for Tracy. Then I say goodbye to the rest of the volunteers, pick up my bag and retrace my steps to the front door of the school. I step out, and my gaze instantly zooms in on him.

# 49

Hunter

She steps out of the school entrance, and her gaze widens. Her body tightens, then she squares her shoulders and heads in my direction. Her scent teases my nostrils, then she walks past me. I follow her out of the school gates then down the sidewalk until she comes to a coffee shop. She walks inside with me in tow. I take the seat opposite her. She ignores me and scans the menu. When the waitress comes, I order her a chai tea latte and a black coffee for myself.

After the other woman leaves, she narrows her gaze on me. "Is there no part of my life that you don't know about?"

"I didn't know you were volunteering with children with special needs."

She glances away, then locks her fingers in her lap. "How did you find me? Did you bug my phone? Is that how you tracked me down?"

When I don't reply, she jerks her gaze in my direction. She spots the expression on my face and her jaw drops. "No way."

"I had to make sure you were safe."

"What did you think was going to happen to me? We live in a first-world country, or have you forgotten?"

"You forget, you are involved with me. The media attention on me is only going to grow, and it's going to bring all kinds of people out of the woodwork. I had to make sure you were protected at all times, which is why I have eyes on you. As long as you are fine, I can focus on my work."

"I assume you also have security on me?"

I tilt my head.

She draws in a breath, then squeezes the bridge of her nose. "This is so fucked up, Hunter. Have you heard yourself? You're obsessed with me. You're stalking me, and you're possibly the next leader of this country."

I set my jaw. "As long as you are kept from harm, I can focus on other things."

"So, you bug my phone and, I assume, my computer, as well? What about my apartment and my office?"

I raise a shoulder.

Her eyes widen. "You bugged my apartment and my office?"

"I have cameras on you, yes."

She stares at me, then holds up her hand. "You've lost it."

"I have. I can't think. Can't focus on my campaign. Can't sleep at night unless I jerk off to images of you under me. Can't eat unless I recall the taste of your pussy when you come all over my tongue."

Her breath hitches. Her eyes flash.

"I compare every woman I meet to you and find them all wanting. Your grit, your tenacity, and your strength fascinate me. I always knew you had a big, giving heart, and what I saw today only confirmed that I have been right all along. There's no one for me but you, Fire. I'd rather spend my days loving you than spend my time pursuing a calling that feels meaningless unless you are by my side."

Our gazes catch and hold through the interval when the waitress arrives and places our drinks on the table.

"I should resent you for intruding into my life. I should hate you for leaking that photo of us and destroying my reputation. I should" —she bites the inside of her cheek— "abhor you for how you fucked me so hard, you've spoiled me for anyone else, how you manipulated me into a place from which the only way out is to join forces with you, to accept your proposal... And yet, I can't find it in myself to do so." She glances between my eyes. "Why is that, Hunter?"

I hold out my hand, palm face up. "You know why."

She swallows, then places her hand in mine. I weave my fingers with hers, and a sense of rightness grips me. A sense of peace envelops me. A sense of...never wanting to let go of her makes me tighten my hold. She squeezes my hand, and my heart stutters. That iron band around my chest—the one I hadn't been aware of—loosens. I draw in a breath, and the rush of oxygen to my lungs makes my head spin.

"I volunteer at the school, at least once in two weeks. A small local charity runs these sports sessions where they train us volunteers to play games with special needs children."

"Because of Olly?"

She nods. "He had ASD, Autism Spectrum Disorder, and he was the most beautiful little boy I've ever known. I was only sixteen when he was born, and he became my entire life.

"My parents were busy with the shop; Cade was already a budding cricketer with the junior English cricket team and traveling to matches. I spent every spare minute I had with Olly. I was responsible for him. That day" —she blinks rapidly— "that day, I took him to the park to play. But I had just gotten my first phone and couldn't stop messing with it. I took my gaze off of him for a few seconds, and when I looked up, he was gone. I searched for him all over the park, and as I reached the exit, I heard the screech of brakes. I knew it right away. I knew what I would find before I even reached the road. He died in a car accident. He'd dashed out into the path of an oncoming vehicle." She firms her lips. "He never had a chance." She pulls her hand from mine. "But you had me investigated, so you probably already know all of this."

I hesitate. "I knew you had a youngest sibling who died in an accident." A tear rolls down her cheek.

My heart feels like it's going to splinter apart. "Zara, baby, please." I wrap my arm about her, and to my relief, she lets me pull her close.

"It was my fault," she says in a low voice.

"It was an accident."

"I should have been more vigilant." Her chin quivers.

"You were barely an adult yourself."

She opens her eyes and looks up at me. "I was nineteen." She sets her jaw. "I knew my responsibilities and I failed him."

"You've been punishing yourself ever since." I lean in, bring her hand to my mouth and kiss her fingertips. "That's why you work so hard. That's why you're so focused on your career."

"You've spent a lot of time analyzing me, haven't you?" She scowls.

"Obsessed with you, remember?"

Her lips kick up. "And I'm obsessed with you, too."

"I know."

"Damn, but that swollen ego—" she murmurs.

"Is not the only thing that's swollen at the moment."

She scoffs. "Keep it in your pants, buster, especially since we're going out there to face the paps, who've already begun to hover outside the door."

I fold her fingers in mine. "Found us, did they?"

"Took them longer than expected. They must be losing their touch."

"Or you're too smart for them."

"You smooth-talker, you."

"Comes with the territory, baby."

I lean in; so does she. I hold her gaze as I lower my lips to hers. I kiss her softly, slowly, gently, and a sigh wafts from her lips. I begin to tilt my head and deepen the kiss, then stop myself.

"You sure you want to do this now?"

She holds my gaze for a second more, then nods.

"Okay."

"Okay."

I rise to my feet, and she follows me, hand-in-hand, as we head out of the café. We step outside, and the questions hit us.

"Are you two together, Mr. Whittington?"

"Are you marrying Zara, Mr. Whittington?"

"Are you pregnant, Zara?"

"Yes."

I hear her answer, and for a second, it doesn't register. And then, it does. It must take the journalists by surprise, too, because for a second, there's silence. I glance at her, trying to keep all expression from my face, and hoping to god I succeed.

"Congratulations, how many weeks are you along, Zara?"

"Are the two of you already engaged?"

"Where's your ring, Zara?"

"Will you be by Mr. Whittington's side when he campaigns, instead of behind the scenes?"

I squeeze her hand, and she returns the pressure. She's pregnant. With my child. And she didn't think to tell me about it? Is this her way of getting back at me for coercing her into a situation where she has no choice but to marry me? And considering she's pregnant, isn't that best for the child, too? I raise my hand and wait until the journalists quieten.

"Zara and I are together. We haven't set any plans for a wedding. When we do, we'll let you know. That's all I'm going to say right now."

I begin to shoulder my way past the first rows of paps, but she tugs on my arm. I turn to find she hasn't moved from her place. She tips up her chin at me. "I have something to say."

"Now?"

She nods.

I frown, trying to read her features, but unable to understand what that look in her eyes means. When she stays silent, I turn to the journalists and, once more, raise my hand. When they fall silent, I gesture toward Zara. "My soon to-be wife wants to share a few words."

I step back by her side. She squeezes down on my hand. Her fingers are cold once more. A tremor runs down her body. Then she lowers her chin. "I'm sorry, Hunter, but it's best for it to come out all at once."

Before I can ask what she means, she's turned back to the journalists.

"I became pregnant when I was sixteen and lost my son when I was nineteen."

# 50

Zara

"You didn't trust me enough to tell me about this before you broke it to the media?" Hunter glares at me from across his office.

After I'd ripped open my past and shared it with the press, we were bombarded by questions. Hunter, however, shouldered his way through the throng with me in tow. His security pulled up in a car, and we made a speedy getaway. All through the trip, we neither looked nor spoke to each other. Our phones vibrating off the hook, but by mutual, unspoken consent, neither of us checked our devices. He also did not let go of my hand.

We drew up to his office, and he led me through a path between desks occupied by his team. Most of them were hard at work, regardless of the fact that it was a weekend. That's the nature of an election campaign. There are no 'off' days, not until the poll results are declared—and not even after that, when the real work begins. Most of them, however, fell silent in our wake. No doubt, seeing their leader pull me along with his fingers threaded through mine was enough to make them realize things had changed.

He barked at his assistant to not let anyone in, then he ushered me inside his office, shut the door, and locked it for good measure. Only then, did he let go of my hand. I avoided his table and the chairs around it and walked over to the sofa pushed up against the wall. I sank into it, placed my bag on the seat next to me, and folded my hands in my lap. Now, I watch as he paces back-forth-back on the carpet.

"I thought you already knew," I finally offer.

He turns on me. "Is that the best you can do?"

"It's a reasonable assumption. You had me investigated. You know everything about me, right down to my hot beverage of choice. Of course, I assumed you knew about my past."

"Apparently, my investigators failed to discover the sibling who died was not your sibling but your son."

I wince, then squeezes my eyes shut. "I suppose I should be grateful that the people I hired to wipe out that particular detail of my past came through." I rub my chest. "My son. I gave birth to him, then watched as he was buried. Then wiped out his connection to me. I am a terrible mother."

"You're not, Zara. You are the strongest, bravest person I have ever met."

Heat flushes my cheeks. I lower my hands to my sides then tip up my chin. "You forgot to say I'm a fixer; it's what I do best. What better use of my talent than to fix my past. I covered up the fact that Olly was my child like it was a dirty secret." My heart squeezes in my chest. My guts churn. "I am a terrible person. I wiped out all existence of my own son. What mother does that?"

"You did what you thought was right. You did what it took to survive. You loved your son. It's evident in how you talk about him. You tried your best to take care of him. You're not to blame for what happened to him."

I chuckle. "Don't go making me out to be something I'm not. Have you forgotten that I didn't tell you about Olly? That I broke the news of him to the press without doing you the courtesy of telling you first?"

"Olly was your secret to tell, when you thought it was the right time. And you did it before you lost your nerve." His gaze softens.

There's so much understanding on his face. So much love. So much everything. The pressure behind my eyes builds. My heart feels like it's going to burst. "I... I could have told you first, when we were on our own." I choke out, "I'm a bad person. You deserve better, Hunter."

He leans forward on the balls of his feet. His blue-green eyes turn that stormy shade of green I now know means he's pissed off. And he has reason to be. If I were in his shoes, I'd break off all relations with me right now. I tip up my chin, and the groove between his eyebrows deepens.

He finally says, "I know what you're doing here."

"Oh?"

He nods. "You think because you sprang that surprise on me, and in front of the media, I'm going to call off our relationship. But you're wrong."

I blink. "I... I am?"

He walks over, then squats down in front of me. "You forget how tenacious I am, Fire. I didn't come this far, only to walk away from you over something that happened in your past."

I jut out my chin. "I kept a lot of things from you, Hunter. I didn't tell you I had a child, that I was a teenage mother of a special needs boy who died because I couldn't care for him."

"You did your best."

A tear squeezes out from the corner of my eye. "You have no idea what I did or didn't do."

He leans forward and scoops up the trail of moisture from my cheek. "In all the time I've known you, you've never—not once—shirked your responsibilities." He brings his moist finger to his lips and sucks on his digit, and my heart feels like it's going to burst.

"You take time out to volunteer with children." He holds my gaze.

"It's nothing."

"You give them your time. It's not like you write a check and forget about it. That means something." He takes my hand in his. I try to pull away, but he tightens his hold on me. "You've gone above and beyond the call of duty. I know how you've supported your friends when they've needed you, how you've given your best to each of your clients and helped them through situations which would have caused anyone else to lose their nerve. But not you, Zara. You face each challenge head on and come out on top. I'm proud of you."

The hot sensation behind my eyes intensifies. "I didn't tell you I was pregnant."

"I knew."

My jaw drops, again. The number of times this man has taken me by surprise is almost as many times as I have tried to pull the rug out from under him...and failed. "You mean—?"

"You refused champagne the last two times. Also—"

"The bug in my mobile phone." I slump into the sofa. "Of course, you knew."

"I'm sorry I spoiled your surprise." He quirks his beautiful lips and a slow fire ignites low in my belly.

"I should be the one saying I'm sorry. I should have told you every-thing—about being pregnant, about Olly. All of it. It's just" —I glance away, then back at him— "it was all too much for me to process. It was such a shock to find out I was pregnant."

He rises to his feet, then sits down next to me. "You should have let me be there for you."

"I've been having morning sickness the last few weeks, so I had a strong suspicion I was pregnant. The test was merely a formality, but seeing that pink line—for the second time in my life—I'm afraid it brought back memories."

He wraps his arm about my shoulders and pulls me close. "I'm sorry you had to go through it alone."

I allow myself to relax against him, muscle by muscle. "I wanted to do it at my own pace. I kept putting off taking a pregnancy test, until I couldn't put it off anymore. And when I saw the positive test this morning, I needed some time to get my head around it all. That's why I knew I had to go to the school and spend time with some of my favorite people."

"The kids."

"The kids," I agree.

We sit quietly for a few more seconds, then I look up at him. "Guess I'm going to marry you after all, huh?"

"Do you want to marry me, Zara?"

"Do you want me to marry you, Hunter?"

He chuckles. "So damn stubborn, but I'm going to wear you down yet." He slides down onto his knee for the second time in our lives, then pulls a ring from his pocket. He holds out his palm, and I place my hand in his. He slips the ring onto my left ring finger. The yellow-gold stone in the center is surrounded by tiny diamonds. I tilt my palm and the light from the window picks up the golden sparks at the heart of the sapphire.

"Fire for my Fire."

"Hunter," I breathe. I'd expected a ring, but this...is beautiful. It's unique, and very much the kind of ring I'd have chosen for myself.

"It's an antique." He rubs his thumb over the shining, golden ball of fire on my finger. "It belonged to my grandmother. She was the one person in my life who truly loved me. She left it for me with instructions to give it to the woman of my dreams. The woman who's my dream, my wish, my fantasy. The woman who's everything I need. You're my hope, my love, my beginning and my end. You're everything I need. I love you more with every breath. You're my reason for living. You give my life meaning. And I want to spend the rest of it giving you and our children" —he places his other palm on my belly— "everything you'll need."

"Hunter." I swallow. There's so much I want to say, but my brain cells seem unable to bridge the connections needed to form the words. "Hunter." Another tear slides down my cheek, and this time, he leans in and kisses it away.

"Marry me, Zara. Marry me, and I'll stand beside you through the years. Although I'll make mistakes, I'll never break your heart. I promise to make you so happy that the only tears you cry will be happy ones. Marry me because I'd rather have one kiss from your lips, one touch of your fingers on mine, one brush of your hair on my skin, hear your heartbeat against mine, than spend any time away from you. Marry me—"

"Yes." I press my lips to his. "Yes."

# 51

Hunter

"Minister, have you and Zara set a date for the wedding?" The journalist asks.

We're in the small conservatory attached to my townhouse in Primrose Hill. We agreed the best way forward was to hold a press conference to which we'd invite a select number of news people.

We drew up a list of those who we knew would be sympathetic to our cause, as well as those we knew would have tougher questions. It was Zara's idea to do that. She also said it would be best to hold the press conference in a location that was personal. It would mellow the media and make them feel like they were our guests, rather than adversaries. I suggested the gazebo attached to my living room, and she agreed. I was delighted. It meant she'd be on my turf, in my house, even though she hasn't yet agreed to move in with me. Something I'm working on. This, I'm sure, will give me a head start in convincing her.

I left it in her capable hands to manage the entire event. She's still the Head of Communications for my campaign. In addition, she's also my partner. After I proposed to her the second time, and she accepted, we ended up kissing and making out, right there in my office—again. The best use I've put my desk to in all the time I've had it.

When we emerged from my office, my entire team clapped. They'd seen the clips from the impromptu catch-up with the journalists at the entrance to the café, followed by me hauling Zara to my office, and had come to their own conclusions. Then there was the ring she was wearing. The ring that announces to the world she belongs to me. That she's mine, under my protection, joined to me, and that I'm never letting go of her. So, it's clear to everyone that we're together.

Now, I turn to my fiancée, who's seated on the chair next to me. "That's for Zara to decide."

The journalists' gazes swing in her direction.

"Given that I like dropping surprises on the minister—"

A titter runs through the group.

"I would only be conforming to my tendency to shock and awe him by saying that I have, indeed, set a date."

Everyone holds their breath. I watch her with pride.

This woman—she could rule the world if she wanted. Yet she's chosen to rule my world, instead. Every day, I thank the powers responsible for making our paths cross. She makes it all worthwhile. She gives me purpose. She's the thread through my thoughts. The rhythm to my walk. The cadence to my words. The color in my dreams. The only reality worth living in. She...belongs to me and that makes me the luckiest man in the world.

"Hunter?"

I blink, realizing she's looking at me. "Whatever you want," I murmur.

"So, you're okay if we get married right now?"

I blink. "Now?"

"We have our attendees" —she nods toward the assembled journalists— "and as for friends..." She smiles at someone past me. I turn my head to find Liam and Isla entering the gazebo from the side door. They also seem to have brought along their dog—a Great Dane who strains at the leash held by Liam.

Behind them are Sinclair and Summer, then Michael and Karma.

Weston and Amelie—both of whom confessed to me and Zara that they'd set us up, and who couldn't be more delighted at how things turned out— wave at us.

Behind them are JJ & Lena and Saint & Victoria.

Bringing up the rear is Cade Kingston, on his own. His gaze is fixed on something—or someone—on the other side of the podium. I follow his line of sight to find Abby scowling at Cade. She tilts her chin. Then, in a deliberate snub, turns her back on him. She leans in to speak to one of her fellow team members, Steve, I think. I glance back to find Cade's brow is thunderous. His jaw tics, and he seems to be having a hard time controlling himself. He takes a couple of steps forward, but just then, Lena turns to say something to him. He tears his gaze off of Abby and replies to Lena. A new face, one I've not seen in many months, walks into the room behind Cade.

"Is that—"

"Edward Chase, one of the Seven," Zara confirms.

"What's he doing back in the country?" The last I'd heard from Sinclair, Edward had renounced the priesthood, and left to travel the world.

"He happened to be visiting, and considering I decided only this morning that we should get married today, it seemed like a sign to ask him to officiate the wedding."

"He's no longer a priest."

"He can still marry us," she points out.

"And as soon as I can arrange it, we're going to the registry office to get our marriage validated."

Her lips curve. "Not taking any chances, are you?"

"Not gonna stop until you're mine in every possible way."

Her golden eyes spark. The pulse at the base of her throat beats faster. I lean in closer, and so does she. Our breaths fuse. I lower my head until my eyelashes brush against hers.

Someone clears their throat. I glance up to find Abby glancing between us. "Uh, we're ready for the both of you."

Zara frowns. "I hadn't planned on anything else."

"But I have." I rise to my feet and hold out my hand. "You're not the only one who can pull surprises, Fire."

She looks taken aback, then chuckles. "I wouldn't have expected anything else from you."

We walk out of the gazebo and into the garden.

"Oh, wow!" She takes in the heaters that have been placed at strategic locations around the lawns. Chairs have been placed in rows, with an aisle in the center. It leads to an arch made of pampas grass, with yellow and purple flowers dotted at intervals.

"When did you do all this?"

"Technically, it's Abby and your team who helped set it up." I nod my thanks at Abby, who clasps her hands together. "I hope you like it."

Kate walks over to join us. "And if you don't, too bad; it's the best we could do in the little time we had while you guys were in the press conference."

"Oh, shush!" Steve draws abreast on the other side of Abby. "We had a fun time doing it, didn't we?"

Kate rolls her eyes. "If you say so. But it's for your wedding, Zara. Never thought we'd see the day, by the way—but since you are planning to be married, I'd say choosing the person who could be the leader of the country is a damn good move."

Zara chuckles. "Thanks, Kate."

The journalists begin to pour out onto the lawns; Abby, Kate, Casey and Steve guide them to the chairs. Our friends take their seats in the front row, and Edward walks around to wait for us at the top of the aisle.

I take Zara's hands in mine and bring them to my lips. "See you on the other side."

# 52

Zara

Had I really thought I could pull another surprise on my man and get away with it? He's known as the sharpest politician of our times for a reason. All along, I thought I was a step ahead of him, but he's outwitted me at every turn. He bugged my phone and my computer, placed cameras in my apartment and office—and I hadn't been aware of any of it. Sure, I got back at him by springing the surprise of my past to the press, and revealing I was pregnant. But he'd already guessed I was.

He proposed to me, and I accepted.

Once more, he's gotten ahead of me. He guessed I had something up my sleeve when I agreed to have the press conference at his place. He roped in my entire team to help with the arrangements for the wedding. Good thing I have this last chance to catch him off guard.

I nod toward Abby, who walks over to Cade. She engages him in conversation. He frowns as she gestures in Hunter's direction. Finally, with reluctance writ in every angle of his body, he follows her to where

Hunter is speaking with Edward. The four huddle in conversation. I step back, and head inside, toward the guest room at the end of the corridor. I step in and, shutting the door behind me, I walk over to where my dress is laid out on the bed. It's a simple white sheath created by an up-and-coming British-Asian designer. Someone whose career I've been following with great interest and whose designs I love. I strip off my pantsuit and step into the dress. As I slide the sleeves over my shoulders, the door opens.

"Am I too late?" Abby bursts in and comes to a halt behind me.

"You're just in time."

She zips me up. I step into the white-satin stilettos, by the same designer. I pat my hair, which I put up earlier this morning, then place the one-tier vintage style veil on my head. Abby helps me fasten it. I draw the netting down over my eyes, then freshen up my makeup.

"How do I look?" I glance at my reflection in the mirror.

"Gorgeous. You look both sexy and understated. Hunter is a lucky man."

"I think we're both lucky we found each other." I meet her gaze in the mirror. "Not to mention, it's a miracle we made it to the altar without killing each other."

"I think you're both going to be very happy," she says in a soft voice.

"As you will be, if you and my brother decide to look past your differences."

"Eh?" She blinks rapidly. "There's nothing like that between us." She waves her hand in the air. "Also, he's my brother's best friend. No way, can we get together."

"Hmm." I decide not to push the point. Each of us has a journey to get through to find our HEA, and given how Hunter and I put each other through the wringer... Well, I'm not sure I'm the best person to give her advice. Still, I can't help but say, "Anytime you want to talk, I'm here, and not just as your boss."

She seems taken aback, then nods. "When I first met you, I thought you were a scary figure. Now, I realize that under all that woman-of-the-world persona, you have a soft heart. You take care of your friends and your team. I'm lucky you took me under your wing."

"Don't count your blessings yet. We have a lot of hard work to be done for the upcoming campaign."

"I look forward to it." She hands me my bouquet. "But first, we have a wedding to attend."

---

"Zara, you look—" Cade shakes his head. For once, my cocky, smartass brother seems to be at a loss for words. "You look absolutely gorgeous." He leans forward and kisses me on my cheek. "I'm sorry Mum and Dad chose not to attend."

I raise a shoulder, trying to pass it off, but in truth, it did hurt that, once again, my parents chose the shop over me. You'd think their daughter's wedding would be more important than keeping the store open, but apparently, not.

"They did message me to say I'm most welcome to visit and bring my new husband with me," I murmur.

"That's something, huh?" He tucks my hand through the crook of his arm. "It's not that they don't love you."

"They just weren't happy about me becoming a teenage mother, and then turning my back on the legal profession to pursue what I love."

"They did support you, though. They were ready to adopt Olly as their own."

"Not that I'd have allowed it." I shift my weight from foot to foot. "You're right, though. When all is said and done, they didn't disown me. They were there for me when I most needed them. They're just not happy with my life choices, that's all."

"Will you go visit them with Hunter?" Cade asks.

"When he's won the election and becomes Prime Minister. He'll probably be good enough for them as a son-in-law then."

We both laugh.

Footsteps sound. Abby reaches us. "We're ready for you." She ignores Cade and addresses her remark to me.

"Thanks, Abby."

She nods, then turns and leaves. Cade watches her go with a frown on his forehead.

"What's that all about?" I nod in her direction. "Something up with the two of you?"

"Nothing's up between us. My best friend, Knight, is her brother. Trust me, he'd be more than pissed off if there was anything between me and Abby."

"When has that ever stopped you?" I scan his features. "Or wait. Maybe you actually feel something for this girl. Is that why you prefer to trade smoldering glances with her than act on what you're feeling?"

"Smoldering glances?" He shakes his head. "Just because you're in love doesn't mean the entire world has to follow suit."

"Aha!" I smile smugly "So you are falling for her?"

"Eh, no, of course not. I don't intend to be romantically involved with anyone, anytime soon."

"Famous last words." I pat his hand. "I'll remind you of it when you're standing in my position."

"I don't think my tastes tend toward white, gowns."

I laugh. "You know what I mean."

"I'm not getting married. Not for a long, long time. And speaking of" —he turns toward the doorway leading to the lawns— "you don't want to be late for your wedding."

# 53

Hunter

The crowd quietens. The hair on the back of my neck prickles. I turn to find her stepping onto the aisle, and my breath catches. Goddamn, she's a vision. A goddess come to life. I'm not sure how she managed to change outfits so quickly, but all of her efforts are worth it. The white gown covers her shoulders then dips slightly to hint at her cleavage. The fabric nips in at her waist then flares over her spectacular hips, before dropping down to her toes. The lace outlines her arms, and her gorgeous skin peeks through the netting. As Cade escorts her up the aisle, she's breathtaking, sublime, exquisite. And I'm the luckiest man on this planet.

They reach me. Cade kisses Zara's cheek, shakes my hand, then places her hand in mine. I kiss her fingertips, and the crowd oohs and aahs. Zara smiles up at me. I lower our arms, then both of us turn toward Edward.

He glances between us and a smile tips up his lips. I see his lips move and must make the appropriate response, as does Zara. Then,

I'm turning to face her again. I pull the platinum band from my pocket and slide it onto her finger next to her engagement ring.

She does the same.

"Guess we both had the same idea, hmm?" I smirk.

She laughs. "Seems we're finally on the same page."

"Does this mean you're going to stop your verbal sparring?" I step closer; so does she.

"What do you think?" she murmurs.

"I think" —I wrap my arm about her waist and pull her into me— "that you'll never stop keeping me on my toes, and I wouldn't have it any other way."

She looks up into my eyes. Her golden eyes lighten until they resemble pools of sunlight. "I love you, husband."

My heart fills my chest. Warmth pulses through my veins. I pull her closer, then dip my head until my lips brush hers. "I love you more than myself. I promise to respect our differences. I swear I'll put you and our family before anything else."

Her chin trembles. "Your country needs you, too."

"And I promise to serve with passion and dedication and do more than my best to steer the course of our future."

"You make me proud." She tips up her chin, and I close my mouth over hers. I kiss her deeply. She parts her lips, and I sweep my tongue over hers. I suck on her mouth, until a moan spills from her lips, until she sways into me, until she melts in my arms, and I pull her even closer into my chest. I kiss her and kiss her until, finally, the sound of clapping reaches me. Then I soften the kiss, brush my lips once, twice over hers, before I pull back. Her chest rises and falls, her skin flushed. Her breathing is ragged, and when she finally flutters her eyelids open, her eyes are more silver than gold.

"That was some kiss." She clears her throat.

"A promise. A pledge. My allegiance to you and my child you carry in your belly."

She swallows. "You're going to make me cry."

"Only as long as they are tears of joy." I cup her face. "I love you, Zara."

A chair crashes to the ground, then, "Tiny!" a woman's voice yells.

We look up to find the Great Dane has broken free from Isla's grasp. He's galloping toward where the drinks are being poured at a table halfway up the garden.

"Tiny!" Isla lifts her skirts and races after him. "Tiny, stop."

The man pouring the champagne into the glass pauses midway. Then Tiny leaps onto the table, which crashes under his weight. The man jumps back. The bottle falls from his hands. Tiny snatches it out of the air, tips it upside down, and into his mouth.

"Tiny, you're a bad boy!" Isla grabs the bottle and tugs it from Tiny's jaws. Liam reaches her and seizes Tiny's collar.

"Did that dog neck a bottle of champagne?" Edward asks in a dazed tone.

Zara and I share a laugh. I turn to Edward. "We have much to catch you up on."

---

"Does that Great Dane have a taste for champagne or am I seeing things?" Edward looks from Isla to Liam.

"It's her mother's dog." Liam raises his hands. As if that explains everything.

"We're baby-sitting him, while my mother is on a trip with her knitting club." Isla explains.

"And he has a fondness for bubbles?" Edward asks in a disbelieving voice.

"From the very first time we opened a champagne bottle in front of him. And it doesn't seem to hurt him, at all." Isla raises a shoulder. "Occasionally, he has a hangover, which is when my mother gets really upset with him."

"He's so cute, though." Abby bends and hugs the Great Dane. Liam's tied Tiny's leash to his chair, and for now, at least, the dog sits on his haunches watching the humans with a long-suffering look on his face.

"He's a darling, except when he's in proximity to champagne," Isla agrees.

"Not that I'm encouraging him or anything, but he can have my share, considering I'm not drinking," my wife announces.

"Oh, my god, I totally forgot to congratulate you." Solene, leans over and hugs Zara.

From across the table, Declan watches Solene with a frown on his face. The two turned up separately to the wedding, have not exchanged a word since, and are seated at opposite ends of the table. Interesting. Not that it's my business. Still, now that I'm married, I can't help but wish the same for my friend.

"I'm so excited for you." Isla flashes my wife a smile. "Marriage and a baby, back-to-back. Who'd have thought you'd beat me to the baby side of things?"

"Umm, it was an accident," Zara mutters.

"But one I'm really excited about," I interject.

Isla straightens, then glances between us. "It's going to be good for the polls as well, right?"

Zara and I look at each other. "It can't hurt," Zara says finally.

"Actually, the coverage has been very positive." Abby waves her phone in the air. "I didn't want to bother either of you, since this is, technically, still your wedding, but the press has lapped it up. There are already gushing accounts of the wedding and the upcoming baby. And the latest polls see elevated approval ratings for Mr. Whittington."

"Call me Hunter."

Abby flushes a little. "Yes sir, Mr. Hunter."

"Just Hunter."

"That's what I meant. Your idea of a surprise wedding with the press invited to it is a hit. Of course, some of them are complaining that they'd have liked to have been told beforehand so they could have dressed accordingly, but other than that, it's one big love fest."

"It's a good way to start our honeymoon, huh?" I tuck a strand of hair behind my wife's ear. *My wife.* How did I get so lucky?

"Our working honeymoon," Zara raises her sparkling juice to her lips and takes a sip. "You still have a campaign to run."

"You're going to keep me on the straight and narrow, hmm?"

"You know that's impossible. You have a mind of your own, baby.

All I'm trying to do is give you options. I know you'll always make up your own mind, but it's not going to stop me from sharing my viewpoint."

I take her hand in mine and kiss her knuckles. "I want you to actively campaign with me. I want you to talk about the causes that are dear to you. I want you to head up a fund that supports the needs of the women, the vulnerable, and children with special needs."

Her features soften. "Are you sure about that?"

"More than anything in the world."

I lean in to kiss her, when someone clears their throat. I look up to find Abby standing next to us. She darts a half-smile in Zara's direction. "Uh, I guess I'm going back to the office."

"You're going back now?" Zara frowns.

"The campaign is still underway, and there's a lot of follow up to be done from the coverage generated by the wedding. It's best to do that now, while interest is high on what the two of you are going to do next. I thought I might—uh— draft a strategy to share with you."

"A strategy?" Zara lowers her chin.

Abby nods. "If that's okay? If you don't mind, I mean—"

"I think it's a great idea."

Abby's features lighten. "You do?"

"Absolutely. I" —she looks at me— "*we'd* be happy to hear your thoughts on how to leverage the publicity for the campaign."

"Absolutely," I agree.

"Oh, great." Abby pulls out a phone from the pocket of her pants. "Let me call for a car pick up."

"There's no need for that, I can drop you." Cade rises from his place on the other side of the table.

"What? No." Abby jerks her chin in his direction. "I mean, you must have had a lot of champagne to drink, so surely, you can't drive."

"I've been nursing water." Cade raises his glass of water in her direction. "I'm in training, so no alcohol."

"Oh—" Abby glances to the left, then the right. "But you must be busy."

"I have nothing on for the rest of the day." He smirks.

"Surely, you have something better to do than drive me to the office."

"Actually, I can't think of anything better than playing chauffeur."

## 54

Eight months later

Zara

"I promise to serve the country with integrity, humility and compassion. I promise to do my best for my country and for you who voted me in. I will deliver on the promises I made to you during my election campaign." The newly elected Prime Minister of the country, who also happens to be my husband, glances about the crowd. "There will be challenges, of course, but I am not daunted. I hope to live up to the demands of my office and deliver on the trust you have placed in me. I stand here before you, ready to lead our country into the future. To put your needs above politics. Together, we can achieve incredible things. We will create a future worthy of the sacrifices so many have made, and fill tomorrow, and every day thereafter, with hope. Thank you."

He moves away from the podium and holds out his hand. I walk over to him, balancing the weight of my swollen belly.

It's been eight months to the day we got married.

Eight months, during which time, I worked side by side with him, campaigning across the country. I continued on as the Head of his PR strategy, until the day he won the elections. At which point, I sold my PR agency to Kate. It was a difficult decision, but the right one. No one knows more than me how all-consuming taking on the leadership role of this country will be. Being married to the Prime Minister means any client I took on would come under a lot of scrutiny. And while I wouldn't be doing anything wrong in holding down a separate job, it could present a conflict of interest with the office my husband holds. So, I decided to make a clean break and embrace my role as the First Lady of the country. I also accepted Hunter's offer of launching a project aimed at looking after the interests of women, the vulnerable, and children with additional needs. That's my passion, and it feels right to use my energy to help those who are weaker.

And all the time we were on the campaign trail, the child I carry in my belly has grown. By now, I'm massive. I should hate just how big I am, but every time I see my stomach, I feel this huge rush of tenderness. This big gush of love that makes my heart swell until I'm sure it's bigger than my stomach.

I promised him I'd hold out until after he was sworn in. Now, as we pose for pictures, he has one arm around me, and the other over my belly. Our wedding and my pregnancy raised a lot of media speculation, but the voters embraced us. Many of the journalists lauded my courage for coming forward with my teen pregnancy and subsequent loss. Of course, there were those who called me unfit to be the wife of the future leader of the country, but overall, the feedback was supportive. Most of the media were excited about our child, and from the time I first made my appearance at Hunter's side, I've been inundated with good wishes.

I'd like to think our child has brought in a rush of good fortune for us, one that paved the way for Hunter to take on the responsibility of being the leader of the country. I smile and wave at the journalists calling to us to pose for them. This goes on for too many minutes. I'd managed to squeeze my swollen feet into heels, and now I'm regretting it.

Sensing my discomfort, Hunter gives a final nod toward the news people. Then, he scoops me up in his arms. Instantly, flashlights go off behind us as the journalists rush to capture the moment.

"Whoa, Hunter, what are you doing?" I gasp.

"Carrying my wife over the threshold, of course." He walks inside 10 Downing Street, and his aides come forward to greet us.

Heat flushes my cheeks and I turn my face into his shoulder. "I think you should put me down now," I say in a muffled tone.

"When I'm ready."

"Hunter, please." I half-laugh, then glance up at him. "Why am I not surprised by your over-the-top gesture?"

"Because you love me?" He smirks.

"That I do, Mr. Prime Minister, so very much."

His features soften. He bends and captures my lips. The kiss is soft and sweet, and firm, and so very hot. I lean into it, open my mouth, and he nips on my lower lip. He deepens the kiss, and that familiar weakness invades my limbs.

Someone clears their throat, and I stiffen. Hunter kisses me for a few seconds more. By the time he raises his head, I'm flushed and my breathing is erratic.

He surveys my features, then nods. "You going to be okay?"

"I'm more than okay as long as I have you by my side."

"You have me baby, always and forever. I love you so very much." He kisses my forehead, then lowers me to my feet.

I take a step back, then nod toward his team. "Go on, your country needs you."

"You always come first, Fire." He searches my features. "You sure you're going to be okay?"

A twinge tugs on my lower belly. I resist the urge to rub my stomach, then nod. "You know I am."

"Hmph." He holds my gaze for a second longer, then bends and kisses me on the lips again, before turning to speak to the assembled people.

I fall back to watch as they line up to speak with him. He shakes each person's hand, giving them his full attention. The full impact of those magnetic blue-green eyes that change with his moods. The country may have his attention now, but I'll have his attention always. I'll have to share him with the world for as long as he's Prime Minister, and probably longer, since he's going to be in some form of public service for most of his life; but I have no doubt, he'll always place me and our family first.

Another spasm squeezes my belly, this time, with enough force that I gasp. I glance around, but no one has noticed me. For once, it pays not to be the center of attention. Hunter is probably the only one I wouldn't begrudge that. After all, I got into PR not only because I like building up the media profile of my clients, but also because I'm an attention whore. The most satisfying time of my life was the last few months, not only because I got to spend so much time with Hunter on the campaign trail, but also because there was a personal connection to the work I was doing. Of course, I gave my best to every client, but with Hunter, I put everything of myself into the PR for his campaign.

I wanted him…needed him to win. I had gotten to know the man behind the public facade, and it was clear to me he would do his best for the country. He has the vision for a future that he will try his best to make happen. More than that, he's genuine and loyal and wanted to use his intelligence and everything he has at his disposal to create a better future for the newer generation.

Sure, he comes from a moneyed background, but it is precisely that which made him selfless. For so long, I held his money and his privilege against him. I judged him, and by doing so, I was guilty of the same kind of mistake that I've berated others for when they've tried to pigeonhole me. I can't be put into a neat category, and neither can Hunter. We're both complex individuals, with many facets to our personalities. Our backgrounds are only one of them.

Now, I realize I was too quick to form an opinion of him when we first met, but Hunter has completely overthrown any preconceived notions I might have had about him. I know now that he's the most tender, most possessive, most protective man I'll ever meet. I also know he's willing to cross the line between right and wrong to take care of me. Perhaps that should bother me, but somehow, I can't hold it against him. The shades of grey to his personality only make him so much more interesting. Am I worried that it will spill over into his professional life? No, because it's only me who brings out that part of his personality.

A third stab of pain cramps the entire lower half of my stomach. The pain is so hard, it's as if I've been buffeted by a wave. I gasp and bend over. Simultaneously, liquid gushes out from between my legs and pools about my feet. I glance down at my now-drenched skirt in horror. I look up to find Hunter has turned toward me. He takes in my stance, and the way I'm gripping my sides. I straighten, draw in a deep breath. In two bounds, he reaches me and sweeps me up in his arms, again.

"Hunter, what are you doing? You'll dirty your suit."

"Fuck that, I'm taking you to the hospital."

---

To say the next few hours were dramatic would be putting it mildly. He asked for the Prime Ministerial car—a massive Jaguar Sentinel—to be brought around the rear entrance. He placed me in the back seat, followed me in, and ordered the driver to take us to hospital. The security vehicle in front flipped on its siren, and I knew we were being followed by another vehicle. Two other members of his protection team on bikes flanked us, and we reached the hospital in under ten minutes.

He insisted on carrying me out of the car and into the emergency room, where we were instantly waved through. He held onto me until the doctors insisted he place me on a bed so they could examine me. They pronounced I was six centimeters dilated, and that we had time for the baby to come. That was ten hours ago.

I've spent the time alternating between the agony of the labor pains and the times in between when I've gathered my energy for the next push. And through it all, he's held my hand, fed me ice chips, and wiped the sweat from my forehead. He didn't even blink when I cursed him soundly for putting me in this position.

Karma and Summer, followed by Isla and Abby, popped their

heads around to let me know they were waiting with me. I told them to go home—it could be hours still, before the baby was born—but they refused. My brother's away on another cricket tour, but Abby mentioned she messaged him, and he's on his way back.

I glance at Hunter's face as he sprawls back in the chair next to my bed.

"You should go get a coffee."

"Not a chance," he growls.

"It could be some more time before—" I wince.

He leans forward, concern in his eyes. "You okay?"

I breathe through that now familiar pain traveling up my spine. Only this time, it builds and builds until it's like a wall that's pushing into me, shoving into me, cutting through me. I gasp, and must scream; perhaps, even black out a little. When I open my eyes, Hunter's features are pale. The shadows under his eyes are pronounced, and there's a drop of blood on his lower lip. "You hurt yourself, did you bite down on your lip?"

He opens his mouth, then closes it. "I'm never putting you through this again." His voice is hoarse.

"Famous last words." I laugh, then gasp again when the pain begins to build once more. "Oh, no, no, no, that's too close."

His gaze widens. He reaches for the switch next to the bed. "I'm calling the midwife."

---

"He's gorgeous." Hunter's warm voice cocoons me like a balm.

After he called the midwife, it took another three hours for the baby to emerge screaming into the world. I was shattered, numb, and shell-shocked. My entire body feels like it was put through a concrete mixer. My insides felt like they were torn out...which, in a way, they were, I suppose. And then, the midwife placed the baby over my chest.

I touch his little nose, take in his eyelashes, the little snub nose, those pink lips, and I fall head-over-heels in love... For the third time in my life. I hold him, and a tsunami of love fills every fiber of my being. I miss Olly so much. He would have loved his younger brother.

I've been given a second chance with this little boy, and I'm going to do everything in my power not to screw it up. The tears slide out of the corners of my eyes. I'm unable to stop them as I gaze at my son. Hunter wraps his arm about me and pulls me into his chest, and that only makes me sob more. Then, the baby opens his eyes and looks at me; my breath catches in my chest, and I nearly swoon. Blue-green eyes. Hunter's eyes look back at me, and I fall for my husband and my son all over again.

When the doctor places my son at my breast for his first feeding, he latches onto my breast with only a little coaxing. The sensation of him suckling at my breast brings forth a fresh round of tears. Hunter holds me until the sobs subside, and my son falls asleep while feeding. I carefully wipe his mouth, pull my hospital gown shut, and both of us stare at the wonder we created.

A buzzing sound fills the room. Hunter ignores it. It stops, then starts again. "I think you should get that," I murmur.

"If I do, it means I'll have to go back to my responsibilities." His eyebrows draw down.

"You can't keep putting it off." I shoot him a sideways glance. His hair is mussed, his shirt creased. A day's growth of stubble shadows his cheeks. He looks crumpled and tired, and so damn delicious.

"You're beautiful, Mr. Prime Minister."

He chuckles. "You, calling me by that name, in that husky voice of yours, might become my new ki— thing," he corrects himself.

"Glad to see you're managing to hold back your four-letter words."

The buzzing of his phone fills the room again. "You really need to get that, Hunter."

"I never should have turned on my phone, is what I should have done." He peers into my face. "I'll never forget what you did for me, for our family. You are the bravest, most courageous person I've ever met. I'm honored you became my wife. I thank the powers that be for the day our paths crossed. If I'm born again, Fire, I hope you'll do the honor of being my wife in that life, and in all our future life's together."

Tears prick the backs of my eyes. I swallow down the lump of emotion that squeezes my throat. "Stop, you're going to make me cry again."

"Don't cry, baby. This is your time to be happy." He leans in and kisses my forehead.

"Oh, hope I'm not interrupting?"

We glance up to find Abby lurking in the doorway of the room. "I could come back." She turns as if to leave.

"You're not interrupting." Hunter rises to his feet. "Actually, I'd be reassured if you kept Zara company while I make a few calls."

With a last glance at me, he prowls out.

"Come on in." I gesture to the girl. She walks over with a big bunch of flowers that she places on a table already overflowing with bouquets and toys. "Wow, this room smells like a garden," she exclaims.

"All of the Seven and their wives have sent me flowers and toys for the baby," I murmur.

"You mean the Seven who run the 7A company—"

"Yes, and the Sovranos."

Her gaze widens. "The Sovranos, as in, the Italian Mafia?"

"As in the Cosa Nostra," I nod.

Her eyes grow even bigger. "Aren't they criminals, of sorts?" she whispers.

"Doesn't everyone have skeletons in their closet?" I retort.

She flushes a little, glances away, then back at me. Huh? That was a guilty look, if ever there was one.

"You're not good at hiding your thoughts, are you?"

Her cheeks grow brighter, if that's possible. "It's the curse of having such fair skin."

"Or a pure mind." I half-smile. "It's okay to be innocent. In fact, it's preferable one retains a core of innocence at heart. Just don't be naive when it comes to making decisions, okay?"

She nods. "Thanks, Zara, I really appreciate you taking me under your wing."

"You've more than pulled your weight over the past few months on the campaign. Without your efforts, my husband couldn't have been elected Prime Minister."

She hunches her shoulders. "Th-thank you so much."

"Raise your chin."

"Eh?" She blinks.

"Raise your chin, girl, and accept the praise. Own it like a mother—ducking—fitch." I stumble over my words. Guess Hunter's not the only one who has to watch his language around the little ears.

Abby laughs. Then peeks down at the little bundle in my arms. "He's sooo small."

"He didn't feel that small when I pushed him out of my va—a—ah—ina. You know what I mean?"

"Jesus, that's too much information," a new voice declares.

I glance up to see my brother inside the doorway. His familiar features wear an unfamiliar, uncomfortable expression.

"You're perfectly aware of how the birthing process takes place," I scold him.

"Yes, but so far, births and anything to do with them have only been a concept. Just like the fact you're a mother now is something I'm still getting my head around."

He walks over to stand on the side of the bed opposite Abby. In his hands, he's holding one pink and one blue balloon, which say 'baby boy' and 'baby girl,' respectively.

"Covering all my bases," he explains to me, then glances down at the baby. "Wow, you really are a mom."

"And you're an uncle."

Cade's face lights up. He thrusts out his chest, pulls back his shoulders, and folds his arms across his chest. "I can't wait to teach him how to play cricket."

"Would you like to hold him first?"

Cade looks alarmed. "Me?"

"Yes, you."

"Umm. He's too fragile. Maybe when he's a little older?" Then he takes a step back to punctuate his words. The balloons flutter above him. "I guess I should tie these somewhere?" He pivots and crosses the room to one of the chairs, then ties them to the back. Apparently, it's going to take my brother a little longer to be completely comfortable with the idea of holding his nephew.

"Oh, now I realize what's wrong, the pink says baby boy," Abby explains.

"I'm aware." Cade spins around, then walks back to take his place on the side of the bed opposite her; this time, putting more distance between the bed and himself.

"Shouldn't it... I mean... Shouldn't it be the other way around...?" Abby chews on her lower lip, and I notice my brother's shoulders tense. His gaze is fixed on her mouth, and there's a look of something I can only define as lust in his eyes. Talk about TMI.

I clear my throat, and my brother seems to snap out of his reverie.

"Who am I coming to visit, hmm?" He addresses his question to Abby.

"You're coming to visit Zara." She frowns.

"Who is...?"

"Your sister?" she replies hesitantly.

"And?"

"Uh, she's very much a feminist, a strong woman, ah—" Her brow clears. "I get it now. You were making a statement that you knew she'd approve of."

My brother smirks. "You're smarter than you look."

Abby's lips firms. "And you're not as dumb as you look, either."

My brother blinks. "Dumb? Did you just call me dumb?"

"You know what they say, when you have a good-looking face, chances are good, there's nothing between the ears."

Cade's jaw hangs open, then he chuckles. "Very good."

"You talk as if you didn't think I could hold my own in a conversation." Abby huffs.

"Oh, I'm sure you can. If not, my sister wouldn't have hired you."

"I took her on because Abby showed a lot of potential. In fact—"I turn to Abby. "I see something of me in you."

Abby's features light up. "You do?"

I nod. "You have the same hunger, the need to prove yourself. That thirst for success that pushes you to try harder, to go that extra mile—"

"Which is why I think you'll be perfect for the role of my new Communications Manager," Cade steps in smoothly.

Abby jerks her chin in his direction. "Wh-what do you mean?"

"I need help managing my social media profiles, as well as my PR, and you heard my sister, you're among the best on her team. So, I've decided you can come work for me."

Abby stiffens. She folds her arms across her chest, mirroring Cade's earlier body language. "And if I refuse?"

To find out what happens next read Cade and Abby's story HERE

Want a bonus scene featuring Zara and Hunter and their baby? Click HERE

Read an excerpt from Cade and Abby's story

Abby

"Oh, hope I'm not interrupting?" I squeeze my fingers around the vase of flowers and peek inside the hospital room.

The woman with the newborn in her arms and the tall handsome man next to her—who happens to be her husband, as well as the leader of the country— glance up at me. I shuffle my feet, hunch my shoulders, and glance away then back at them. *Why do I have to be so shy? Why can't I feel half as confident as the dark-haired woman who fixes me with her unblinking gaze? Don't flush now, you didn't do anything wrong. You're only here to update them on the new campaign you are working on. Why can't I find it in me to be courageous? To hold my own and face the world head on?* The silence lengthens. My cheeks turn fiery. "I could come back

"You weren't interrupting." Hunter rises to his feet. "Actually, I'd be reassured if you kept Zara company while I make a few calls." He kisses the woman on her forehead then prowls past me.

"Come on in." Zara, who's also my boss, gestures to me.

I walk over to the table pushed up against the wall and place my flowers amongst the many bouquets and toys scattered there. The scent of roses, lilies and other flowers meshes together to form a heady floral perfume that embraces me. No hint of antiseptic or any of the smells one would associate with a hospital dare intrude here. After all, Zara is the wife of the Prime Minister, who also happens to be one of the richest men in the country. "Wow, this room smells like a garden!" I can't stop the words from escaping. *Gosh, did that make me sound gauche? Hope not.*

"All the Seven and the Sovranos, and of course, their wives, sent me flowers and toys for the baby," Zara says in a soft voice.

I turn to face her. Not only because I've never heard my boss sound so...feminine, so womanly, so...gentle. Not that she isn't all three of those. It's just, she's the woman who recruited me to her company when no one else would give me a chance and for that, I'll always be grateful. It also means I'm in awe of her.

She's the hardest working person I know, and definitely the cleverest. If only I had a quarter of her talent and confidence, I'd be so much more successful. Yeah, I may have a bit of a girl-crush on Zara Chopra Whittington. Which means I should be tongue-tied in her presence, which would be more in keeping with my character. Only, I've gotten to know Zara well over the last few months. Besides, my curiosity is riding me hard. Enough that I can't stop myself from asking: "You mean the Seven who run the 7A company—"

"And the Sovranos." She nods.

I stare. "The Sovranos. As in, the Italian Mafia?"

"As in the Cosa Nostra."

I widen my gaze. "Aren't they criminals of sorts?" I whisper.

"Doesn't everyone have skeletons in their closet?" She raises a shoulder.

The flush which had receded comes back with a vengeance. This time it's accompanied by the flip-flop of my stomach. My guts churn. *Stop feeling guilty, you have nothing to be afraid of.* I glance away then back at Zara.

"You're not good at hiding your thoughts, are you?" She tilts her head.

My cheeks burn, and I lock my fingers together in front of me. "It's the curse of having such fair skin," I mumble.

"Or a pure mind." She half smiles. "It's okay to be innocent. In fact, it's preferable that one retains a core of innocence at heart. Just don't be naive when it comes to making decisions, okay?"

If she only knew of the decisions I had to make to get here, she wouldn't think I'm that innocent. Guess I'm a better actress than I gave myself credit for. I bite the inside of my cheek. "Thanks, Zara. I really appreciate you taking me under your wing."

"You've more than pulled your weight over the past few months on the campaign. Without your efforts, my husband couldn't have been elected Prime Minister." She smiles.

I hunch my shoulders. "Th-thank you so much."

"Raise your chin," she orders.

"Eh?"

"Raise your chin, girl, and accept the praise. Own it like a mother—ducking—fitch." She glances down at the still sleeping baby in her arms, then back at me. "Oopsie."

I can't stop myself from laughing. I move closer, then take in the little bundle in her arms. "He's sooo small."

She scoffs, "He didn't feel that small when I pushed him out of my va—a—ah—ina. You know what I mean?"

"Jesus, that's too much information," a deep voice rumbles.

The hair on the nape of my neck rises. I know who that is. I know that sinful baritone belongs to a man whose soul is as dark as his voice. *Don't turn around. Don't turn around.*

It's as if I have no control over my body anymore. As if I'm the puppet and he's the puppeteer to whom I've handed over control. I pivot and take in the man lounging in the doorway. Dark hair that's cut short at the sides and long on top. Square jaw, blue eyes so bright they seem to draw every inch of light in the room. High cheekbones, the makings of a five-o-clock shadow on his chin, even though it's not even noon. He straightens and his shoulders fill the doorway. Then he prowls toward me, and the rest of the room recedes. Wide chest, sculpted enough that the grey Henley he's wearing stretches across his pecs. His waist is narrow, his powerful thighs straining the worn jeans he's wearing. His gaze locks with mine, and as always, it's as if he's reached into my mind and learned every dirty fantasy I've harbored about him all these years. For a second, those blue eyes flare with cold fire. Then, just as suddenly, he wipes all expression from his face. He looks away, and my muscles sag. It's as if I've been released from a tractor beam. He glances toward his sister and his features form into an uncomfortable expression.

"You're perfectly aware of how the birthing process takes place," Zara scolds him.

"Yes, but so far, births and anything to do with them have only been a concept. Just like the fact that you are a mother now is something I'm still getting my head around," he drawls.

He walks over to stand on the side of the bed opposite me. Which leaves the entire expanse of the bed between us, *thank god*. His fingers are looped around one pink and one blue balloon, which say, 'baby boy' and 'baby girl,' respectively.

"Was covering all my bases, since you kept us guessing until the last moment," he explains, then glances down at the baby in her arms. "Wow, you really are a mom."

"And you're an uncle."

Cade's face lights up. He thrusts out his chest, pulls back his shoulders and folds his arms across his chest. "I can't wait to teach him how to play cricket."

"Would you like to hold him first?" Zara asks.

Cade looks alarmed. "Me?" There's so much panic in his voice that I have to press my lips together to stop myself from snorting out loud.

"Yes, you." Zara tilts her head.

"Umm. He's too fragile, maybe when he's a little older?" Cade takes a step back to punctuate his words. The balloons flutter above him. "I guess I should tie these…somewhere?" He crosses the room to a chair pushed up by the window and ties them to its back.

"Oh, now I realize what's wrong. The pink balloon says baby boy," I exclaim.

"I'm aware." Cade spins around, then walks back to take his place on the opposite side of the bed, this time, putting more distance between the bed and himself. Not that I'm complaining. The farther away from me he is, the better.

"Shouldn't it… I mean… Shouldn't it be the other way around?" I chew on my lower lip, and his gaze lowers to my mouth. His nostrils flare and he looks annoyed. *With me? With himself, maybe?* He raises his gaze to mine, and my breath catches. There are sparks of something I can only define as... Lust? *Nah, not possible, he doesn't find me attractive, does he?*

Zara clears her throat, and Cade seems to snap out of his reverie.

"Who am I here to visit, hmm?" he drawls

I frown. "You're coming to visit Zara."

"Who is…?"

"Your sister?" I offer.

"And?"

"Uh, she's very much a feminist, a strong woman, ah—" I tip up my chin. "I get it now. You were making a statement that you knew she'd approve of."

"You're smarter than you look." He smirks.

I firm my lips. "And you're not as dumb as you look, either."

His gaze widens. "Dumb? Did you just call me dumb?"

"You know what they say" —I thrust out a hip— "when you have a good-looking face, chances are, there's nothing between the ears."

Cade's jaw hangs open, then he chuckles. "Very good."

"You talk as if you didn't think I could hold my own in a conversation," I scoff.

"Oh, I'm sure you can." He raises his shoulder. "If not, my sister wouldn't have hired you."

"I took her on because Abby showed a lot of potential. In fact—" Zara turns to me. "I see something of me in you."

A warmth suffuses my chest. "You do?"

She nods. "You have the same hunger, the need to prove yourself. That thirst for success that pushes you to try harder, to go that extra mile—"

"Which is why I think you'll be perfect for the role of my new Communications Manager," Cade steps in smoothly.

*Eh, excuse me? Did he just say what I think he did?* I jerk my chin in his direction. "Come again?"

"I need help managing my social media profiles, as well as my PR. And you heard my sister, you're among the best on her team. So, I've decided you can come work for me."

No way, he's offering me a job. Cade Kingston, my brother's best friend, the man I've had a crush on for, like, forever, the asshole who turned down my advances and left me feeling humiliated. The grumptwat who walked away and never bothered to keep in touch with me—until I ran into him a few weeks ago. The world's most sought-after sportsman who has a reputation for being a man-whore.

That Cade Kingston is offering me a role on his team? *And why? Because he wants to see me fail and laugh at me again, no doubt. Like it wasn't enough for him to snub me all those years ago? Apparently, he wants to destroy what little is left of my confidence, eh?*

Of course, it'd mean I'd finally get a chance to see him every day; and how agonizing would that be? To watch him from up-close as he fucks his way through the beds of every supermodel and actress he meets. Because those are the only kinds of women he dates. *No, I haven't been keeping track of him. Not at all. I only monitor his social media feeds because it's part of my job as a communications expert. What? Don't you believe me?* I hunch my shoulders. *Yeah, neither do I.*

Nah, if I accept this job, I'm setting myself up for failure. Or worse, I'll end up giving my heart to someone who'll never reciprocate how I feel about him. It's best to stay as far away from him as possible. It's the only way I'm going to hold on to what dignity I have left.

I fold my arms across my chest, mirroring Cade's earlier body language. "And if I refuse?"

## Cade

*She's here. Of course, she's here.*

Zara's her boss, and the two of them share a unique relationship where my sister clearly considers herself a mentor to Abby.

Abigail Warren. My best friend Knight's little sister, who he explicitly warned me off. Not that she's my typ. At all.

I prefer my women to keep their mouths shut and spread their legs wide, on my command. That way, they're merely need-fulfilling orifices and not much else. There's no danger of developing any feelings for them. No messy relationship drama. I can focus on my mission of becoming the greatest batsman in the world of cricket. Of banking those sponsorship dollars and watching my wealth and power grow.

Whoever said money has nothing to do with influence has, clearly, not experienced firsthand just what money can get you. Wine and women, with sex and rock'n'roll thrown in for good measure. Not to mention, the ability to live life on my own terms. To get what I want, when I want it. Be it my choice of pussy, or the choice of buying what and who I want off the sports-field.

No living life afraid of being successful; afraid of standing out too much and being knocked down; afraid of spending my hard-earned money because it might attract too much attention from the community. No, I left those fears to my parents. My goal from when I was very young was very simple. To be everything they're not. To be fearless. To go after what I want.

A fierce focus, combined with the determination to succeed, was topped off with a natural ability to play cricket. It had me getting a sports scholarship to the American International School in London, and later, to Oxford. It meant I left home when I was eleven. It also meant I wasn't there as much as I wanted to be for my sister Zara. Which is why I'm determined to be there for her now as she embarks on this new role as a mature and responsible mother.

What I didn't reckon with was that one tiny, curvy woman would also be on the scene. A gorgeous beauty, no longer the skinny little girl who followed Knight, and by extension, me, everywhere when we went home for school holidays. More often than not, I'd go along with him because I didn't want to go see my parents. My folks were never unkind to me. But they also weren't the demonstrative, affectionate type. Not like Knight's parents, who always welcomed me with open arms. Their house was more of a home to me than my own. Knight was the brother I never had. And Abby… She was the little sister—no…

She never felt like my sister. The relationship between us has always been fraught with…a kind of uncomfortable frisson I've never been able to ignore. Probably because she was always an annoying add-on to the games Knight and I played as young boys—football and cricket and tennis and occasionally, holing up in his treehouse, where we pretended to be pilots. Activities she was always on the fringes of. She's always been the annoying, little sprite who tagged behind us. I didn't expect her to grow up to be so…alive, so potent, so gorgeous… So…everything. Now, I look into her big green eyes and purse my lips.

"Don't recall giving you a choice," I drawl.

Her gaze widens. "Choice? You're giving me a choice?"

"I'm not," I clarify.

Color flushes her cheeks. "Who are you to tell me what I can and cannot do?"

"The man your brother charged with taking care of you."

"Excuse me?" Those big eyes of her grow enormous, until they seem to fill her face. "My brother?"

"Knight, your older brother, remember?"

"I know my brother's name. What I mean is, he never mentioned anything about you taking care of me. Besides, I'm a full-grown woman."

*Yea, trust me. I noticed.*

"And who are you to take care of me anyway?"

"You're brother's best friend?" I offer.

"Someone I haven't seen in ages. I barely know you."

"We don't have to know each other for me to do my duty toward my best friend."

"Well, I absolve you of your duty." She cuts the air with her palm. "You can rest assured I can look after myself. I've been doing it all these years since I left home, after all."

"Apparently, you're not doing a good enough job of it though."

"King!" Zara protests, but I ignore her.

Abby stiffens. "What do you mean?"

I look her up and down. "Clearly, you don't eat enough. Have you seen just how skinny you are?"

"Wh-what?" She opens her mouth, then shuts it. Then opens it again. "What did you say?"

"As for your dress, did you buy it at the charity shop?"

Zara makes a strangled noise at the back of her throat.

I ignore her; so does Abby.

She glances down at her dress, then at me. "This one's from Mango," she says in a low voice.

"Could have come from a charity shop, the way it hangs on you."

"Okay, that's enough," Zara snaps. The baby stirs, then begins to cry. She hushes the kid, who only begins to bawl louder. "It's okay darling. Mommy's here. You're hungry, aren't you?" She pushes down the neckline of her dress and I get a flash of breast—*my sister's breast*—before I hastily turn away.

The baby stops crying; clearly, because it's latched onto her boob. *Ah hell, should I be associating the word boob with my sister? Sisters aren't supposed to have breasts or get married... Or spawn babies, for that matter. Jesus, where has the time gone?* I remember Zara as being a feisty girl who matched me when it came to running, or playing cricket, or standing up to my parents when they insisted she behave more like a 'girl'. *When did she grow up enough to have kids of her own? How much did I miss in the time I was away from home.* I rub the back of my neck. *Why am I having all of these misgivings? I made my choices a long time ago. And so far, they've been working for me. So why am I questioning them now?* Clearly, seeing my sister with her newborn, not to mention meeting the woman who has a way of getting under my skin, has thrown me off kilter.

"I think, uh, I need a cup of coffee." I turn toward the door.

"I'm not done with either of you," Zara announces.

I blow out a breath. I may be only a few minutes younger than her, but she's always been the bossy one. And when my sister commands, you don't ignore it.

I exchange glances with Abby, who looks a little embarrassed, as well. She glances at Zara. "Sorry about that; didn't mean to wake up the little one."

"Oh, he was hungry, anyway. He'll be okay once he's had his fill." She turns to me. "You, on the other hand, need to apologize."

"Eh?" I scowl. "For what?"

"For being rude and saying things you don't mean, for one."

"I meant everything I said." I draw myself up to a full height. "Also —" I turn to Abby. "I promised your brother I'd look after you while he's away on duty."

Yep, Knight joined the army. He had the chance to join the national cricket team with me. He is, in fact, the only person I'll concede is better at the game than I am. But he turned down the opportunity of making the big bucks for a chance to serve his country. Something which makes me proud of him, and makes me realize just how much of a selfish motherfucker I am. The least I could do was promise him I'd look over Abby while he's gone. A promise I intend to keep.

Abby folds her arms across her chest, her jaw set in stubborn lines that take me by surprise. The Abby I remember was sweet to a fault. Perhaps, she was even somewhat of a crybaby. She was very young, not even a teenager, when I'd met her. The Abby in front of me is, as she just pointed out, a grown woman. She has the figure of a siren— albeit, with gentler curves—and a strong backbone, which she apparently acquired along the way. She narrows her gaze on me. "I do not need you."

"Oh, but you do. You just don't know it yet," I say in a casual tone.

Her eyes flash, and color flushes her cheeks. "Anyone told you how condescending you are?"

"I can afford it."

She gapes at me. "You're such an asshole."

"Thank you. Also, I prefer alphahole."

"Why you—"

"Enough already," Zara's steely tone cuts between us.

Abby takes a deep breath. She seems to get a hold of herself, and by the time she turns to face Zara, all traces of anger are wiped from her face. "Sorry about that. I don't normally lose my temper."

"Don't I know that?" Zara looks at her speculatively. "It's good to see you stand up for yourself."

She shuffles her feet. "It's just, he— I—"

"Don't worry about it." Zara's features soften. "I think it would be good for you to accept this role with King."

Abby blinks. "Y-you do?"

Zara nods. "You've done a great job with the Prime Ministerial campaign. But that's over now and you need something else to challenge you so you can grow. And becoming King's Communication Manager would give you all of that, and more."

*Did my sister just insult me?* "Are you saying my reputation is in need of repair."

Zara snorts. "It would help if you weren't seen with a different woman every week. Not to mention, that pub brawl you got into; you could have done without that."

I smirk. "You should see the other man."

Zara shakes her head, but her lips curve up a little. "You're right. You need a professional in charge of your image. Someone who'll also help keep you in line."

"Hold on." I raise my hands. "Who said anything about keeping me in line?"

"If I were to become your Communications Manager, it means you'd need to follow the ground rules I lay down." Abby draws herself up to her full height.

"I make the rules, doll; I don't follow them."

"Also, I have a name. You'd do well to call me by that," she says primly.

"I'm the person paying you. Do I need to remind you of that?"

"And I'm the person who'll be managing your public facing profile. So remember, I have the power to also cast you in a bad light."

I stare at her, then bark out a laugh. "Touché, kitten. Apparently, you have claws."

She glances at her nails then rubs them on her sleeve. "They're sharp and lethal and can cause enough damage that you'll wear the scars for a lifetime."

The thought of her marking me sends a ripple of heat racing through my veins. I may have agreed to keep an eye on Abby as a promise to Knight. I hadn't thought the assignment would turn out to be quite this interesting. Of course, there's no way I'm going to break the trust Knight placed in me. Doesn't mean I can't have a bit of harmless fun with her in the meanwhile, hmm?

I walk around the bed, then hold out my hand to her. "So, *Abigail Warren*, you're taking the job?"

To find out what happens next read Cade and Abby's book **HERE**

Read Summer & Sinclair Sterling's story **HERE** in The Billionaire's Fake Wife

Read an excerpt from Summer & Sinclair's story

Summer

"Slap, slap, kiss, kiss."

"Huh?" I stare up at the bartender.

"Aka, there's a thin line between love and hate." He shakes out the crimson liquid into my glass.

"Nah." I snort. "Why would she allow him to control her, and after he insulted her?"

"It's the chemistry between them." He lowers his head, "You have to admit that when the man is arrogant and the woman resists, it's a challenge to both of them, to see who blinks first, huh?"

"Why?" I wave my hand in the air, "Because they hate each other?"

"Because," he chuckles, "the girl in school whose braids I pulled and teased mercilessly, is the one who I—"

"Proposed to?" I huff.

His face lights up. "You get it now?"

*Yeah. No.* A headache begins to pound at my temples. This crash course in pop psychology is not why I came to my favorite bar in Islington, to meet my best friend, who is—I glance at the face of my phone—thirty minutes late.

I inhale the drink, and his eyebrows rise.

"What?" I glower up at the bartender. "I can barely taste the alcohol. Besides, it's free drinks at happy hour for women, right?"

"Which ends in precisely" he holds up five fingers, "minutes."

"Oh! Yay!" I mock fist pump. "Time enough for one more, at least."

A hiccough swells my throat and I swallow it back, nod.

One has to do what one has to do... when everything else in the world is going to shit.

A hot sensation stabs behind my eyes; my chest tightens. Is this what people call growing up?

The bartender tips his mixing flask, strains out a fresh batch of the ruby red liquid onto the glass in front of me.

"Salut." I nod my thanks, then toss it back. It hits my stomach and tendrils of fire crawl up my spine, I cough.

My head spins. Warmth sears my chest, spreads to my extremities. I can't feel my fingers or toes. Good. Almost there. "Top me up."

"You sure?"

"Yes." I square my shoulders and reach for the drink.

"No. She's had enough."

"What the—?" I pivot on the bar stool.

Indigo eyes bore into me.

Fathomless. Black at the bottom, the intensity in their depths grips me. He swoops out his arm, grabs the glass and holds it up. Thick fingers dwarf the glass. Tapered at the edges. The nails short and buff. *All the better to grab you with.* I gulp.

"Like what you see?"

I flush, peer up into his face.

Hard cheekbones, hollows under them, and a tiny scar that slashes at his left eyebrow. *How did he get that?* Not that I care. My gaze slides to his mouth. Thin upper lip, a lower lip that is full and cushioned. Pouty with a hint of bad boy. *Oh!* My toes curl. My thighs clench.

The corner of his mouth kicks up. *Asshole.*

Bet he thinks life is one big smug-fest. I glower, reach for my glass, and he holds it up and out of my reach.

I scowl. "Gimme that."

He shakes his head.

"That's my drink."

"Not anymore." He shoves my glass at the bartender. "Water for her. Get me a whiskey, neat."

I splutter, then reach for my drink again. The barstool tips in his direction. This is when I fall against him, and my breasts slam into his hard chest, sculpted planes with layers upon layers of muscle that ripple and writhe as he turns aside, flattens himself against the bar. The floor rises up to meet me.

*What the actual hell?*

I twist my torso at the last second and my butt connects with the surface. *Ow!*

The breath rushes out of me. My hair swirls around my face. I scramble for purchase, and my knee connects with his leg.

"Watch it." He steps around, stands in front of me.

"You stepped aside?" I splutter. "You let me fall?"

"Hmph."

I tilt my chin back, all the way back, look up the expanse of muscled thigh that stretches the silken material of his suit. *What is he wearing? Could any suit fit a man with such precision?* Hand crafted on Saville Row, no doubt. I glance at the bulge that tents the fabric between his legs. *Oh! I blink.*

*Look away, look away.* I hold out my arm. He'll help me up at least, won't he?

He glances at my palm, then turns away. *No, he didn't do that, no way.*

A glass of amber liquid appears in front of him. He lifts the tumbler to his sculpted mouth.

His throat moves, strong tendons flexing. He tilts his head back, and the column of his neck moves as he swallows. Dark hair covers his chin—it's a discordant chord in that clean-cut profile, I shiver. He would scrape that rough skin down my core. He'd mark my inner thighs, lick my core, thrust his tongue inside my melting channel and drink from my pussy. *Oh! God.* Goosebumps rise on my skin.

No one has the right to look this beautiful, this achingly gorgeous. Too magnificent for his own good. Anger coils in my chest.

"Arrogant wanker."

"I'll take that under advisement."

"You're a jerk, you know that?"

He presses his lips together. The grooves on either side of his mouth deepen. Jesus, clearly the man has never laughed a single day in his life. Bet that stick up his arse is uncomfortable. I chuckle.

He runs his gaze down my features, my chest, down to my toes, then yawns.

*The hell!* I will not let him provoke me. Will not. "Like what you see?" I jut out my chin.

"Sorry, you're not my type." He slides a hand into the pocket of those perfectly cut pants, stretching it across that heavy bulge.

Heat curls low in my belly.

Not fair, that he could afford a wardrobe that clearly shouts his status and what amounts to the economy of a small third-world country. A hot feeling stabs in my chest.

He reeks of privilege, of taking his status in life for granted.

While I've had to fight every inch of the way. Hell, I am still battling to hold onto the last of my equilibrium.

"Last chance—" I wiggle my fingers from where I am sprawled out on the floor at his feet, "—to redeem yourself…"

"You have me there." He places the glass on the counter, then bends and holds out his hand. The hint of discolored steel at his wrist catches my attention. Huh?

He wears a cheap-ass watch?

That's got to bring down the net worth of his presence by more than 1000% percent. Weird.

I reach up and he straightens.

I lurch back.

"Oops, I changed my mind." His lips curl.

A hot burning sensation claws at my stomach. I am not a violent person, honestly. But Smirky Pants here, he needs to be taught a lesson.

I swipe out my legs, kicking his out from under him.

### Sinclair

My knees give way, and I hurtle toward the ground.

What the—? I twist around, thrust out my arms. My palms hit the floor. The impact jostles up my elbows. I firm my biceps and come to a halt planked above her.

A huffing sound fills my ear.

I turn to find my whippet, Max, panting with his mouth open. I scowl and he flattens his ears.

All of my businesses are dog-friendly. Before you draw conclusions about me being the caring sort or some such shit—it attracts footfall.

Max scrutinizes the girl, then glances at me. *Huh?* He hates women, but not her, apparently.

I straighten and my nose grazes hers.

My arms are on either side of her head. Her chest heaves. The fabric of her dress stretches across her gorgeous breasts. My fingers tingle; my palms ache to cup those tits, squeeze those hard nipples outlined against the—hold on, what is she wearing? A tunic shirt in a sparkly pink... and are those shoulder pads she has on?

I glance up, and a squeak escapes her lips.

Pink hair surrounds her face. *Pink? Who dyes their hair that color past the age of eighteen?*

I stare at her face. *How old is she?* Un-furrowed forehead, dark eyelashes that flutter against pale cheeks. Tiny nose, and that mouth—luscious, tempting. A whiff of her scent, cherries and caramel, assails my senses. My mouth waters. *What the hell?*

She opens her eyes and our eyelashes brush. Her gaze widens. Green, like the leaves of the evergreens, flickers of gold sparkling in their depths. "What?" She glowers. "You're demonstrating the plank position?"

"Actually," I lower my weight onto her, the ridge of my hardness thrusting into the softness between her legs, "I was thinking of something else, altogether."

She gulps and her pupils dilate. *Ah, so she feels it, too?*

I drop my head toward her, closer, closer.

Color floods the creamy expanse of her neck. Her eyelids flutter down. She tilts her chin up.

I push up and off of her.

"That… Sweetheart, is an emphatic 'no thank you' to whatever you are offering."

Her eyelids spring open and pink stains her cheeks. Adorable. Such a range of emotions across those gorgeous features in a few seconds. What else is hidden under that exquisite exterior of hers?

She scrambles up, eyes blazing.

*Ah!* The little bird is trying to spread her wings? My dick twitches. My groin hardens, *Why does her anger turn me on so, huh?*

She steps forward, thrusts a finger in my chest.

My heart begins to thud.

She peers up from under those hooded eyelashes. "Wake up and taste the wasabi, asshole."

"What does that even mean?"

She makes a sound deep in her throat. My dick twitches. My pulse speeds up.

She pivots, grabs a half-full beer mug sitting on the bar counter.

I growl, "Oh, no, you don't."

She turns, swings it at me. The smell of hops envelops the space.

I stare down at the beer-splattered shirt, the lapels of my camel colored jacket deepening to a dull brown. Anger squeezes my guts.

I fist my fingers at my side, broaden my stance.

She snickers.

I tip my chin up. "You're going to regret that."

The smile fades from her face. "Umm." She places the now empty mug on the bar.

I take a step forward and she skitters back. "It's only clothes." She gulps. "They'll wash."

I glare at her and she swallows, wiggles her fingers in the air. "I should have known that you wouldn't have a sense of humor."

I thrust out my jaw. "That's a ten-thousand-pound suit you destroyed."

She blanches, then straightens her shoulders. "Must have been some hot date you were trying to impress, huh?"

"Actually," I flick some of the offending liquid from my lapels, "it's you I was after."

"Me?" She frowns.

"We need to speak."

She glances toward the bartender who's on the other side of the bar. "I don't know you." She chews on her lower lip, biting off some of the hot pink. How would she look, with that pouty mouth fastened on my cock?

The blood rushes to my groin so quickly that my head spins. My pulse rate ratchets up. Focus, focus on the task you came here for.

"This will take only a few seconds." I take a step forward.

She moves aside.

I frown. "You want to hear this, I promise."

"Go to hell." She pivots and darts forward.

I let her go, a step, another, because... I can? Besides it's fun to create the illusion of freedom first; makes the hunt so much more entertaining, huh?

I swoop forward, loop an arm around her waist, and yank her toward me.

She yelps. "Release me."

Good thing the bar is not yet full. It's too early for the usual office-goers to stop by. And the staff...? Well they are well aware of who cuts their paychecks.

I spin her around and against the bar, then release her. "You will listen to me."

She swallows; she glances left to right.

*Not letting you go yet, little Bird.* I move into her space, crowd her.

She tips her chin up. "Whatever you're selling, I'm not interested."

I allow my lips to curl. "You don't fool me."

A flush steals up her throat, sears her cheeks. So tiny, so innocent. Such a good little liar. I narrow my gaze. "Every action has its consequences."

"Are you daft?" She blinks.

"This pretense of yours?" I thrust my face into hers, growling, "It's not working."

She blinks, then color suffuses her cheeks. "You're certifiably mad—"

"Getting tired of your insults."

"It's true, everything I said." She scrapes back the hair from her face. Her fingernails are painted... You guessed it, pink.

"And here's something else. You are a selfish, egotistical jackass."

I smirk. "You're beginning to repeat your insults and I haven't even kissed you yet."

"Don't you dare." She gulps.

I tilt my head. "Is that a challenge?"

"It's a..." she scans the crowded space, then turns to me. Her lips firm, "...a warning. You're delusional, you jackass." She inhales a deep breath before she speaks, "Your ego is bigger than the size of a black hole." She snickers. "Bet it's to compensate for your lack of balls."

A-n-d, that's it. I've had enough of her mouth that threatens to never stop spewing words. How many insults can one tiny woman hurl my way? Answer: too many to count.

"You—"

I lower my chin, touch my lips to hers.

Heat, sweetness, the honey of her essence explodes on my palate. My dick twitches. I tilt my head, deepen the kiss, reaching for that something more... more... of whatever scent she's wearing on her skin, infused with that breath of hers that crowds my senses, rushes down my spine. My groin hardens; my cock lengthens. I thrust my tongue between those infuriating lips.

She makes a sound deep in her throat and my heart begins to pound.

So innocent, yet so crafty. Beautiful and feisty. The kind of complication I don't need in my life.

I prefer the straight and narrow. Gray and black, that's how I choose to define my world. She, with her flashes of color—pink hair and lips that threaten to drive me to the edge of distraction—is exactly what I hate.

Give me a female who has her priorities set in life. To pleasure me, get me off, then walk away before her emotions engage. Yeah. That's what I prefer.

Not this… this bundle of craziness who flings her arms around my shoulders, thrusts her breasts up and into my chest, tips up her chin, opens her mouth, and invites me to take and take.

Does she have no self-preservation? Does she think I am going to fall for her wide-eyed appeal? She has another thing coming.

I tear my mouth away and she protests.

She twines her leg with mine, pushes up her hips, so that melting softness between her thighs cradles my aching hardness.

I glare into her face and she holds my gaze.

Trains her green eyes on me. Her cheeks flush a bright red. Her lips fall open and a moan bleeds into the air. The blood rushes to my dick, which instantly thickens. *Fuck.*

Time to put distance between myself and the situation.

It's how I prefer to manage things. Stay in control, always. Cut out anything that threatens to impinge on my equilibrium. Shut it down or buy them off. Reduce it to a transaction. That I understand.

The power of money, to be able to buy and sell—numbers, logic. That's what's worked for me so far.

"How much?"

Her forehead furrows.

"Whatever it is, I can afford it."

Her jaw slackens. "You think… you—"

"A million?"

"What?"

"Pounds, dollars... You name the currency, and it will be in your account."

Her jaw slackens. "You're offering me money?"

"For your time, and for you to fall in line with my plan."

She reddens. "You think I am for sale?"

"Everyone is."

"Not me."

Here we go again. "Is that a challenge?"

Color fades from her face. "Get away from me."

"Are you shy, is that what this is?" I frown. "You can write your price down on a piece of paper if you prefer." I glance up, notice the bartender watching us. I jerk my chin toward the napkins. He grabs one, then offers it to her.

She glowers at him. "Did you buy him, too?"

"What do you think?"

She glances around. "I think everyone here is ignoring us."

"It's what I'd expect."

"Why is that?"

I wave the tissue in front of her face. "Why do you think?"

"You own the place?"

"As I am going to own you."

She sets her jaw. "Let me leave and you won't regret this."

A chuckle bubbles up. I swallow it away. This is no laughing matter. I never smile during a transaction. Especially not when I am negotiating a new acquisition. And that's all she is. The final piece in the puzzle I am building.

"No one threatens me."

"You're right."

"Huh?"

"I'd rather act on my instinct."

Her lips twist, her gaze narrows. All of my senses scream a warning.

No, she wouldn't, no way—pain slices through my middle and sparks explode behind my eyes.

To find out what happens next read Summer & Sinclair Sterling's story HERE
Read an excerpt from Mafia King – Michael and Karma's story

## Karma

*"Morn came and went—and came, and brought no day…"*

Tears prick the backs of my eyes. Goddamn Byron. His words creep up on me when I am at my weakest. Not that I am a poetry addict, by any measure, but words are my jam. The one consolation I have is that, when everything else in the world is wrong, I can turn to them, and they'll be there, friendly, steady, waiting with open arms.

And this particular poem had laced my blood, crawled into my gut when I'd first read it. Darkness had folded within me like an insidious snake, that raises its head when I least expect it. Like now, when I look out on the still sleeping city of London, from the grassy slope of Waterlow Park.

Somewhere out there, the Mafia is hunting me, apparently. It's why my sister Summer and her new husband Sinclair Sterling had insisted that I have my own security detail. I had agreed… only to appease them… then given my bodyguard the slip this morning. I had decided to come running here because it's not a place I'd normally go… Not so early in the morning, anyway. They won't think to look for me here. At least, not for a while longer.

I purse my lips, close my eyes. Silence. The rustle of the wind between the leaves. The faint tinkle of the water from the nearby spring.

I could be the last person on this planet, alone, unsung, bound for the grave.

Ugh! Stop. Right there. I drag the back of my hand across my nose. Try it again, focus, get the words out, one after the other, like the steps of my sorry life.

*"Morn came and went—and came, and… and…"* My voice breaks. "Bloody asinine hell." I dig my fingers into the grass and grab a handful and fling it out. Again. From the top.

*"Morn came and went—and came, and—"*

*"…brought no day."*

A gravelly voice completes my sentence.

I whip my head around. His silhouette fills my line of sight. He's sitting on the same knoll as me, yet I have to crane my neck back to see his profile. The sun is at his back, so I can't make out his features. Can't see his eyes... Can only take in his dark hair, combed back by a ruthless hand that brooked no measure.

My throat dries.

Thick dark hair, shot through with grey at the temples. He wears his age like a badge. I don't know why, but I know his years have not been easy. That he's seen more, indulged in more, reveled in the consequences of his actions, however extreme they might have been. He's not a normal, everyday person, this man. Not a nine-to-fiver, not someone who lives an average life. Definitely not a man who returns home to his wife and home at the end of the day. He is...different, unique, evil... Monstrous. Yes, he is a beast, one who sports the face of a man but who harbors the kind of darkness inside that speaks to me. I gulp.

His face boasts a hooked nose, a thin upper lip, a fleshy lower lip. One that hints at hidden desires, Heat. Lust. The sensuous scrape of that whiskered jaw over my innermost places. Across my inner thigh, reaching toward that core of me that throbs, clenches, melts to feel the stab of his tongue, the thrust of his hardness as he impales me, takes me, makes me his. Goosebumps pop on my skin.

I drag my gaze away from his mouth down to the scar that slashes across his throat. A cold sensation coils in my chest. What or who had hurt him in such a cruel fashion?

*"Of this their desolation; and all hearts*
*Were chill'd into a selfish prayer for light..."*

He continues in that rasping guttural tone. Is it the wound that caused that scar that makes his voice so... gravelly... So deep... so... so, hot?

Sweat beads my palms and the hairs on my nape rise. "Who are you?"

He stares ahead as his lips move,

*"Forests were set on fire—but hour by hour*

*They fell and faded—and the crackling trunks*
*Extinguish'd with a crash—and all was black."*

I swallow, moisture gathers in my core. How can I be wet by the mere cadence of this stranger's voice?

I spring up to my feet.

"Sit down," he commands.

His voice is unhurried, lazy even, his spine erect. The cut of his black jacket stretches across the width of his massive shoulders. His hair... I was mistaken—there are threads of dark gold woven between the darkness that pours down to brush the nape of his neck. A strand of hair falls over his brow. As I watch, he raises his hand and brushes it away. Somehow, the gesture lends an air of vulnerability to him. Something so at odds with the rest of his persona that, surely, I am mistaken?

My scalp itches. I take in a breath and my lungs burn. This man... He's sucked up all the oxygen in this open space as if he owns it, the master of all he surveys. The master of me. My death. My life. A shiver ladders along my spine. *Get away, get away now, while you still can.*

I angle my body, ready to spring away from him.

"I won't ask again."

Ask. Command. Force me to do as he wants. He'll have me on my back, bent over, on my side, on my knees, over him, under him. He'll surround me, overwhelm me, pin me down with the force of his personality. His charisma, his larger-than-life essence will crush everything else out of me and I... I'll love it.

"No."

"Yes."

A fact. A statement of intent, spoken aloud. So true. So real. Too real. Too much. Too fast. All of my nightmares... my dreams come to life. Everything I've wanted is here in front of me. I'll die a thousand deaths before he'll be done with me... And then? Will I be reborn? For him. For me. For myself.

I live, first and foremost, to be the woman I was... am meant to be.

"You want to run?"

*No.*

*No.*

I nod my head.

He turns his, and all the breath leaves my lungs. Blue eyes—cerulean, dark like the morning skies, deep like the nighttime...hidden corners, secrets that I don't dare uncover. He'll destroy me, have my heart, and break it so casually.

My throat burns and a boiling sensation squeezes my chest.

"Go then, my beauty, fly. You have until I count to five. If I catch you, you are mine."

"If you don't?"

"Then I'll come after you, stalk your every living moment, possess your nightmares, and steal you away in the dead of night, and then..."

I draw in a shuddering breath as liquid heat drips from between my legs. "Then?" I whisper.

"Then, I'll ensure you'll never belong to anyone else, you'll never see the light of day again, for your every breath, your every waking second, your thoughts, your actions... and all your words, every single last one, will belong to me." He peels back his lips, and his teeth glint in the first rays of the morning light. "Only me." He straightens to his feet and rises, and rises.

This man... He is massive. A monster who always gets his way. My guts churn. My toes curl. Something primeval inside of me insists I hold my own. I cannot give in to him. Cannot let him win whatever this is. I need to stake my ground, in some form. *Say something. Anything. Show him you're not afraid of this.*

"Why?" I tilt my head back, all the way back. "Why are you doing this?"

He tilts his head, his ears almost canine in the way they are silhouetted against his profile.

"Is it because you can? Is it a... a," I blink, "a debt of some kind?"

He stills.

"My father, this is about how he betrayed the Mafia, right? You're one of them?"

"Lucky guess." His lips twist, "It is about your father, and how he promised you to me. He reneged on his promise, and now, I am here to collect."

"No." I swallow... *No, no, no.*

"Yes." His jaw hardens.

All expression is wiped clean of his face, and I know then, that he speaks the truth. It's always about the past. My sorry shambles of a past... Why does it always catch up with me? *You can run, but you can never hide.*

"Tick-tock, Beauty." He angles his body and his shoulders shut out the sight of the sun, the dawn skies, the horizon, the city in the distance, the rustle of the grass, the trees, the rustle of the leaves. All of it fades and leaves just me and him. Us. *Run.*

"Five." He jerks his chin, straightens the cuffs of his sleeves.

My knees wobble.

"Four."

My pulse rate spikes. I should go. Leave. But my feet are planted in this earth. This piece of land where we first met. What am I, but a speck in the larger scheme of things? To be hurt. To be forgotten. To be taken without an ounce of retribution. To be punished... by him.

"Three." He thrusts out his chest, widens his stance, every muscle in his body relaxed. "Two."

I swallow. The pulse beats at my temples. My blood thrums.

"One."

## Michael

"Go."

She pivots and races down the slope. Her dark hair streams behind her. Her scent, sexy femininity and silver moonflowers, clings to my nose, then recedes. It's so familiar, that scent.

I had smelled it before, had reveled in it. Had drawn in it into my lungs as she had peeked up at me from under her thick eyelashes. Her green gaze had fixed on mine, her lips parted as she welcomed my kiss. As she had wound her arms about my neck, pushed up those sweet breasts and flattened them against my chest. As she had parted her legs when I had planted my thigh between them. I had seen her before... in my dreams. I stiffen. She can't be the same girl, though, can she?

I reach forward, thrust out my chin and sniff the air, but there's only the damp scent of dawn, mixed with the foul tang of exhaust fumes, as she races away from me.

She stumbles and I jump forward, pause when she straightens. Wait. Wait. Give her a lead. Let her think she has almost escaped, that she's gotten the better of me... As if.

I clench my fists at my sides, force myself to relax. Wait. Wait. She reaches the bottom of the incline, turns. I surge forward. One foot in front of the other. My heels dig into the grassy surface and mud flies up, clings to the hem of my £4000 Italian pants. Like I care? Plenty more where that came from. An entire walk-in closet, full of clothes made to measure, to suit every occasion, with every possible accessory needed by a man in my position to impress...

Everything... Except the one thing that I had coveted from the moment I had laid eyes on her. Sitting there on the grassy slope, unshed tears in her eyes, and reciting... Byron? For hell's sake. Of all the poets in the world, she had to choose the Lord of Darkness.

I huff. All a ploy. Clearly, she knew I was sitting next to her... No, not possible. I had walked toward her and she hadn't stirred. Hadn't been aware. Yeah, I am that good. I've been known to slit a man's throat from ear-to-ear while he was awake and in his full senses. Alive one second, dead the next. That's how it is in my world. You want it, you take it. And I... I want her.

I increase my pace, eat up the distance between myself and the girl... That's all she is. A slip of a thing, a slim blur of motion. Beauty in hiding. A diamond, waiting for me to get my hands on her, polish her, show her what it means to be...

Dead. She is dead. That's why I am here.

A flash of skin, a creamy length of thigh. My groin hardens and my legs wobble. I lurch over a bump in the ground. The hell? I right myself, leap forward, inching closer, closer. She reaches a curve in the path, disappears out of sight.

My heart hammers in my chest. I will not lose her, will not. *Here, Beauty, come to Daddy.* The wind whistles past my ears. I pump my legs, lengthen my strides, turn the corner. There's no one there. Huh?

My heart hammers and the blood pounds at my wrists, my

temples; adrenaline thrums in my veins. I slow down, come to a stop. Scan the clearing.

The hairs on my forearms prickle. She's here. Not far, but where? Where is she? I prowl across to the edge of the clearing, under the tree with its spreading branches.

*When I get my hands on you, Beauty, I'll spread your legs like the pages of a poem. Dip into your honeyed sweetness, like a quill pen in ink. Drag my aching shaft across that melting, weeping entrance.* My balls throb. My groin tightens. The crack of a branch above shivers across my stretched nerve endings. I swoop forward, hold out my arms, and close my grasp around the trembling, squirming mass of precious humanity. I cradle her close to my chest, heart beating thud-thud-thud, overwhelming any other thought.

*Mine. All mine.* The hell is wrong with me? She wriggles her little body, and her curves slide across my forearms. My shoulders bunch and my fingers tingle. She kicks out with her legs and arches her back, thrusting her breasts up so her nipples are outlined against the fabric of her sports bra. She dared to come out dressed like that? In that scrap of fabric that barely covers her luscious flesh?

"Let me go." She whips her head toward me and her hair flows around her shoulders, across her face. She blows it out of the way. "You monster, get away from me."

Anger drums at the backs of my eyes and desire tugs at my groin. The scent of her is sheer torture, something I had dreamed of in the wee hours of twilight when dusk turned into night.

She's not real. She's not the woman I think she is. She is my downfall. My sweet poison. The bitter medicine I must partake of to cure the ills that plague my company.

"Fine." I lower my arms and she tumbles to the grass, hits the ground butt first.

"How dare you." She huffs out a breath, her hair messily arranged across her face.

I shove my hands into the pockets of my fitted pants, knees slightly bent, legs apart. Tip my chin down and watch her as she sprawls at my feet.

"You... dropped me?" She makes a sound deep in her throat.

So damn adorable.

"Your wish is my command." I quirk my lips.

"You don't mean it."

"You're right." I lean my weight forward on the balls of my feet and she flinches.

"What... what do you want?"

"You."

She pales. "You want to... to rob me? I have nothing of consequence.

"Oh, but you do, Beauty."

I lean in and every muscle in her body tenses. Good. She's wary. She should be. She should have been alert enough to have run as soon as she sensed my presence. But she hadn't.

I should spare her because she's the woman from my dreams... but I won't. She's a debt I intend to collect. She owes me, and I've delayed what was meant to happen long enough.

I pull the gun from my holster, point it at her.

Her gaze widens and her breath hitches. I expect her to plead with me for her life, but she doesn't. She stares back at me with her huge dilated pupils. She licks her lips and the blood drains to my groin. *Che cazzo!* Why does her lack of fear turn me on so?

"Your phone," I murmur, "take out your phone."

She draws in a breath, then reaches into her pocket and pulls out her phone.

"Call your sister."

"What?"

"Dial your sister, Beauty. Tell her you are going away on a long trip to Sicily with your new male friend."

"What?"

"You heard me." I curl my lips. "Do it, now!'

She blinks, looks like she is about to protest, then her fingers fly over the phone.

Damn, and I had been looking forward to coaxing her into doing my bidding.

She holds her phone to her ear. I can hear the phone ring on the other side, before it goes to voicemail. She glances at me and I jerk my chin. She looks away, takes a deep breath, then speaks in a cheerful voice, "Hi Summer, it's me, Karma. I, ah, have to go away for a bit. This new... ah, friend of mine... He has an extra ticket and he has invited me to Sicily to spend some time with him. I... ah, I don't know when, exactly, I'll be back, but I'll message you and let you know. Take care. Love ya sis, I—"

I snatch the phone from her, disconnect the call, then hold the gun to her temple, "Goodbye, Beauty."

TO FIND OUT WHAT HAPPENS NEXT READ MAFIA KING **HERE**

WANT A BONUS SCENE FEATURING ZARA AND HUNTER AND THEIR BABY? CLICK **HERE**

WANT TO FIND OUT HOW **WESTON AND AMELIE** MET? READ THE BILLIONAIRE'S CHRISTMAS BRIDE **HERE**

FOR THE LATEST READING ORDER OF THE BOOKS INCLUDING FINDING OUT WHEN EDWARD'S BOOK RELEASES JOIN MY READER GROUP **HERE**. MAKE SURE YOU ANSWER THE QUESTIONS TO GAIN ENTRY

WANT TO BE THE FIRST TO FIND OUT WHEN L. STEELE'S NEXT BOOK RELEASES? SUBSCRIBE TO HER NEWSLETTER **HERE**

READ ABOUT THE SEVEN IN THE BIG BAD BILLIONAIRES SERIES

US

UK

OTHER COUNTRIES

CLAIM YOUR **FREE** CONTEMPORARY ROMANCE BOXSET **HERE**

CLAIM YOUR **FREE** PARANORMAL ROMANCE BOXSET **HERE**

FOLLOW L. STEELE ON **AMAZON**

FOLLOW L. STEELE ON BOOKBUB

FOLLOW L. STEELE ON GOODREADS

FOLLOW L. STEELE ON FACEBOOK

FOLLOW L. STEELE ON INSTAGRAM

JOIN L. STEELE'S SECRET FACEBOOK READER GROUP

FOR MORE BOOKS BY L. STEELE CLICK **HERE**

# FREE BONUS EPILOGUE

WANT YOUR **FREE** EXCLUSIVE BONUS EPILOGUE FEATURING ZARA AND HUNTER AND THEIR BABY? CLICK **HERE**

WANT TO FIND OUT MORE ABOUT KARMA AND SUMMER'S BABIES AND ISLA'S CHILD? YOU'LL FIND THIS AND MORE IN THE AGREEMENT.

WANT TO FIND OUT HOW **WESTON AND AMELIE** MET? READ THE BILLIONAIRE'S CHRISTMAS BRIDE **HERE**

WANT EVEN MORE CHRISTMAS BOOKS? READ A VERY MAFIA CHRISTMAS, CHRISTIAN AND AURORA'S STORY **HERE**

FOR THE LATEST READING ORDER OF THE BOOKS INCLUDING FINDING OUT WHEN EDWARD'S BOOK RELEASES JOIN MY READER GROUP **HERE**. MAKE SURE YOU ANSWER THE QUESTIONS TO GAIN ENTRY

WANT TO READ THE OTHER BOOKS IN THE SERIES? CLICK **HERE**

FOLLOW ME

ON **FB**

ON INSTAGRAM

ON TWITTER

ON AMAZON

ON BOOKBUB

ON GOODREADS

# MORE CHRISTMAS ROMANCE BOOKS FOR YOU!

Want to find out how WESTON AND AMELIE met? Read The Billionaire's Christmas Bride HERE

Want even more Christmas books? Read A very Mafia Christmas, Christian and aurora's story HERE

# FREE BOOKS

❀ Created with Vellum

Printed in Great Britain
by Amazon

16286428R00210